The Last Election

—ᖬᖬ—

A Novel of Politics

Gary H. Collins

2 1st Century Publishing

Telling the stories that matter

ISBN: 0990568377
ISBN: 978-0990568377
Library of Congress Control Number: 2014945590
21st Century Publishing East Berlin, CT

For Amy

Acknowledgments

I stand on the shoulders of so many that I don't know where to start to thank everyone who has helped to make my life possible. The vast majority of my benefactors fought for me even though they'd never meet me. And in many cases, were standing up for me before I was even born. My unending appreciation goes to the engineers of the Underground Railroad who pushed forward in the darkness with bloodhounds and hate on their heels, to Goodman, Schwerner & Chaney who stared evil in the face that horrific night in Mississippi and to the millions of others who have and continue to risk their livelihood and lives to advance the human condition. Perhaps this book and its pages will serve as a small "thanks" for your immense sacrifice.

I likewise thank the many artists who toiled through the ages to inspire me. I love you all equally and fear that to identify any of you by name would be taken as an indication of favoritism, so I will just say thanks to everyone from Mozart to Steinbeck to Oprah. I very much hope that my work will provide the same type of inspiration and companionship that you've given me through life's journey.

Much of what I have learned on this journey has come as the result of being a brother to my loving siblings, Brenda, Kevin and Kenneth. I can't imagine what life would have been like without your love and support. Thank you.

To my amazing kids, Harrison aka Hawkeye and Grant aka The General. You make me feel like the luckiest Dad in the world every day with your insights, energy and wisdom that is far beyond your years. Thank you for the incalculable way you enrich my life.

To my beautiful wife, Amy, your love is the bedrock of my life. Thank you for your support, encouragement, and patience. I'm perpetually awed by your passion, care and work on behalf of people forgotten by everyone else. I love and adore you.

To Mom & Dad, I seem to miss you both even more as each day passes. Your love, patience and teachings continue to make all the difference in my life. Doing my very best to make you proud. Thank you for everything.

Contents

Every man is guilty of the good he did not do.

Voltaire

I

I don't like politics.

I don't like what candidates have to do to get elected. Once they get elected, I don't much care for what they have to do to get anything done.

I tolerate the sexting scandals, falsified resumes and corruption trials each election cycle because I know the most important thing in the world is the outcome of an election.

I'm living proof of it.

The result of a single election saved my life.

That's probably why, as much as I've always tried to keep a comfortable distance from politics, it always seems to find me. The way it found me at lunchtime on my first day in the second grade at Willingham Elementary School.

That was the day I met Aidan Coyle.

"Awww, your glasses broke?" a big blonde kid asked, speaking in baby-talk. He and his two confederates stood over a pale, nerdy-looking red-headed kid. I couldn't tell which one of the three had knocked the nerdy kid to the ground, but they had him surrounded like a hungry pack of hyenas.

The nerdy kid grabbed his glasses and struggled back to his feet. He pushed the twisted frames onto the bridge of his nose and slowly backed up as much as the wall of kids looking on would allow.

"Think your daddy can help you now, Danny boy?" the blonde kid taunted.

The three instigators looked awful big to me. Too big to be in the fourth grade— that was the highest grade at Willingham Elementary. Danny didn't even look old enough to be in the second grade. That was my grade and I stood nearly a head taller than him.

The crowd that gathered engaged in the sad childhood ritual of egging on a conflict. Danny was trapped and had no means of escape. He held up his fists to fight as the trio of bullies moved in for the kill.

Mom and Dad had tried to prepare me for just such a moment a few hours earlier that very same morning. Mindful that moving us from Garden Street in Hartford's rough-and-tumble North End to the outskirts of the affluent suburb of Willingham was going to present certain challenges, Dad sat me on the hood of his car in the parking lot to explain them to me.

"You're the first of our kind to go to school here," he said, pointing over my shoulder to the school's front doors. "That means you've got a fair amount of trouble coming your way. There's no point in talking about it or complaining on it. It just is."

"Not from everyone," Mom said. "But there may be a few kids that you're going to have to avoid."

I could tell from the glare Dad shot over to Mom that they weren't in complete agreement on this point. Dad leaned forward to look into my eyes.

"Mind your own business," he told me. "You can avoid most trouble by just minding your own business. But when that trouble comes, you *must* throw the first punch." He showed me his gigantic fist for emphasis. "And don't ever let them get you to the ground. If they get you to the ground, they'll stomp you."

I looked up to Mom for help. She was biting her lip so hard I thought it was going to bleed. Her arms tightly crossed over her stomach, I could tell that she wanted nothing more than to scoop me up and take me home.

I was scared to death.

"Can I go home with you?" I asked.

"No. Get that out of your head," Dad said sternly. "We're not like other families and you have to learn this now. I wouldn't make you do it if you weren't ready."

"But why do I have to go to school here?" I asked, looking to Mom.

"Because these kids are going to be the future leaders of Connecticut," she said. "And you have to get to know them."

I remember it making absolutely no sense to me that I had to go to a school filled with a bunch of kids who didn't want me there when there was a perfectly fine school waiting for me back in Hartford. More to the point, I didn't understand how I was supposed to make friends with kids who didn't want me there.

Dad wasn't interested in debating the matter. He grabbed my chin to draw my attention back to his lecture. "Quinn, here's the most important thing to know: There may come a time in a fight when defeat looks certain. If that time comes, I want you to remember my face and fight harder."

"Why do I need to remember your face?" I asked.

"Because I'll be fighting with you—even if I'm not there."

He pulled me down off the car and knelt in front of me. He rubbed my arms and shoulders as if he was trying to warm me up on a cold winter morning. "We love you and your brothers more than anything in the world. So, please, just follow my instructions."

I nodded.

Mom kissed me on the forehead.

Dad turned me around and patted me on my backside. Petrified, I gripped my book bag to my chest and started the long walk to the front doors.

I managed to make it to recess without conflict. In fact, I was pretty sure that Dad had misjudged the whole situation. The girls could not have been nicer. Some of the boys stared but I figured they'd warm up to me sooner or later. There was a bit of snickering and whispering coming from behind me as I walked down the hallways: "His hair looks like a big Brillo pad," or "Those jeans *must* be hand-me-downs," and

"He's cute but he's just soooo black." It bothered me but I figured I could stand it if it was going to make Mom and Dad happy.

I probably could have made it clear to the end of the day without any trouble but for these three bullies on the playground at lunchtime. With Dad's instructions ringing in my ear, I held my ground hoping providence, in the form of a teacher, might intervene on behalf of this underdog. Unfortunately, Daniel's plight only grew worse while I waited for someone else to do something.

The leader delivered a sharp blow to Danny's nose. I knew what that kind of punch felt like from growing up in Hartford. It hurts deep inside your head and makes you dizzy. It knocked Daniel's glasses from his face again but he stayed on his feet.

"How's that feel, Danny boy?" the blonde kid asked.

Dazed but holding his fists up in defiance, Danny braced himself as the three moved in to finish their work. I couldn't stand to watch.

I got involved.

I immediately drew all three boys' attention by stepping into the ring. Outnumbered, I took a deep breath and prayed for courage. As soon as I heard the largest of the boys mutter, "Skinny nigger," I had all I needed.

Following Dad's fight instructions to the letter, I punched wildly in every direction and didn't stop. Even as painful blows to my face and body mounted, I just kept swinging. Oddly, their blows fed my determination to keep fighting.

When the dust cleared, I knew I was in big trouble.

Each of the three boys had been laid flat alongside the patches of weeds that littered the dry cracked dirt. The biggest one had blood dripping from his nose and mouth. Our gym teacher, Mr. Buckman, nearly choked me to death as he dragged me to Principal Ramsey's office.

When we arrived, he shoved me onto the wooden bench outside the principal's door and directed that I was not to move for any reason. Buckman proceeded into Principal Ramsey's office to obtain my indictment and conviction.

From the uncomfortable bench, I could hear every work spoken.

I was relieved to hear them discussing what would be my swift expulsion. It was clear that Willingham Elementary was not for me. I longed to be back in my old neighborhood in Hartford. My spirits actually rose until I saw the disappointment in the faces of Mom and Dad as they came walking down the hall. It got worse when they entered Principal Ramsey's office and I had to listen to them beg for me.

No matter what they said or how much they pleaded, the outcome was the same. I was to be expelled immediately. That is, until Aidan Coyle arrived.

"Now you must be Quinn," Mr. Coyle said warmly. I could barely understand him through what I would later learn to be a thick Irish brogue. "That's a good Irish name, you know."

Aidan Coyle was larger than life. Six foot four and with hands that seemed as long as my arms, he sported a fancy, gray double-breasted suit and mint-colored silk tie. His outfit left no mistaking to my eight-year-old eyes that he was a very important man.

I strained my neck to look up to him even after he sat on the bench with me.

"What you did for my boy Daniel today took a mountain of courage." Mr. Coyle put his arm around me. "There are hundreds of boys in this school and you're the only one that had the courage to fight. And do you know what made that fight special?" he asked.

I shook my head from side to side.

"You were fighting for someone who was a complete stranger to you." Aidan tightened his grip on my shoulder. "These people . . ." he said, pointing to the principal's office with contempt, "These people have no idea how special a boy you are to do such a courageous thing."

"But I wasn't fighting for your kid," I said. "I was fighting for me."

"You were fighting for yourself?" he asked, smiling. And amused.

"Yeah," I said. "I'd be hating myself if I didn't do anything."

"Oh, Sonny. That's what just makes you even more special. And different." Mr. Coyle moved forward on the bench, putting his elbows on his knees. "You know that voice inside your head?" he asked. "The voice that pushed you to fight?"

I nodded.

"Most people never hear that voice," he said. "They live long lives and they never once hear that voice."

From the moment I laid eyes on Aidan, I felt a special connection. Even on that first day, he seemed to know precisely what I was thinking and feeling.

"It's the hardest thing in the world to be different from everyone else," he said.

"I don't like it," I said. "It makes everything hard."

"Well, life is hard for everyone," he said, leaning in. "But you're right, it's gonna be hell for you. For a while. A long while. You're gonna be God-awful lonely and make yourself crazy trying to figure out what's wrong with you. Because every day the world's gonna remind you that you're not like everyone else." Aidan rubbed my shoulder the way I imagined he would embrace his own son, Daniel. "Am I scaring you?" he asked.

"No," I said matter-of-factly. "My Dad says the same thing."

"It's better to learn it now."

"He says that, too."

Aidan slipped his hand to the middle of my back to buck me up.

"The good news is that one day," he said, "a long time from now, you're gonna see that there's a power in being different. It's a special power that can help you become a ferocious lion. And there's no stopping a ferocious lion . . ."

The principal's door burst open. I sat straight up. I stopped trying to figure out what Mr. Coyle was talking about and turned my attention to my parents and whether they had made any progress with Principle Ramsey.

The tear slowly making its way down Mom's cheek confirmed the verdict.

Aidan stood and tightened the knot on his tie.

"Principal Ramsey," Aidan said, firmly placing his hand on Ramsey's back. "Let us all have a chat."

Everyone reversed course.

After the door closed, Aidan stated my case.

But Aidan didn't beg.

He told Principal Ramsey directly and without emotion that I would not be expelled. And if I were to be expelled, Mr. Ramsey would no longer be the principal at Willingham Elementary or any other school. He then told Buckman that from that day forward, his job responsibilities included making certain no harm came to me.

"If I find out a hair on that child's head is ever pushed out of place," Aidan said, "the least of your troubles will be finding a new job."

I'd never heard someone speak with that kind of confidence. Aidan was so sure of himself that I figured he must have been some kind of school superintendent. I soon learned that Aidan was far more powerful than any school official.

Aidan was a Democratic Party boss.

The son of Irish immigrants, Aidan got his start selling bricks on Hartford's Albany Avenue in the 1940s. He worked his way through college and law school tending bar downtown. By age twenty-five, he was on a first-name basis with every banker, lawyer and politician in the city.

Aidan Coyle went on to build his legal and political empire the old-fashioned way. He carefully and obsessively doled out small favors in exchange for larger ones. He wielded power—particularly as a younger man—by always playing hardball.

"If someone comes at you with a stick," Aidan liked to say, "you hit them with a brick. And hard."

Anyone who threatened his interests had a significant problem on his hands. And on that day, I had officially become one of Aidan's most important interests.

Throughout my childhood, Aidan paid special attention to almost everything I did. He came to my Little League games and sat with Mom and Dad, regardless of whether Daniel was playing. He gave me my first job when I was eleven, copying briefs in his law office. There were even times when he somehow arranged to see my report cards before I brought them home to Mom and Dad.

Dad loved Aidan and the two of them became thick as thieves. Their idea of a weekend well spent was sitting on Aidan's deck reviewing the Normandy invasion's strategic nuances or debating whether

Copernicus did more than Da Vinci to advance mankind's ascension. My most vivid childhood memories are of playing baseball with Daniel in Aidan's backyard while our fathers laughed and hollered over Miles Davis's *Midnight in Tunisia* blaring from the house. On the nights they imbibed too much whiskey, Aidan liked to try to dance to the jazz legend. It was truly a sight to behold.

There was never any doubt that Aidan was a part of our family—and that we were a part of his—but it was confirmed in a way that I could have never imagined during my freshman year of high school. Dad was hit by a drunk driver on his way home from working the graveyard shift at Drummond Aerospace. And it was bad.

Aidan actually got to the hospital before us and was able to talk to Dad. By the time we arrived, Dad had slipped into a coma. The doctors predicted that he wouldn't make it through the night. Aidan put his life on hold like the rest of us to tend to him.

When Mom took breaks each midnight, Aidan took her place reading him books, playing his favorite music and just talking to him. When Mom returned in the mornings, Aidan spent the day on the phone with specialists from across the country to be sure we weren't missing anything that could even slightly help Dad's chances.

"Do you understand what's going on deep inside your father?" Aidan asked me after finishing a call with a doctor from California.

"He's busted up inside," I said. "I suppose his body is just trying to rest."

"Like hell," Aidan said. His eyes were bloodshot and glassy. "He's fighting. He's scratching and clawing at a thousand devils to get back to his family."

Dad held on for almost four weeks until his body finally succumbed to his injuries. Aidan was with us when the end came. That day, and every day forward, I've regretted that we didn't get to the hospital sooner the night of the accident so I could have spoken to him one last time. It's one of my many irrational regrets. The longing to change something I had no control over. I know it probably wouldn't have made much difference in how things turned out but nonetheless it gnaws at me.

I remember being angry with Aidan even as he sat at Dad's death-bed, drowning in tears. It was the only day I've ever seen Aidan cry about anything, but all I could think about was how he had robbed me of something that belonged to me. The one last opportunity to talk to my Dad.

I was angry with everyone for the next couple of years. Losing Dad was a big part of it but it was also the age when I started to see how my world was changing—and that there was no escaping it.

I was the same kid who loved sports and *Star Trek* and wanted to run for class president. But all of a sudden, the world didn't see me as a cute little kid anymore. When I achieved, I was questioned about whether someone had helped me (or whether I was cheating). When I tried to socialize, there were suddenly lines I wasn't allowed to cross—especially with girls. When I just tried to walk down the street, women gripped the shoulder straps of their purses or moved to the other side to avoid me.

When the world sees you as a menace you start behaving like one. It wasn't long before I was cutting out of school to spend my days back in my old neighborhood in Hartford. I reconnected with Titus, one of my best friends from grade school. Titus was in a gang by that time and it made sense that I should also join.

"You belong with your family—with us," he told me a week before my fifteenth birthday.

I agreed.

I was done with Aidan. And everyone else.

But Aidan wouldn't let go.

The night of my "beat-in" on Park Street to mark my initiation, Aidan appeared out of nowhere to stop the whole thing. Unfortunately, my would-be gang brothers were unaware of Aidan's status as a party boss. He took a hell of a beating to get me out of there.

When we finally made it back to his Buick, he looked at me—with blood still dripping from his mouth. "I could tell you that thousands of people—including your father—sacrificed everything so that you wouldn't have to be a prisoner to your past. But that's not gonna mean anything to you tonight." Blood and spit jumped from his lips while he hollered at me. "So I'm just gonna tell you this: I understand that when people hate you for no good reason, it makes you want to blow your brains out. I . . . understand . . . it," he said slowly. "You're asking, 'What's wrong with me that people treat me like this?' And it's making you hate yourself." He grabbed the front of my t-shirt, his fists trembling. "I'm gonna make you see this. I *have* to make you see this or you're gonna destroy yourself. And one of the things I promised your father was that I'm not gonna let that happen. If I have to drag your skinny ass around all day every day until I leave this earth, I will not let that happen."

That was probably the most important moment of my life. I feel guilty about it, but it's true. I should probably be able to point to a moment I had with my Dad or one of the many sacrifices Mom made to try and make my life better. But the truth is that this one moment with Aidan changed everything for me.

It wasn't just that Aidan cared about me. I figured that lots of people, including my Mom and my siblings, cared about me. It was that one other human being understood exactly what I was feeling at the precise moment that I needed someone to understand. And knowing that gave me hope that I might get through it.

There was nothing that I wouldn't have done for Aidan after that night. He didn't need to keep hovering but he did anyway.

When I earned a football scholarship to attend Connecticut State, he came to every one of my games and most of the practices—even during the years when I didn't play much. In fact, the most memorable image from my four years in college came when I was a senior and had to play a meaningless late-season game in a terrible blizzard in Buffalo. There wasn't a single person in the stands—except Aidan.

Over the years, Aidan taught me all the rules of politics. Aidan believes politics are everywhere. He insists that anyone who doesn't understand politics—the art of reading and understanding people and getting them to see things your way—can never be successful in business, get along in a big family or accomplish just about anything. And Aidan flat-out loves politics. He revels in the deal making and strategy. And always used politics to help me get prepared for life.

"You can win any race and defeat any foe *if* you're prepared and willing to fight like your life depends on winning," he told me, over and over again. "If you ever find yourself in a situation that looks hopeless, you're simply not thinking hard enough."

He repeated this teaching so many times I could often hear him saying it even when he wasn't around. Like today, as I crossed Asylum Street, rushed through the lobby of Hartford's CityPlace building and rode the elevator up twenty-one floors.

As I stepped off the elevator into Coyle & Coyle's law offices, I realized that in over thirty years, this was the first day that one of Aidan's teachings had ever failed me.

Aidan was dying and there was nothing I could do about it.

II

"Hi there, Quinn," Aidan's receptionist, Annie, said. "He's waiting for you." She opened her hand in the general direction of Aidan's conference room at the far end of the hall. She smiled her perfect smile. The one I'd seen a thousand times since I was in grade school. But I could see through this one. Like everyone else in Aidan's world, she was worried. I just smiled back.

I typically talk to Aidan two or three times a day, including weekends. Sometimes we talk about our cases. Sometimes we talk about my kids. Most of the time we talk about politics. But Aidan hadn't returned any of my calls in over a week. That's what he does when things aren't going well for him—he retreats into a cave. It's probably why he's been divorced three times. I always sort of understood it. I even understood why he never told anyone he was sick until it was too obvious to hide anymore. He just didn't see the point.

Aidan sat at the far end of a long mahogany table that could accommodate twenty others. His only company was Daniel.

With his body ravaged by the late stages of pancreatic cancer, he looked like a small man in a big suit. And that he'd completely lost his appetite. He didn't notice my arrival until I was halfway across the room.

"Sonny!" His roar defied his frailty. "Thanks for coming over so fast."

Aidan slowly got up from his chair. He delivered a bear hug, followed by running his hands up and down my back. It was how he would greet a friend he hadn't seen in years. I took it as a signal that he was coming to grips with the fact that we would have fewer and fewer opportunities to embrace—and he wanted to savor each one.

"How you feeling?" I asked.

"Great coverage of your pro-bono case," he said, tapping his hand on the front page of the *Hartford Journal* spread across the conference room table. "I knew the jury would come back with a not guilty."

Aidan always taught me to try to talk more about the person you're meeting with than yourself. But with Aidan, this was next to impossible. He was only interested in information flowing in his direction. After he got himself caught up on the events of the past few days—my fight with Judge Shea over jury instructions and the kids' Little League games—I tried again.

"What do you say we take some time off?"

"And do what?" he asked, smirking. "Sit on my couch and wait?"

"We could take a trip and relax." I looked to Daniel to enlist him as an ally. "We could take a week and visit a bunch of baseball parks."

His face soured and he waved at me like I'd just pushed a plate of cauliflower in front of him.

"Sonny," he said to me, "I'm gonna be dead for quite a long time. I'll have plenty of time to rest then. And I have too much to do right here, right now."

"Like what?"

"Glad you asked." Aidan used his finger to signal for Daniel to pour him a glass of ice water from the crystal pitcher sitting between us.

Daniel poured. Aidan was slow to get the glass to his mouth. His hands trembled noticeably. I wanted to help him but I knew that would only annoy him. Daniel and I just waited patiently for him to lower his glass to the table and neatly fold his hands in a tent before continuing the discussion.

"I can't sleep," he said.

"How long has this been going on?" I asked.

"Almost three weeks."

"Can't your doctor prescribe something?" I looked to Daniel for details.

"It's not that kind of thing," Daniel said, looking at me deadpan.

"No doctor can help," Aidan said. "I'm being haunted by my mistakes and there's no pill for that."

"Aidan, you've made a difference in the lives of thousands of people across this state," I said. "Whatever mistakes you've made, you've made up for them a thousand times over."

"I've helped a lot of people," he said, nodding in agreement. "But I've made some terrible mistakes—and there's one in particular that's still hurting people."

"I'm not sure I understand. Or know how I can I help."

"Only you can help."

"Then I'll take care of it."

"This is no small favor."

"Just tell me what you need."

Aidan leaned back and slipped his thumbs behind his black suspenders before revealing his mystery.

"I need you to primary Saul Berg in August."

Aidan's request was so far out of context that I didn't understand his words as they escaped his lips. Before I could get over the shock of his request, he added an important qualification.

"And I need you to win. You *must* win."

Aidan probably understood better than anyone in Connecticut that my chances of curing his illness were, sadly, better than those of defeating Senator Saul Berg in a primary.

Saul Berg is a Connecticut institution. His political career began in 1967 when, at the age of 23, he was elected to the State House of Representatives. He was sworn in just months after his graduation from Yale. He was a U.S. Congressman before the age of 32—a fairly big accomplishment for most, but Saul had his sights set on even higher office. He spent every day of his tenure in Congress lining up what for him was the ultimate prize in politics. He celebrated his 40th birthday on election night in 1988, thanking his supporters for delivering it to him in the form of a ticket to the U.S. Senate.

Once in the Senate, Saul got to work ensuring his reelection.

He kept his campaign coffers overflowing by leveraging his committee assignments to tap every special interest from Wall Street to

Silicon Valley. He painstakingly worked to secure federal funding for new Connecticut parks and libraries and then made certain that virtually all of them bore his name. He treated members of the mainstream media as his most important constituents, doling out favors and leaking stories, to gain what was nearly on-demand coverage of any issue he wanted to promote.

After twenty-four years of perfecting the science of incumbency, Saul wasn't simply the best-known politician in Connecticut; he was probably the best-known person in the state.

"Aidan, I can't do that."

"You must."

I didn't need to ask why.

Aidan had given nearly every politician in Connecticut their start. His reign, which spanned almost five decades, marked the heyday of Connecticut's Democratic machine. He handpicked the candidates; lined up the unions and the party machinery behind them; and single-handedly developed and deployed the strategy to propel them to victory. Saul was no different.

Back in '87, Saul begged Aidan to support his Senate run. I was in law school when Aidan was grappling with that decision and I remember his reservations well. On the one hand, the incumbent, Mason Charles III, was a Rockefeller Republican who Aidan actually liked and felt was pretty good on issues that were important to Democrats. On the other hand, Saul touted himself as the relentless liberal and promised he could do better. On balance, Saul was the Democrat and Aidan gave him the benefit of the doubt.

Within the first year of Saul's first term, Aidan had come to consider his support a mistake.

Like all politicians, Saul worked hard to get into the spotlight and keep himself there. It was the way he did it that troubled Aidan so much. Saul obsessively sought a portfolio of issues to endear him first with conservatives and more recently the Tea Party. Saul's strategy ensured his regular appearance on the front pages of national newspapers and on Sunday talk shows, but the state suffered. When Connecticut started hemorrhaging jobs in '02, struggling with plummeting graduation rates, and battling nationally led efforts to dismantle organized labor, Saul was busy maintaining his national profile and nowhere to be found in Connecticut.

The more power and notoriety Saul amassed the more extreme he became. When the shooting massacre at Columbine devastated the country, Saul blamed violent video games and the coarsening of the American culture. As the war in Iraq raged on, Saul wildly and falsely maintained, "We are at war with a brutal enemy who attacked us on 9/11 and we must stay the course." When the "fiscal cliff" approached, he locked arms with the Tea Party and declared, "There are no circumstances under which I would vote for a single dollar in more taxes."

Aidan and Saul's relationship had ended years ago, but as long as Saul held his Senate seat, the matter would never be over for Aidan.

"You've said it a thousand times," I said, reaching for the pitcher. "Incumbents are virtually unbeatable. Voters are like shoppers. They buy the same product over and over again without even thinking. How would we even begin to break into his market share?"

"You're gonna find new voters: young people, college students, hard-core activists that have given up on the process," Aidan said, calmly. "The largest block of primary voters is still people that don't vote. You're gonna figure out a way to get 'em to vote for you."

"It's Patriots' Day today. There are less than two weeks left in April. How could we possibly raise the money we'd need for an August primary?" I asked, this time looking over to Daniel for a lifeline. "Even putting the time frame aside for a second, no big donor would dare contribute to us and risk having their name appear on our FEC report."

"I'll raise you money from my own Rolodex," Aidan said. "You'll have plenty of money."

"What about the attorney general, the secretary of state or our treasurer?" I asked. "Even a state senator would be a stronger candidate . . ."

"No elected official would ever do this," Aidan said. "It's too risky for a sitting politician."

"Sounds like you checked," I said.

"I have not," Aidan said, sharply. "If there's one thing that fifty years in politics has taught me, it's that true change will never come from someone inside the system."

"Are we overlooking that I've never been elected to anything?"

"Gary Hart, Paul Wellstone, Jim Webb, Al Franken, Herbert Kohl, Frank Lautenberg." Aidan ticked off half a dozen more names in staccato fashion, confirming that while his disease may have decimated his body, his mind remained razor sharp. "None of them had even been elected so much as dog catcher before their Senate runs."

"And your experience lines up fine with any of them," Daniel said. "You were a federal prosecutor. You're a law professor and a partner at the oldest and largest firm in Connecticut."

Aidan reached for his water. "And you threw the winning touchdown in the greatest college football game this state has ever seen."

"We've all seen strong candidates lose because they didn't have a winning issue," I said. "What's our issue?"

Aidan and Daniel looked at each other as if I had just asked the single dumbest question in the history of American politics.

"We're the most unequal state in America," Aidan said, his hazel eyes burning bright. "We've now officially got more low-income housing projects sitting blocks from multi-million dollar mansions than you'd see in some third world countries."

"No state in the country has grown more unequal as fast as us," Daniel said. "The General Assembly's about to put out a report that says the income and employment gap between rich and poor is widest it's been in twenty years."

"And while we're sitting around here watching," Aidan said, "the Plopper twins and Patriot Partners are pumping over $250 million into races for incumbents serving on key defense and energy committees—*the two committees that Saul now chairs.*" He grabbed the *Journal* while he was talking and flipped it over to show me a back page headline: "Plopper Twins to Funnel Hundreds of Millions to Corporate Allies in Upcoming Cycle."

"American Crosswinds says they're going even bigger," Daniel said. "They're pledging to spend $300 million. They're buying Congress plain and simple—and Saul's at the top of the list." Daniel swirled the water in his glass like he was about to sip aged bourbon.

It was a small thing, but it distracted me.

Daniel's a recovering alcoholic. I took a double take at the glass to check its contents before turning my attention back to Aidan.

"The level of greed is like nothing I've ever seen," Aidan said, his face bright red. "It stands to be the ruin of us. This is the defining moment of a generation."

"Guys," I said firmly, trying to slow their rant. "I know all this."

"Then do something about it," Aidan said, jaw clenched.

Someone who didn't know him would have thought he was angry with me. I understood that he was just angry.

"Do the big thing," he went on. "Be the one person in all this insanity that says, 'No more.'"

"I obviously agree with everything you've said, but—"

"Well, then let us join together one final time to do something historic." Aidan struggled to his feet to announce that the discussion was over. "Will you do this favor for an old man who loves you to death?" he asked, extending his hand to mine.

"Let me talk to Brooke—and the kids—over the weekend."

"But you're on board?"

"The timing could not be worse." I hugged Aidan and could feel his bones through his suit jacket.

"I love the excitement of launching a campaign." He showed his fists to playfully spar with me.

"Don't do anything until we talk again," I said.

"I won't."

III

"Let's go, Eliza," Pierce hollered to his little sister from the hillside. He formed a bullhorn with his hands and yelled, "Fight to the end!"

Pierce's twin, Benjamin, stood beside him. "Keep battling," he said, hopping on his toes.

Eliza stepped out of the batter's box after swinging and badly missing for strike two.

She was in a tough spot.

Her team, the Cardinals, was down to its final out. The hopes of a season opening come-from-behind-victory rested on her small shoulders. And she looked overmatched.

Fear hung all over her face. It made me second-guess my decision to let her play with the boys. Brooke was against it from the beginning. An outstanding athlete in her own right, Brooke understood competition, but Eliza was young for her grade, and Brooke thought this put her at too great a disadvantage. She was concerned that if Eliza didn't succeed, she'd feel like she couldn't live up to her brothers' successes, and that might permanently damage her confidence.

I disagreed.

I knew she had enough talent to succeed—and would benefit from playing against top competition. I just had hoped she would get through the season without having to face such a daunting challenge.

Tommy Coughlin was oversized for a nine-year-old and could throw as hard as any kid three years his senior. After the tying and go-ahead runs reached first and second base, he was brought in to finish us off.

He struck out the first two batters he faced with six pitches. Then he severely dampened the odds of Eliza's driving in the winning run as he hurled a blazing fastball past her to register strike two. She barely had the bat off her shoulder when the ball reached the catcher's mitt.

I called a timeout from my post in the third base coach's box and waved her over. We met halfway between third and home plate. I knelt.

"I'm scared, Daddy."

"I know. It's okay. Even grown-ups get scared."

"He throws fast. And he's wild."

"I know that too," I said, her face a few inches from mine. "You just have to pretend that it doesn't bother you."

"Can we just go home?"

"No. This is hard but you have to learn how to do hard things." I put my finger on her chin to lift her head. Her bright emerald eyes locked on mine. "Let's talk about our plan . . . ."

Eliza looked up to me for hope. The muscles in my neck were knotted so tight, it felt as if I couldn't turn my head.

"He thinks he has you," I said.

"He does."

"No, he doesn't. But he thinks he does so he's going throw it fat—right over the plate. I want you to move back in the batter's box—toward the catcher—and try to slow everything down."

"How do I do that?"

"Close your eyes." Eliza obeyed. Her hands gripped the knob of her bat. I put my hand over hers. "I want you to see the ball coming at you. But it's in slow motion. It's coming so slow you can see the laces slowly turning over. Do you see it?"

The blonde and brown curly locks sprouting wildly from the back of her helmet moved up and down.

"Good. Now see yourself hitting a bammer like no one has ever seen." I rubbed her back, tracing the number 1 on her red and white jersey. "Now, open your eyes for me."

I turned her around to face home plate. I patted her on the backside and left one final word of encouragement in her ear.

"You're a warrior. Go fight him. Be quick with your bat—stay level—and hit it hard."

"I'm still scared. But I'll try."

Eliza hustled back to home plate and settled herself just outside the batter's box reserved for left-handed hitters. She took two hard practice swings, touched the top of her batter's helmet and dug into the batter's box. If she was frightened, no one could tell. She stared at Tommy with the grit of a champion prizefighter as she readied her bat.

My stomach churned. I knew what she had no way of knowing. A million things could go wrong. Tommy could throw a wild pitch—and she surely would fish for it and miss. Even worse, he could throw off target. Maybe even at her head. And she wouldn't have time to get out the way.

I knelt on one knee and crossed my arms over my chest. I gave Tommy a final look and then turned back to Eliza to see if there was room for a final bit of instruction. She looked ready. I held my tongue.

Tommy twisted his body in his trademark contortion before hurling the ball toward the plate. I could tell it was going to be a strike as it left his hand because his throwing motion was picture perfect.

So could Eliza.

She turned on the pitch and sent it just a few feet from my head, down the third base line. The fifty or so onlookers erupted in applause. It sounded as loud as a crowd of five hundred.

My eyes followed the ball as it landed just a few feet in foul territory.

I sent her teammates back to their bases. When I turned to home plate, Eliza was already in her pre-pitch ritual, taking hard practice swings. She didn't even glance in my direction.

She had a chance.

I could have sworn that lightning flashed from her eyes as the next pitch approached the plate and she started her swing. Had Tommy not ducked, he surely would have spent the evening in the emergency room. The ball rocketed over his head and then over the head of the center fielder—never rising more than ten feet from the ground.

Eliza held onto her helmet as she rounded second and headed toward me at third. She sped around the bases as if her life depended on safely making it to third—not realizing she had already won the game.

Tommy and his Blue Jays threw their mitts and caps to the ground. A sea of miniature red and white Cardinal jerseys waited for Eliza at home plate for the post-game celebration. I let her enjoy the moment until the Blue Jays lined up to shake hands. Most of her opponents gave her an extra pat on the shoulder as she made her way through the line.

She was still beaming when it came time to help me pack the gear. She dragged the oversized black equipment bag—which was longer than she was—to the parking lot without complaint. She couldn't wait to take her place between her two brothers in the back of our Jeep Wrangler Unlimited to replay each pitch of her game-winning at-bat. Her hair, unbound by her cap, filled the rear-view mirror as she turned from side to side to review the finer points of hitting with her brothers.

"How about ice cream?" Brooke asked, slipping into the passenger's seat.

"How about dinner at Frescas?" Eliza asked.

Ordinarily, I would have vetoed a request for a casual Thursday evening bite at a five-star restaurant. We live in a small town like Pentfield to keep the kids from becoming and behaving entitled. It was probably a bigger issue for me than for Brooke. I decided not to make a big deal out of it under the circumstances. We headed down to Main Street toward Frescas for dinner.

Pentfield is quintessential small-town New England. It's stocked with scores of historic 18th century homes. We live in one on Beecher Street—which is the second-to-last street at the far end of Main Street. Built in 1768 by a Presbyterian abolitionist, it's one of the oldest homes in town. Like most Connecticut homes on the Underground Railroad, ours has a number of secret rooms that hid runaway slaves. The kids love to use them to play hide-and-go-seek.

Pentfield sits atop the east side of the Connecticut River Valley. It has a town green and a dozen or so boutiques and antique stores.

A brownstone statue at the center of the green commemorates the soldiers who died putting down the Great Rebellion. Our town hall sits on the east side of the green; the largest art gallery in Middlesex County is on the west. Frescas, with the trademark elegant white lights that frame its sidewalk café, is positioned to the north.

My iPhone started buzzing from its perch in the cup holder as we pulled up to the restaurant.

"I'm going to need just a few minutes," I said.

Brooke didn't acknowledge me and just opened the passenger's door.

"Let's go, kids," she said lightly.

Brooke's tone telegraphed to me what she really wanted to say, "I don't want to have the same argument we've been having for twelve years but it's rude to me and rude to the kids. You don't always have to answer that damn phone when it rings."

Thinking about it irritated me.

It made me want to say, "Do I have to remind you every fifteen minutes that I'm from Hartford and not Greenwich? The only way I know to maintain this lifestyle is to work twice as hard as everyone else."

Nowadays, that's kind of what I'm always doing. I play out a full-blown argument inside my head based on the real ones we've had the past several years, and it puts me in a foul mood—or makes me feel like pulling my hair out.

Brooke and I are from different worlds. Brooke Elizabeth Wolcott is the eleventh generation of her family from Connecticut. She descends from Oliver Wolcott, a signer of the Declaration of Independence. She was raised in Guilford, the crown jewel of the Connecticut Shoreline. Her mother is a tenured psychology professor at Yale and her Harvard-educated father is one of New England's leading cardiologists.

None of this mattered when we met. We never even gave it any thought. But raising three kids introduced issues into our marriage that neither of us could have foreseen. While we snipe about lots of things, the core issue is how we raise the kids.

Last summer, Pierce came home in tears because two older kids from a neighboring town stole his bike at the park. I made him go back and fight them to reclaim it. Brooke was mortified. She didn't talk to me for a month. When Benjamin broke his nose in his basketball league's season opener last November, I had him fitted for a mask and tried to put him in the following week's game. Brooke threatened to call the Department of Children and Family Services and held him out for almost the entire season. I didn't talk to her for pretty much the entire season. And there's Eliza. I basically treat Eliza the same way I treat the boys. When she's sick, I push her to go to school anyway. When she's upset because she can't win a one-on-one basketball game against a boy, I tell she has to work harder to get better. When she falls down and is hurt, I make her get up on her own.

The incident that seemed to fundamentally change things between us occurred about two months ago. I was supposed to be watching the kids while Brooke played tennis with her friends. She came home early to find me teaching the boys how to defend themselves. How to fight. Unbeknownst to me, she watched as I showed them how to use their knees and elbows as weapons. When I started to educate them on the pressure points of the body that can incapacitate an aggressor, she stormed in and put a stop to it.

She didn't say a word to me as she gathered the kids under her arms and led them upstairs. When she reached the top of the staircase she looked back at me like she was looking at a monster.

I'm mindful that people from Guilford don't raise their kids this way. But that's because they don't have to. I, on the other hand, know something that Brooke may never fully appreciate: This world isn't going to treat our kids the way it treated her. It's going to be mean and brutish—especially to the boys—in a way that will break them if they're not prepared for it.

Aidan always had a sharp sense about it. "Sonny, the one percent rule is real," he told me on my ninth birthday while I opened his gift in his kitchen. "If just one percent of white people hate you because of your skin color—and it's gonna be a lot more than one percent— they're gonna come after you and you have to be ready to fight."

"So how many kids is that in my school?" I asked him, as I tried on the new pair of red Everlast boxing gloves.

"Twenty to twenty-five kids. Maybe more," he said. "But it's not just your school. It's everywhere you go."

"And it's not just about your body," Dad said, from the chair next to him. "Your mind has to be stronger than steel." Aidan nodded in agreement. "Hate can be so powerful that it can make you hate yourself," Dad went on. "And you have to develop a state of mind that says, 'Nothing can defeat me—NOTHING.' If you had to climb Mount Everest with no shoes and a piano on your back, you have to know you could do it—on your own."

"On your own!" Aidan repeated. "Don't depend on anyone but yourself."

That's what I was always taught. That's what I believe. And I can see now that it was making Brooke question whether I was the best choice of a husband.

"Thanks, Honey," I said, turning to Brooke. She fixed her hair beneath the interior light. "I'll be quick."

Eliza placed her miniature hand on my shoulder.

"Daddy, do you want us to order for you?"

"Yes, and thank you. I won't be long."

They piled out and asked the maître de for a table outside, near the sidewalk.

I pulled around the corner to park.

My phone rang again before I could even check my messages.

"Quinn Barnes here."

"Jonathan Q. Barnes!"

I didn't recognize the voice.

"This is Quinn," I repeated.

"Lucy B. McCann here," the voice on the other end announced, still yelling.

I wasn't sure what to say.

Lucy McCann's presence on the Connecticut political scene was a mystery to both local and national pundits. The founder of the Worldwide Wrestling Confederation, headquartered in toney Fairfield County down in the state's southwest corner, she made her billions peddling fake sporting contests with the assistance of steroid-enhanced athletes. A household name amongst lovers of faux cage fighting, she was unknown to the world of politics until six months ago when she announced she would be seeking the Republican nomination for U.S. Senate.

Born and raised in South Carolina, Lucy was the survivor of a bankruptcy, a federal indictment for the trafficking of illegal steroids and a philandering husband. Now divorced, the sixty-one-year-old grandmother of nine loves to spend her Sunday afternoons during the summer months navigating her 47-foot yacht, luridly named the *Sexy Bitch,* down the Connecticut River.

I had never actually met Lucy but much to Brooke's chagrin, I found her to be eminently likable. Outsiders to politics typically have one advantage when they enter the ring: They talk and sound like normal people. Politicos call it being authentic. Unlike Saul, who was born on third base and spent his life believing he'd hit a triple, Lucy was born into poverty in the rural South and had to fight for everything she earned, including her gaudy yacht. She probably couldn't articulate a single issue that I could subscribe to, but I respected her.

"Cat got your tongue, Sweetie Pie?" Lucy asked, the remnants of a Carolina accent still discernible in her voice.

"In a word, Yes. You're about the last person I'd expect to be calling me."

"Now you know Lucy McCann won't stand to be last at anything," she said flirtatiously. "How 'bout we flip that to making me the first person you couldn't stand not to hear from?"

"I suppose."

"Now we're cooking."

"What can I do for you?" I walked to the corner and watched the hostess seat Brooke and the kids. The boys book-ended Brooke. Eliza took a seat by herself opposite them. She started coloring while the waitress distributed the menus.

"I wanted to congratulate you on getting into this race," Lucy said.

"I'm not sure where you heard that, but it's doubtful that I'll do it."

"Oh, don't be silly. There are three things men simply can't resist: power, women and bacon—and not necessarily in that order." Lucy paused. It sounded like she was taking a drink. "Lucy McCann understands the psyche of men."

She referred to herself in the third person as easily as most people breathe.

"I promise," I said, "you'll be the first person I call once I make a decision."

"You do that. 'Cause I got about five million dollars in my pocket that's gonna get unloaded on Saul's head once you get in."

"Really?" I asked.

"You bet. I can take you down, but that Saul would be a tough dog to castrate," she said. "You know what that makes us?"

"I'm not sure."

"Partners. Well, temporary partners."

"You mean until after the primary."

"Not much gets past you, Quinn. You're gonna be real good at this political game."

Brooke craned her head looking for me.

"Bye, Lucy."

"Bye-bye, Sweetie Pie. You go spend some quiet time with your family and know that we're thinking about you."

I hurried down the street and settled in next to Eliza.

"Daddy, why do people always stare at us?" she asked. She spoke loud enough that the silver-haired culprits at the table next to us quickly looked down at their food.

"We're different," I said. I didn't look up from my menu.

"It's mostly the old people," Pierce said. "You just have to get used to it."

"How are we different?" she asked. "And why do I have to get used to this? They're the ones staring."

Eliza was continuing to live up to be every bit of her namesake.

We named Eliza before she was born. Brooke was restless throughout her pregnancy. We were convinced that our newborn was going to be a placekicker due to the constant stirring and kicking. Brooke couldn't sit comfortably for more than a few minutes when she got close to her due date so one Sunday afternoon we headed up to the Stowe House in Hartford to walk around.

The boys had a high time. In between running around and slamming a few doors, they took in every bit of the guide's instruction on *Uncle Tom's Cabin.* They were mesmerized by the tale of Eliza's leap over the frigid Ohio River, her baby clutched in her arms, in her quest for freedom.

"Her feet were being cut to shreds and bleeding on the jagged ice but she refused to give in," the guide told them. "Eliza was endowed with the kind of courage and strength that God gives only to the desperate."

So impressed by Eliza's "fight," the boys resolved that she would make a great sister. It was decided on the car ride home that if we had a girl, she would be Eliza. Brooke went into labor that same night and the boys had their Eliza the next morning.

"They may have been staring because you're a stunning beauty." Brooke's smile covered the table like a warm blanket.

But Eliza would not relent. "But I still don't get how we're so different?"

"Open your eyes!" Benjamin shot from across the table. "Are you blind?"

"Please don't talk to your sister like that," Brooke said. "She's trying to understand something that's even hard for adults to understand."

"Yeah," Pierce piled on. "Don't be a butthead."

"I'm a butthead?" Benjamin asked. "Well, then you're a smelly butthead."

"If I'm a smelly butthead, you're the crown prince of the kingdom of the smelly buttheads," Pierce retorted.

I suppressed a laugh at what I thought to be a clever turn of phrase for an eleven-year-old. Brooke was not amused. Creases gathered on her forehead and she admonished me with her eyes for laughing.

"Let's talk about this later," I said, handing Benjamin my iPad to play a word game. Eliza put her crayons down and took my arm to pull it over her shoulder. She rested her head on my side.

"How's Aidan?" Brooke asked.

"He finally called me back." I tasted the iced tea waiting for me in front of my plate. "I saw him this afternoon."

"Where's his hospice?"

"He's at work."

"Aidan's still working?" She asked. "What's wrong with him?"

Brooke never really understood Aidan. She applauded his life's work. She credited him with ensuring the election of the nation's first female governor and stocking our Supreme Court with justices who ruled that all citizens—regardless of race or economic standing—have a constitutional right to a quality education. She had even worked with him to help build the necessary majorities in the state legislature to abolish the death penalty and legalize same-sex marriage. She just always questioned whether the cost to his family was worth it.

Brooke doesn't respect anyone who doesn't put their family first.

And she viewed Aidan's personal life as a total mess.

"What did you guys talk about?" she asked.

"You, the kids, politics . . ."

"I would think that politics would be the last thing on his mind right now."

"Politics is his life."

"Now's the time when his family should be his life." Brooke sipped her sparkling Perrier. "Why is he worrying himself about politics?" she asked, softening her tone.

My pulse quickened. After twelve years of marriage, there's not much that I don't know about my wife. And I know it's generally better to tell Brooke about complicated issues in stages. I usually drop a clue here, offer a hint there and let it marinate a bit before dropping the bomb. I didn't have that kind of time and this opening looked heaven-sent. Regardless, I proceeded with caution because I know my wife and once I even mentioned a campaign, she'd be thinking about Rosalynn Carter.

Blessed with a photographic memory, Brooke can instantly recall the names of the signers of the Declaration of Independence or the battles of the Civil War in chronological order with the ease that most of us recite the letters of the alphabet. With all those facts and figures swirling in her head, her favorite political anecdote—which she loved to share with our friends—was about former First Lady Rosalynn Carter.

Apparently Rosalynn Carter never strayed far from Plains, Georgia before marrying Jimmy. His Naval career afforded her the opportunity to live in Virginia, New York, Hawaii and New London, Connecticut—all the while developing a love for classical music, art and studying Spanish.

In 1953, Jimmy came home from work one day and announced that they were returning to Plains, Georgia so he could take over the family's peanut farming business and start his political career. According to Brooke, Rosalynn's response was to stop speaking to her husband—for more than a year.

"Can you imagine that?" Brooke asked, as she retold this tale last year at our holiday party, "Your wife not speaking to you for over a year?"

And Brooke could be a lot more stubborn than Rosalynn Carter.

Our waitress dropped off our food. Brooke took the iPad away from Ben, made sure the kids had all their condiments and ordered everyone another drink. When the waitress stepped back from the table, Brooke turned back to me.

"So why's he worrying himself about politics?" she asked again.

"He wanted to talk to me about running against Saul," I said casually, as if I thought the proposition were a silly one.

She laughed. "You're kidding."

I honest-to-God had no desire to become a candidate but could have done without the laugh.

"Saul is making him nuts. And hurting the country," I said. "And this morning had to be the last straw."

"What happened?"

"He gave the keynote at the Conservative Union luncheon and said that the Occupy Wall Street protestors need to 'take a bath and get a job.'"

"How can the state that voted for Jerry Brown in '92 keep sending this man to Washington?" she asked, sampling her salad.

"If we're not willing to do something about it, we have no business complaining."

"We do enough," she returned firmly. "Besides, why would he ask you?"

"Probably because no one else will do it," I said. "He also knows that real change can only come from outside the system."

"Aidan doesn't believe that and you know it. He's no idealist; he's a cold, calculating party boss."

"Well, I believe it."

"You want to do this, don't you?" she asked, putting her fork down.

"No."

The waitress gave us a break by setting down our drinks.

She sipped her sparkling water but kept her eyes locked on me until the waitress retreated.

"If you don't want to do it, why are we having this conversation?" she asked.

"Because I feel like I have to do it."

"Well, I have no interest in explaining to the world why I paid a bill late twenty years ago—or refuting the details of conversations that never occurred." Brooke picked up her fork and stabbed into her salad. "Besides, do you really want to jeopardize your law practice and your family for nothing?"

"For everything. These are the most important times since World War II."

"For nothing. You can't win."

"What?" I asked.

Brooke looked at me straight and repeated herself without emotion. "I said, You, Quinn Barnes, cannot win."

Her opinion was probably no different from any other political professional. It was just hard to hear it from her.

"That's not positive!" Eliza said.

Brooke and I had both forgotten, for a moment, that the kids were with us.

"What's not positive?" Brooke asked calmly.

"You're not supposed to say you can't do something, or that you're not going to win, or you can't get an A."

"You're right," Brooke said. "But this is different."

"How's it different?" Eliza asked with a mouth full of spaghetti.

"No offense, Dad," Benjamin said, chiming in, "but you're not famous. Saul is famous. Everyone knows Saul."

"Does this mean we don't have to visit all the state capitols of New England for summer vacation?" Pierce asked.

"No," Brooke said, emphatically, "because there's not going to be a campaign."

Pierce and Benjamin rolled their eyes. They didn't care about my running for the Senate. They simply couldn't bear the thought of spending any portion of their summer break in Augusta, Montpelier or Concord when they could be home playing baseball and swimming in the pool.

Eliza looked up at me. "So you're not going to try, Daddy?"

"I'm sorry, Eliza, but I can't."

IV

My eyes open every day at 4:00 a.m. Brooke thinks it's a curse and that it's going to take years off my life. I've always thought of it as a competitive advantage. Over the course of a week, the two extra hours each morning give me an extra full day to get things done. The early morning hours also allow me to watch Brooke sleep, which is still one of my favorite things to do. Brooke smiles when she sleeps. Sometimes she even laughs aloud.

Today she just tossed and turned.

I moved to her side and ran my hand the length of her back. After she settled down, I left a long kiss on her forehead and got up to start my day.

I love the quiet of the morning. It usually brings clarity. Problems that seemed insurmountable in the darkness seem to untangle themselves overnight. I keep a journal next to my bedside to jot the insights and strategies that come to me in the night. My subconscious failed me on this morning and there was nothing to write. I was no closer to finding a solution for Aidan than the day before.

I dressed quickly and stepped outside to inhale the crisp New England air. The thermometer hadn't yet touched 60 degrees but I took the top down off the Jeep before setting off to the office. As I made my way through the sleeping town, the only sign of life was on Main Street. It was from the workers starting the early shift in the bakery.

I crossed the Connecticut River via the green metal Arrigoni Bridge. It delivered me to the north end of Middletown. I waited for a red light in the left turn lane to jump on Route 9 and get up to Hartford. Off in the distance to my right, a man hobbled down the sidewalk near Washington Street. I thought I recognized his limp but couldn't be certain in the darkness. I checked my watch and took a detour to investigate.

I pulled up behind him.

"I thought you were set up in the shelter," I said.

Gene just scowled and made his way over to the small historic cemetery wedged between the soup kitchen and the Community Arts Center. He lay in the grass and turned his back to me.

I've known Gene since I was in grade school. He's a year younger than me but he was nonetheless one of my best friends growing up in Hartford. By the time he was a junior in high school he was six foot six and 280 pounds, which made him one of the most sought-after recruits at offensive tackle in the country. He was the one-in-a-million kid who could have played at almost any school in the Dixie Conference, but he chose to stay home and attend Connecticut State with me. He was a first team All Yankee Conference player his first two seasons in the mid-80s. Most experts thought he'd be a shoo-in first-round draft pick in the professional ranks, until he suffered the injury that left him with his limp.

He hurt himself trying to protect me.

It happened on a Saturday night down in Ohio against Bowling Green. The Bowling Green squad featured a standout lineman of their own, six foot five Dex Powers. We only had two wins that year and Bowling Green had three, but both Gene and Dex were headed for professional football. And the papers were excited about the match-up.

Bowling Green was controlling the game, but we were only down by a touchdown as halftime approached. Dex, however, was dishing out an awful beating to me. Like a martial arts expert, he broke my body down with each blow. In the first quarter, he slipped around Gene and used his shoulder pads to hit me low, leaving me with a hip pointer that hobbled my legs. Early in the second, he beat Gene to the inside and drove his helmet into my midsection, bruising my ribs and making it hard to breathe.

"I'm sorry, man," Gene said, sweat pouring down from his face as he extended his big mitt to help me from the turf.

"Stop apologizing and just hit that guy!" I shouted back. "He's gonna kill me."

Bowling Green had the ball at mid-field with only a few minutes left in the first half. I was hoping they would just run out the clock so I could get in the locker room to lie down. But they fumbled.

I was slow getting up off the bench and back on the field.

"C'mon Quinn," Aidan said, from the stands behind me. "Keep going. Just keep going."

My legs felt like lead. Each breath was a labor. But I put one foot in front of the other to try and tie things up before halftime.

I dropped back to pass on the first play of the drive and found myself defenseless—as quarterbacks often do—waiting for a receiver to clear before delivering a pass. Dex hit me so hard my helmet popped off my head. When he followed up with a shot across my nose, Gene lost it.

It's one of the worst fights I'd ever seen in a game. When it was over, Gene was at the bottom of a pile, unconscious, with a twisted knee and ankle.

Because he couldn't play, the school refused to renew his scholarship the following year. Gene took a tumble he never recovered from.

My first pro-bono case after law school was representing him in a possession of heroin rap. He climbed on the wagon for about six or seven years but the next time I heard from him was after he'd picked up a federal distribution case. Gene had scored some heroin and given half to one of his junkie friends. The prosecutor said that made him a distributor. Even worse, they were getting high in the woods behind an elementary school, which doubled the penalty. He went away for almost nine years.

I hadn't seen or heard from him until last fall when I took Eliza to the opening of the Community Arts Center. She took a painting class and spent the better part of the morning on an impression of the small garden in the courtyard. She was very proud of her work.

As we left the Center we found a homeless man sprawled on the sidewalk.

It was Gene.

He was wearing a dirty white t-shirt and black carpenter pants. He had no shoes, which exposed the ankle that had never healed correctly. His deformed foot jutted awkwardly toward the outside of his leg.

Eliza studied the man carefully. Her eyes welled up.

"Help him, Daddy," she said.

Gene opened his eyes, stood and hobbled away down the busy sidewalk. I followed with Eliza in tow but when I caught up to him and placed my hand on his shoulder, he turned on me with the kind of lightening reflex that had made him a standout on the gridiron. He just said, "Leave me. Now."

We let him go. But when we returned home, Eliza announced she was not going to bed that night until one of us took her to make certain Gene had somewhere to sleep. I wasn't going to sleep well either, so we obliged and spent the evening at the city shelter. The director assured Eliza that she knew Gene and that he would have a place to sleep. That was almost seven months ago. I hadn't seen him since then.

I ran back to my Jeep and grabbed a Connecticut State sweatshirt from the back. Gene rolled over on his stomach as I returned to him. I tried to blanket him with the sweatshirt but it only really covered his back. I tucked the sleeves beneath his body to keep it in place. I returned to the Jeep and found a protein bar and a bottle of water in the console. I returned to Gene and left both items behind his head.

I hopped behind the wheel, made a U-turn and headed up Route 9 to Hartford. And started talking to myself.

I'm always talking to myself. It started out as something I'd do to plan for a big meeting or an argument that I had to make in court. But over time it just became something I couldn't stop doing. I try to keep it under control when other people might be around—which just makes me mumble. The kids have caught me doing it too many times to count. It typically sets off an imitation contest and lots of laughter. I don't tell them that these days I only do it when I'm worried.

I tried listening to the morning news on NPR but found myself practicing what I might say to Aidan later in the day. "'There are other people to consider . . .' No, that's stupid. He'll just say something like, 'Yeah, the three and half million people who live in this state.' I'll just tell him I don't *want* to do it. I'm an idiot; I can't say that. I wish he'd just ask Daniel to do it; maybe I could ask him." And so it went. Each sentence typically ending in an unintelligible mass of garbled nonsense.

I sped through the empty parking garage, hurried to the elevator and marched through the dark hallways to my office. I settled in behind my desk and opened my contacts. I ignored the small stack of mail and a draft brief awaiting my review to give my full attention to finding someone that might satisfy Aidan.

Without knowing who Aidan may have already contacted, I didn't take anyone off the table: legislators, former legislators, town committee chairs, convention delegates, prominent activists, not-so-prominent activists, television personalities. It's not easy to find the right candidate to run for statewide office in Connecticut. It's a complex place.

There's a little bit of everything in Connecticut. Private equity moguls, hedge fund managers and insurance executives operate alongside dairy farms, sunflower farms and even tobacco farms. Its economy is anchored by manufacturers of firearms, helicopters, micro-processor boards, and even nuclear submarines.

Connecticut is well more than a hundred years older than America but it's not just populated with old-stock New England Yankees. Italian-Americans are the largest ethnic group in five of the state's eight counties. French-Canadians are the largest group in Windham County up in the northeast, while the Irish dominate in Tolland County to the north.

Blacks make up 13 percent of the population and Hispanics almost 17 percent, with both groups mainly residing in urban areas. Migrants from Laos, Vietnam, Thailand, Indonesia, Mexico, Brazil, Guatemala and Panama are all fast-growing groups that likewise tend to gravitate to the cities. Connecticut's a third Catholic but Jews, Baptists, Episcopalians, Methodists and atheists are all well-represented.

And then there's the wealth—alongside the poverty. The most expensive American home ever offered for sale, the $190 million Copper Beech Farm in Greenwich, leads a remarkable assembly of waterfront homes and estates that track the more than 300 miles of winding southern coastline, Connecticut's Gold Coast. On the other end of the spectrum, more than 725,000 people—21 per cent of the state's population—live in households at double the poverty level or lower. Hartford, our capital city, leads the way. It's one of the poorest cities in the nation, with three out of ten families living below the poverty line.

Running for statewide office in Connecticut calls for candidates who can navigate the overlapping ethnic and socioeconomic circles without stumbling over themselves. I had three ideas for potential candidates after getting through about half my contacts: a former state controller who wasn't happy in her law practice, a former state treasurer who'd made a lot of money after leaving office, and a sitting federal prosecutor who I knew to have political ambitions.

"Have you decided anything?" Keisha asked.

She startled me. My secretary always stops in at about 7:45 a.m. But today she was fifteen minutes early.

I first met Keisha when she was only fifteen. Her brother, Lane Jackson, was one of the tri-state area's most infamous drug dealers. When she was barely nine, he enlisted her to keep the numbers of his mammoth drug organization. She tracked every delivery, sale and distribution channel with incredible precision—all without reducing a single number to writing.

When Lane learned that Keisha was going to be a co-defendant and tried as an adult if he pushed for a trial, he did something I had never seen a defendant facing a life sentence do. He thought of someone other than himself, and pleaded guilty.

Keisha started in Clay Pittman's mail room after her high school graduation. She was running it within a year. More than a few eyebrows were raised when I brought her upstairs to work as my secretary. Keisha's high heels and immodest wardrobe didn't quite match the decorum of a white-shoe law firm, but no one could challenge her performance. She was the most talented secretary in the building. Had she been born under different circumstances, she'd be one of my law partners.

"Who've you been talking to?" I asked.

"Daniel dropped me a line after you left there yesterday."

"Great."

"And then Aidan called me himself."

"Wonderful."

"And Brooke sent me a text last night."

"Fantastic."

"They want me to watch to see if you were paging through your contacts," Keisha said, leaning on my desk. "Aidan and Daniel want a call if you're searching for someone else. Brooke wants to know if you're not searching."

"What do you think I should do?" I asked.

"Your partners will never let you run around the state making their friend look like a fool," she said, "or getting in the way of their money."

"Plenty of lawyers here have run for office: state Senate, treasurer, Congress—"

"Money. Those people were all Republicans and weren't getting in the way of your partners' money." She sipped her coffee. "They'll vote you out of here in about ten seconds flat if you do this."

"We have rules about that stuff," I said. "They're in our partnership agreement."

"Well, that agreement ain't gonna help you one bit if they think even one company or client would complain about you."

"So you don't think I should do it."

"Oh, no. I think you have to do it."

"For Aidan?"

"I don't care about Aidan," she said, her lips twisted. "You have to do it because people like us don't have anyone like you: Someone that knows them and how they operate. There's no union for poor people."

"Even if I can't win?"

"I think you can beat him," she said. "But even if I thought you weren't gonna win, I'd say you have to do it anyway."

My phone rang. She reached over me and lifted the handset from its cradle.

"Mr. Barnes' office. Can I help you?" Keisha asked, immediately transforming her voice to speak with diction that would make the Queen of England proud. "Great," she said to the person on the other end of the line before hanging up. "The Kincaids are here," she told me.

Alistair Kincaid is one of the three wealthiest men in Connecticut, which makes him one of the wealthiest men in the world. The 54-year-old self-made private equity titan got his start as a junior trader on Wall Street in the early '80s. The son of a painter and public school teacher, his net worth stands at $2.4 billion.

The only things Alistair Kincaid doesn't own are things he doesn't want to own. He has three mansions, a home on four different continents, part of a professional baseball team and a collection of fine art that includes a recently purchased Picasso, for which he paid a modest $47 million. He's a man who has spent the majority of life in firm control of his destiny—until today.

I had to tell Alistair that he was about to be indicted.

"Is his wife with him?" I asked.

"Yes." Keisha straightened up. "They're on their way up. I'm gonna meet them at the elevator."

"What conference room do we have?"

"The Reagan."

"Where are the copies?"

Keisha pointed to the stack of paperwork on the corner of my desk.

"I'll be there in a minute."

An indictment is the government's formal filing of charges against the accused. In the federal system, the only body in the entire country that has the power to issue an indictment is the grand jury—which does so at the behest of the prosecutor. In a white- collar case, months—sometimes years—of work precede the issuance of an indictment. There's almost nothing a criminal defense attorney will not do to ward off an indictment; that's because the conviction rate of indicted defendants is an astonishing 97 percent.

I grabbed the copies of the indictment and Alistair's case file. I made my way down the hallway of mahogany-framed office doors and gold nameplates to the Reagan conference room. Normally, I would have a half dozen or so partners and associates with me to discuss a case with a client like Alistair. On a day like today it was best to keep it intimate.

Alistair wore a black pinstripe suit with a silver tie. His slick black hair was parted neatly to the side. A touch of gray slowly encroached from his sideburns. Scarlett's platinum-blonde hair was neatly pulled back in a bun. A beautiful set of pearls accessorized her tailored hound's-tooth blazer. Alistair and Scarlett matched.

There was little small talk. Alistair and Scarlett sat like anxious patients at the oncologist's office.

"You're going to be indicted," I said, instantly dashing their hopes of any sense of normalcy for the remainder of their lives. "The lead charge is insider trading. There are six counts. There are other charges, mail and wire fraud, making false statements, but the principal charge is insider trading."

Alistair lifted his hand to his head and ran his fingernails down the side of his face. He dug so deep into his skin that a thin line of blood trickled down his cheek. I handed him a handkerchief. Scarlett moved to his side and draped her arm over his shoulder.

Alistair recovered quickly. He stiffened his posture, firmly wiped the side of his face, and got down to business.

"Is this a final decision?" he asked.

"Yes," I said.

"This is no longer secret, right?" Scarlett asked.

"Correct. Everything that happens in front of the grand jury is secret, but the indictment is a public document."

"When will it be made public?" Alistair asked.

"About three weeks. All the indictments under consideration by the grand jury are presented together to the chief judge. After she accepts them, they're made public."

"Three weeks?" he asked, squinting.

"I'll get you the exact date."

Alistair removed the handkerchief from his cheek. The bleeding had stopped but he looked like the victim of an awful shaving accident. He sipped the coffee Keisha had left for him and leaned back, passing his hand over his hair.

"What's the penalty?" he asked.

"The insider trading counts each carry a potential penalty of 20 years in prison and a $5 million fine. The federal sentencing guidelines can adjust those numbers up or down."

"We hired you because of your relationships with the people in that office," Scarlett said angrily. "You worked there. What about your relationships?"

Alistair stepped in. "Is there anything that can be done in these three weeks to stop this process?" he asked.

"No."

"Are you sure?" Alistair asked.

"In theory, the prosecutor could withdraw the indictment before it's presented to the judge but he would probably have to get the grand jury to agree. In more than 20 years of practice, I have never seen that happen."

"This is because of all this nonsense with Saul," Scarlett said. Her face reddened.

"I'm not sure I understand what you're saying." I put my pen down.

"Everyone is talking about your running against him," she said. "He associates us with you."

"Scarlett, I know this is terrible news but it has nothing to do with a race that I'm not going to run."

"You're making his life miserable," she went on, "and he's going to make life miserable for you and anyone who associates with you."

"I can assure you that a federal prosecutor is not influenced by an election," I said. "And that these decisions were made weeks ago."

"He's our friend, you know," she said.

"More than that," Alistair said. "He's a client."

"Quinn, you're naïve," she said, her voice cold. "Any decision can be influenced."

My phone buzzed on the corner of the conference room table alerting me to the arrival of a text. Seconds later, there was a knock at the door.

Keisha stuck her head in and pointed to my phone.

"Excuse me," I said, picking up the phone and activating it with my thumb to read the text:

There's been a shooting.

Mr. Coyle needs you to get to East Haven ASAP! K

"Can I come out to the house either this afternoon or this evening to continue this discussion?" I asked. "There's been a—"

"That's not necessary," Alistair said. "We're done here."

V

One of the first history lessons every Connecticut child is taught in grade school is the story of Sarah Harris. In the fall of 1832, Harris, a nineteen-year-old woman from rural eastern Connecticut, was trying to figure out what career to pursue so that she might lead a meaningful and purposeful life. The daughter of a local farmer, she was certain that farming was not for her. She loved books and was passionate about learning, so she set out to become a school teacher.

Sarah soon learned that another woman, Prudence Crandall, had recently opened a boarding school for girls in nearby Canterbury. She paid Prudence a visit. Sarah was astonished to find that the school was one of the best in the state—perhaps even the country. Students at Prudence's school learned everything from reading and writing to advanced mathematics and astronomy.

Sarah asked Prudence for admission so that she, in turn, could teach others these marvelous things. Prudence had reservations but ultimately pushed past them and admitted Sarah. In doing so, she created the first integrated school in the United States.

There was hell to pay for both Sarah and Prudence. The school didn't last long, due to among other things, repeated threats of violence. But these two young women nevertheless put the state—and the country—on the long road to integration an entire generation before the Great Rebellion.

This is why Connecticut's current racial tensions are such an embarrassment.

It's easy to miss if you stay close to the affluent shoreline communities in the south like Clinton, Madison and Guilford—or behind the walls of the Fortune 500 companies that call southwestern cities like Fairfield, New Canaan and Greenwich home.

I don't have that luxury.

I have to live in and navigate all of Connecticut, including the towns like East Haven.

First settled by Puritans in 1638, East Haven poses as a cozy suburb of urban New Haven. In its center are a simple town green and an 18th-century stone church. This mostly working-class town would largely go unnoticed but for its reputation for promoting racial strife.

East Haven is run by the tough-talking Mayor Jay Brocco, Jr. An electrician before getting into politics, he took the helm at the mayor's office in the late '70s at the height of Connecticut's efforts to desegregate its schools. Brocco ran on a platform that opposed busing black kids from nearby New Haven to integrate East Haven's public schools.

"What right does the state have to force someone to be bused against his will, to sacrifice the interests of any individual to a vague social plan?" Brocco told the *New England Free Press* during his first campaign. "Each person has the right to do what he wants with his own life, including the free choice of which school he should attend."

I've always remembered that quote. I read it to my parents at the dinner table in October of 1977.

Aidan taught me that politicians like Jay Brocco are like weather vanes. They don't really believe in anything except staying in office. They'll go with whatever direction they believe the wind is blowing to hold onto power. And Mayor Brocco has spent a lifetime attending every pancake breakfast, high school basketball game and wedding reception—whether he's invited or not—so he always knows which way the wind is blowing in East Haven.

In '97, a member of Brocco's all-white police force followed an unarmed 21-year-old black man named Malik Jones from East

Haven to New Haven and shot him to death following a traffic stop on Grand Avenue. Brocco figured he'd best stand with his white working-class constituents and against the community activists who cited the tragedy as the inevitable result of Mayor Brocco's hostility toward the growing minority and immigrant population in his community.

After the shooting, protests raged. Tensions heightened. Brocco dug in.

"East Haven represents faith and family values," he told his supporters as his police force took racial profiling to new heights. It didn't take long before there were reports of detainees being slapped, kicked and beaten while handcuffed. When a local priest tried to document the brutality, he was also arrested. The Feds got involved in '09, issuing a report detailing "widespread biased policing, unconstitutional searches and seizures, and the use of excessive force" by his department. Brocco stood defiant and largely ignored the report—until this year, 2012, when the Feds arrested and indicted four members of his police department for harassing, beating and retaliating against Hispanics and other people in town who complained about their viciousness.

When Mayor Joseph Brocco Jr. was asked again if he stood behind his police department and what he was going to do to address the Latino population's concerns, his answer was simple: "I might have tacos when I go home."

Those words were ringing in my ears as I pulled up to a small white Cape on Currier Street in the heart of East Haven's Dominican community. It looked like all the other houses on the block, which all stood about twenty feet from each other. People milled about on the tiny front lawn. No one really noticed me as I walked to the front door.

A woman stepped onto the porch before I could knock.

She was tall—as tall as me. She wore bright red lipstick but no other makeup.

Long curly black hair draped the shoulders of a blue pants suit. Her striking beauty was dampened only by the redness in her brown eyes, making it clear that she'd been crying.

"You are Attorney Barnes?" she asked, her accent thick.

"Yes," I said. I extended my hand.

"My name is Nancy Perez." She firmly shook my hand and gestured for me to follow her inside.

The small living room was crammed with people I assumed to be friends and family members. I had to turn my body sideways to pass through the room. I nodded to the people who made eye contact with me as she led me into the kitchen.

A young boy sat alone at the kitchen table. He wore a black hoodie and leaned back in his chair. His hands were jammed into the hoodie's front pouch. He stared blankly at the center of the table. His jet-black hair draped over his face. I couldn't see his eyes.

"Attorney Barnes, this is my youngest son, Carlito. He was there."

I slipped out of my coat jacket and loosened my tie. I placed my leather briefcase on the floor. I didn't take out my iPad or any paper to take notes. I didn't want to make the kid nervous.

"Hi, Carlito. I'm Quinn."

I received no response.

Ms. Perez barked something to him in Spanish. I didn't understand what she said, but Carlito magically came to life. He sat up, brushed his hair from his eyes and placed his palms on the table. He stared right at me—and looked like he wanted to fight.

"How old are you, Carlito?"

"Eleven."

"My boys are eleven," I said. "They're both baseball players. You play ball?"

"Not today," he said.

I rolled up my sleeves.

"I need to understand what happened today."

"I was with my brother, Alarico," he said. "We were in My Country. It's a store on Main Street."

"It's owned by Dominicans," Nancy said. "We're Dominican."

"Who else was with you?" I asked.

"It was just me and Al."

"Did you buy anything?"

"He bought a bunch of licorice and some orange soda. On the way home, we got stopped."

"By who?"

"I think it was a cop . . . I'm not sure."

"Why aren't you sure?"

"We have a neighborhood watch," Nancy said, leaning back against the counter. "They carry guns."

"The guy had on a dark blue coat. I just figured he was a cop," Carlito said.

"What kind of questions was he asking you?"

"Where we were going—stuff like that. Al answered his questions and I thought he was gonna just let us go home."

"But?" I asked.

"But he started asking me questions and Al got mad. He told the guy that he was responsible for me and that I didn't have to answer any questions."

"How old is Al?"

"He was seventeen," Nancy said. Her eyes welled up. She grabbed a tissue from a box on the counter behind her.

"Did you answer any questions?"

"No."

"Why?"

"Because Al told him we were leaving and we started walking away. The guy says, 'You're not going anywhere.'"

"Did you stop?"

"Kind of. Al grabbed me by the arm and whispered, 'Remember the rule,' but he said it in Spanish, 'Recuerde la regla.'" Carlito leaned back in his chair. He started crying. "The guy got real mad. He started yelling for us to step away from each other and to get on our knees. He had his hand on his waist."

"Was there anyone else around?" I asked.

"No." Carlito rubbed his eyes with the sleeve of his hoodie. "We got on our knees and put our hands up—but only for a second."

"Why for only a second?"

"'Cause the guy called us a 'pair of banana niggers.'" Carlito took a deep breath. "Al went nuts. He got up and started fighting the guy."

"What did you do?"

"I followed the rule: If something like that happens, the older kids stay and fight so the younger kids can make it home."

"Whose rule is that?"

"Mine," Nancy said. "I work two jobs. I'm a nursing aide at New Haven hospital and work third shift at Nutmeg Medical here in town. That's what I need them to do if I'm not here."

"Did you ever see a gun?" I asked.

"No, I saw Al body slam the guy and I just ran. When I got to the end of the block, I heard a shot—and then two more."

"Was your Mom home?"

"I was working third shift," Nancy said. "I came home as soon as he called."

"Have the police asked to speak with Carlito?"

"No," she said. "Can you help us? I don't want them to get away with this the way they did with that other boy."

"How did you find me?" I asked.

"I'm in the service employees union. My shop steward told me to call Mr. Coyle. Mr. Coyle said he was sending you."

"The police are going to call you either tonight or tomorrow for a statement." I reached into my pocket for a card. "When they call, I want you to call my cell so I can come back. I need to be there for the interview."

"So this means you're gonna help us?"

"I'm going to try."

VI

I leaned against the wall and waited for Brooke in the hallway outside her office in Middletown. There's no reception area. The double doors to family court sit at the end of the hall. The tiny offices for all the assistant attorney generals who work in the child protection unit line both sides of the hallway. Brooke's office is about fifteen feet from the courtroom.

All sorts of characters made their way in and out of the place. Social workers led abused children out of the courtroom. Investigators ducked into the AAGs' cramped offices to prepare their cases. Parents accused of abusing their kids argued their cases to their lawyers up and down the hallway. Couples hoping for adoption walked around with confused expressions as they tried to navigate the unfamiliar surroundings of family court.

Brooke complains a lot about her job. Not the people in the courthouse or the kids—she carps about the spartan office space and lack of resources. About six or seven years ago, I tried to set her up in a big firm in New Haven but she turned it down flat.

"Stop trying to fix everything," she told me when I had suggested the idea of switching jobs. "I just need you to listen to me vent about the place sometimes."

"I just think there's a lot of about law firm life that you'd like," I said.

"I'm obviously okay with you doing it—working in one of those firms," she told me. "But I need to be connected with people. To do something with purpose. I can't think of anything I would enjoy less than helping people fight over money."

"You know there's more to it than that. And you can have a pro-bono practice."

"Quinn, I don't want to do this work as a sideline—something I pick up for a few hours when things are slow with a corporate client. This is a real thing. Real people with real problems."

"But I can see it wearing on you. The broken bones . . . the baby homicides . . . It's human tragedy heaped upon human tragedy."

"You're not the only one who needs to live in the real world. This is part of it."

"But I don't want to. I have to. I don't have any choice."

"That's not true and I wouldn't have married you if it was."

Brooke emerged from her office with two social workers in tow. They wrote while she talked.

She always looks a little out of place here. She loves her designer clothes and at five foot ten, it's hard to miss her in them. She always looks like someone overdressed for a party—but doesn't care that she is.

I put my phone away, picked up my picnic basket and waited for her to walk down to me.

"Are you a lawyer?" a short teenager in a Middletown High School t-shirt asked me.

"I am."

"Wanna be my lawyer?" she asked.

"Traynique, he's not the kind of lawyer you need," Brooke said from behind her. "Mr. Cohen is going to be your lawyer." Brooke passed her and planted a kiss on my cheek. She looked excited to be getting out to lunch.

"That's your man?" Traynique asked.

"Well, I don't own him, but yes, this is my husband, Quinn Barnes." I shook Traynique's hand.

"But your last name is Wolcott . . ."

"It is."

We slipped out a side door and held hands while we made our way down DeKoven Drive toward the Connecticut River. Sun splashed on the storefronts and restaurants decorated by school children for Earth Day. Brooke made us slow down so she could take in the drawings of moon jellyfish, hummingbirds, chameleons, puffer fish, dung beetles and other creatures from across the globe. When we finally made it to the Route 9 underpass and then up to Harbor Park, we found a small sailboat slowly making its way down the river and framing a picturesque view of the Connecticut River Valley.

We found a picnic table with a large red rectangular umbrella next to the water. She sat. I unpacked our basket.

"Benjamin's class needs a chaperon for their field trip to the Amistad museum next Wednesday," she said. "I told his teacher you'd do it."

"During the week?"

"That's typically when schoolchildren have school trips—during the school day."

"I can't do that."

"You have to do more with them than sports," she said, helping me spread a white cloth over the table.

"I'm aware."

"They're empty vessels—"

"I know that also."

"–something's going to fill them up. Us or video games."

"Well, the Amistad museum will have to fill them up for an afternoon. I can't take an entire day in the middle of the week."

"How do you know? You didn't even look at your calendar."

"I don't need to look at my calendar to know that I can't take a day off in the middle of the week." I placed a glass and a green bottle of Pellegrino in front of her. "You know that."

"I do it. You can do it. Please look at your calendar."

"I have a different job." I pulled out my phone to check my calendar.

"I know you just didn't mean to suggest that somehow your job is more important than mine," she said, digging into the basket. "So I won't take offense to that." She retrieved a platter of grapes, artisanal cheeses and wheat crackers. "I know you didn't make this yourself," she said, plopping a grape in her mouth, "but it doesn't look like you bought it in a store."

"Keisha put it together for me."

"Love that Keisha."

"I have two arraignments in the morning," I said, looking at my calendar. "A guilty plea after lunch and then I have to meet with Aidan." I returned my phone to my pocket.

"Okay, great. Any first-year associate can say, 'My client enters a plea of not guilty,'" she said in a husky fake voice, "and 'Yes, your Honor, we waive our rights to a trial.'" She dropped another grape in her mouth. "I just saved your clients thousands of dollars," she added, smiling.

"I can't do it," I said, unwrapping our salads.

"Okay," she said lightly. "I'll call my mother."

Keisha had outdone herself. I slipped a tossed salad with sliced grilled chicken breast, tomatoes, avocado, scallions and sunflower seeds in front of Brooke. Keisha had prepared the same for me but remembered to add bacon to mine.

I poured us both water and sat.

"What's the Aidan meeting about?"

"The campaign."

"What is there still to be talking about?"

"I still haven't found him a candidate."

"I thought this was settled. It's not your responsibility to find him a candidate. It's his idea. He can find himself a candidate."

"It's not that simple."

"He's manipulating you."

I didn't respond. She knows what buttons to push to make me angry. And I know hers. I dug into my salad for a slice of chicken and some greens.

"You're about the smartest man in this state," she went on. "You have to see how he's manipulating you."

I picked up my water and drank, slowly. Now I was looking at her. Not getting a response, she jabbed again.

"It's now more important than ever that you see him for what he is."

"Brooke, the man is dying," I said.

"He's an alcoholic. His own son hates him. And he's about to die without a family. You're the only one who can't see it. You still treat him like some kind of savior—and believe everything he says is the gospel."

Deep breath.

When we were newlyweds and Brooke said something that filled me with rage, I would holler and wonder if our marriage would endure. After we settled into marriage a good bit, I took it as a sign that I had married the right person. I figured that only destiny could have brought me to a person who I loved so intensely that I sometimes feel physically ill when we're apart, and who at other times could fill me with white-hot anger requiring herculean restraint to avoid throwing a piece of furniture through a window. Now, I wasn't sure what to think.

Another deep breath.

"Okay," I said. "You just said that because you're afraid that I'm actually going to do this and you're trying to get my attention."

"Wrong. And don't patronize me." She put her fork down. "I'm saying this because it's true. And I'm not going to let him ruin your life and our family."

I put my own fork down. "Is this about money? You're worried that we won't be able to live like this if I'm not at the firm?"

"You say things like that and it's like punching me in the stomach. It honestly makes me want to throw up," she said, her face reddening. "And I know that's Aidan talking. If our marriage doesn't last, it's because you've let him paint a picture of me in that head of yours that you won't let go of."

"If our marriage doesn't last it's because you can't bring yourself to accept what I am."

"You can be as cruel as you want but I'm going to make you sure you hear this." She gripped the edge of the table with both hands. "I've let you look at him adoringly through rose-colored glasses all these years—even though I know how he's hurt you."

"Aidan has *never* hurt me. Never!" Brooke lowered her head and scratched her scalp with all ten fingers. "And if the way he's gotten me to this point in life offends you, well then, that's your problem."

"You're right," she said, looking up. "Aidan is and has always been my problem."

"The person who has me in position to be a senator is a problem?"

"I knew you wanted to do this," she said, gritting her teeth.

"Brooke, how many times do I have to tell you? I'm . . . trying . . . to . . . find . . . someone . . . to . . . do . . . it."

"Give me enough credit to know that no sane person is going to take a flying leap into the teeth of a buzz saw. And you're so obsessed with him and with pleasing him that it's all a done deal, and you don't even see it yet."

"You're not making sense."

"I'm the one not making sense?" she said, her face now bright red.

"Even if you're right, we're talking about three and a half months. The primary is August fifteenth. We'll be on the Cape together before Labor Day."

She just kept shaking her head.

The light bulb went off in mine.

"You think I'm going to win."

She looked at me, her eyes welling up. "I think you *could* win."

"Well, then, that's one of the meanest things you've ever done to me—laughing at me, telling me I was a joke."

"Oh, grow up. And don't try and turn this back on me. You're the one who's about to break up our family. I'm doing what I have to do."

"I'm not going to break up anything."

"Name for me one single politician who has a normal family life. A politician is a person who will attend a fundraiser while his child is battling pneumonia. They're the kind of people who spend their wedding anniversaries speaking at rubber-chicken dinners. They literally go months without seeing their spouses and kids and behave like it's normal to catch up for fifteen minutes backstage at a fundraiser. I'm not going to be married to a politician. It's no marriage at all."

"I can't believe we're having this conversation."

"Believe it. I am not going to let a lonely, sad, pathetic man destroy our family."

"You know what Aidan would say to that?"

"Why don't you keep that one to yourself."

I stood.

And left her sitting there.

—⚮—

Night fell on the Hartford skyline while I worked alone inside my office. I lost track of time catching up on emails and voice mails from clients and other lawyers. A pile of pleadings drafted by associates needed to be reviewed before being filed in court in the morning. And I was still no closer to finding Aidan a candidate. I sent Brooke a text to let her know I wouldn't be home for dinner. I stared at the phone waiting for a response, but none came.

I rolled my chair to the window and put my feet up on the ledge. With the office now deserted, the only noise was the tick of the clock to keep me company. I got to thinking about what life would be like when Aidan was finally gone. I watched the white lights crawl north on I-91 along the Connecticut River and turn to a trail of red rubies as they curved onto I-84 west out towards Waterbury.

Waterbury always reminds me of one of Aidan's most important teachings.

When I was a teenager, Aidan always made a point of dragging Daniel and me with him whenever he had to go to a funeral. I always protested.

"I'm missing basketball practice, and I have homework to do," I said from the back seat of his Buick as we headed west on I-84 to attend the funeral of a former Waterbury mayor I'd never met. Daniel paged through a comic book in the passenger's seat.

"I love a good funeral," Aidan said happily from behind the wheel, decked out in the dapper black suit he always wore to these events. "A funeral always lifts my spirits."

"But I don't even know this guy," I said.

"He was a good Irish soul. That's all you need to know."

"But I'm not Irish."

"The Irish are the Blacks of Europe," he said, still smiling. "That means he's your cousin. Think of him as your cousin."

Daniel just shook his head.

"How can a funeral make you happy?" I asked. "Didn't you even like this guy?"

"I loved Mayor Scully," Aidan said. "Got him elected and helped him keep gettin' elected." Aidan used the rear view mirror to pick up my gaze. "Funerals remind me about the meaning of life."

Aidan had my undivided attention. He was always saying funny and amusing things—things that would make me think and want to better understand history and the world. But this was the first time he'd ever revealed that he knew the meaning of life. I sat up, leaned forward and marked every word.

"Well, don't stop," I said. "I've got to hear this."

Aidan gave me a wry smile through the rearview mirror.

"Well, first," he said, "you need to understand that the past is never dead—it's not even the past."

"What the heck does that mean, Dad?" Daniel asked from the passenger seat.

"Quinn, what do you think it means?" Aidan asked.

I was as lost as Daniel and just guessed. "That there's no such thing as history?" I said meekly.

"That's exactly what it means," Aidan said. "Faulkner said it. It means that no person, no place, no civilization can escape its history. So when you boys are studying your history lessons and learning about something that happened fifty years ago or five hundred years ago, you have to think about it like it happened this morning."

"Are you sure that's what it means?" I asked.

"I'm certain." Aidan held up his right hand to let me know there was nothing to debate. "Next," he said, "you have to think of all the people who've ever lived on this planet."

"You mean today?" I asked.

"No. Think bigger," Aidan said. "I'm talking about since the beginning of mankind. Since the first human being ever walked on this earth." He gave us some time to consider it. "More than one hundred billion souls have been born," he went on, "all over the course of tens of thousands of years."

"Okay," I said, slowly. Not really understanding where he was going.

"Well, when you figure you're only gonna live about seventy or eighty years—if you're lucky—you probably feel pretty small."

"When you put it that way," I said, "I do."

"And that there can't be much point to your itty-bitty little life," he said.

"I suppose not," I said.

"Here's what I want you to always remember." Aidan looked back at me again through the mirror. "Everything all those people have ever done brings us to this moment right here today. All those people are singing a song. And they're singing together."

"What song are they singing?" I asked.

"He doesn't mean it literally," Daniel said, smirking at me in a way that made me feel kind of stupid. I got the sense that he'd heard this part before.

My eyes darted back to the mirror to find Aidan's face.

"Think of it like they're chanting," Aidan said. "Some people are chanting soft. Some are loud. Some of them can barely be heard."

"Why are they singing?" I asked.

"To push us all forward," he said. "All those people are connected to each other through this song and they're trying to improve things. To make life a little better for everyone that comes after them."

"Is this what the Catholics believe?" I asked.

"Not exactly. This is our own kind of religion," he said. "But don't worry about what other people believe. I just want you two boys to look back on your lives someday and be able to say that you sang as loud as you could."

"Are you singing loud?" I asked.

"That's why I'm in the politics business, Quinn."

Tired, I rubbed my eyes and then rolled back over to my desk to unplug my office phone, power down my cell phone and lay my head down for a catnap.

Within a matter of minutes, I slipped into a deep sleep. I dreamed about the weekend before Mom and Dad moved us to Hartford. Together with my two best friends, Gene and Titus, we rode our bikes through the August heat to the park on Hudson Street for a day of basketball. We played "Winners," the game that always got played on Hudson Street. We couldn't be stopped. We dispatched the kids our own age without letting up a single basket. Gene was a terror down low beneath the basket and Titus was always the fastest kid on the court. We managed to win four consecutive games against the older kids by playing in perfect sync. After we finally got knocked off the court, we pooled our money and stopped at the fruit stand on Park Street to buy a cold iced watermelon. We worked together to break it on the curb into five or six pieces for consumption, then used the bottoms of our t-shirts as baskets to transport them to a bench behind the sidewalk. We sat in the shade and dug into the jagged pieces of melon while we watched the afternoon go by.

The bliss of kids playing and laughing all around me was interrupted by what sounded like crying. I hovered between sleep and consciousness, trying to figure out if I was still dreaming or whether I needed to wake. I battled to open my eyes to find three members of the evening cleaning staff circled around my desk. Carmen and Magdalena were deploying tissues to brush back their tears. Sam, a forty-year veteran of the night crew, stood beside them, smiling from ear to ear.

"We're so proud of you," Magdalena announced.

"You're going to be for us," Carmen added.

Confused, I looked to Sam for an explanation.

"It's been all over the news," he explained. "I've spent every one of my seventy-one years in this state and I can't believe I'm gonna tell my grandchildren that I know a United States senator—and that he looks just like them."

I plugged in my office phone with my right hand and powered up my cell with my left. They both rang immediately. I tapped the space bar on my computer to bring the screen to life. My heart raced uncontrollably as I read the headlines in the subject bar of the first three emails. The blogosphere was running wild.

The *Left Nutmeg* was reporting, "Hartford attorney and activist pledges to take on Berg." "Longtime democratic operative to challenge Senator Berg," *My Blue Connecticut* announced. Finally, Sludge Hammer from *The Sludge Report* led with, "Former Connecticut State QB hopes to connect on a Hail Mary against Berg." Reporters from the major dailies, the *New England Free Press*, the *Ledger* and the *Gazette* were trying to reach me for comment.

I didn't need to conduct an investigation to figure out that this was Aidan's handiwork. He'd used the blogosphere in a countless number of campaigns to get a story to bubble up into the mainstream media. He also knew that he could get something like this on the web without a blogger calling me first for confirmation. They all knew about our relationship and probably figured I had asked him to leak the news.

I grabbed my car keys and rushed past Carmen, Magdalena and Sam. They followed me all the way to the elevator as if it was their responsibility to get me aboard safely. When I reached the parking garage, I bolted for my Jeep with a singular focus: get to Brooke.

The car clock read 10:42 p.m. as I sped onto the on-ramp to southbound I-91. I scanned through the news channels on the AM dial as I pushed the Jeep up to 80 mph. It was worse than I thought. Aidan hadn't anonymously leaked his musings about my candidacy; WTIC played an audio clip of him declaring that, "Saul will have a primary opponent and his name is John Quincy Barnes."

I turned off the radio and drove faster.

The house was dark when I pulled into the driveway. I slipped in the side door and tiptoed into the kitchen. It was spotless and in perfect order. I held out hope that everyone was peacefully sleeping upstairs until I noticed the note bearing the seal of Brooke's stationery in the middle of the counter. I read it beneath the dim counter lamp.

Quinn:

I have no words for you.

I've taken the kids down to the shoreline to give you the time that you obviously need to figure out what is most important to you.

Brooke

I collapsed into a chair at the kitchen table. I tried Brooke's cell, although I figured she wouldn't answer. I hung up before the voice-mail activated. I called the house phone at our summer place in the Fenwick historic district of Old Saybrook. As I waited for someone to pick up, I thought about how I never really wanted a summer house. I just didn't think the kids needed it or that we'd use it much. I suppose it was coming in handy now. The announcement on the voicemail came on. I hung up and dialed again.

Same result.

I didn't leave a message.

My body felt tired and heavy. Unable to muster the energy to stand and go to bed, I sat motionless for the better part of a half hour. The sharp ring of the house phone shot a small dose of adrenaline through my heart.

"John Quincy, it's me."

"Hi, Mom."

"Are you okay?" she asked.

"I'm fine," I said. "It's just been a very long day."

"Well, go ahead and get up to bed," she said. Her Louisiana drawl always sounded more pronounced to me late at night.

"Is everything okay?" I asked.

"I'm fine. I just wanted to tell you that I'd be sick if you were doing this to please me."

"How could you have possibly heard about this in Opelousas?"

"We have the internet in Louisiana, John Quincy."

Mom was born and raised in Opelousas, Louisiana, which is about as Deep South as the South gets. She descends from a long line of sharecroppers. Sick of working someone else's property with her eight brothers and sisters, she thought the good Lord had answered her prayers when she met my Dad back in '55.

Dad was in the Air Force, stationed at a nearby base. The only time he took away from his work at becoming a first-rate jet mechanic were his dates with Mom. When providence created a job opportunity at Drummond Aerospace in Connecticut, Dad jumped on it. Mom was an enthusiastic partner, but she never did really take to Connecticut, and didn't have much interest in staying after Dad died.

When I received my signing bonus from Clay Pittman, the first thing I did was buy her some land down in Opelousas. I bought the same property that our family had sharecropped for more than five generations.

"Mom, don't worry about that. I know there's stuff on the internet but I'm not even going to—"

"Because I've been proud of you every minute of every day that we've had together."

"I know, Mom."

"Well then, you should also know that the only reason your father was able to tolerate so many indignities for so many years is because he believed that a day like today would come." I could hear her voice breaking. "I know he's watching," she managed to add, "and he now knows that his life's work had meaning. His dreams are finally coming true."

VII

Self-doubt always seems to have perfect timing. Just when you manage to cobble together the courage to take on the new challenge or dare to do the unconventional thing, the doubt appears like clockwork to elbow bravery and mettle out of the way. Self-doubt works hard to break your spirit. It nearly paralyzed me once.

During the fall of my freshman year in college, my coach told me he was going to name me the starting quarterback the following day. In just a few short hours, I was going to be transformed from a generic member of the 16,000 member student body at Connecticut State, to the person everyone on campus would be discussing.

A unique challenge awaited me in six days. The defending national champions were coming to Connecticut State. Most of their players were the elite athletes being groomed for careers in professional football. Our team didn't have a single player who could even make their team, let alone start on it. It was the kind of game that small-time programs like ours scheduled to try to raise money and build their profile. We had no business getting on the field with the seven-time champions of the Dixie Conference. Mismatches like this one in football usually mean people are going to get seriously hurt.

I suppose it was the perfect ending to what were the hardest four months of my four years of college. Training camp had been a sober reminder of how harsh the real world could be.

I walked into the locker room for the first day of practice to find the depth chart for each position staring me in the face. Each player was ranked from first to worst for each position. Eleven quarterbacks were listed. My name appeared eleventh.

"Hope you didn't unpack your bags, rookie," Boomer Heathcut said, tapping his fist on my shoulder pads from behind me. "Doesn't look like you're gonna be here with us long."

Boomer was the pride of Wilton, Connecticut. I'd never met anyone from affluent Wilton, but he looked pretty much what I imagined a person from Wilton to look like. Tall and blonde, his body looked to be sculpted by Greek gods. Boomer's name was number one on the list.

"Well, I may start slow but I'm sure I'll move up," I said timidly.

"There are no slow starts, buddy," he said. "You start slow and you're out."

"But I'm on scholarship," I told him.

Boomer laughed, showing me his big white teeth. "There's no such thing as a four-year scholarship. We all have one-year options. All of us. That's how it works. If they want you out, you're done."

I went to my locker, pulled a quarter out of my pants, and called Aidan from the pay phone outside the trainer's room.

"I'm sunk," I said, explaining the situation to him. "They have me last and they haven't even seen me play. How's that fair?"

"Stop with the 'fair' crap," Aidan snapped at me. "Nothing's fair. Especially for you. You know that."

My voice started to break. "But how the hell am I gonna pay for college if they can me?"

"Sonny, you buck up right now before I come down there and buck you up," he said angrily. "Do you understand me?"

"Yes, sir." I covered the handset so he couldn't hear me sniffling.

"Now, this is all politics."

"Politics?"

"Yes, politics. Remember that in any competitive situation where you could be cut or fired, the decision maker will keep you around longer—give you every chance to prove yourself—if they like you."

"Whaddya mean like you?" I asked.

"It's all like grade school," he said. "If they like you, they'll give you a chance."

"Okay. How do I get them to like me?"

"Well, it's kind of like same way you got the teachers to like you. The coaches are like the teachers. When you speak to them, do what your mother taught you, always use perfect English—no contractions—and call them 'sir'. Say hello to them when you see them."

"What does diction have to do with football?"

"Sonny, you're different. And people like other people that they think are the same as them. If you sound like them, you can get 'em thinking you're like them."

"Isn't that racist?" I asked.

"Do you want to get what you want and stay in college or make some kind of protest that no one will care about or remember?"

"Okay. What else?"

"Remember that people are watching you even when you're not playing. Never turn your back to the field. Even when you're getting a drink of water, always look like you're paying attention. And ask questions. Talk to your coaches. People tend to vilify people they don't really know. If you can have at least one real conversation with each coach and they feel like they know you, they'll probably at least give you a fair shake. Remember, politics aren't just local—they're personal."

"How do I do all that during practice?"

"Go to the locker room early. And stay late. Just always be hanging around. Get dressed and undressed by the door so you can meet people."

"Does it have to be every coach?"

"Yes. All of them. But here's the thing. It has to be a real conversation. If it comes off as something that's manufactured, they'll just think you're a kiss-ass and it won't help. You're an A-plus communicator. You'll be fine."

"But what about the football?" I asked.

"Is Boomer slated as the starter?"

"Yes," I said. "But shouldn't I be worried about the guy who's number ten before I worry about catching up to the guy's who's number one?"

"No!" Aidan yelled. "Your goal isn't to become the tenth-best quarterback. You want to be number one. Compare yourself to the best," he said. "Now what are Boomer's weaknesses?"

"That's what I'm trying to tell you. This kid can throw a football through a brick wall. He has no weaknesses."

"Sonny, every person has a weakness. You just have to be patient and watch people to figure it out." I could hear him puffing on his cigar. "Can this kid run?" he asked after he exhaled.

"Boomer?" I asked. "He's about as mobile as the Statue of Liberty."

"Okay. Whenever you get a chance to run, you get on your horse and run like the wind."

"But I hate running the football."

"He's the incumbent. You can't unseat him by trying to be a lesser version of him. You have to create contrast. Give them another option. Be a better option."

The phone was quiet while I took it in. I was actually starting to feel better but knew doubt would crash down on me as soon as I hung up the phone.

"Are you sure this will work?" I asked.

"Only if you can do one more thing. It's the most important thing." Aidan paused. I could hear him puffing on his cigar and exhaling again. "You have to embrace your desperation."

"Embrace my desperation?"

"Yes. You have no safety net. If you fail, you'll probably be off that campus by December. And if you fail, there will be no one to blame but yourself. You're desperate. But desperation can be a gift if you channel it in the right direction."

"What direction is that?"

"Use it to stay motivated. To fight. I want you to perform every task like you're fighting for your life. Because you are."

The phone was silent. I knew what I had to do. I wanted to tell him that I loved him for helping me figure it all out but that's not something we ever did.

"Thanks, Aidan," I said. "I'm ready."

"Okay, Sonny. Call me tonight so I can hear about practice and we'll strategize some more."

"I will."

Aidan was actually waiting for me at the field that night after practice was over. He debriefed me on everything from the drills I was put through to the names of every coach on the staff. He wrote their names down on his note pad.

By the end of the first week, I was moved up to seventh. After our first inter-squad scrimmage a few weeks later, I was promoted to fourth. By the time the season started, I was third and traveled with the team down to Vanderbilt for our season opener, a privilege rarely afforded a freshman.

The team was a disappointing 2-4 when Boomer went down midseason with a pair of bruised ribs. His back-up was a fifth-year senior, John Mings, the likely choice to replace him. With our chances of making it to a bowl game gone, they looked to the future and handed the starting job to me. Along with taking on the task of leading the team against the Mighty Tide scheduled to roll into Hartford that Saturday.

I was so scared I didn't hear a single word spoken by any of my professors or anyone else that week. I tried to be brave at practice, because Aidan had always preached never to show fear. Regardless, I could tell my teammates were thinking exactly what I was thinking: We were about to take a terrible beating that weekend and several of us would likely have our seasons ended by injury.

Game day was an absolutely glorious fall New England Saturday. As I led the team onto the field for our warm-up, I couldn't stop thinking about how tragic it was that such an awful thing was about to happen on such a beautiful day.

And then I saw Aidan.

He stood alone in the corner of the end zone with his sideline pass prominently hanging from his neck. Dressed in a dark blue suit with a royal blue and silver tie that matched our school colors, he could have been mistaken for a coach. As the team lined up in military fashion on the yard lines to stretch, Aidan did something he'd never done in all his years of watching me play. He motioned me over to him.

I darted in between our opponents conducting their calisthenics to get to Aidan, looking like a puppy trying to make his way through a pride of hungry lions.

"Son, I know you're scared," he said. "I know exactly how you're feeling, because I'm scared every day. It's been like that my whole life and it never ends."

Aidan had never said anything that stunned me the way this admission knocked me back. It never occurred to me that he could fear anything.

He placed his palms over the ear holes of my helmet to make certain I could hear him above the music blaring from the stadium speakers. "You have a strength in you that can move mountains, but you have to believe in it. It's not enough for me to believe it. *You* have to believe it," he said, his hazel eyes focused on mine. "I need you to grow up today. To be the person I know you can be. That means that today and every day after this one you have to stare fear in the face and fight like hell. I know you better than you know yourself. And you're ready to do this."

I wanted to hug him but just nodded. I had never been more determined to make him proud.

"And take chances," he added before I pulled away. "The only way to win against someone that's bigger and stronger than you is to take chances. You can't win playing it safe."

I did my best to incorporate Aidan's directives into the game plan. I threw deep when they expected me to throw it short. I ran the ball when the circumstances dictated I pass. Most important, I focused. I was so focused that I had completely shut out the noise of the crowd going berserk as we closed the deficit to seven points at halftime, trailing only 21-14. It was as if I were playing in the biggest game Connecticut had ever seen while wearing sound-proof headphones.

There's a funny thing that happens when Goliath realizes even the possibility that he could fall to David. Doubt seems to switch sides to wreak havoc on the favorite. The longer our rag-tag assembly of second-rate players managed to keep the game close, the more the champions from the South seemed to press and make mistakes. The second half was a roller-coaster ride that delivered us within inches of victory. With six seconds remaining and thirty-one yards from the end zone, we had cut the lead to four points in what was now a 28-24 contest.

What transpired next marked another one of the most important moments in my life—and it had nothing to do with football. As I stood behind center in the middle of a stadium filled with more than forty thousand people, I experienced a moment of clarity—and a wave of confidence—that I've spent every day since that one trying to regain. I knew the outcome of the game before the Hail Mary pass ever left my hand. When my teammates and the crowd poured onto the field to celebrate our miracle victory, I rejoiced only in having driven self-doubt from my presence—for at least a day.

As Aidan prophesized, I have never been able to drive doubt from my life. I doubt myself every day. I doubt whether my next opening statement is going to be any good despite the fact that I've delivered scores of them. I doubt whether I can do an effective job at Little League practice, even though I've coached hundreds of practices and games. It never ends. I wake up most days doubting whether I'll be able to tie my shoes.

I doubted whether I could even share the stage with the likes of a political legend, let alone beat him. Self-doubt was back and petrifying me in a way that I haven't experienced since my days at Connecticut State.

I arrived at my office before dawn to wrestle with my doubts in the quiet hours before the day's chaos commenced.

I feared so many things it was hard for me to count them all.

Building a law practice is like starting and maintaining a small business. It takes years of nurturing and constant attention. Even after years of success, you still always feel like you're barely keeping your head above water. The process of making the right contacts and then convincing high-priced clients that they should trust you with their secrets is a long and slow one. The instant you let up or fall into even the slightest complacency, the clients dry up and the practice dies. Even if I could talk my partners into a long leave of absence, the time away would likely prove fatal to all I had toiled for decades to build. I had seen others try it and fail spectacularly.

Hanging a shingle and trying to start over wasn't a viable option, either. My contacts would be gone along with the clientele that feeds my practice. The white-collar bar is a club. The elites that feed it, the ones that pay more than eleven hundred dollars an hour for our services, have certain expectations. Ideology matters. They don't hire or tolerate lawyers who don't believe in them or their causes. A populist campaign for Senate would place me in permanent exile.

And then there was Brooke. We'd had enough fights for me to be certain that she was at the end of her rope. There was no pushing her any farther and she was right about things—at least, the campaign. Politics demands twenty-hour days for weeks on end. Every waking moment is filled with an endless stream of fundraising calls, followed by long nights with town committee and union meetings. Brooke wouldn't stand for it. And I didn't want a divorce.

Finally, there was the blood sport of politics. Running for elected office these days means entering into an agreement to let your opponent and his henchmen tell lies about you and your family that are extreme, outrageous and shocking to the conscience. These are the kinds of lies that can ruin you—and Saul was the master of the politics of personal destruction.

Saul had first won our Senate seat by defeating one of the most experienced and qualified lawmakers in the country, a moderate Republican, Mason Charles III. It was a campaign that was ingenious for its wickedness. Saul won by repeatedly characterizing Charles as old, tired and lazy. He bombarded the electorate with ad after ad depicting Charles as a fat, slothful bear that didn't care about anything other than feeding his rotund face and sleeping in his cave. Charles never recovered. He retired from politics after the election.

The Republicans thought they finally had Saul cornered twelve years later when they nominated Buck Starr, a triple amputee from wounds suffered during his service in Vietnam, to run against him. Saul was quickly becoming the nation's leading foreign affairs hawk and Starr's very presence on the campaign trail highlighted Saul's deafening hypocrisy: Saul Berg had sought six deferments to escape service in the Vietnam War. Unfortunately, the Republicans sorely underestimated what Saul would say or do to hold on to power.

When Buck took a position early in the campaign in favor of allowing a local religious group to build a mosque near Connecticut's 9/11 Memorial, Saul pounced. He ran an ad warning that, "As Americans face terrorists and extremist dictators abroad, Buck Starr wants to let our enemies build a monument to their conquest on 9/11." As photos of Saddam Hussein and Osama bin Laden came together with a picture of Buck, the ominous tone from the voice-over closed out the ad by declaring, "Starr doesn't have the courage to lead." Putting pictures of Saddam Hussein and Osama bin Laden next to the picture of a man who left three limbs on the battlefield was worse than disgraceful, but it worked. Saul was propelled to victory. Buck's career in politics was over before it began.

Six years later, Mark Doane figured he would take a shot at Saul. Doane had left a lucrative job on Wall Street to volunteer his time working for the federal government. His task was to reorganize conglomerates that nearly fell under the weight of the financial crisis. Doane was wicked smart and had a proven record of success. In fact, he was widely credited with saving the government $6 billion by conducting forensic audits of each failed institution and identifying wasteful spending. While Doane's intellect was impressive, he simply could not match Saul's cunning and shrewdness.

The first tactic in Saul's playbook is always to attack his opponent's greatest strength. Saul's ads lampooned Doane as an "egghead" who wasn't qualified to help lead the country through the financial crisis because he had no experience operating the "machinery of government." Saul—who wouldn't recognize a derivative if one fell from the sky and landed on his head—convinced the electorate that he knew more about the cause of the financial crisis than a world-renowned financial expert. He accomplished this by reducing Doane to a cartoon day after day on the airwaves. Doane's professional reputation was in shambles after the election.

I'm not a perfect person, but I have no skeletons in my closet. I always pay my taxes, I've never had an affair and I've spent the better part of my life trying to help people who need help. But I know that won't matter to Saul. A professional politician will say or do anything to hold on to power. As Aidan liked to say, "Saul plays for keeps." He'd figure out some way to twist an innocent, innocuous fact into a horrific scandal that would render me unfit to serve in the eyes of the electorate.

"They're waiting for you," Keisha said.

"Where?" I asked, checking my watch. I'd lost track of time and would have forgotten altogether about the executive committee's demand for a meeting.

"In the Bush conference room," she said.

Clay Pittman's executive committee consists of three partners, each of them every bit the politician. Other partners in the firm had larger books of business but none of them managed their clients with a politician's touch. Dudley Saltonstall, Albert Chapman and Gershom Burr—ominously referred to by the rank and file as "The DAG"—ensured their re-election to the committee each year by strategically doling out work (and clients). By that patronage, they built and maintained the voting blocs necessary for victory.

Dudley Saltonstall learned how to play the political game from none other than Saul himself. He bragged whenever the opportunity arose that he volunteered to work on Saul's first campaign while still in law school and he continued in his role as an operative since then. Born into one of the nation's wealthiest families, he is delusional enough to tell anyone who might listen about his being "self-made." Aidan called Dudley and people like him peacocks. Full of bluster but no substance or grit. He reminded me of everything I've been fighting my whole life.

Life is a race. Dad and Aidan made sure I understood that before I learned the alphabet. Dudley comes from the kind of generational wealth and obscene privilege that allowed him to start that race a thousand miles ahead of me. I've had to outperform all the Dudleys in my world for decades just to achieve something close to equal footing. I don't resent him for it. But I can't stand that he doesn't see it, or acknowledge it.

I always managed to navigate my way around Dudley at the firm but there was no avoiding him now. My supposed threat to his political benefactor placed me directly in his sights.

"We want you to resign," Dudley said, before I could even take my seat. He was calm and measured but his smirk showed his delight in spearheading my ejection from the partnership. "Today," he added. "We want you to *resign today.*"

"Why?" I asked.

"Because you're running for Senate and you can't do that while you're working here."

"You shouldn't believe everything you read in the papers," I said.

"I read this morning that you're going to be meeting with reporters today to talk about the race," Dudley said.

"Talk about the race," I said calmly, looking to Gershom and then Albert. "I haven't made a decision about this." I crossed my legs. "That said, I don't understand your concern. We've had all kinds of people run for office while maintaining their partnerships."

"I think what we're trying to say is that we don't see how you can run a full-time Senate campaign while keeping up your practice," Gershom said. He sounded almost apologetic.

"And there's a pretty significant business conflict," Albert said. "We don't need to point out to you that the senator helps us maintain relationships with three of our largest clients."

"Listen," I said, "it doesn't escape me that the firm throws two fundraisers a year for Saul for a reason—"

"It's not about that," Albert said.

"Do you plan on suggesting that there's something inappropriate about that?" Gershom asked.

"You're out of the race or you're gone today." Dudley said, before I could get a word in edgewise.

"Dudley, the partnership agreement says the partners would have to vote on this," I argued evenly. "You don't have the authority to do this on your own. You need a two-thirds vote."

"You're right, I don't," he said, smugly. "And the second you announce you're in this race, we'll be having that vote."

You didn't need to be an experienced trial lawyer to be able to read Dudley's cocky grin. He obviously believed he had the votes to push me out the door and any rational person, when presented with the choice of risking a lucrative partnership in the state's most prestigious firm over an election that was impossible to win, would back off.

I didn't underestimate Dudley or Saul but felt pretty sure I could cobble together one-third of the partners to keep me. It would be ugly, though. Big clients feed a lot of lawyers and purchase considerable leverage in a law firm. My friends—and their practices—would suffer for supporting me. I didn't want to put them and their families through that.

Dudley had me backed into a corner.

When caught off guard or surprised, I, like most people, tend to revert to my core—the unvarnished version of myself that I would probably just as soon keep hidden from the world. When challenged, all of my instincts are to lash out and fight.

Aidan always coached me carefully about aggression. When Daniel and I were in sixth grade, one of the girls in my class, Mary Beth Pfeiffer, told her friend—in front of all the other kids in our class—that she didn't want to play with the clay because "Quinn had his dirty black hands in it." I would have decked her if the teacher wasn't in the room. That afternoon, Daniel and I were in Aidan's law office copying briefs and I told him about it.

"Were you there?" Aidan asked Daniel.

"Yeah," he said, standing on a step-stool in front of a copier.

"What did you do?" Aidan asked him.

Daniel just shrugged. "I really didn't know what to do . . ."

"Don't worry," I told Aidan from my own step-stool in front of the other copier. "I'm gonna take care of it tomorrow. I'm gonna settle it on the playground."

"Leave it," Aidan said sternly.

"Leave what?" I asked. "If someone comes at you with a stick," I said, parroting his own words back to him, "you hit them with a brick. Mary Beth just hit me with a stick and I'm coming back tomorrow with a—"

"No!" he hollered. "That's not what it means." He grabbed the brief I was about to load into the copier from my hands. "I don't want to discourage you from being aggressive. It's your greatest strength—"

"That's why I'm gonna—"

"But it has to be measured." Aidan's face was getting red. That always happened when he was irritated and we always irritated him when he had to repeat something he'd already told us. "You only fight at the right times and only about things that matter. This doesn't matter."

Aidan handed me back the brief.

He was done talking.

"It matters to me," I said, loading the brief into the copier.

"Well, it shouldn't. These people are all gonna be working for you some day. It doesn't matter."

"But it bothers me."

"I'm gonna tell you one more time, this doesn't matter and that's the . . . end . . . of . . . it," he said.

I thought he'd left the copy room. I shook my head and sucked my teeth while watching the papers run through the machine. "It's not the end of it for me," I said, under my breath.

The next thing I knew I was laid flat on my backside. Aidan had hauled off and knocked me clear off the stool with the back of his hand. I was still seeing stars when I looked up at him, but I remember what he said.

"Not one more word out of you!" he shouted. "If you don't learn this, you'll screw up everything—everything that's being planned for you. Do you understand me?"

I looked back across the table at Dudley. There was nothing to be accomplished by lashing out at him right now.

"Let me give this some thought," I said, nonplussed.

"We need an answer now," Dudley said.

"The by-laws of the partnership agreement say that you would have to give me seventy-two hours' notice before taking a vote on expulsion," I said, looking to Gershom and Albert, ignoring Dudley. I stood. "If you take your vote before then, I'll sue the partnership and we'll have a judge sort this out. I think we all know how that would turn out."

"Can't we come to some agreement here?" Albert asked.

"Not if you want me to resign today." I turned the door. "Just let me know what you guys decide," I said, with my back to them.

VIII

You ready?

Aidan's text displayed prominently on my phone. Before I could slide my thumb across the screen to reply, he sent another.

We're waiting for you . . .

I slipped my phone into the breast pocket of my shirt, pulled my suit jacket over my shoulders and headed for the elevator.

The cavernous lobby at 90 State House Square was unusually quiet for mid-morning. The only other persons present were the two security guards sitting behind the ornate brown and gold desk at the end of the elevator bank. I nodded at the two guards as I made my way between the Roman columns leading to the front door.

A small phalanx of reporters waited on the red brick plaza twenty or thirty feet beyond the front doors. Aidan's black Cadillac Escalade sat in front of Hartford's historic Old State House, framing the background.

I could see him seated in the back seat. He was using his right hand as a visor to battle the sun's glare while peering into the lobby looking for me.

My phone buzzed again to alert me to another text. I pulled the phone from my pocket. Brooke's name appeared atop the screen.

I want to speak with you.

I stepped between two columns to ensure I wasn't in view of the group gathering outside. I stared at the message a good while before swiping the screen to unlock the phone. My wallpaper photo is of Brooke and the kids at Harper's Ferry last summer. Brooke wanted to tour John Brown's fort. The kids were miserable in the hundred degree heat and just wanted to go tubing down the Potomac, but each managed a smile.

I slipped my phone back in my pocket and bowed slightly—my forehead resting on the cool column—and closed my eyes. I drew in a dozen or so deep breaths.

The answer to my predicament wasn't much clearer when I opened my eyes and straightened my back. I wanted to turn right and head back to the elevator bank. I gathered myself, turned left and headed to the doors to face the chaos that waited on the other side.

The building's overhang and dark brown pillars kept me in near darkness from the intense sunlight. It wasn't until I neared the line separating the darkness from the light that the reporters all lurched toward me.

Jack Crowe from the *Free Press*, Connecticut's oldest newspaper, fired first.

"What makes a neophyte who's never as much as run for dog catcher think he can do as much for this state as Saul Berg?" he asked.

After four terms in the Senate, Saul had most newspaper reporters in his corner but the majority are at least careful about appearing impartial. Jack, however, never found it necessary to even put on a pretense of objectivity. The *Free Press* is owned by Patriot Enterprises International, a multi-national conglomerate run by the Plopper twins. Each of their newspapers, which now cover most of the globe, is in the advocacy business on behalf of conservative causes.

"Well, I should probably first make clear that I haven't made a final decision just yet regarding a candidacy," I said evenly. "That said, you're right, Jack. I'm just a regular citizen—"

"Who's never been elected to anything," he said, unapologetic about his interruption.

"Any citizen is entitled to challenge the ideas and the ideals of any member of government. In fact, citizens have an obligation to question their government—especially at a time like this when there's so much at stake."

"You're sounding awfully like a candidate!" Mark Conner from the *Fairfield Clipper* shouted from the rear of the crowd.

"Please don't say that," I pleaded with both hands raised. "My wife may be watching."

They laughed.

But they didn't let up.

I looked for a friendly question, or at least a fair one, from Sue White with the Associated Press, but Pamela Foggerty, a television reporter from WMEG cut her off.

"Why do you want to be a U.S. senator?"

I could see Aidan in the background just over Pamela's shoulder. Like a father watching his child in his first Little League at-bat, he bit his lip and crossed his arms. He'd prepared me for this question years ago.

—⚬—

In 1979, Aidan took off for the entire summer to raise money and organize for Ted Kennedy for president. That meant that Daniel and I had to put our summer vacations on hold to help him.

Kennedy was poised to achieve something that had never been done in American politics: Wrestle the party nomination away from a sitting president. Jimmy Carter was paralyzed by soaring gas prices and a hostage crisis, and the last surviving brother of America's most storied political dynasty was in position to knock him out.

Aidan pulled some strings with the campaign to provide me with an early Christmas gift—a pass to join him at the Kennedy Compound in Hyannis Port. The occasion was to watch as Kennedy gave the first television interview of his nascent campaign to Roger Mudd of CBS. I knelt at Aidan's knee as we watched Kennedy's aura of inevitability unexpectedly shatter with the first question: "Why do you want to be president?" Kennedy's rambling and incoherent answer ended the campaign before it began.

—⚬—

"I'm giving a candidacy for the United States Senate careful consideration because I believe you can change people's lives through public service," I said. "It's that plain and that simple." I took my time, the way I would with a jury. I looked directly to Pamela and then to Jack to finish my answer.

"The point of government is to help give people a fighting chance," I said. "To advance the human condition. When politicians stop working toward those ends, it's time to re-examine our government and the people running it."

"Are you actually saying that Saul Berg is against the human condition?" Sludge Hammer from *The Sludge Report* asked, his face contorted to show his incredulity.

"I suppose there was a time when Saul was just like me—filled with idealism and determined to make life better for as many people as possible. But I've never met that Saul." I stepped right to Sludge to take him on. "The Saul I know is choosing billionaires over college students drowning in student loan debt. The Saul I know is continuing to support subsidies for big oil and claims that there's no money to put people to work rebuilding roads and bridges. The Saul I know puts his friends and his own interests first. And if you're putting yourself first, you're not doing the business of government."

"How can you seriously argue that you could do more for Connecticut than a national figure who has directed tens of millions of dollars in earmarks to the state in just the past year?" Pamela asked.

"Those resources are important to the state, but at what cost do we accept them? Do earmarks give Saul a license to advocate for a constant state of war across the globe? Or work against true marriage equality? Or mislead the public as to the threat that historic rates of income inequality pose to our state and country? Saul is on the wrong side of history and we need to make a change."

"Lucy McCann says your platform is 'Socialism Now,'" Jack said. "Your response?"

"I think all this name-calling is unfortunate because it stops us from having a discussion about an issue that stands as the single greatest threat to our economy and our country."

"But are you a socialist?" Jack pressed.

"I'm not going to take the bait and get upset by any name or label that you or anyone else wants to put on me during this campaign. I'm going to spend my time talking about facts, and here are the facts that I know. Since the credit crisis in 2007, every major investment bank and multi-national company that we were told was on life support is now doing fine. In fact, they're all posting record profits and their stock is going through the roof." I noticed a blogger from *The Left Nutmeg* standing next to Jack. He nodded while I spoke. I took a half step toward them and tried to find the right balance between passion and anger. "The same people who live in my little town of Pentfield who were struggling to keep their jobs and pay their mortgages during the crisis are all still struggling to find work and stay in their homes. I'm asking the people of this state to ask themselves, How is this possible? How is it that five years after the crisis, we could have successfully bailed out a bunch of multi-nationals but turned out backs on our neighbors?"

"You never answered Jack's question," Sludge said, holding up his pen.

"I'm a capitalist. But I can't cheerlead for a system that's becoming more rigged and corrupt by the hour, that's allowing companies and their wealth to purchase a Congress to fatten their bottom lines by getting subsidies they don't need and killing the regulations that they do need. So I, like Thomas Jefferson, James Madison and John Adams, oppose the generation of wealth by manipulating our democracy. Name-calling, cute sayings and pithy campaign slogans are not going to address the greatest challenge of this generation. If that's what Saul Berg decides to rely on during this primary, I'll be serving as your next senator."

"So you're in the race for sure?" Sue White from the AP asked.

"I suppose I am."

The print reporters wrote furiously. The television reporters checked with their crews to make sure they had captured what might provide a sound bite for the evening news.

I knew Brooke had reached her end with me. I wasn't sure whether I had failed her or she failed me.

"The calendar is about to turn to May," Sue noted. "Senator Berg already has all the endorsements, all the town committees and all the money." Sue almost sounded as if she had genuine concern for my welfare. "What do you have?"

"Youth and idealism."

Jack laughed along with the crowd.

"You can't win this race," he said. "Everyone here knows it and I think you know it too."

"Well, Jack," I said, "I suppose we'll both find out the answer to that on primary day."

Reporters tweeted. Bloggers uploaded video to YouTube from their smartphones and tablets. I made my way toward the curb to shake a few hands and join Aidan and Daniel in the back of their Escalade.

"Superb!" Aidan exclaimed. He put up his fists and feigned to shadow box with me again. "I absolutely, positively have never been more proud."

Daniel patted me on the back and smiled but I saw more hurt than happiness in him. He looked the way he looked when we were kids and Aidan praised my grades or a ball that I caught—one that Daniel knew would always be beyond his grasp.

I could see the pain in Daniel now as clear as I saw it then but wasn't going to let it bother me. It felt good to please Aidan. For him to be proud of me. Part of me even thought that seeing him so energized was worth going through what I knew to be the hell to come.

IX

A idan always liked to say that a successful campaign is first con-
ceived in the candidate's mind. By that he meant the candidate
is the person who has the vision, sets the strategy, and endures through
the thicket of problems and obstacles that would render a normal person incapable of lifting his head from their pillow each morning.

I had no strategy. Only the hope that I could keep up the pretense
long enough to prevent Aidan from figuring out that I was just going
through the motions.

"Are you excited?" he asked as we cruised south down Main Street
together in the back of his Escalade to our campaign headquarters.

I replied much the way a child would while being directed to piano
lessons that he knows cost his parents a lot of money. "This is great."

Hartford changes fast. The doors of the most prestigious law firms
and Fortune 500 companies are just three-quarters of a mile from the
half-way houses and drug rehab facilities that surround South Green
Barnard Park. Daniel pulled up to the Circle of Life transition house
situated across the street from the park. Aidan had rented office space
next door.

The counselors and clinicians from the Circle of Life waved to me
through their front window as we walked up to our building. I could
read the support and hope in their smiles. I felt worse than awful.

Aidan led me through the long, drab gray-blue hallway toward an
open space at the end. Volunteers had already decorated the hallway
with 11x14 pages, all with a single giant-sized "Q" printed on them.

Gary H. Collins

Someone had taken a black Sharpie to one of the pages near the end of the hall to write: "The Right Side of History."

Aidan stepped into the vast open office space. Daniel and I followed.

A small army of volunteers milled about, moving desks and setting up computer equipment. There was a big flat screen in the corner that looked like the one from Aidan's office. It was playing *Star Trek: The Undiscovered Country.*

Several volunteers had brought their small children with them. None of them appeared to be school age and they seemed to be having fun coloring together in the far corner. They were drawing Qs and taping them to the wall. One little girl had made a peace sign inside her Q.

Aidan used his cane to lead me along the wall toward the largest of the first-floor corner offices. Volunteers nudged and whispered at one another as they gestured in my direction. It wasn't long before everyone stopped working and stood to applaud.

"Where did all these people come from?" I whispered to Aidan.

"You brought them here," Aidan said, looking back over his shoulder.

He stopped and placed one hand on my shoulder and leaned on his cane with his other. "This is how people that care about this country respond to a first-rate candidate," he said. "Someone that inspires them."

I mouthed, "Thank You," several times to all the strangers who had signed up to champion our lost cause, most of whom looked barely old enough to be in college. Seven or eight came over to nervously shake hands. For a brief moment, it made me feel that I was great and that we could win.

But only for a moment.

I stood on the nearest chair.

"I want to begin and end every day—and every campaign meeting—the same way: by thanking you. Our country endures because of special people like you who stop and take the time to consider the direction the country is heading and which leaders are best qualified

to steer its course. I'm humbled to have your support, and I'll do everything in my power to make our shared vision for a more peaceful and
just world a reality."

More applause.

I kept thinking about all the long nights they had ahead—the
sleeping beneath desks while they sustained themselves on cold coffee and stale pizza. All the money that would be raised and wasted on
something that they have to know could never happen. I pledged to at
least do my best to keep them inspired so they might have something
to take away with them after I led them all to the slaughter.

Aidan tried to usher me to an office in the corner, but we were
interrupted by a pale, thin young man wearing a t-shirt with Einstein's
face on the front. He cradled a laptop like he was holding a baby. "Sir,
I just want to say that I'm here because you inspired me today," he said,
stammering.

"Thank you. What's your name?"

"Graham. I'm a freshman at Connecticut College."

"Well, thank you for volunteering for the campaign, Graham. Let's
try and get out to Connecticut College soon to find more volunteers
like you."

"Could I show you something?" he asked, turning his laptop screen
to Aidan and me. "It's a new program that counts voters. It micro-
targets them."

"We've got an old system that works pretty well," Aidan said, "It's
called knocking on doors and dropping polls. But as soon as we have a
campaign manager, you can show it to them."

Aidan shooed a few more people away and led me into the corner
office. Daniel stayed back to go over some paperwork with a volunteer.

"This is gonna be your campaign manager's office," he said. "You
can use it for today."

Candidates don't have offices. They are either making fundraising
calls or out campaigning.

"I've got Daniel setting up your bank accounts," Aidan said,
enthused to brief me about our newly minted campaign. "He's gonna
be your treasurer."

I sat in the chair behind the plain walnut-colored desk. I motioned for Aidan to get off his feet, which he ignored. He leaned on the front of the desk.

"One of the kids has put together a skeleton website. It's up now to ask for money," he said. "We're gonna use the video of you from today to cut a bio piece."

"Do we have any leads on a campaign manager?" I asked.

"Keisha is organizing resumes and we're gonna show you some people tonight."

"Absolutely not."

"Absolutely not what?"

"Keisha lives paycheck to paycheck," I said, standing. "She can't afford to take a leave from the firm to work on the campaign."

"Leave?" Aidan asked, grinning. "She already quit."

"When did she do that?"

"I suppose right after your partners voted you out of the partnership."

"When was I voted out of the partnership?" I asked, eyes wide.

"Probably about ten seconds after your press conference was over."

I sat beside Aidan on the corner of the desk shaking my head. He put his arm on my shoulder. "Quinn," he said in a low tone that always soothed me, "we knew this was coming. We can't be thrown off by this. This was his strongest card and we both knew he was gonna play it."

"I worked so hard for that partnership."

"It doesn't matter anymore and I'm glad it's gone."

"You're glad," I said, chuckling but not laughing.

"It's a safety net that would hold you back," he said. "Desperation keeps you hungry."

"I've now got all the desperation I need, thank you." I stood and moved to the chair behind the desk. "It makes me sick that Keisha quit."

"Son, you have to let people make these decisions for themselves."

I stayed mute. I knew exactly what Aidan would say and he was well aware how I would counter; we were like an old married couple. There was no point in arguing. I was relieved to see Daniel enter to help us change the subject.

"Senator Barnes," he said, dropping a small stack of papers on the desk. Four or five yellow Post-Its with arrows pointed to the places where I needed to sign.

"That's bad luck," I said, looking over the papers. "Don't say that."

"That ain't bad luck," Aidan said, rubbing his hands together. "That's confidence." He reached into his coat pocket for his Mont Blanc.

I pulled the paperclip from the upper left corner of the stack and reviewed the papers while Aidan and Daniel hovered over me. They went quiet, as if they were afraid any discussion might result in me changing my mind.

It takes a year to plan a winning Senate campaign and two full years of campaigning to execute it. The idea of running and winning a race in less than five months was comical. I scribbled something illegible on the paper as some small protest. When I finished I handed the pen back to Aidan.

"Congratulations, Quinn," Daniel said, his hand on my shoulder. "You're a candidate."

"I'm proud of you," Aidan said. "I can't wait to see you out there."

Daniel gathered the papers and went on his way.

My phone vibrated from the top of the desk. Aidan saw Brooke's name, raised his eyebrows, and backed out of the office to afford me some privacy. After the door closed behind him, I pressed the bottom of the screen to answer.

"Hi Honey." Blood rushed to my face as I waited to hear her voice.

"Hi, Daddy!"

"How's my little girl?"

"I made All-Stars!"

"That's awesome," I said. "Who's coaching the team?"

"Well, I guess 'cause you're not coaching, Mr. Robinson is gonna coach it."

"He's a great coach,"

"He yells too much."

"You can always just ask him to not yell so much."

"Mommy already did."

There was a knock at the door followed by Keisha's head peering through the crack.

"Your first interview is here," she whispered.

I showed her the palm of my hand with five fingers extended.

"Do you have to go, Daddy?"

"I'm okay for a few more minutes. Where are you?"

"In Old Saybrook—at the summer house."

"What are your brothers doing?"

"Wrestling and tackling each other."

"You say that like it's bothering you."

"It is. Why are they always climbing on each other, play fighting—and real fighting?"

"I supposed it's innate."

"What does 'annate' mean?"

"Innate," I said slowly. "It means there are some things that are deep inside us that make us behave a certain way and want to do certain things."

"Is that why you're trying to be a senator?"

"I don't think so but your Uncle Aidan does."

"I saw him with you on TV."

"Good. Was Mommy with you?"

"Yup, we all watched it together."

"Is she there with you now?"

"She's sitting right next to me."

"Can you hand her the phone?"

"She said she will speak with you 'in due time.' How long is 'in due time?'"

"I'm not sure but tell her I love her and give a big hug for me."

"I will. She also said you have to smile more."

"Smile?"

"Yeah, she said you looked too serious on TV. You have to smile more. She says it has to look like you're having fun."

"I'll try."

"Are you coming to my practice for All-Stars?"

"When is it?"

"Friday. Mommy said if you pick me up from school and take me, she will pick me up after."

"I'll be there."

"I love you, Daddy."

"Love you too, Eliza."

—⚘—

I rarely need much more than a half hour to interview any candidate for any role. Whether someone is looking for a job as admin, a new associate to the firm or hoping to join a board of directors, I can typically get a feel for whether it's going to be a good fit within the first five to ten minutes.

Interviewing a campaign manager was going to have to be different. The campaign manager is the first voice a candidate hears in the morning and the last voice he or she hears at night. If the candidate is responsible for setting the campaign's vision, the campaign manager is responsible for finding a way to harmonize the myriad of voices and personalities to make that vision a reality. A good campaign manager is part task master, part strategist and part psychologist. The manager is also the only person working for the campaign who sleeps less than the candidate.

I reached across the desk for the binder that Keisha had prepared for the interviews. I opened it to find a note from Aidan:

Sonny:

I know this feels messy. Stay focused on the challenges directly in front of you. Don't worry about problems five miles down the road. Adapt to the situation. Simplify everything for everyone. Play to your strengths.

Aidan

I put the note in my suit jacket. Aidan was like the uncle who puts a five dollar bill in your birthday card long after it's necessary to put a five dollar bill in your birthday card. He had told me these things so many times that they were ingrained in my psyche—like all his other teachings. Regardless, his note made me feel a touch better and wonder more about how I'd manage without him.

There were no surprises in the resumes. Most of the candidates were young enough that I could be each of their fathers. No sane person would choose to make a career out of managing campaigns. When you factor in all the late nights and seven day work weeks, they're barely earning a minimum wage.

The first candidate was an enthusiastic twenty-four year-old graduate of Providence College, Brady Mulhern. He had managed a campaign for a candidate running for Boston's City Council before doing advance work for Elizabeth Warren's Senate campaign. Not enough experience to run a campaign, but I figured he could lead our advance effort and maybe do some work in communications.

Next was Melissa Torres. She was somebody I knew. A mom at age 14, she graduated from Weaver High School in Hartford, best known for its graduation rate of 49%. She went on to get a degree from Middlesex Community College and then battled her way through the night program at University of Hartford. Aidan tried to recruit her to organize Latinos in the First District Congressional race three years ago but she was already organizing for the Working Families Party. She was on my short list until the last few minutes of the interview.

"Do you have any questions for me?" I asked.

"Are you going to water everything down?"

"I'm not sure what you mean."

"I left the Party—the Democrats—because they were watering everything down. They don't want to argue for real universal health coverage that doesn't cost people money because they're all afraid to be called socialist, so we're stuck with this half-ass health care bill. They don't want to push for publicly funded elections because they're all afraid to lose their own seats, so we're stuck with McCain-Feingold and *Citizens United.*"

Melissa didn't take a breath in between thoughts. It all came out in one long stream. "They're letting the public school system be privatized and dismantled by charter schools because they don't know how to simply say, 'The job of an elected official is to educate all the kids, not just the top thirteen percent,' and now it's all watered down to a system that tolerates the failure that comes from chronically under-funded public schools. You sounded like a candidate today who might be different, but I'm asking you whether you're just going to water everything down because you're too afraid to 'offend anybody,'" she said, making quotation marks with her fingers.

"Melissa, I think I'm about as close to a candidate as you're going to find who supports what you believe in—"

"For a Democrat—" she interrupted.

"—but if we were to work together, you'd have to understand and accept that I'm the candidate. I set the agenda. I decide the message."

"Let's do each other a favor," she said as pleasantly as if we were discussing the weather. "I want to help you but I'm probably not the right fit to manage your campaign. I'm not one of these kids looking for a job or to move up in the Party—"

"That's why I want you here."

"But it also means that I'll probably embarrass you at some point if I'm around your communications or messaging. How about I organize your signature drive to get you on the ballot and your GOTV effort?"

GOTV is shorthand for Get-Out-The-Vote. It's the hundreds of minute tasks that cover everything from registering voters to driving them to the polls. A strong GOTV operation could make the difference in a close race, and I figured I'd be lucky to have Melissa run it and whatever else she might be willing to take on.

"How about you also coordinate our Convention strategy?" I asked.

"There's absolutely no way you're getting on the ballot by going to that Convention," she said, confidently.

There are only two ways to get your name on the Democratic primary ballot in Connecticut. Most candidates take what is considered the easier route of going to the Party Convention in July and securing the support of fifteen percent of the delegates during a roll call vote. The only alternative is to petition your way onto the ballot by obtaining the signatures of three percent of all registered Democrats in the state. That's about twenty-five thousand signatures that I wasn't sure we had time to gather.

"If Aidan and I can't get fifteen percent of the Convention delegates, there's no point in pushing this to a primary vote," I said aloud. As soon as I spoke the words I wanted to gather them out of the air and put them back in my mouth. I believed them but shouldn't have shared them with someone who was little more than an acquaintance.

"Aidan's not relevant anymore."

I put my pen down. Melissa noticed.

"I'm sorry," she said, "but this is politics, right? We can't be emotional about this stuff."

"Go on," I said evenly, pretending that I wasn't bothered.

"You can win the primary but Aidan can't help you. He's not gonna have any leverage with donors. It's not exactly like anyone will feel like there'd be consequences for not donating to you." She paused and lowered her voice as if she was suddenly concerned about being overheard. "I hate to say it but he's not going to be around much longer and everyone knows it."

I folded my hands on the desk. And labored to keep my emotions in check. "Keep going," I said.

"And it'll be same with the Convention delegates. These are elected officials, town chairs—people who aren't gonna like you primarying another Dem regardless of what they think about Saul. But more to the point, the ones who might be in play will know that Saul's wrath will come if they support you. And that Aidan won't be around to protect them when it does."

"But some of the delegates are activists," I countered.

"Not enough to get you to fifteen percent," she said, shaking her head. "Listen, your biggest need right now is boosting your name recognition. You should be blanketing every train station, grocery store and shopping center in the state with kids armed with palm cards getting you signatures. It's good campaigning *and* it will get you on the ballot."

I took a note.

Melissa kept talking.

"But you have to do it today. I take that back. You have to do it yesterday."

"So you're on board to lead volunteer coordination, ballot access and GOTV?"

"Will get started today." She stood and offered me her hand. "And don't pay me," she said while we shook. "Save your money for TV."

"That's a hard offer to turn down . . ."

Keisha brought me three more candidates, along with a salmon salad and black coffee for lunch. I wasn't in the position to turn anyone away and did my best to keep staffing the campaign during the interviews. There was a fifteen minute break in the schedule, which I suspect Keisha placed there to afford me time to eat. I used it to call Aidan.

"How you doing?" I asked.

"I'd be doing better if you had a campaign manager."

Keisha knocked on the door that was already partially open. She didn't wait for me to say anything before entering. She had my next interview with her.

"I meant, how are you feeling?" I asked.

"I'd be feeling better if you had a campaign manager."

"How do you know I don't?

"Because you would have started this call off by saying, 'Aidan, no worries. I found the perfect person,'" he said, imitating what sounded like a ten year-old version of me. "I'm trying to raise some cash. Call me back when you have a campaign manager."

"Will do." I thought about telling him that I loved him before he hung up. I knew it would make him uncomfortable but I wanted to get it in before time ran out. "Will call you later," I said. And hung up.

"Quinn, this is Monica Metzler," Keisha said.

Monica marched directly to my side of the desk and extended her hand.

"Hi, it's actually Monica McKay Metzler." She looked straight into my eyes through her black horn-rimmed glasses. "There's no hyphen; just Monica McKay Metzler. My friends call me Triple M. Well, not really my friends, just people who are probably too lazy to say my full name, or think that Triple M sounds cool, which it doesn't."

I probably held on to Monica's hand a beat too long while I tried to figure out what to make of her. She relied on three ball-point pens to keep the unkempt bun atop her head together. She wore a white shirt with a black tie loosely draped around her neck. The sleeves of both her shirt and black jacket were rolled up to her elbows. She wore black pants that were not quite the same tone as her jacket and I could tell they weren't part of the same outfit.

"I really want to manage this campaign," she said, still standing.

"Okay."

"Yeah. My grandpa taught me that if you really want a job you should come straight out and say it. So, I'm saying it. I really want to be your campaign manager."

"I appreciate that. Please sit, relax."

Monica dropped an oversized brown leather knapsack from her shoulder onto the visitor's chair and took the open seat.

"Great job this morning," she said, starting off.

"Thanks, but what could I have done better?"

"I'd never tell you that."

"If you want to be my campaign manager you'd have to be able to critique me."

"Do you like baseball?" she asked.

"I'm a Little League coach."

"Well, I'm from California and my Dad's been a high school base-ball coach in my town for thirty years. When I was just a little bitty thing, he had a kid on his team who used to make him nuts. He had the craziest batting stance you've ever seen but could crush the ball. His nickname was 'B-1' because all he did was hit bombs."

Monica pulled a bottle of water from her knapsack. She drank while keeping her eyes on me. It made her look deranged. I doodled in the margin of her resume until she was done.

"Anyway, Dad was worried sick that the college coaches would be scared to take a chance on someone with such a crazy stance. One day I asked him, 'Dad, why don't you just try and fix him?' He said, 'I'd never risk screwing up such a natural talent, and a good college coach will see his greatness.'"

"That's all interesting, but let's assume that I'm a touch more self-assured than a 17-year-old baseball player. Tell me what you would change."

"I probably could have found a dozen things about it that I'd tweak, but they would all take away from your greatest strength."

"Which is?"

"You don't sound like a politician. Saul is an automaton—one of those politicians who talks and talks and no one ever really knows what he said when he's done. You sound like a real person and there's no way that I'm aware of to make someone authentic."

"Tell me about the last few campaigns that you've worked on?"

Monica took me through the hills of North Carolina, the base of Rocky Mountains and the banks of the Mississippi as she described her work during the last five election cycles. Her trials and tribulations showed a resourcefulness that I figured would be valuable to a renegade campaign. There was only one issue that was a fatal flaw.

"How many campaigns have you managed?"

"Seventeen," Monica said without a moment's hesitation.

"And you didn't win any?"

"No siree. Not one."

"Ever close?"

"Got to within single digits once in South Carolina and again in Alabama but lost both those by twelve."

"Do you have references?"

"Plenty." She reached into her bag to retrieve a folded piece of paper and handed it to me across the desk. "They should all be able to get back to you right away," she said, curling her lip. "It's not like any of them are busy serving in Congress."

I made some notes on the margin of her resume and then flipped to preview the next candidate's credentials. I still didn't think we could win but wasn't going to be reduced to a laughingstock.

"Can I point something out to you?" she asked, probably sensing her opportunity was slipping away. "I'm different."

"'Different doesn't bother me." I rolled my pen between my thumb and forefinger. "I'm about the most 'different' person you have or will ever meet in your life."

"Well then, you of all people should understand me. I don't take on easy races—or causes. The few times the millionaire candidate has fallen into my lap, I've passed. The times when I could have managed a race in a blue district, I left it to someone else. And God knows I've never once had the better candidate. I do the hard races and only the hard races."

"That's not so great for your career advancement."

"I don't spend ten seconds thinking about advancing my career. I'm in the races that no one else wants because those are the most important ones. If Progressives keep talking to just themselves, nothing is going to change. There's a reason why no candidates are talking about what you were talking about today."

Monica looked down at her lap.

She looked like she was in pain.

"Are you okay?" I started to get up to make sure she was okay.

She put me back in my seat by holding up her hand.

"I'm having a Hillary Clinton in New Hampshire moment—just give me a second."

"You're crying?" I asked.

"She *wasn't* crying. Please don't tell me that you're one of those jerks who thinks Hillary won the New Hampshire primary because she cried."

"I'm not. I don't."

"God forbid a woman shows some real emotion about something that just might be the most important thing on the planet: the outcome of an election about the defining public policy issue of a generation—" Monica cut herself off and snatched her knapsack from the visitor's chair. She pulled the strap over her shoulder and stood.

"Where are you going?"

"To Wyoming. There's a liberal running for Congress who would be perfect for me."

"But you're hired."

"I can't work for you now."

"Why?"

"'Cause I just did the most stereotypical thing in the world and couldn't bear the thought that you hired me just because I showed a little emotion."

"Can you forget about Hillary Clinton for a second?"

"I *will not* forget about the Eleanor Roosevelt of my generation!"

I got up and guided Monica back to her chair. She plopped down and put her knapsack on her lap. She folded her hands over the knapsack. I sat next to her.

"Okay, this is going to be an outsider, renegade, against-all-odds campaign. We're going to have no money and from what I can tell, we'll struggle to find a dozen volunteers who've actually worked on a campaign before." I crossed my legs. "You're the most qualified person for this job and our only hope of victory. Would you please accept my offer to manage this campaign?"

"On one condition."

"Which is?"

"That neither of us speaks of this interview again."

"Done," I said.

I extended my hand. She gave me hers back.

"Well, this has been weird," she said.

"Interesting choice of words," I said. "It reminds me that I have to let you know that my family's not going to participate in this campaign."

Monica tilted her head slightly. "Not even your wife?" she asked, squinting.

"My wife in particular. And you're not to ask her."

"But you can't do this by yourself. You'll need her help."

"Those are the terms," I said, standing to return to my chair on the other side of the desk. "Can you accept that?" I asked.

"Okay," she said.

"Great. I need you to take this binder," I said, pushing it from my side to Monica's side of the desk, "and interview all the people who have stars next to their names." Monica pulled one of the pens from her hair and put it to work as I gave instruction. "I think they should all work for the campaign in some capacity but I'll leave that to you."

"I'll get started right away."

"I've hired a few people already. Keisha will fill you in but it's all yours now."

"Great," she said, nodding.

"One more thing. I want you to sit in the bullpen with the senior staff and volunteers, and I want you to keep campaign meetings open to everyone."

"You want to leverage everyone. I get it."

"Exactly. We have so little time to put this together and we need to hear every idea that might possibly help us win."

"Great idea." Monica tucked the binder under her arm. "I'm going to fight for you harder than you fight for yourself."

"I don't doubt that for a second. Now go win us an election."

X

I opened my eyes and turned my head.

With Brooke gone, the time on the clock was in full view. It was 4:12 a.m. I was running late, but I buried my nose in her pillow to breathe in the scent of her hair and the even fainter smell of her Clive Christian perfume. Even on our worst days—the days when she makes me feel like I'm going to go nuts—that smell calms me. It reminds me of when we first met and what I've been trying to recapture in our relationship every year since.

Brooke and I met in a bar. I was a senior in college and Connecticut State was playing a Memorial Day game against rival Northeastern. Our team was perfect that Saturday and cruised to a 42-7 win. After the game, Aidan took about a half-dozen of my teammates and Daniel out for dinner to celebrate in Boston's Back Bay. After dinner, Aidan had to get back to Hartford. We obviously wanted to go bar-hopping.

"Whatever you do," Aidan said, "stay out of Southie. It's racist and I don't want to be back up here sorting out a mess in the morning."

I didn't know my way around Boston but Daniel did. As soon as Aidan drove off, he was leading us across Route 1 to hit a nearby bar, the "Dock N Dive." I figured not much could go wrong with six teammates by my side, but by the time the clock hit midnight our crew had thinned out to just Daniel and our punter, Kerry Drinkwater. Kerry was a great kid but not exactly packing the kind of muscle that would be needed if trouble came our way. And it did.

Daniel was talking to three girls at the bar. One of them was wearing a tight-fitting blue polo shirt with a Northeastern sweater draped around her neck. At about five foot ten, she was almost a full head taller than Daniel. She stood with an air of confidence that reminded me of Aidan. Her two friends, both fit-looking brunettes, were striking beauties, but the blonde girl in the polo shirt stood out among them. She was the kind of girl who naturally seems to draw your attention.

But back then she was precisely the kind of girl I assumed I'd have nothing in common with and tended to avoid. I focused my attention on the game of Pop-O-Shot that Kerry and I were playing in the corner. After I finished what I thought was going to be my last game I heard a voice hollering behind me.

"Who let the monkey in?"

The bar quieted down to just the music playing. I knew there was going to be a fight before I turned around to find four muscle heads staring us down.

"Figures the monkey would want to come in here to play a monkey game," he said in a grotesque Southie accent.

The four of them were between us and the door. Kerry and I moved close together so we could get back to back. "No matter what happens," I told him, "don't let them get you to the ground—they'll stomp you. Stay on your feet until the police get here."

I pulled my silver watch from my wrist and wrapped it around my knuckles—a trick Aidan had told me about. The inevitable conflict was suspended by screaming coming from the bar.

It wasn't hysterical screaming. It was more like the way a police officer might yell a command. The three girls who had been talking to Daniel had jumped up on the bar and were determined to rescue us.

"Get away from him, you friggin' coward," Brooke shouted from the middle position, pulling her Northeastern sweater from her neck.

"One more step and I'm going to be the witness at your trial that sends you to jail," her friend Michele hollered.

The third of their crew, Sarah, jumped behind the bar and pushed her way past the bartender to get to the phone. "I'm calling the police! You people make me sick!"

The whole thing was bizarre. The three of them could have passed for runway models and the last people I probably would have picked out of the crowd to come to our defense. But there they were.

When Brooke realized from her perch atop the bar that neither Kerry and I, nor the muscle heads, were going to back down, she jumped down and went right up to the guy who called me a monkey and said, "I'm not moving. And if you so much as brush me I'm the kind of person who can make sure your racist Southie piece of shit ass will *never* see the light of day."

The commotion gave us just enough of an opening to get to the door and make our exit. The six of us ran and then grabbed a cab back to the Northeastern campus. Brooke and I ditched everyone else and spent the night talking in her room until sunrise.

I couldn't wait to tell Aidan about her.

He wasn't impressed.

"Sounds like your run-of-the-mill blue blood to me," he said from behind his desk the next day.

"Did you hear a single word that I said?" I asked. "What about what she did? It was the most incredible thing I've ever seen."

"Sonny, you have a purpose. A destiny," he said, his elbows resting on the front of his desk. "Do you know what kind of destiny a girl like that has waiting for her? Counting her money at her country club on the shoreline."

"I think she's different."

"A woman like that is never gonna understand you or your purpose."

"So what are you saying?"

"I'm not gonna get exercised about some girl you spent one night with in Boston."

"But she touched my heart. I think I'm in love."

"Well, Sonny, all I can say then is that there are three things in life that always cause lots of trouble: gambling, drugs and women. I've managed to keep you away from the first two and I've never held out hope that I could save you from the third."

Back then, I was certain Aidan was wrong about Brooke. Sure, she and her friends are the kind of people who grew up with summer houses on the Connecticut shoreline and Cape Cod, took trips to Europe each fall and had real Monets and Matisses hanging in their houses. But true-blue Old Stock New England Yankees also have no tolerance for intolerance. They descend from the thinkers who built this country and they're all fiercely libertarian. Not the kind of libertarians who want to abolish the IRS (or the government); they're libertarian in the sense that they fervently oppose anything that even remotely smells of persecution—probably because their ancestors were escaping it. Brooke's family crest was commissioned in 1768 and reads *Sub libertate quietem* at the bottom. It means Rest Under Liberty.

Now as I lay with my face buried in Brooke's pillow, I couldn't help but wonder whether Aidan had been right all along. And whether this was all inevitable. I battled the temptation to pull the covers over my head and curl up.

"Keep going, Quinn," I said aloud before throwing the covers off and jumping out of bed.

I went downstairs to do a half hour on the treadmill before an abbreviated shower and getting dressed. I would have made it to the office by 5:00 a.m. but for a driving miscalculation. I pulled up to the parking garage of Clay Pittman out of habit and didn't mark the error until my key card was rejected at the gate.

A pile of briefing books waited for me in the campaign office. Under ordinary circumstances, briefing books are carefully compiled under the supervision of leading experts in the fields of education, health care, foreign affairs, defense spending, energy and anything else that could potentially come up on the campaign trail. Keisha had done a first-rate job of recycling information from books that were put together from the past few election cycles and updating key data and statistics.

I did triage on the pair of gigantic binders. Sections that covered issues that I was certain would come up in the next few weeks got a complete, albeit speedy reading. Issues on the periphery got a lighter touch.

I pulled out a few facts to commit to memory that I could weave into a stump speech. I underlined and then highlighted them, which is what I do when I'm trying to memorize something:

- ❖ *Connecticut has the most multi-million dollar homes in the Northeast, and the second most in the nation after California.*
- ❖ *One in seven kids in Connecticut lives in poverty.*
- ❖ *The gap between Connecticut's overall high school graduation rate (83%) and the graduation rate for economically disadvantaged students (62%) is the largest such gap in the nation.*
- ❖ *In 2001, U.S. defense spending was $400B; it's now $728B —almost double.*
- ❖ *The incarceration rate in the U.S. is the highest in the world. While the U.S. represents about 5 **percent** of the world's population, it houses around 25 **percent** of the world's prisoners.*
- ❖ *The U.S. ranks 10th worldwide in upward/class mobility.*

It felt like I was studying for a calculus exam by browsing through my notes, but without doing the work and practice problems to ensure success.

"Ms. Perez is here," Keisha said.

She startled me and watched me jump, but didn't pause as she breezed into the office and placed a hot cup of black coffee on the corner of my desk.

I checked my watch. It was 7:40a.m.

"Here?" I asked.

"At my desk."

"What do I have this morning?"

"Call-time starts at eight."

Nancy Perez appeared at the door. She knocked on the door frame even though we both obviously saw her standing there in full view.

"I'm sorry, Mr. Barnes," she said, "I've never done anything like this, but please understand that I'm fighting for my children." The area beneath her eyes was puffy. "I called your office yesterday and they said you don't work there anymore. Is everything okay? Are you still gonna be able to help me?"

Keisha took her arm and sat her down in the chair in front of the desk. I moved to the opposite side of the desk and sat next to her.

"Do you need some coffee—or something to eat?" Keisha asked.

"No, I'm fine, thank you."

"I'll get you something anyway," Keisha said.

Weary, Nancy still looked defiant. She sat with perfect posture as she ran her hand over her hair, which was pulled back into a tight ponytail. Her eyes were as red as her lipstick and nail polish but she didn't look or sound timid.

"Again, I'm sorry."

"Please don't apologize," I said. "I'm the one who owes you an apology for not calling this week."

"Did I cause you some kind of trouble?"

"Why would you say that?"

"I'm not exactly part of the one percent; I figured that when you work at a firm like that you can't represent many people like me."

"Everything is fine," I said. "It has nothing to do with that and more to do with a campaign I have in front of me."

"I saw you on the news and figured that's why you haven't called."

"What going on with the investigation?"

"They're not gonna arrest him."

"Who?"

"The neighborhood watchman guy."

Nancy read my confusion. She drew a deep breath and took a step back.

"The guy's name who shot Al is Simon Greeneli," she said. "He's not a cop. He's part of the neighborhood watch."

"How do you know that?"

"It's in the paper today." She pulled a neatly folded copy of the *East Haven Press* from her bag and handed it to me. "That's why I came here."

"Did the police try and speak with you?"

"No. I went down to the police station every day for the last three days and the guys just said, 'We're getting to you.'"

"Or Carlito?"

"No, but I'm not even sure they know he was there."

Keisha appeared with a bagel and cream cheese and coffee. She sat on the corner of the desk while Nancy took a bite.

"We're going to go to the police station today," I said, "but this time we're going to tell them you want to file a formal complaint."

"You're gonna be with me?"

"No. I'm going to have to send one of my colleagues, Daniel Coyle, with you." I looked to Keisha. "Can you set this up?"

Keisha picked up my phone. "I'm texting him now," she said.

"Can you come?" Nancy asked.

"I can't today."

"Daniel will be fine," Keisha said, while she typed. "I can come along also."

"What exactly do you want me to say?" Nancy asked.

"Daniel will go over it with you but you're going to tell them that you're reporting a crime: The homicide of your son Alarico."

Keisha handed me my phone back to show me an incoming text.

I'm waiting for you!

It's call time!!

MMM

I stood.

"I have to step out."

Nancy started to get up but I placed my hand on her shoulder to keep her seated.

"You're in good hands," I said. "I'll get a report from them tonight and we'll talk tomorrow."

The average price of winning or holding a seat in the United States Senate is $10.4 million. I know and keep track of that number because I've spent more than twenty years making calls and bundling checks for candidates to raise it. That means that a candidate must raise more than $14,000 every day of an election cycle, including Saturdays and Sundays, to win.

I'm kind of ashamed of it. Not kind of ashamed, just ashamed. Aidan always rationalized it all as the necessary evil to get the right people elected.

"The first step is to get our candidates to Washington and then they can change the system," he'd say.

I found that once candidates become incumbents, they have little to no incentive to change a system that ensures their re-election. With incumbency comes the power to vote in Congress. The power to vote in Congress attracts cash from the more than 12 thousand lobbyists in Washington alone. And incumbents know that money is the single greatest factor in determining the outcome of an election.

I settled into my call center, which was simply a small colorless office with a gray metal desk wedged in the corner. A white plastic card table impersonated a conference room table.

I couldn't help but think about the irony. I had contributed mightily to the very system that would likely enable Saul to stay in office. He'd raised over $20 million last cycle and would obliterate that figure if he felt threatened by us.

"We've blocked out five hours a day for call time for you," Monica said. She adjusted the flat screen in front of me with the care a mother might use to prepare a meal for an infant.

"Can we talk about paring that back?" I asked. "I'd actually like to spend some time talking to voters."

"No. And it's actually six to seven hours a day," she said, as she navigated the mouse to open the program holding our digital call sheets. "You have to make delegate calls and speak with union officers. We're trying to block them all together toward the end of the day."

"When do I get to read the newspaper?" I asked, playfully.

"You don't." She handed me a headset. "We'll tell you what's in it."

I paged through the lists on the screen. The names on the first several pages were family members. The next group was my friends, who were followed by my neighbors.

"I don't want to call this list today," I said. "Give me the activists list. I'll call this list when we get desperate."

"Absolutely not. We're desperate now," Monica said. "This is the difference between being an operative and a candidate. This is what winning candidates do. You're calling this list today."

"You're forgetting I'm your boss," I said, leaning back with my hands behind my head.

"I'm not forgetting. I just know that we need this money. We're dead without it." She sat on the white plastic table in the center of the room and rested her feet on one of the folding chairs around it. "If you don't call them today, you'll never call. We're getting more and more volunteers every day—a bunch of them are going to sleep on that dirty carpet upstairs these next four months because they believe in you. Do it for them."

On cue, four volunteers appeared at the door with laptops and iPads under their arms. None of them looked like they were old enough to drive. I wasn't sure if they had overheard our exchange.

Monica stood and waved them in.

"Here's how it's going to work. They're going to work to get a live call on the line," she said, gesturing to our volunteers as they took a seat at the table. "As soon as they have one, the call sheet for that person will appear on your screen, the call will come on your headset and you're on."

"You do realize that I've done this a time or two," I said.

"Not as a candidate—and everyone needs to hear this." Monica stepped back to the door so she could view the five of us together. "This is Rachel," she said, pointing to a thin brunette in a Wesleyan sweatshirt.

"Do you have a last name, Rachel?" I asked.

"Saunders, sir," she said, her brown eyes darting back and forth between Monica and me. "I'm Rachel Saunders."

"Rachel is going to listen to every one of your calls to make sure each donor gets asked to double max out to the campaign," Monica said. "That means $2,600 for them and their spouse for both the primary and the general."

"But that's $10,400," Rachel said.

"That's right. Saul has about seven and a half million dollars of cash on hand. He has that money because everyone who shakes his hand gets asked for $10,400—and he makes sure they give it."

"Let the games begin," I said.

Monica retreated. I slipped my headphones over my head. We got to work.

There's no such thing as an easy fundraising call—at least not for me. I'd rather stick needles in my eyes than ask a relative for money, especially on Brooke's side of the family.

"We're not the kind of people who care about money," her Dad would remind me at what seemed like every holiday gathering.

That's because they've always had it. I've never asked them for a penny and had no plans to start now.

I did my best to embrace call time. I spent the five or ten minutes with each person to catch up on what were typically long-overdue conversations. I didn't always follow Monica's instructions. I could see Rachel nervously recording my breaches in protocol. I liked that they took Monica so seriously.

Everyone offered congratulations but most calls went downhill from there. My friends asked what I planned on doing after losing to Saul. The politicos flat-out told me I was crazy for challenging a sitting senator, and that I would surely pay a hefty price for trying to upset the natural order of party politics.

"This isn't a game to Saul," the mayor of Oxbow told me. "He's so pissed he can't see straight. You will never recover from what's about to happen to you. Never."

"That's why I need your help," I said.

"You need to figure a way out of this race—right now."

And so it went. Over and over again. The only group of people with whom I had any success was the hard-core activists, but they weren't in position to write big checks. They all gave beyond their means but no way near the numbers we needed to meet our daily goal.

I wrapped up my first six-hour session feeling as if I had just served a long prison term. I was on my way out the door to get caught up on the day's events when Rachel summoned me back to my desk.

"Lucy McCann is on the line," she said, her face so twisted that she looked as if she'd eaten a lemon whole.

I slipped my headset back on and sat on my desk.

"Hello, Lucy."

"John Quincy Barnes, you got yourself an angry woman on this end of the phone. I'm jealous and fit to be tied!"

"Jealous?"

"Yes! I'm jealous of all these other people who are apparently much more important to you than little ole' Lucy McCann. You've hurt me, John Quincy Barnes. I'm terribly hurt."

"Socialism Now?" I asked, reminding her of her assessment of our campaign.

"Well, that's just like a man to try and flip things around when they're in the wrong. Besides, that was just a nudge; a love tap."

"What can I do for you, Lucy?" I asked.

"That's the wrong question, sir. You're supposed to be asking me for the help."

"Help?"

"Yes, help. That public school education really did you a disservice. You want to ask me for help."

"Why would I do that?"

"Goodness gracious," she said, exasperated. "How did your fund-raising calls go today?"

"They went."

"And who has more money than anyone you know?" Lucy didn't wait for me to respond. "I'll tell you who. Lucy McCann."

"Lucy, I really am glad to hear from you. It's been the highlight of my day—"

"Now you're talking."

"—but I have to get upstairs for a meeting. I'm looking forward to seeing you on the campaign trail."

"Real quick, have you seen Saul's financial disclosures? A fella in your position should be studying them."

"Take care, Lucy."

"Sweetie Pie, please call me back. I've taken a liking to you and I can't bear to think about what you're gonna look like when that ol' Saul is done with you."

"Bye, Lucy."

"I'm sending you a gift."

"Lucy, really, I'm just not interested in any funny stuff."

"Oh, don't be silly. It's not that kind of gift." She lowered her voice to a whisper. "I'm gonna send you a little something just to keep you thinking about me—and to remind you that I have a unique insight into the male psyche."

"Bye, Lucy."

"Bye, Sweetie Pie."

XI

"Campaign meeting!" Monica announced as we made our way through the bullpen. She waved everyone toward the back of the cavernous room as she continued her imitation of a town crier. "Campaign meeting! Campaign meeting!"

The forty or so volunteers followed. Most of them moved slowly, not sure what they were supposed to do or whether they were invited.

"Everyone!" Monica assured them. "Grab a chair and let's go."

Monica grabbed a large white board from the middle of the room and dragged it behind her. She set up her makeshift classroom in the corner while our volunteer staff pushed their chairs behind her. There was no order to the assembly of chairs.

Aidan and I followed. I resisted the temptation to lead the meeting and settled next to Aidan on a table in the rear.

I figure I can probably do a better job at every task the campaign has to perform—from distributing lawn signs to making coffee—than any staffer or volunteer. I'm also aware that a candidate can't run a successful campaign if he's busy distributing lawn signs and making coffee.

Monica rubbed her hands together to announce she was ready to get things started.

"It's getting late but we have something important to get done before we close our first full day of the campaign. Let me start by saying I've got some good news for you and some bad news."

Monica's audience took notes as if they were in a classroom.

"The good news is that you're about to do something great—and are going to be part of something great. Without getting all mushy, Quinn and I are mindful that we could not do this without your help. So thank you." Monica adjusted her whiteboard's position while she spoke. "Now the bad news. We have to take on one of the most powerful men in the country with little or no resources, and we don't have much time to do it."

The diverse congregation, ranging from retirees to college students, nodded almost in unison.

"We're going to have to be super organized and figure out how to do things that cost lots of money—on our own." Monica started writing on the board.

"Should everyone be in this meeting?" an elderly African-American gentleman in a crisp white button-down shirt asked from the far left side of the room.

Monica turned. "Your name, sir?" she asked.

"Raymond. Raymond Austin."

"Thank you, Raymond. We're going to do things differently. We have less than four months to defeat a political giant. We're taking all comers."

"But that lady right there is a Republican," Raymond said, pointing to a comely silver-haired woman holding a note pad in the front of the room. She was petite, slim and wore a simple pair of pearls over a cream-colored silk blouse.

Mildred Butterworth has been involved in nearly every statewide GOP campaign in this state since 1976. Politics, however, always seemed to be more of a social affair for Mildred. She hosted any number of cocktail fundraisers from her estate in New Canaan—and was probably just as interested in socializing with her friends as with the candidates who appeared at her doorstep for campaign dollars. I thought I had recognized her earlier in the day but concluded that my eyes must have deceived me.

"Is that right?" Monica asked, stepping toward Mildred.

Mildred stood and introduced herself to the group. She confirmed the accusation with the assuredness of a queen. "It's my pleasure to work with you all," she said before returning to her chair.

"Well, welcome to the campaign." Monica said matter-of-factly.

"So she's staying?" Raymond asked.

"Again, we're taking all comers."

"But she could tell them our secrets," Rachel said, her Wesleyan sweatshirt now wrapped around her neck.

"The other side doesn't send well-known people to serve as moles," Monica said. "They send college kids like you."

"If you say so," Rachel said, the left corner of her mouth turned up in a slight frown.

"I just did. And one more thing . . ." Monica used her teeth to pull the cap from the erasable marker before stepping to her whiteboard, "We're the good guys. We're not afraid to do things out in the open."

"You mean 'good persons'," Rachel said. "You said 'good guys' and I think you meant to say 'good persons.'"

"Rachel," Monica kept talking while she wrote on her board, "I suspect you're going to be a colossal pain in my ass." She stopped for a moment to look over her shoulder at Rachel, "but I like you."

There was a smattering of laughter.

Mildred reached over to pat Rachel on the back.

"Now," Monica continued, "campaigns usually pay consultants zillions of dollars to come up with a pithy message that might 'capture the hearts and minds of a generation.'" She stopped talking and stepped back to read her work. She finished her thought after returning to the board. "But we have no money at the moment and we can do this just as well ourselves if we ask the right questions."

Monica stepped aside to reveal her work:

What They Say About Us   *What We Say About Us*
What we Say About Them   *What They Say About Them*

"Okay. First question: What are they going to say about us?" she asked.

Monica waited at the board to record the team's input. When she didn't hear anything, she turned back to the room. "There are no wrong answers," she said. "We're running a renegade campaign and need to hear every idea: good, bad or crazy. Just shoot."

"Well, he's black," Raymond said.

"Well, I don't think they'll say it quite that way, but good."

"And he's married to a white woman," he added.

"This is Connecticut, not Mississippi," Mildred said from the front row.

"Still matters," Raymond insisted. "He's a black man married to a white woman."

"No one cares about that," Rachel said, creases covering her forehead. "Should we even be talking about this?"

"In politics, we talk about everything." Monica wrote 'not like us' on the board. "Why does that matter to you?"

"Not sure," Raymond said, shrugging. "I don't think about it until I see them together. She's just so blonde. It kind of shocks me."

"I'm going to leave if this continues," Rachel said.

"Oh, c'mon," Raymond said, raising his voice. "You wouldn't stare if you saw some blonde-haired high society looking woman walking around with a dark-skinned black man?"

"I'm leaving." Rachel stood. "Every person in this world over thirty is crazy."

"But this is a Democratic primary," Mildred added.

"You're not going anywhere," Monica said firmly, to Rachel. "Your job is to figure out how to get Quinn Barnes elected in the real world, not on an Ivy League campus. This is how people think in the real world."

"Not in my world," Mildred said.

"And Mildred, you're right that this is a Democratic primary, but Lucy doesn't have a primary opponent so we're running a primary and a general election at the same time. Let's keep our eyes on all of it so we can win this primary first and then go beat the pants off Lucy in the general."

Aidan touched my hand with his index finger. He looked at me with a wry smile and winked a wink that said, "I like her."

"And one more thing," Monica said, returning to her board. "We're going to disagree on lots of things over the course of four months but no one is 'quitting' the campaign; we have to stick together to win this thing—especially when we're making each other a little nuts."

Rachel slowly returned to her chair.

"Now," Monica said, "give me more."

"Unpatriotic," hollered a red-haired middle-aged man from the back of the room.

"Neophyte," a well-dressed thirty-something female offered from the side.

Acclimated to the process, our room of volunteers opened up from all across the room. Monica wrote furiously, with her back to her audience, to keep up.

"Trial lawyer."

"Football player."

"Dumb football player."

"No experience."

"Naïve."

"Naïve Liberal."

"Extreme Naïve Liberal."

"Untried."

"Untested."

"Never been elected to anything."

Monica showed the group the palm of her hand to stop them. She backed away from the whiteboard to study the group's work. She ran her fingers through her hair and asked, "Why is he unpatriotic?"

"He helped Aidan Coyle organize all those rallies to protest the Iraq War," the red-haired man said.

Rachel sucked her teeth loud enough to get everyone's attention. "How does that possibly make him unpatriotic?" she asked.

"Well, a lot of people from my part of the state lost their lives in 9/11," he said.

Rachel held both palms against her cheeks in frustration. "What does the Iraq War have to do with the people that attacked us on 9/11? How can you possibly be a Democrat?"

"I'm not," he said calmly. "I'm an Independent like most people in this state."

"And that's exactly why 'unpatriotic' stays on the board," Monica said, refereeing. "Why is he 'extreme'?"

"I heard him say once that the only way to improve graduation rates in Hartford is 'to take the kids away from their parents' or something like that," Raymond said.

Monica didn't react but I could tell she had her poker face on and wanted to know more about this. She unfolded her arms and went back to the white board.

"Okay, what will we say about ourselves?" she asked.

"Aren't we going to say the same things?" Mildred asked back.

"I certainly hope not," Rachel said.

"Well, I just mean he can't run away from who he is. He *is* a trial lawyer. But we're just going to emphasize that he's been both a prosecutor and a defense attorney." Mildred stood. Most people would feel uncomfortable standing to offer their ideas in such an informal meeting but Mildred did it with ease and grace. "He's been a partner at the state's oldest firm. And a law professor. He's clearly involved in his community. He has experience. It's just a different kind of experience."

My phone vibrated. I recognized the 202 area code. I wasn't expecting a call from Washington, D.C. but stepped back so as not to disrupt the meeting.

"Quinn Barnes," I said in a hushed tone.

"Mr. Barnes?"

"Mr. Barnes, can you hold for the majority leader?"

"Leader Steed?" I asked.

"Yes, that's right. Can you hold?"

I slipped into the first office I could find. The only furniture was a gray metal chair and a card table pushed against the wall.

I activated the speaker and placed the phone on the desk. I hovered over it like a question mark and waited for Senator Grange Steed's voice on the other end of the line.

"Quincy," he said, as if we were old friends, "how are things going up there?"

I had only met Senator Steed a handful of times at fundraisers in Washington and Connecticut. I was certain he couldn't pick me out of line-up. Regardless, I played along.

"Good. I'm sure you've heard that we're getting things started, so it's busy."

"Yes, that's why I'm calling. But let me first ask, how is Aidan doing?"

"Thanks for asking," I said. "He's feeling a bit better. The biggest challenge is keeping him off his feet."

"Good luck with that," Steed said. "I remember the first campaign in Connecticut that we partnered on. He must have knocked on a thousand doors himself. Come to think of it, that was Saul's first campaign."

"What can I do for you, Senator?"

"I'm going to get right to the point." Steed drew a deep breath. "We don't want you to do this. It's actually stronger than that. I can't have this right now."

"The campaign?"

"Yes. You know we're barely holding on to a majority down here and this stands to jeopardize everything: judicial nominations, the budget, our entire legislative agenda."

"I'm not sure what to say."

"Do you really want to be the guy who costs the party the Senate, which by the way means losing the balance on the Supreme Court, the Affordable Care Act and just about everything else that you say you care about?"

"Leader Steed, wouldn't you be better served by a senator who actually voted with the caucus?"

"Quinn, we don't know each other well and that's my fault. I'm going to try and change that but we're trying to run a country during a very difficult time and this is not helping the situation. I'd consider it a personal favor to me—that I'd remember—if you could step aside."

I've heard Aidan use the "personal favor" appeal too many times to recount. It was his genteel way of saying, "give me what I want or I'm going to make it my personal business to pound you into submission." I don't think I ever once heard someone pass on the opportunity to do a "personal favor" for Aidan.

"Senator Steed," I said evenly, "I greatly appreciate your leadership and would consider it a tremendous honor to work with you. But I can't do what you're asking."

"Why?" he asked tersely.

"Because we believe in what we're doing."

"I'm sorry to hear that."

We exchanged our goodbyes. He was cordial. I was nervous.

Rather than rejoin the meeting, I took advantage of the time alone to catch up on my emails and texts. I scrolled through the 200 or so messages to see if Brooke had written. I made it through about half of them—which were mostly words of congratulations from friends and clients—before Monica stuck her head in.

"Are you guys done?" I asked.

"Just taking a break. They're a great group." She leaned against the wall clutching her iPad to her chest. "Listen, there's a ginormous black man who just showed up out there. After he spent five minutes apologizing to me for his appearance—he's obviously homeless and could use a bath and some fresh clothes—he says he wants to work for the campaign. He says he knows you."

"How big is ginormous?"

"Do you know more than one enormous homeless man?

"Actually, I do."

"Well, this guy's name is Gene . . ."

"Gene Allen. We need to give him a job—and a place to stay."

"Well, Mildred said if he really knows you that she'd set him up in a hotel but can I suggest that we limit our paid roles to people—"

"No. Not on this. Let's pay him two thousand a month."

"Two thousand, sir?"

"But pay him weekly. And don't give him large sums of money."

"Sir, can I suggest that we be careful about—"

"Take out the money for his hotel and food before you pay him."

I could tell Monica was put off. Regardless, she opened her iPad to note my instructions.

"What's our slogan?" I asked when she looked to be about finished.

Monica immediately livened up. "Well, let me just say that I love it. And Aidan loves it."

"Don't build it up so much," I said. "Suppose I don't like it."

"Aidan said he'd make you love it." Monica showed me the palms of her open hands like a young screenwriter pitching a film idea to a room full of studio executives.

"John Quincy Barnes: The Right Experience. For the Change We Need."

"That is pretty good," I said.

"Don't you love it?"

"Drop the 'John Quincy' and just make it 'Quinn' and it's a deal."

"Great."

Monica noted my directive.

"Also, I'm going to want Mildred with me when we're on the road for town committee meetings, town halls—"

"Sir, I would have to strongly advise against that." She put her tablet down. "This is a primary. We're trying to get liberals to vote for you and that's the wrong message to be sending them. She can work with me in the office and we can roll her out in the general."

"She's coming with me."

"Can we talk more?"

"Not about this. I've decided."

"Okay, sir. Have you decided anything else?"

"Can we find something important for Rachel to do?" I asked.

"Fundraising is about as important as it gets."

"Does she like doing that?"

"No one likes fundraising."

"Okay, but let's also have her write some position papers for the website. Keisha has all the briefing books. She can use them to get started." Monica nodded. "And let's have Gene be my driver," I said.

"And let's have Gene be my driver," I said.

"Does that guy even have a driver's license?"

"He used to," I said. "Let's have someone figure that out—or help him get it renewed if it needs to be renewed."

Monica used her thumbs to make some more notes. "I forgot to mention I got a heads-up from a contact in D.C. You're going to get a call from Senator Steed." She spoke while she typed. "I had some thoughts on how you can avoid the call for a few days to give us some time to get things going."

"Too late."

"He called?"

"During the meeting."

"What'd he say?"

"That he's going to come down on us like a ton of bricks."

"That reminds me. Can we talk about whether we're going to spearhead a plan to take children away from their parents?"

"No."

"No?"

"I'll take care of it myself. If I can't handle a question like that, we're already dead in the water."

XII

"Mr. Gene, are you feeling better?" Eliza asked, from the back seat of our Jeep.

Gene gripped the steering wheel hard. He had finally settled in after his first few days of employment with us but I could tell her question made him uncomfortable.

"He's feeling a lot better, Eliza," I said from the front passenger's seat.

"That's right, Ms. Eliza," Gene said. "A lot better."

"'Cause you didn't look like you were feeling too good when I saw you on the street," she said.

"That's enough, Eliza," I said turning my head to look back at her.

She suspended her work trying to cram her hair under her baseball cap and looked back at me. "Enough what?" she asked.

"Ms. Eliza," Gene said. "I need to apologize to you."

"Shouldn't you just call me Eliza?" she asked. "I'm only eight."

"Well you're special—like your Daddy—so I'm gonna just keep calling you Ms. Eliza." Gene turned from Pentfield's Main Street onto Bartlett Street. "I'm sorry I scared you," he said.

"When?" she asked. Her frown displayed her confusion.

"When you saw me on the street," he said.

"Oh, I wasn't scared," Eliza said, back to work on her hair. "My Dad says that sometimes people stumble. He says it's what's called a metaphor." She squinted, looking confused again. "Dad, is it still a metaphor if the person actually *does* the metaphor?" she asked.

Gene and I both laughed quietly.

"Yes, Eliza," I said.

"Interesting," she said to herself. "Anyway," she said brightly to Gene, "my Uncle Daniel used to stumbled like that. Dad says we're not supposed to just watch when somebody falls down. You have to try and help them get up. I just wanted him to help you up."

"Well, thank you then," Gene said.

"But why did you run away from us?" she asked.

Gene paused as he turned right on High Street. "'Cause I look up to your Daddy," he said, looking straight ahead. "And didn't want him to see me so low."

Gene pulled into the parking lot of Valley View elementary. Eliza grabbed her baseball glove and jammed it into her red and black Easton bag. He pulled up to the field.

"Go have some fun at practice," Gene said, looking back at her, fist extended.

She bumped his fist with her tiny one. "Go have some fun working with my Daddy."

"I will," he said with a chuckle.

I walked Eliza over to the dugout. A few of her teammates were warming up out by the left field line. She hung her equipment bag and searched for her cleats.

"How's practice been going?" I asked.

"Okay," she said. "I don't think Coach Robinson likes me." She kept her voice low so as not to be overheard.

My phone rang. I pulled it from my pocket. "Don't be silly," I said. Nancy Perez's name was on the screen. I made a mental note to call her later and looked back at Eliza. "Of course he does."

"He's nice but says there are seven different parts to a swing. I'd do better if he would just let me 'See the ball' and 'Hit the ball.'" She handed me her cleats and sat on the dugout bench.

"I'll talk to him." I knelt in front of her to lace up her cleats.

"Mommy already did," she said.

"Well, I'm sure that will take care of it."

"Tie them tight," she said, pointing to her foot. "It makes me faster."

I went to work.

"When are we all going to be back together?" Eliza asked. "I like Old Saybrook but not without you."

"I'm not sure. We have to give Mommy more time."

"I don't think she's mad anymore."

I finished her left cleat but stopped before working on the right. "Why do you say that?" I asked, looking up.

"Because she reads everything about the campaign." Eliza pulled her glove out of her bag and slipped it over her right hand. "She reads the newspaper in the morning, and stories on the internet at night, and we have to be quiet if there's something about it on the news so she can hear."

"Well, I suppose that's progress."

"She writes down everything you do wrong."

"How long is the list?"

"Long. Like three pages long."

I went back to work on her right shoe. "I'm not sure I want to know what's on those pages."

"She says, 'Daddy's all over the place.'"

"All over the place?"

"Yeah, she says you're supposed to be saying the same thing."

"I know, but that's boring."

"Well, she says you have to keep saying the same thing so people know what you're for."

"What else did she say?"

"She says you need something called 'rapid response.'"

My phone vibrated. I pulled it from my shirt pocket to read the text from Monica.

Need you back right away.

Emergency!

MMM

Gene appeared in the dugout. "Q, they need us back," he said.

"I have to go," I told Eliza. "Mommy will be here to pick you up after practice."

"I need you to stay."

"I can't, Honey. I'm sorry."

—⚏—

When I returned to campaign headquarters, the long, drab gray-blue hallway leading to the bullpen was being brightened up by a volunteer fixing the overhead light. Three other volunteers were replacing the 11x14 "Q" signs with sleek looking posters reflecting our new campaign slogan and brand. A giant blue letter "Q" sat on a white background. The "Q" encased our campaign slogan written in red: "The Right Experience. For the Change We Need." Someone had also placed a new handwritten sign over the door leading into the bullpen: "Geek Zone: Authorized Personnel Only!"

The entire campaign staff, several of whom were already wearing t-shirts bearing our campaign slogan, was huddled in the middle of the bullpen like tourists gathered on a sidewalk to watch a street performer. I couldn't make out the cause of the commotion from the doorway but could see that the men seemed to be standing closer to the table than the women.

"I think I'm going to be sick," Rachel said, holding her hand over her mouth as she headed past me on the way to the bathroom. She handed off a white envelope embossed with red trim.

I stepped into the middle of the huddle.

Like a pride of hungry lions, the men—along with Keisha—were tearing into the roasted pig like nothing else in the world mattered. Gene pushed past me to start filling a plate with pork, potato salad and collard greens. Mildred and Raymond looked to be having a picnic in the corner. A contingent of vegans—who looked to be mostly college kids—had started a support group on the far side of the floor. "I can't even stand the smell," one of them in a Yale t-shirt said.

I opened the envelope.

John Quincy:
Hope you and your team like what my Momma used to call a Pig Pickin'. Nothin like a plate full of bacon to keep a man happy, I always say. Men are such simple creatures!

The poke you're going to get today means that I'll have to take things into my own hands. Never leave a man to do a man's job I suppose.

Love you!

Lucy

Lucy added a postscript on the back of the card.

PS In case you decide to grow a pair, you can beat Saul by just figuring out the one thing someone who spent his life in politics doesn't have . . .

"Where's Monica?" I asked Mildred and Raymond.

They both pointed to the conference room next to her office. Raymond grinned from ear to ear.

Monica waited for me at the end of the table with her iPad propped up on its case. Two people I'd never seen were sitting on the radiator behind her.

I turned to the two strangers and extended my hand. Monica introduced them to me while we shook.

"Quinn, this is Dean Rand and Donavan Price. They're two of the best image and media guys in the business."

"It's a pleasure to be on board," Dean said.

"Looking forward to working with you," Donavan added.

I glared at Monica. The most important thing any organization does is hire employees—especially high-level consultants. I wasn't at all happy about her doing this without my approval.

"Where's Aidan?" I asked her.

"Daniel says he's not up to coming to meetings anymore," she said.

"But he has to be here if we're talking about something important."

"Do you want me to try and get him?" Monica asked.

"No," I said flatly.

My phone rang again.

"It's Nancy," I said, looking to Monica.

"Don't answer that!" Donavan yelled.

"Why wouldn't I answer my own phone?" I asked, my voice cold.

"There was a press conference this morning," Monica said. "The State's Attorney declined prosecution."

"Apparently, Alarico Perez isn't a model citizen," Donavan said. "In addition to being kicked out of school for all kinds of things, he's a reputed gang member."

There was a knock at the door. Gene opened the door and filled the door frame.

"Q, I'm headin' out to pick up your mom from the airport," he said. "Graham is gonna drive for you tonight."

"You're going to pick up who?" I asked in disbelief.

"I thought you knew," he said, looking to Monica to save him.

"She wanted to come," Monica said. "She wants to help."

"My mother is seventy-six years old!" I looked at Monica. "You don't do something like that without talking to me. What the hell were you thinking?"

"We thought you'd be glad that your mother was coming," Monica said.

"I'm sorry," Gene said, stammering.

"Just go," I said.

Gene pulled the door behind him. I sat down and pinched the bridge of my nose. I took a deep breath and then grabbed my phone. The three of them just stared at me while I texted Brooke.

> *My Mom is coming. Can you please come home? Things are so chaotic and I don't know how I'd explain that you and kids are gone …*

I hit "send" and took another breath.

"Okay," I said. "Why exactly is Nancy trying to get me?"

"She's calling 'cause she wants you to come to speak at a protest for Alarico," Monica said.

"We told her that you couldn't make it," Dean said. "We're advising you against going. At least until some of these facts get sorted out."

"So let me get this straight," I said, gripping the table with both hands. "Two people who've never met me and another who barely knows me have decided this for me?"

"We know this is an adjustment," Donavan said, "but it's part of playing in the major leagues. You have to let us handle these things."

I thought my head was going to explode. I stood and headed for the door.

"Quinn," Monica said. "We have to show this to you."

"Show me what?"

The room stayed silent for a beat. Dean jumped in.

"Quinn, this ad just hit the net and TV." He reached for the iPad sitting in front of Monica and touched the screen to bring it to life. "You'll want to have a look."

The ad started with a black screen and ominous music playing in the background. The screen faded up from black and displayed a grainy close-up photo of me. Text then appeared in the center of screen:

Quinn Barnes: In His Own Words

A narrator—who sounded a lot like me—then read along with text rising from the bottom of the screen.

> "The story of America is a simple one."
>
> "A small group of people decided that they wanted all the capital for themselves: all the land, all the property and all the opportunity."
>
> "So, they set up a system whereby only they could own property, exercise the right to vote or even learn to read."
>
> "They've kept the system in place by running a three hundred year campaign designed to convince everyone else that they are genetically inferior—less intelligent—than the people in their small group."
>
> "Anyone who believes in an alternate view of our country's history is either a fool, never read a history book or both."
>
> "This is the story of America."

The picture faded to black as the ominous music reached its crescendo. A baritone voice asked the question, "Do you know the real Quinn Barnes?" The spot didn't include the legally required disclosure from Saul that he approved the message. Instead, it just said, "Paid for by the Citizens for a More Responsible America."

I pushed the iPad back towards Monica.

"Did you say this?" Dean asked.

I ignored him and spoke to Monica.

"That's not my voice," I said. "Is this Patriot Partners money doing this?"

"Probably." Monica said. "But did you say that?"

"Ever?" I asked.

"Yes, have you ever said that?" she asked.

The truth was that it sounded an awful lot like something I would say—or Aidan or Daniel. It's the kind of thing we'd rant about over drinks or if one of us was reading Howard Zinn. I never spoke like that in mixed company, but Aidan rarely held his tongue.

"Listen, that's not my voice and there's no speech—or paper—or anything else that anyone can come up with where I said that." I placed my knuckles on the table. "Let's just say that it's not my voice and move on."

"I'm not sure we can do that," Donavan said. "Do you believe that statement?"

"How much are we paying you?" I asked.

"Our standard rate," he said, without a hint of defense. "But we have to tackle these issues. The campaign's failure to vet this stuff is making this look like amateur hour."

"Really?" I said.

"The shit storm has just begun if we don't start working through this," Dean said. "We have to start game planning on how we're going to answer these questions."

"Quinn, why don't you take a few minutes to decompress?" Monica stood to meet me at the door. "Maybe you can go check in with Aidan and we can reconnect?"

"Do you know what Aidan would say?" I asked with my hand on the door handle. "Any candidate who can't answer a question about crap like this without a consultant doesn't deserve to win anything, and has wasted a lot of money."

The door slammed behind me.

XIII

What started off as a brutal week somehow morphed itself into a horrendous month, and I could feel our insurgent campaign falling apart.

The Memorial Day weekend started on Saturday with three consecutive days of parades from dawn to dusk. For the life of me, I don't understand why politicians go to parades. Kids want to see clowns, Shriners in their go-carts and fire trucks at a parade, not politicians. But Monica said I had to go, so I went.

The marathon started early Saturday morning in Willimantic's "Unique People's Parade" on the east side of the river and ended on Monday in the Naugatuck Valley in the west; all towns in Saul's stronghold.

Saul and his supporters were in full glory all weekend in their red "Stickin' With Saul" t-shirts. His advance people made sure he was well positioned for each event, and secured the lead spot in the more populated cities like Waterbury, Norwalk and Meriden. Saul happily made his way across the state wearing his trademark perma-smile that people hadn't seen in six years—which was the last time he'd set foot in any of these towns.

Lucy was a hoot. Her campaign constructed a massive Mayflower boat covered in red, white and blue sequins. She sat at the helm dressed up as Uncle Sam—with cleavage. Instead of handing out palm cards, she threw tea bags and copies of the Constitution from her boat. "Make 'em follow the Constitution!" she hollered into a bullhorn. "Fight the

Socialists." She was a big hit in some of the more rural towns but got booed in Hartford and New Haven. But she kept on smiling.

Gene, Raymond and Melissa organized our volunteers to put together a cute little school bus float to highlight my education plan. Unfortunately, the wheels of our bus kept falling off. On Saturday evening, the *Free Press* led with the headline, "Wheels Falling Off the Barnes Bus." On Sunday, they went with "Barnes Campaign Stuck in Reverse." On Monday, they went back to "Wheels Still Falling Off Barnes Bus."

By the time I was able to get back to my fundraising calls during the first week of June, it was clear that Saul's air attack was taking its toll.

"You have to answer this stuff," one of my former law partners pleaded with me. "He's making you look like a nut job."

"We're trying to get him to debate," I said.

"Why would he debate you?" he asked. "He's too busy kicking dirt on your grave."

And then their next ad hit.

I knew it was bad even before Monica appeared in the basement during call time to show it to me. A hard core activist, Gina Proia, from toney West Hartford had told me about it during a fundraising call earlier in the morning.

"It's bad, Quinn," Gina said.

"How bad?" I asked.

"You just really need to start hitting back," she said.

"I want to try and lift people up," I said. "Not just tear Saul down."

"You're not being realistic."

"If you can just help me raise more cash, we'll be able to start getting our message out."

"Well, you can forget me hosting a fundraiser."

"Oh, c'mon, Gina."

"You're not viable at this point," she said. "It's actually worse than that. He's successfully defining you and the definition is crazy."

Monica took a chair next to me while I finished up a call. She had her iPad in her hands with a set of headphones plugged in. When I wrapped up my call, she pulled off my phone headset and replaced it with the headphones from her iPad. She activated the screen and hit "play."

It had the exact same look and feel as the piece from weeks before. It started with same black screen and ominous music. The first image was the same grainy close-up photo of me, although I could have sworn the producer had sharpened my teeth to look like fangs. The title was the same: **Quinn Barnes: In His Own Words**. The narrator, still impersonating my voice, read the text rising from the bottom of the screen.

"Capitalism is theft."

"It always has been and always will be."

"And the wealth of America is based on theft."

"America was born by first stealing the country from Native Americans. We then developed that land by stealing labor off the backs of blacks through a system of slavery that lasted for more than 250 years. Still looking to line their pockets, our 'wealth creators' invaded Mexico and started the Mexican-America war to steal the Southwest."

"In fact, the entire Western world acquired its wealth by theft. It had almost nothing to do with investment and innovation and everything to do with colonialism. The theft of the world's riches and natural resources."

"Even today, capitalism is robbing people of their fair share. And their dignity."

"This is the story of America."

The piece closed with the Citizens for a More Responsible America asking the same question, "Do you know the real Quinn Barnes?"

"Where the hell is this stuff coming from?" I asked Monica.

"Only you would know," she said. "I'm certainly in the dark."

The next several days of call-time were an exercise in futility.

The pledges—the folks who had promised to contribute to the campaign but hadn't yet sent in their money—were becoming harder and harder to chase down. When I managed to get any of them on the phone, I had to help them through their amnesia.

"Did I pledge that?" my law school roommate asked. "I should have checked with the Mrs. before doing that. Let me get back to you." The small donations were still coming in on-line and helping us keep the lights on, but prospecting for new money was pretty much over.

"Are you that socialist guy?" I kept hearing over and over.

Without money, we couldn't make our first media buy to get on television. Without television, we couldn't change the narrative about me—and Saul's handiwork to define me as an extremist was hardening. And making it next to impossible to raise money.

"I need to understand our earned media strategy," I told Monica during one of our daily lunchtime catch-ups.

"We're working on something."

"How can we be 'working on something'?" I asked, shaking my head. "We have to have a game plan every day for how we're going to get us on the news. Every day."

"When we're always on defense, it's kinda hard to drive a strategy," she fired back. "We have to get on offense."

"So get us on offense," I yelled back.

The only positive throughout the four weeks was that home was starting to get back to normal. Brooke had spared me the embarrassment of trying to explain to my mother why we weren't all living under the same roof and had brought the kids back home. The two of us still weren't talking much but since I was hardly ever home, I was hoping Mom wouldn't really notice.

My mother was a great help with the kids. She knows her way around Connecticut and jumped right in to help get them to their summer camps and baseball practice while Brooke and I worked. Mom's only condition was that I be home every other day to eat dinner with the family.

"What did you guys do today?" I asked while Mom poured a ladle full of gumbo on my plate.

"Grandma showed us how to make this gumbo so we can make it for you when she's gone," Eliza said.

"It was either this or something call bow-den," Pierce said.

"Boudin," Mom said, pronouncing it "boo-dahn" to correct him.

"You know what's in boudin, Dad?" Ben asked, taking his place between his siblings on the bench that runs the length of dining room table.

"I do," I said from my Windsor chair opposite them.

"It's a sausage with pig blood and a pig heart in it." Ben said, dying to say it aloud. "And when you cut it open, the blood comes pouring out and you're supposed to use bread to soak up the blood and eat it!"

"It's absolutely disgusting," Eliza said, her face deformed by her frown.

"Your Daddy used to love a good boudin," Mom told them, while she filled their bowls.

"Have you ever tried it, Mommy?" Ben asked, looking to Brooke.

"No," Brooke said from the head of the table. "Boudin is not for me."

"Is that why we live in New England, Mommy?" Eliza asked. "So we don't have to eat things like boudin?"

"Don't be silly," Brooke said. "It's just not something we ever ate growing up here."

"Mom only likes things in New England," Ben said to my mother, as if he was telling on Brooke. "She says we all have to go to college in New England."

"And work in New England," Eliza added.

"And die in New England!" Pierce said.

"Will you three pipe down and eat your dinner?" I said.

"That's okay," Mom said from her chair opposite Brooke. "That's what you're supposed to do at the dinner table. Talk. And ask questions."

"Did my Dad ask questions at the dinner table when he was little?" Ben asked.

"My Lord!" Grandma said. "He was always full of questions. He'd ask them non-stop. Some days all he did was ask questions. Your grandfather and I used to call him our little question mark."

Eliza giggled. "Like what kind of questions?" she asked.

"When he was your age," she said, looking at Eliza, "he wanted to know all about the moon and what he had to do to become an astronaut."

"He still loves the moon," Eliza said as if I wasn't there. "And planets and stuff like that."

"And then there was a long time when he'd ask us what he had to do to become a professional football player or baseball player or basketball player," Mom said, holding up her spoon as she thought back on it. "Mostly a football player, I suppose."

Ben and Pierce looked at each other and laughed. "He still talks about playing football," Pierce said, cackling.

"He's so crazy," Ben said. "He says he's gonna start working out and play in college again. We keep telling him he's an old man and would get broken!"

My mother laughed along with them.

"And when he got to be your age," she said, looking at Pierce and Ben, "he'd ask us how to handle people in school that were mistreating him. That went on for a bunch of years."

"Do you feel bad about sending Daddy to those schools where people were so mean to him?" Eliza asked.

"Eliza Rose Wolcott-Barnes," Brooke said sternly. "What has gotten into you? You don't ask a question like that."

"That was a long time ago," I said. "It's all way in the past."

"Sometimes I do," Mom said. "It was hard for him."

"Did he have friends?" Eliza asked.

"Not really." Mom reached out and touched Eliza's curly locks. "He was always very popular but never really had any friends beyond your Uncle Daniel."

"So why'd you make him do that?" Pierce asked.

"Well, we all have to do hard things. And everyone in our family has had to suffer. My parents suffered and the Lord knows life was just about hell for their parents." Mother put her elbows up on the table and looked at each of the children. "But I suppose we made him do it because I knew he was strong enough to suffer through it. And if he could suffer through it, he could do something big like be a senator someday."

"Are we gonna have to suffer?" Pierce asked, concerned.

"No, not like that," Brooke said. "You'll have different challenges."

"So Grandma," Eliza said. "Would all that suffering have been for nothing if Daddy doesn't win?"

"Not for me," Mom said. "I'll always know that he was good enough, strong enough and smart enough to be a senator."

"But do you want him to win?" Eliza asked.

"More than anything in the world."

"But Dad's doing bad," Ben said. "He's doing bad every day."

"We all have more bad days than good ones," she said. "So he just needs to do the same thing we told him to do when he was your age and having a bad day."

"What's that?" Pierce asked.

Mom looked at me. "Just keep goin', John Quincy. One foot in front of the other and keep going."

XIV

"Did you read this?" a graying middle-aged man asked before stepping into the aisle of the plane. He handed his traveling companion the morning edition of the *Free Press*.

"About the Senate race?" the second man asked before joining his colleague in the aisle to depart.

"Yeah, it's unbelievable."

Monica froze in her seat. She took out her iPad and waited to hear if there was anything worth writing down. I waited patiently from my window seat to watch the whole thing play out.

"Dick, you know I don't trust anything that rag prints. It's all advocacy—and crappy advocacy."

"Well, you need to read this. It says Quinn Barnes was once a member of a gang that was involved in narcotics trafficking and murder."

"Okay, you're a serious person," the first man said. "A CEO."

"Sure," Dick said.

"Well, then, you can't actually believe that a guy who was a federal prosecutor and then a partner at Clay Pittman was a gang member?"

"I don't know anything about this person," Dick said. "It's the point Saul is trying to make. He's different and none of us know him."

"But you can't believe that—"

"How do you know he wasn't?" Dick asked.

"Because I'm not a friggin' moron."

The cabin door opened and the line started to move. Monica scrambled and elbowed her way to the front to ensure she could stay within an earshot of her serendipitous focus group. Like a cub reporter chasing a big story, she hurried to keep pace with the two men. I trailed, but not too far behind.

"Go ahead and bury your head in the sand," Dick said.

A bottleneck stopped them about ten feet short of the terminal.

"I'm not burying anything. I just want to see this happen."

"To assuage some kind of liberal guilt?" Dick asked.

"I'm no liberal. It's just that he's qualified and I want to see this happen."

"He ain't qualified if he's a gang member," Dick said, looking over his shoulder. "And I for one am not willing to hand the keys to one of the most important offices for this state to someone who could be a drug dealing murderer for all we know . . ."

I couldn't help but look at Dick. He noticed and returned my gaze.

"I agree," I said, shrugging, "we just don't know this guy."

The bottleneck cleared. We all continued into the Reagan National terminal.

"This is a waste of time," I said to Monica.

We made our way, shoulder to shoulder, through the growing crowd of early morning travelers.

"I don't like you when you're grumpy," Monica said, pulling the strap of her leather knapsack over her shoulder. "You know what your problem is?" she asked.

"Today? Today my problem is that I'm on a hopeless mission in Washington to raise money from people who will never give it to me."

"You refuse to do the dance."

We stopped at a café along the promenade leading to the DC Metro. I ordered two cups of black coffee. Monica dumped what looked to be a fistful of sugar and then cream in hers.

We stopped at a deserted row of benches near the exit.

"What dance exactly would you like to see me doing?"

"You're not going to get any money if you don't ask for it."

"Political action committees are in the incumbent business," I said, crossing my legs. "I could do a hundred interviews and we won't get an endorsement. We're wasting a day in a race in which we have less than sixty left."

"It's not always about the endorsement. Sometimes you can keep money on the sidelines. Keep someone from endorsing Saul."

"Over the course of thirty years, every PAC in Washington has endorsed Saul Berg. Besides, he's probably raised more than $15 million by now. He doesn't need any money."

"We could benefit from people seeing and understanding that you're not a murdering gang member."

"You're not listening to me," I said.

"You have to try."

Monica handed me the itinerary for the day.

"Are you coming with me for all these?"

"No. We're spreading out. Where do you want to reconnect?" she asked.

"I'll text you."

I headed to the double doors of the Metro. I was relieved to be by myself.

I rode the Metro red line to Union Station and emerged at one of Washington's political action committee hives: the ten-block area behind the Capitol where the northeast and southeast sections meet. If you just randomly knocked on the doors of ten brownstones you would likely find yourself on the doorsteps of the National Women's Network, Disabled Persons United, Clean Energy Connection or some other group with keys to a treasure chest of dollars to help fund a campaign.

It's not the $5,000 contribution—an amount that is limited by federal law—that candidates seek from PACs, or even the stamp of approval that might come with an endorsement from political professionals in the areas of education, arms control or tax reform. Candidates beg for PAC endorsements to leverage their bundling prowess. Every PAC has members—tens of thousands of them—sometimes even hundreds of thousands or millions of them. A call to make a contribution on behalf of a candidate—even a small one of five to ten dollars—from the PAC's faithful can yield enough money to fund an entire campaign. But PACs only like sure bets.

I motivated myself to endure a day of rejection from PAC boards and executive directors by simply trying to enjoy the policy discussions—which I actually like. Political professionals, however, aren't always interested in policy discussions.

"What's your fundraising budget, Mr. Barnes?" the chairman of the Council for a Livable World asked from the head of the table.

"Three million dollars," I said.

"You're going to run a Senate race on three million dollars?"

"That's the primary," I said. "Three million dollars for the primary. The economics obviously change after the primary."

"But you've raised less than two-hundred thousand," the co-chair said from the chair next to him. She didn't say it with disdain. I got the sense she was actually rooting for me.

"You understand that you have to establish yourself as a viable candidate," the executive director said.

My phone rang just a few inches from my right hand on the conference room table. Brooke flashed across the top of the screen. I didn't turn my phone off but instead tried to keep talking.

"I do, and thank you," I said. "We're trying to do something very difficult against a very unique candidate."

"Be that as it may," the chair said, "you have to show us that you're viable. Or that you have a plan to be viable. And that means money."

"We believe in a world free of nuclear weapons, the co-chair said, changing the subject. "Zero. None."

"I'm aware of that. That's also the position of Henry Kissinger, George Schultz and Sam Nunn. It also happens to be my position."

"Good," she said, appreciative that I had at least had a working knowledge of their issues. "Well, then, Mr. Barnes, who would be the last country to have a nuclear weapon?"

The phone rang. Brooke again.

"Excuse me, but I have to take this call."

I heard a gasp.

I didn't care.

"You're not coming to my game?" Eliza asked, distressed.

I was instantly sick.

"Is it tomorrow?"

"Daddy, the game starts in a half hour." She started crying. "I told you I needed you to be there. You said you were gonna be there."

"Hold on just one second," I said. "Just give me a second and we can talk."

I took a deep breath and stood.

"I'm sorry but I have to go," I said, heading to the door.

The chair stood and scratched the back of his head. The directors exchanged silent glances. One shrugged. Another turned his palms to the ceiling.

I was halfway out the door before I stopped to answer their question.

"There won't be one single country," I said.

"One country?" the co-chair asked.

"Yes. There won't be one county with the last nuclear weapon. There'll be a small number—may three or four—and they would all disarm together. Kinda like turning out the lights of a room and leaving together."

Several board members made notes, including the chair.

"The U.S. would be one of those three or four countries," I said. "Probably the one that would turn the light switch off for everyone. That's the only way it would work. Again, my apologies."

I stepped out of the conference room and then the front door to try to console Eliza from the cobblestone on Fourth Street.

—∭—

"How we doing?"

"Not so well," Monica said, out of breath as she climbed the top three steps of the Lincoln Memorial.

She dropped her knapsack hard next to my leather briefcase and sat with me on the top stair. We looked out at the reflecting pool while she caught her breath.

"So by 'not so well' you mean we have no commitments for an endorsement," I said.

"That's right, sir."

"And we've lost an entire day when we could have been home retooling the campaign?"

"This isn't a city council race. It can't be won just on social media."

"It's not—never mind. I'm tired of arguing about it."

I leaned back on my elbows and stared out over the reflecting pool. Monica followed my lead and tried to do the same. Not able to get comfortable mirroring my pose, she sat up.

"Can I ask why we're sitting here, sir?"

"This is about my favorite place in the world."

"How many times you been here?"

"Too many to count," I said. "Did you ever notice that Lincoln's hands are spelling his initials in sign language?"

Monica craned her neck to check. I continued looking out over the Mall.

"His left hand is sculpted to spell *A*," I said, "and his right is in the *L* position."

"Oh yeah," Monica said, nodding. "Interesting."

"Did you also know that Robert E. Lee's profile is sculpted in Lincoln's hair? And faces south?"

Monica studied his stone locks.

"I don't see it," she said.

"You have to walk over to the side."

Monica got up to have a look.

She was back by my side within a minute or so.

"That's amazing," she said. "How come I've never heard this?"

"The Park Service denies it—or that it was intentional."

We watched children scurry around the reflecting pool. Some ran up and down the stairs playing tag. Tourists passed us on their way to and from having a look at Abe and the Gettysburg Address.

"Can I tell you about your biggest problem?" Monica asked, finally breaking the silence. She kept her eyes on the Mall.

"You've already told me. I won't 'do the dance.'"

"That's one of your problems," she said. "I'm talking about your biggest problem."

I turned my head and looked her in the eye.

"You live in a bubble," she said.

"Can't say I've ever thought about it exactly that way before . . ."

"You're trapped in your bubble."

I turned back to look out over the Mall.

"I bet you Saul's been here as many times as you," she said, "and loves it just as much—but Saul doesn't confuse idealism with politics. Saul understands that Lincoln was a politician first; and a damn good one."

"I know that."

"Maybe you do but you don't understand what it means." Monica pulled her knees to her shoulders and drew a deep breath. "This guy that you revere was sitting in his office one evening trying to figure out how to get the 13th Amendment passed. He didn't have the votes so he decides that the only way to get it done was to bribe members of Congress. An outright corrupt and contemptible act."

"He didn't actually bribe people," I countered.

"Oh, yes he did," Monica said. "The history books sugar coat it but it was bribery plain and simple. And you sit here looking up at him all starry-eyed and mushy trying to live up to a standard that doesn't exist."

"What do you want me to do?" I asked. "Accuse Saul of being a wife-beating pedophile?"

"Stop being so extreme," Monica said.

"You sound like Brooke."

"Well, then, Brooke is a smart woman," she said. "I'm just asking that we at least hit him on all the deferments from Vietnam since he's backed military action in every conflict since then, including his calls now to bomb Iran. Or that he's always claiming he went down to Mississippi during Freedom Summer and the people that actually went say it's a bunch of bullshit."

"You want me to spend time talking about stuff from the 60s?" I asked. "Really?"

"Pointing out to people that their senator is a hypocrite or a liar isn't toilet politics," Monica said. "It's just politics. And a public service, if you ask me."

"Even if I don't even know whether half that stuff you want me to say is true?"

"Quinn, a guy walks up to a presidential candidate on the eve of primary day and says, 'I got good news and bad news for you. The good news is that I've found a way to make you president. The bad news is that it's going to require us to promote bigotry by falsely accusing your opponent of fathering an illegitimate black child and being a closet homosexual.' The candidate did it. And he won." She grabbed my arm to get me to look at her. "This is a dirty business, Quinn. From George Washington to Abraham Lincoln to Saul Berg, the people in it have found the strength to do things that disgust them so they can win on the big issues—the important ones."

"I can't do that."

"I know." Monica exhaled. "This is your religion," she said, sounding defeated. "You do realize that most of the people you worship wanted you to be a slave."

I didn't get the sense that she was trying to make a point as much as she was looking to give me a good jab.

"You've been in this business so long that you just don't see it," I said.

"Apparently, I'm blind as a bat when it comes to understanding you or what the hell we're doing."

"Our job is to just try and make it all a little bit better—a little less dirty. I'm not trying to make this system perfect. I'm just trying to push us closer to it. He was trying to do that," I said, gesturing over my shoulder. "It was all just messier in his time."

Monica's phone rang.

"Barnes for Senate," she said in a way that the caller might wonder whether any life was left in the campaign.

"I think I can arrange that," she said, immediately changing her tone. "We'll see you in 45 minutes."

"We really can't take another meeting," I said. "We might miss our plane and I really have to get home."

"You'll take this meeting," she said, standing and fixing her hair.

"Who are we going to see?"

"Senator Berg."

—⁂—

The Hart Office Building is the largest of the Senate office buildings and is home to about forty-five senators. Built in the '70s, it has a high central atrium that is bridged by walkways on each floor. Alexander Calder's fifty-one foot sculpture, *The Mountains and the Clouds*, dominates the atrium's vast space. I've never really cared for it. It looks to me like an oversized version of Darth Vader's helmet, but I keep my opinion to myself out of respect to the artist who died the evening he finished working on it.

We passed the elevator banks on the east side, opting for the semicircular staircases on the south end to make our way up to Room 322.

Monica knocked on the doorway to the reception area and entered like she owned the place.

"Quinn Barnes and Monica Metzler to see the senator," she said. She hovered over the receptionist like she wasn't going to tolerate waiting long for her meeting.

"Welcome. I'll let them know you're here," Saul's receptionist replied, nice as pie. "Can I get you something while you wait?" She opened her palm in the direction of the couch against the wall.

"We're fine," Monica said.

I sat. Monica paced back and forth. Neither of us spoke or even gestured to one another. Now that we were deep into the belly of the beast, we both assumed that everything we said or did was being monitored.

Ivan Crapp, Saul's chief of staff, emerged from behind the door leading to the interior office. He extended his hand to me and then to Monica. "Nice to meet you both," he said warmly.

"Let's go see Saul," Monica said, uninterested in offering even a modicum of courtesy.

"This is just going to be the senator and Mr. Barnes," he said.

"Like hell," Monica said loudly. "The lies and the smear and the . . . crap—it's gonna stop today and we're both gonna hear it from his mouth."

Monica looked to me. I couldn't tell if I was supposed to play the good cop or whether she was serious.

"Let's try this," Ivan said, his voice not raising a decibel. "You guys have a flight to catch, right?"

"We do," I said.

"Let's just have a five-minute conversation to get a dialogue started and if we need more time we can set something up in Hartford."

"That's fine," I said.

Monica turned her back on us, took out her phone and started typing. I followed Ivan into the interior of the office. My phone buzzed as he led me through what felt like a maze. I grabbed it from my breast pocket while trying to keep up with Ivan. The incoming text was from Monica:

No bullshit!

Call him the frickin' liar that he is and tell'em you're going to rip his balls off if it doesn't stop!

"Do you need to respond to that?" Ivan asked. His hand rested on a polished brass door knob.

She sent a second text while Ivan was waiting for my answer.

Hardball! It's all he understands!!!

"No," I said to Ivan, powering down my phone.

Saul's office was chock-full of the accoutrements of power that come from climbing to the top of the political world. The textured cardinal red wallpaper was barely visible behind his collection of photos with world leaders, Hollywood stars and little leaguers from Stamford. The navy blue carpet in the center of the office bore the Seal of the U.S. Senate. The coffee and end tables were decorated with expensive looking pewter figurines and historical memorabilia.

The shelf mounted next to the doorway featured a bust of Abraham Lincoln.

The window behind Saul's desk perfectly framed the Capitol dome. He emerged from behind his desk to meet me.

"Quinn!" He greeted me the way Aidan greets people. He extended his right hand to mine and used his left to grip my forearm. "Thank you for coming," he said.

I stood nearly a foot taller than Saul but he carried himself with a confidence that made him appear like a leviathan to me. I felt small.

"Quinn drinks an iced tea with no sugar," he said to Ivan. "Can we have someone bring him one?"

Ivan nodded and backed out the door.

"Heard you had a busy day," the senator said.

He sat on the couch that bordered the seal in the carpet and crossed his legs. I sat on the couch situated on the opposite side of the seal. A mahogany coffee table with a glass top divided us.

"It was a good day," I said.

"Sure it was. It never hurts to get in front of people—let them get a sense of you. You have to have a long view of things."

A knock at the door was followed by Saul's secretary appearing with my iced tea. She also had an amber-colored drink in a glass with a heavy bottom for Saul. It looked to be a neat bourbon.

She placed the glasses on the table. "Mr. Barnes," she said. "Ms.— I'm sorry, I can't recall your colleague's name."

"Metzler."

"Yes, Ms. Metzler asked me to remind you to check your phone."

"Tell her I got the message, thank you."

I sipped my iced tea. Saul's receptionist left. Saul got down to business.

"How's Aidan doing?"

"Thank you for asking. As well as can be expected under the circumstances."

"I'm sure he's not resting one bit. He's worrying about you."

"He obviously has more pressing issues than worrying about my campaign."

"Oh, I'm certain there is nothing more important to him right now than you and this election." Saul re-crossed his legs. "Do you know I remember the week you were going to find out if you made law review?"

"Law review?" I asked, narrowing my eyes. "From law school?"

"I was trying to convince Aidan to support my first Senate run. He was sick to his stomach worrying about it."

"About me getting on law review?"

Saul chuckled.

"Yes. In fact," Saul said, looking off in the distance for a moment as he reminisced about that day, "I was in his office when you called to tell him that you made it; there were about four of five of us having a campaign meeting." Saul's belly jiggled as he laughed about the episode. "He had us sit quietly like schoolchildren while he took the call."

"He never mentioned that to me," I said.

"He teared up after he put the phone down. He hid it from the others but I could tell." Saul drank from his glass. "You don't forget things like that. Real emotion. Worry and pride for someone you love. That's why I wasn't surprised when you announced."

I wasn't sure what to say. He had me totally off balance.

"What did you want to talk about?" I asked.

"Oh, you know what I want to talk about." Saul leaned back easily and tasted his drink again. "I want to see if there's a way for both of us to get what we want."

"I don't see how that's possible at this point."

"Anything is possible; you just have to think hard on it."

"Well, what are you thinking?" I asked.

"I think you've got everyone's attention, including me. I'd like to come to an agreement that would ensure the things that are important to you get their proper attention so that you can get back to your law practice that you worked so hard to build."

"I was already voted out of my partnership."

"That could be reversed. Or you could do something else. I'm prepared to help you attain anything that's within my power that you might want."

147

"Why would you do that?" I sipped my iced tea, working to appear as smooth as Saul.

"I'm a senator because I *always* take the long view," he said. "I'm no different than Aidan."

"I'm not so sure about that."

Saul exhaled. He placed his glass on the table and folded his hands on his right kneecap.

"Quinn, whether you want to believe it or not, Aidan and I are the same person. And right now we're both thinking about our legacies—what people are going to say about us after we're gone—the meaning of our precious time here on this earth. You tend to do that when you're our age—or facing what he's facing."

He grabbed his glass and walked over to the photos hanging near the window. I followed and leaned on the corner of his desk, still struggling to look suave. Like someone who was worthy of working in an office as elegant as Saul's office.

"I'd like to find a way to rightfully applaud your courage, he said, "get you back on track with the firm—and maybe set you up to be a senator someday."

"Why in the world would you do that?" I asked.

"Because Aidan Coyle is responsible for helping me get to this office." Saul used his chubby knuckle to tap the photo on the wall, "and serving in this office has made me a part of history. That's my legacy. And I honestly don't want to spend my last election destroying his."

I moved next to Saul and peered into an eight-by-eight photo on the wall. It was my law school graduation photo. It was me standing in front of the library. I even remember Aidan taking it. I would have chalked the whole thing up to some kind of hoax to get me out of the race but for one thing. There was handwriting on the photo and I was one-hundred per cent certain it was Aidan's:

> *Saul:*
>
> *Don't forget about him.*
>
> *Aidan*

Saul let me drink it in. He didn't make a move or say anything until he was certain I had connected the dots he wanted me to connect. I backed away from the photo and returned to the couch. Saul followed and sat beside me.

"I honestly don't want to spend my last election destroying the person he's hoping to carry on the legacy that he's earned."

"That's why you're trying to convince the state that I'm a murdering drug dealer?"

"Son, you need to understand something," Saul said, calmly. "I've earned certain things. And if you're thinking for even a second that I'm not going to do what's necessary to keep what I've earned, you're in the wrong business."

"Well, there's no way to call this off," I said. "He wants you gone."

"He doesn't want me gone. He wants you in this office. There's a big difference. There's a way to accomplish both things."

"You're wrong."

"I don't know what Aidan's told you but his dying wish isn't to stir public debate over income inequality. He's not even a liberal." Saul took a slow steady gulp from his drink. "Aidan wants his son to be a U.S. senator. That's the legacy he's fighting for; that's why he's doing this."

"What exactly are you proposing?"

"Go home and talk to your family. Call a press conference—say next Wednesday or Thursday. That will give you more than a week to think about it."

"No one will be there."

"Oh, every news outlet in New England will be there. I'll see to it." Saul tapped the side of his glass with his index finger while he stared into my eyes. "Tell them the truth: that you fought the good fight to raise issues that are important to working people but you can't continue for family reasons. I'll jump right in—the same day. I'll applaud you and let folks know you've inspired me to revisit raising the national minimum wage and that I'm going to be introducing a bill in Congress within a week to do just that."

"How about apologizing to Occupy Wall Street? And doing something on student loan debt?"

"I can do that too."

"How can I be certain you'll hold up your end of the bargain?"

"Tell them you're suspending the campaign for a week. If I don't do everything I promised, you can just jump right back in." Saul put his hand on my shoulder. "But if I do everything I promise—and I will—you'll have a victory that will make you the leading candidate for my seat after I retire. This is win-win."

A knock at the door was followed by Saul's secretary's head appearing through the opening. "You're late for the Majority Leader," she said to Saul.

"Tell him I'll be right over."

She nodded and retreated.

We stood together.

"Quinn, someday you're going to make a great senator—or whatever else you decide to do. This is a gift. Please take it. If you think these past few months have been rough, you won't survive the last two—"

"Because of the Plopper twins—"

"I don't control them or any of the other companies or lobbyists that don't like what you're doing. But I'll tell you this: The easiest thing in the world for me to do is just wait two months and beat you. You'll have nothing after that."

We walked together to the door.

"What's your thinking?" he asked before opening the door to lead me out.

"I'm not sure. I have to give it some thought."

"Don't think too long."

We shook hands. I went on my way.

His secretary helped me find my way back to the receptionist area. Monica was pecking away at her phone. She put it away when she noticed me and opened the door to the hallway.

"How'd it go?" she asked, leading me to the elevator.

"Fine."

"You let him have it, right? Told him we'll go after his family if we have to?"

"Yes."

"I don't trust that bastard as far as I can throw him, but that's good. At least we can say he acknowledged all the slander. Did you get him to agree to a debate?"

"Not really."

"Figures. But at least we can say we took the issue to him personally and he refused—and that it's un-American and all that." Monica pressed the button to call the elevator. "Seems like you were in there for a long time. What else did he say?"

"We got to talking about Aidan."

Monica whipped out the notepad on her phone. "We need to figure out how to leverage this meeting. It puts us on stage with him. We can show people we're on the same level, meeting with him in Washington."

"How about a press conference?"

"Great idea," she said. "We can pound on his refusal to debate you. Have some of the kids dress up as chickens."

"Not sure about the chicken part but let's shoot for Thursday of next week."

"Will get the kids on it."

"At the state Capitol."

"Fine."

The elevator doors opened. I pressed the button for the lobby while Monica texted the staff back in Hartford.

XV

"Tonight," Aidan announced, cradling his glass of neat Irish whiskey. "I'm gonna teach you two boys the lesson of hubris." He pointed at Daniel and then me.

That's how our night started on New Year's Eve of 1975. Daniel and I were both twelve. The age when part of you still wants to be a kid but the rest of you feels ready to drive and do just about anything else that grown-ups do. It's also when you start learning that adults aren't perfect. Some of them are pleasant and amusing. Some of them are wretched and low. Most of them are both.

I suppose it's natural to think your own parents are dumb. I never felt that way about Mom and Dad and definitely not Aidan. Aidan held the keys to something I wanted and I figured he was handing them over to me with every lesson, anecdote and experience that I wouldn't have had without him. Daniel didn't see things that way. By the time we were twelve, he was pretty much finished listening to Aidan.

"Hubris, Dad?" Daniel asked, smirking as he leaned on his elbow in front of the fire in the Coyle living room.

"That's right, boy," he said to Daniel. "Hubris. And self-destruction."

"You think we want to destroy ourselves, Dad?" Daniel said, stopping just short of openly mocking him.

"Some things are innate."

"What does innate mean, again?" I asked.

"It means something that's deep inside you."

"Deep!" Dad hollered from the corner of the room with his nose in Aidan's collection of jazz albums.

"What's hubris?" I asked.

Daniel rolled his eyes and leaned back on a pillow.

"Well, that's the point of the story." Aidan kicked Daniel to get him to pay attention but Daniel closed his eyes and kept still as a cadaver. "There was this boy who was just about the same age as you and Daniel," Aidan said looking at me. "His father was just about my age and the two of them were stuck in prison."

"Where was this?" I asked skeptically. Aidan had taught me more about criminal law than a first year law student by that time and it didn't make sense that a judge would put a kid in prison with his father.

"In Crete," he said

"Crete?" I asked.

"It's one of the Greek Islands," Aidan said.

Daniel opened his eyes and came back to life. "It's not a real story," he said. "It's fake."

"It's a myth," my Dad corrected.

"Which means it's fake," Daniel said.

"Don't back-sass, young man," Aidan said to Daniel. The threat of a backhand quieted him. "Myths inspire us," he said, calm again but slurring his words.

Aidan's eyes were glassy and I was pretty sure he was drunk. It didn't bother me. I just wanted him to get on with the rest of the story before he was no longer able to tell it.

"How'd they get out of prison?" I asked.

"Well, the boy's father built him a pair of wings," Aidan said. "But the wings are a metaphor—a symbol."

"For what?" I asked.

"Education," Dad said as he flopped on the couch behind me.

"But not just school education," Aidan added. "It's everything we're trying to teach you two boys." Daniel slipped his headphones over his head to tune Aidan out. "About politics and people and why they behave the way they do."

"And passion," Dad said.

"Passion?" I asked.

"Yup," Aidan said. "Love, fear and hate. If you can figure out what someone loves, fears and hates, you can get 'em to do just about anything."

"We need to get these boys reading some Shakespeare," Dad said to Aidan, taking us even further off topic and making me pretty sure he was drunk too.

"*Julius Caesar*," Aidan said, falling back on a pillow.

"*Othello*," Dad said, snapping his fingers.

"*Taming of the Shrew*!" Aidan hollered.

They both laughed. I didn't see what was so funny.

"So what's the hubris part of the story?" I asked, trying to extract the teaching that was escaping me.

"The wings were made of wax," Dad said, finishing off his wine. "The boy flew away and got out of the prison but flew too close to the sun—"

"He disobeyed his father," Aidan said, glancing at Daniel who was laying with his eyes closed, hands over his chest and earphones still on. "His father warned him about it, but the boy did it anyway and crashed to the ground."

"So you think the boy wanted to destroy himself?" I asked Aidan.

"That's not the main point of the story," Dad said. "The point is that you have to be confident—but humble at the same time—all the time."

"Don't let yourself get too high or too low," Aidan said. "Just keep flying straight."

"But what would make the boy want to destroy himself?" I asked, looking to Aidan.

He shrugged.

"Probably something he loved, feared or hated."

"Or all three," Dad said.

"Is that possible?" I asked. "You can love, fear and hate the same thing?"

"Oh, you better believe it," Aidan said. "You just keep on living. You'll see . . ."

After that lesson, I've always been fascinated with people who self-destruct. I knew that's not what they wanted me to take away from it but it's what I latched onto. I can still entertain myself for hours thinking about it—probably the same way a physicist can lose himself pondering the theory of relativity.

Gene fascinates me. I'm always wondering what combination of love, fear and hate pushed him over the edge that night at Bowling Green. And hoping that it wasn't the love he felt for a brother, which would make the whole thing even more tragic. There were many others over the years that made even less sense: a friend in his forties who left his four small children to take up with a teenager; a former client who gambled away his kids' college fund out at the casinos; a law school classmate who, after putting down two bottles of wine at dinner, headed the wrong way up the off-ramp on I-84 in Hartford and killed a family of three.

And then there was Daniel.

Daniel had gotten a start in life that was like winning the lottery. And self-destructed. The way I see it, alcoholism cost him nearly twenty years of his life. He spent more time in the bars in Harvard Square than he did in his constitutional law classes. It was a miracle that his marriage lasted as long as it did, considering he spent the better part of six years imbibing a whiskey before lunch. His law practice was a constant roller coaster, the low point of which included his falling asleep drunk at the counsel table during a hearing in federal court.

I suppose he recovered and deserves credit for getting himself cleaned up. He just always seemed unappreciative about getting a second chance in life. The older I get the more it bugs me. Probably because I know if the shoe was on the other foot, the world wouldn't have given a second chance to me.

"We have to talk," he said, interrupting Thursday morning's busy call-time. He said it like he had all the power—like I worked for him.

"When?"

"As soon as possible. You free tonight?"

"Not really, but if it's important, I can make time early."

"It is. Meet me at the Pattaconk in Chester at five-thirty."

I stewed all the way down Route 9 to Chester. I'd have to rush back to Hartford after we were done and would be running late for the rest of the night. All for a meeting that I suspected we could have had over the phone. I was mad at myself for agreeing to it. I suppose I made the effort out of respect for Aidan.

"The blogs are reporting the thing about the black pastors," Daniel said before I could sit down at the patio table. "Have you seen it?"

"What blogs and what thing?" I ordered an unsweetened iced tea from the waiter on his way to the kitchen. Daniel already had a Diet Coke in hand.

"The *Left Nutmeg* says the Coalition of African-American Pastors opposes your same-sex marriage agenda. They're supporting Saul."

"So?"

"So, you're going to let that happen?" he asked.

"This is a Democratic primary. I'm not losing votes over my position on gay marriage."

Daniel gulped his Diet Coke. "But you're not going be able to peel away any of the older moderates from Saul," he said, putting his glass down on the sturdy wooden table. "Besides, the real story is going to be your lack of support in the black community. You need the blacks."

"I've been black for a long time. I don't need help from a bunch of pastors to talk to black people."

"Dad's worried about it."

"I'll talk to him," I said. The waiter delivered my iced tea. "How'd we do today?"

The waitress dropped two Cobb salads in front of us. Daniel picked up a piece of turkey from his plate with his hands.

"The money's not coming," he said. "I certainly hope you had fun yesterday playing hooky in D.C. because there's no money coming in here."

"I know the call center hasn't been strong, but aren't you and your Dad pulling down commitments?"

"Dad is sick, Quinn. He can't sit up for more than a few hours at a time," he said, stabbing into his salad for a fork full of ham and turkey. "And I'm not feeling so great right now about him spending his final days making fundraising calls for your Senate campaign."

"I think you're forgetting whose idea this whole thing was."

"Be that as it may, I'm telling you how things are now."

"What would Aidan say if he heard you say that?"

"He'd probably throw me off a roof top. But I'm just telling you what I think."

Daniel just stared at me while I sipped my iced tea.

"We've only been at it for a few months," I said, not even sure why I spoke the words. I knew my argument made no sense.

"There are barely eight weeks left to this thing," Daniel said, sneering. "If you don't do something now, this is gonna be a total embarrassment."

"So what are you saying? You think I should get out of the race?"

"I'm just saying the money's not coming in. I'm not seeing that changing. And this campaign is killing him."

—∞—

Mildred waited for me in a black Lincoln town car outside campaign headquarters. Gene was behind the wheel. The air conditioner was turned up full blast to shield us from the unseasonably warm late-June evening.

"Whose car is this?" I asked.

"Mine," she said, handing me our itinerary for the evening. "We need to start looking like we're an actual campaign. Consider this my contribution."

"Nice ride, huh, Q?" Gene said, winking at me through the rear-view mirror and running his hand across the plush tan leather passenger seat.

Mildred and I were settling into a nice routine on our evenings criss-crossing the state. It was one of the few things that was going well—or at least working the way it was supposed to. When we started back in April, she'd put together a briefing book with the news I missed while making my fundraising calls. Now she had an intern summarize each article into fifty words or less and she would just talk me through them. We then turned to polling. We still didn't have a real pollster but Mildred worked with Monica and Keisha to cobble together information from our voter ID efforts with data available on the web. They taught an intern—Samantha—how to compile the data and run a report each day, and this provided us with a pretty good daily tracking poll, which I got to see each night.

"We're 57 to 32 today," Mildred reported as we cruised up rural Route 66 toward Marlborough.

"I suppose that's progress," Gene threw out from behind the wheel.

"Not really," Mildred said, pointing to the bottom of the spreadsheet as I studied it. "Neither Saul's nor your numbers have moved more than three points in the last four days."

"Does that mean the cement's drying?" Gene asked.

"Yes," Mildred said. "The numbers are solidifying."

"How is tonight looking?" I asked Mildred.

"After the Marlborough town committee we're due at the Manchester town committee and then we head up to Coventry—," she held a piece of paper between her index finger and thumb like it had been sprayed by a skunk and handed it to me—"for the ALF-CIO meeting."

"I suppose they'll have to revoke your Grand Old Party membership card if you walk into that union hall with me tonight."

"That card's already been revoked." Mildred pointed to the paper to prod me to unfold it. "That's hot off the press and you need to read it now."

ALF-CIO is 'Stickin' With Saul'

Coventry—On Wednesday morning, the Connecticut ALF-CIO endorsed Senator Saul Berg for the Aug. 13 Democratic primary. With the endorsement, the labor federation, which represents some 180,000 members in the state and across New England, went on record supporting the Democratic senator

*most identified with his recent vote with the Republican caucus
to filibuster the health reform bill.*

*Tom Cold, chairman of the state ALF-CIO, said the union
"proudly endorsed" Berg in a special meeting by a two-thirds
voice vote.*

*Berg, a four-term incumbent, is facing a challenge for the
Democratic ticket for the first time since entering the U.S.
Senate in 1988. Quinn Barnes, a Hartford lawyer, is oppos-
ing Berg on an income inequality platform, trying to tap into
growing concerns about worsening economic and social conditions and class mobility.*

I balled the paper up in my fist. "I can't believe this guy!"

"I know," Mildred said in a high pitch.

"I've spoken with him . . . every . . . single . . . day . . . for the past
month."

"I know," she repeated.

"He promised me every which way to Sunday that they were either
going to endorse me or stay neutral." I punched the back of the
driver's seat. "And now they're endorsing the guy who just voted to
filibuster a piece of legislation that their members have been waiting
for—forever!"

"They get what they deserve," Mildred said. "Do you still want to
go?"

"Do they still want me to come?

"They say they do."

"Then we're going."

The ALF-CIO news left me furious—and distracted. During my
stop in Marlborough, I sounded like I'd never given a stump speech.
I was so mad by the time I got to Manchester that I said, "I love being
in Rocky Hill" twice.

"Q, he's throwing you off your game," Gene whispered in my ear
with his hand on my shoulder as he guided me from the Manchester
town committee meeting. "Forget him," he said, patting me on the
back. "Just keep playing."

I thought about it more on the way up to Coventry. Gene was right. It wasn't a coincidence that news of the ALF-CIO endorsement was announced hours before I was supposed to speak to them. Saul wanted to upset and embarrass me. And I was upset and embarrassed.

He was sending me a message. Reminding me about what he'd told me in his office the day before. That he had it within his power to help me or hurt me. And regardless of whether I decided to keep fighting him or accepted his offer, there was no way beat him.

Understanding it didn't make me feel any better. I was still thoroughly disgusted. The whole episode crystallized what I hate most about politics. Most people have no courage.

Tom Cold was a good enough guy. A family man with a mortgage to pay and two kids in college. Under ordinary circumstances, he'd probably always lead his flock in the right direction. But when Saul told Tom to do something that goes against everything he's supposed to be fighting for, Tom got in line. Even if it meant driving his membership to vote against their own interests.

"Quinn, thanks for coming," Tom said, using two hands to shake mine. "Tough decision on the endorsement but you know how those things go. It's not personal—just politics."

I shook Tom's hand but didn't say anything. I just took my seat in the front of the union hall and stewed while waiting to be introduced. After Tom stumbled through my bio, I took the floor.

"Whether you want to admit it or not, you're in a fight," I said, rolling up my sleeves, "And you're gettin' the holy hell beat out of you." I had a few nods in the front but most of the hall just looked up at me with blank stares. "Every time you turn around, someone else is kicking you in the teeth. Your salaries are being renegotiated down. Your health benefits are getting cut. Your work conditions are becoming more hazardous by the day." I walked down the hall's center aisle. "I'm the guy who worries about it—who lies awake at night in his bed worrying about it. But you know what?" I stopped in my tracks for effect. "I'm not worrying about it tonight. Because you just endorsed the very guy who's kicking you in the teeth."

"Wait a second," Tom said from behind me with both hands raised.

I kept talking.

"Saul doesn't care about you. He'd rather be caught dead than stand on a picket line with you, and you just keep on endorsing him and politicians like him in hopes of trying to live off the scraps from their table." I made my way back up to the front of the room and grabbed my jacket. "There was a time when this organization was bold—when it was proud—when it spoke truth to power and fought for its members. When you're sitting around next winter trying to figure out how you're going to pay your oil bill, or make ends meet at the supermarket, or pay to get your kid's toothache fixed, you remember what you did here and how you're getting exactly what you voted for."

No one clapped. They just sat and stared at me. One guy in the front had his jaw open.

Neither Tom nor any of the members offered me a handshake and I didn't go looking for one. I just followed Mildred and Gene out the door.

Gene started the car. Mildred dipped her head while she activated her phone.

I'm always kicking myself at night about the things I say to people. Sometimes I worry about having been too curt—or even rude. More often, I'm obsessing about having been too nice. Tonight, I felt just fine. I said exactly what needed to be said.

I grabbed a bottle of water from the arm rest and gulped half of it down.

"How'd I do?" I asked Mildred, wiping my mouth with the back of my hand.

She didn't seem to hear me. She sat there mouthing the words she was reading from her phone.

"What are you looking at?" I asked.

She held up her palm to quiet me while she finished reading. Her phone lit the bottom of her face and its wry smile.

"Have you ever heard of Nutmeg Medical?" she asked.

"Sure. Why?"

"Because Nutmeg Medical might make you a senator."

XVI

Saul stepped to a lectern bearing the Seal of the U.S. Senate to meet a bank of cameras and photographers in the Hart Office building's lobby. Monica stood on a chair in our campaign office trying to shush our team crowded in front of the largest of our flat-screen televisions. Keisha looked under papers and binders in search of the remote to turn up the volume. Gene eyed the side of the flat screen, mounted near the ceiling, for the button to do it manually. He didn't need a step stool after he found it. I sat next to Aidan, who had finally let me put him in a wheelchair.

"Thank you for joining us on such short notice," Saul said in his best baritone senatorial voice. "Good to see you all here today."

He looked cool and in command after a two days of playing defense through his spokesmen. Late Thursday night, Saul had his office issue the standard press release, basically telling everyone to move on, that there was nothing to see. The final paragraph noted, "This office has never and will never feel the need to respond to unfounded accusations from bloggers." By mid-morning on Friday, the Washington papers had picked up the story. The *Washington Record* led with the headline, "Berg Tangled in Conflict of Interest: Filibusters Health Bill the Same Month Wife Rivka Sells Interest in Nutmeg Medical." By Friday evening, local television stations were reporting on it and asking hard questions: Who bought Rivka's interest and were they lobbying Saul? How much money did the Bergs stand to gain from the sale? Was there anything illegal about the sale? Saul couldn't ignore what our campaign was internally dubbing "Nutmeg-Gate" and called a Saturday morning press conference.

"In case you haven't noticed," Saul said from the lectern, sounding like everybody's idea of a grandfather, "there's an election going on. And with elections come scurrilous allegations—allegations from my opponents in their effort to defame my beautiful wife, Rivka, myself and our family." On cue, Saul threw a loving gaze at Rivka, who was sitting dutifully behind him. "So I'm here today to take all your questions, as many as you have until we get them all answered."

"That's good," Aidan said, tapping my knee.

"Good for him or good for us?" Rachel asked from a chair behind him.

"It's just good politics. He's gonna make this a marathon bore fest. After today, he will have positioned himself to just say, 'I answered all your questions—let's move on.'"

I tried to take in both Saul's comments and Aidan's commentary, but my mind was tied in a pretzel trying to figure out the positions of all the pieces on the political chessboard.

I figured Saul had to know about these allegations when he met with me just days before and made his promise. My best guess was that he'd kept it out of the papers by applying pressure and by leveraging long-standing relationships. I'd seen Aidan do the same thing over the years. Bloggers are different animals. Most of them were beyond Saul's reach as he didn't have anything they might want. They operate outside patronage circles. It made sense to me that bloggers would run with the story and mainstream media would hold off until they simply couldn't hold off anymore.

It wasn't clear to me, however, that the allegations changed the overall calculus. I was pretty sure there wasn't going to be a formal investigation. Senators nominate the U.S. Attorney and ours was hand-picked by Saul. There'd be no federal investigation unless the case was a slam dunk. State prosecutors are experts at bringing drug, gun and theft cases, but complicated white-collar matters are not their forte. Moreover, Saul was sure to have considerable influence inside the halls of the State's Attorneys' office. If Saul had a plausible explanation for the whole thing, I'd be in exactly the same position I'd been in when I left his office.

I did my best to concentrate on Saul's remarks. And judge them through the eyes of the average voter.

"Let me start off with a few facts," Saul said, pulling out his note cards. "First, Nutmeg Medical is a private company and I do not have any holdings in it; my wife does. But it's a nominal interest of less than one-tenth of a percent. Second, even though I don't have any holdings in Nutmeg Medical, I disclosed the details of the transaction—in an abundance of caution—in my annual financial disclosure statements. Finally, and perhaps most importantly, contrary to what my political enemies allege and what has been reported by bloggers," Saul shook his head to show his disbelief that anyone would take a blogger seriously, "there is nothing illegal about this transaction."

"That's the new standard?" Mildred asked, standing off to my right. "Blatant conflicts of interest are okay as long as you don't break the law?" She received nods from the room.

Aidan tugged on my jacket sleeve to pull my ear down to his mouth. "Let's pull the adults together to strategize after he's done," he said.

Saul put his index cards down. "Let's start with the questions."

Saul pointed to the back of the room for his first question.

"Jack Crowe from the *Free Press*," Jack hollered from off camera. "Senator Berg, can you explain to us why this doesn't violate insider trading laws?"

Aidan slapped his forehead with his palm. "Lord have mercy!" he said. "Is there one legitimate independent reporter left on this planet?"

Saul clobbered Jack's presumably planted question.

"That's a good question," Saul said, finger raised. "Let me start off by reminding everyone that I sponsored the STOCK Act last year—the Stop Trading on Congressional Knowledge Act—to put an end to the terrible practice of members of Congress trading on inside information from *public* companies. It wasn't against the law until I made it against the law and I'm darn proud of that. In fact, I stood next to the president while he signed it. This is an allegation about a *private* company—which is why the allegation makes no sense . . ."

And so it went. A first-rate political professional, Saul dodged and dismissed question after question with the authority of one of those silver-haired doctors you see on TV commercials. When questions were raised about his involvement in the transaction, he cited concerns about breaching confidentiality of private parties. When he was pressed about the increase in his net worth, he cited facts and figures from his index cards about his position at the bottom of the income scale vis-à-vis his colleagues in the Senate. He got downright indignant when a reporter showed the audacity to ask whether the Senate Ethics Committee would be conducting an investigation.

"The Senate Ethics Committee has said over and over again"— Saul picked up another index card to read—"'A member of Congress *must* take official action with regard to all matters, unless they are the lone beneficiary of that action.' And that has been the rule since the beginning of time. This whole thing has been manufactured by my political enemies."

It looked to me like Lucy's fingerprints were on this. I figured she'd have the business contacts and resources to dig it up. Regardless, I wasn't sure it was something I'd be able to use in the campaign.

Saul kept his promise and stayed on the podium until everyone was bored to death. After it was clear to Aidan that Saul was just working to find different ways to say the same thing, he pulled me back to him. "Let's meet," he said.

I tapped Monica and Daniel on their shoulders and pointed to Monica's office. Monica grabbed Mildred. I pulled Aidan from the crowd and pushed his wheelchair into the office. Keisha followed.

It was cramped. I stood behind the closed door. Daniel and Mildred took the two visitors' seats. Monica and Keisha stood against the wall behind the desk. Aidan's wheelchair rested just in front of them.

"What do you think?" I asked, looking to Monica.

"I think it's all we should be talking about from now to Election Day," she said, crossing her legs. "If it's not illegal, it should be."

"We have to be careful," Daniel said. "What Saul said is generally correct—and this could backfire on us—especially if Quinn has positioned himself to be above attack politics."

Mildred raised her hand to jump in. "But this goes to exactly what our core message has been: Our democracy is being manipulated by companies and politicians to fatten their pockets. This is the issue that inspired me to even be a part of this campaign."

"But we don't know that for sure," Daniel said. "We don't even know who the buyer of the company is. What if it turns out that they have no connection to Saul?"

"Really?" Monica asked, her mouth twisted. "You think this is all just a coincidence? There's a health bill that puts price controls in place for half the procedures Nutmeg Medical performs; he filibusters the bill; and then the company gets sold."

"And his wife cashed the check for the two of them," Keisha said.

"Apparently a very small check," Daniel countered. "And you have the order wrong. The sale happened first and then he filibustered the bill."

"So what?" Monica demanded.

"So everything," Daniel hollered back across the desk. "If the sale happened first, he's got no motive to help the buyer with the filibuster."

"Unless it was arranged beforehand," Mildred said evenly. Monica nodded in agreement.

"But we don't know that." Daniel stood and moved in front of the whiteboard against the wall. "In fact, the tonnage of what we don't know scares me. What if it turns out that Quinn's firm represents the buyer?"

"Why would you even say something like that?" I asked. "Any firm could have done this work."

"Because Alistair Kincaid and his private equity brigade are in every serious deal in this state—and they're also a big part of why Saul now has more than twenty million in cash on hand."

"Who the hell's Alistair Kincaid?" Monica asked.

"A former client of mine," I said.

"But you didn't represent him on something relating to this?" she asked.

"No," I said. "It was a different matter."

"So then, who friggin' cares!" Monica said. "If someone from his stupid white-shoe firm was involved in the transaction, it doesn't touch Quinn."

"Yes, it does," Keisha said, looking at me. "It's what they call 'collective knowledge.' If one partner knows a client's secret, all the partners know it. He could be disbarred for saying anything about a client's secret."

"Or prosecuted," Daniel said.

"So we can't talk about this?" Monica asked, scratching her head.

"But someone else could," Mildred said.

"Maybe," Daniel said. "They'd have to be totally unaffiliated with the campaign.

Even then it would be tricky. Quinn would be accused of misconduct."

"What do you think, Aidan?" Monica asked.

"I'm not the one running for Senate," he said.

Aidan was speaking in code. I knew what he wanted me to do. He just didn't want to undermine what I might say to the group. Aidan doesn't care about wading in gray waters. If something was arguably legal, he'd do it to win a race. In fact, it got me to thinking whether he was behind the whole thing.

I'd seen Aidan pressure poll workers to remove observers stationed by an opponent's campaign to thwart their attempts to track voters. In another race, I stood right next to him while he twisted the truth to reporters about a candidate's voting record, claiming he wouldn't "stand up and protect" a women's right to choose because he had not voted on an abortion-related bill in the Connecticut legislature. The candidate in question was under the knife having arthroscopic knee surgery when the vote was taken.

If this was his handiwork, he wouldn't tell me about it. He knew the law and that Keisha was right. I'd be in big trouble if any of this was traced back to me.

"This is what we're going to do," I said. "Let's give it a couple days to see what shakes out."

Monica slammed her right hand down on the desktop.

"Just a couple of days," I said, holding my hands up. "Reporters are looking at this now. Let's just give it a little time to see if an independent source comes up with any new facts. If they do, I promise it will be open season on Saul."

XVII

" Good morning, I'm Hank Daniels. It's Sunday morning and that means it's time to Face Connecticut."

I drew in a deep breath, relieved that the interview was finally starting. I'd probably built the thing up way too much in my head. A single Sunday morning interview in a race in which I was down by 25 points probably wasn't going to move the needle much, but it felt good to be in a television studio. Like we were running a legitimate campaign. I had to personally call in a favor to make it happen.

"I could really use this," I'd told Hank a week before as I was frantically working to line up interviews between fundraising calls.

Hank Daniels is just about my age. I was a regular on his show during election cycles whenever he needed an operative or a strategist to analyze a campaign. He kept his politics close to his vest, but my sense of things, based on his questions and guests over the years, was that he leaned conservative. Regardless, he was about as fair as they come.

"I can't do a puff piece," he warned. "You're a good guy and all, but I'd have to ask you the hard questions."

"I wouldn't expect anything less," I said.

The studio had two sets to accommodate a cooking show, *In Connecticut's Kitchen,* as well as *Face Connecticut.* Monica, Mildred and Gene stood shoulder to shoulder at the kitchen counter behind the cameras pointed at Hank and me on the *Face Connecticut* set. They all looked nervous. Hank studied his notes and wasn't very talkative.

"I'm going to ask you tough questions," he said again as the producer went into her countdown.

The show opened with a three-minute pre-taped package that summarized the campaign. Balanced, it started by summarizing Saul's career and highlighting that, "Senator Berg's greatest strength may also be his weakness in a Democratic primary." It continued with recent photos of Saul hugging Texas Senator Ted Cruz and Kentucky Senator Rand Paul backstage at C-PAC, and more dated ones of him sitting side-by-side with then-presidential candidate John McCain at a laptop. There was another of him poking fun at the former North Carolina senator, John Edwards, combing his hair. "These are the images that linger and continue to anger Connecticut Democrats," Hank's voiceover explained.

The piece gave short service to Lucy. There was a quick reference to her humble beginnings. This was followed by some analysis of how the money she's been spending has cleared the GOP field for her; and it questioned the impact the Worldwide Wrestling Confederation's considerable financial corporate contributions might have on the campaign. The vignette about Lucy ended with muscle-bound wrestlers flying across the screen.

The summary of our campaign was fair. Hank walked through my bio, working in that I'd been a federal prosecutor, law professor and partner at a big law firm. There was even footage of my Hail Mary pass at Connecticut State, but the synopsis bluntly stated that ours was a "campaign that simply could not get any traction—or get out of its own way." The final image was of the wheels falling off our school bus.

"With me here in the studio is the man trying to unseat four-term Senator Saul Berg." Hank turned to me. "Quinn, welcome to the show."

We had a few moments of friendly banter before getting down to the campaign.

"Why do you think your campaign has stalled?"

"Well, I'd start by pointing out that we've made considerable progress since April—"

"You've gone from being initially down 38 points to being down 25 points," he said, correcting me. "And some tracking polls show that 25 number going back into the 30s—indicating that Senator Berg's press conference in which he addressed Nutmeg Medical was effective."

"In an August primary people aren't going to really settle in and focus until the week before the election. We're confident we'll pick up ground before then as we continue to get our message out."

"Does it complicate the campaign that there's in essence a primary going on at the same time as a general election with Lucy McCann wrapping up the Republican nomination and running a campaign that's already in high gear?"

"Not for me," I said. "My message will be the same for the general electorate as it is with primary voters. There's not going to be a pivot to change our message."

"I thought you'd say that," Hank said. "Let's talk about messaging and an issue that will likely be part of both the primary and the general in light of a recent Supreme Court's decision." Hank turned over a copy of a highlighted press release. "We've received an advance copy of an ad from American Crosswinds that we're told will be rolled out next week. Let's have a look after which I'd like to get your reaction."

A dark grainy picture came into focus showing the hands of a white man. It pulled back just far enough to see him reading a letter. "In a time when jobs are scarce and you're struggling with how to pay the mortgage, you needed that job and you were the best qualified, but they had to give it to a minority because of set-asides and racial quotas," the baritone voice stated. "Is that really fair—almost a hundred and fifty years after the Civil War? Quinn Barnes supports racial quotas. Do you?"

"Quinn, before you give us your reaction, let me just say we asked the Berg campaign for a comment and they didn't have one." Hank picked up an index card and readied himself to read from it by putting on his glasses. "The McCann campaign, however, said this: 'Quinn Barnes is the former chair of the Commission on Human Rights and Opportunities and in that post was charged with managing Connecticut's affirmative action program and enforcing racial quotas. This ad raises a fair question and I'd like to hear the answer.'" Hank pulled the glasses from his face and placed the index card back down on his desk. "Your response?"

"Hank, thank you for showing me that ad, and thank you for raising the question. Let me start off by saying that quotas have always been illegal and I have never supported quotas—"

"But you support affirmative action," he said. "It's part of your family's history. It could actually be said that you wouldn't be sitting here were it not for affirmative action."

Hank had done his homework.

—⁂—

Life dealt both my parents an awful hand. It was the same hand that their parents and every Barnes before them had received. They were born at the intersection of race and poverty and the odds of escaping that place weren't simply heavy, they were next to impossible.

Dad hails from Washington, D.C.'s southeast section. Having spent his formative years steering clear 0f drug peddlers and petty thieves, he figured he'd join the military to learn a trade. He was certain the skills he gained would pave the way to a good paying job at an airline after his service was complete. And he'd hoped it would finally get the family on the road to realizing the American dream of entering into the middle class.

"Mr. Harry S. Truman desegregated the military after Dubya-Dubya-Two and you know what that meant for me?" Dad would ask whenever he reminisced about his start in life. "Opportunity."

In the spring of 1953, he walked straight from his high school graduation ceremony to a recruiter's office to join the Air Force. It wasn't long before he was shipped down to Chennault AFB in Louisiana where he spent the next four years mastering the F-86 fighter and B-52 bomber from tip to tail. The only breaks he afforded himself on the path to becoming one of the finest jet mechanics the Air Force had ever seen were his dates with a local girl from Opelousas, who would eventually become his bride, and my Mom.

Mom always believed that the Almighty himself brought her together with Dad. That God destined her and the family to break free from generations of sharecropping through her love and union with Dad. They were certain that, working together, they would rise above their circumstances and make it to the middle class.

"I'd never met a colored man with so much fire in his eyes," Mom would tell us years later. "I just knew the world would see right away that he was special."

Unfortunately, Mom was dead wrong.

They lived in a system that was rigged against them and there was no way possible to beat it.

In 1957, Dad was honorably discharged at the rank of first lieutenant. The two of them packed their bags the same day to move back to his hometown of Washington, D.C. They rented a cold-water flat on South Capitol Street, just two blocks from the one he was raised in.

Mom and Dad spent the bulk of their savings—which they kept in a mason jar—on a typewriter. They worked together late into the night for weeks on end to perfect the applications he would submit to area airlines.

At first, Dad received several calls for interviews. But the hiring process always ended abruptly when he appeared and the interviewers learned he was colored. By the time my brother Lincoln was born that winter, Dad had been rejected by half a dozen airlines without ever being given the opportunity to finish introducing himself.

"They would just openly say, 'Sorry, you didn't sound colored on the phone.'" I remembered that Dad always smiled when he recounted this episode but there was a discernable pain behind the grin.

Dad wasn't going to give up on his dream—or the family—easily. He took a night job washing dishes at the Willard Hotel, where influential Washingtonians have come for generations to conduct their business, so he could continue his job search during the day. For the next year and a half, Dad limited himself to one meal a day so Mom and Lincoln would have enough to eat. His daily meal came from the scraps off the plates he washed.

Mom got pregnant with my other brother, Franklin, in 1958. The timing couldn't have been worse. The family was on the brink of being homeless.

Determined to provide for his growing family, Dad started driving a cab full time. He told himself it was only temporary. Dr. King was marching. JFK was talking about his high hopes that the country would change. Mom and Dad believed somehow things would get better and Dad would find a job that would change our family's luck. But before they knew it, the days had turned into weeks and the weeks into months and it became clear that their fate would be the same as every Barnes and Guillary who had come before them.

Mom wasn't sure how Dad would take the news of my expected arrival. They were facing problems far greater than running out of money. Mom and Dad were living in a prison, and regardless of how hard they worked, there was no hope of escape. The worst part of it was knowing there wasn't anything they could do to save yet another child from suffering the same fate.

When I was born at 4:12 a.m. on June 21, 1963, at the National Hospital Center, it was it was pre-ordained that I, like my brothers, would be named after a President. As bad as things were, Mom and Dad were still looking to help us gain any potential advantage in life. They figured an association with the majesty of the Presidency would somehow help.

With a hospital bill to pay and an extra mouth to feed, Dad didn't have the luxury of resting on my birthday. He was back in his cab by 7:30 that same morning. He headed over to the Capitol and sat in line to wait for a fare.

"My stomach was turning something fierce that morning," Dad recounted years later. "The last thing I wanted to see that morning was that dome."

Dad believed deeply in this country. Not the way people who wave the flag at Independence Day parades and backyard barbecues say they love it. He believed in America and the principles on which it was founded the way people believe in their religion. In fact, it was his religion. And he always had complete faith that a steadfast commitment to it would enable him and our family to realize the dream of entry into the middle class—until that day. As he sat in line that morning waiting for a fare, he was forced to accept that his religion had forsaken him.

When he finally reached the front of the line, a slender man in a plain black suit slipped into his cab. He asked to go to the White House before turning his attention to the documents in his briefcase.

Dad quickly learned the man's name was Hobart Taylor, Jr. and it didn't take long before Mr. Taylor was asking Dad about where he was from and what he did.

Dad told Mr. Taylor all about his plan and how hard he had worked to execute it. He spoke of his service to our country and how he had done everything it asked of people to be successful only to learn that it didn't matter how hard he worked or how many degrees he earned. Dad even told Taylor how he was growing to despise this country for what it was about to do to his children.

"I told him straight out"—Dad never had a problem mustering up real anger whenever he relived this conversation,—"this country isn't gonna let my kids do much of anything besides cleaning food off plates or driving a cab—and the politicians running it don't give a damn about people like me or my family."

Dad picked up Mr. Taylor's furrowed brow in the rearview mirror. Fearing that he'd killed his chance at a tip, he quieted down. Neither man spoke for the remainder of the ride.

When they arrived at the White House, Taylor grabbed his briefcase and stepped out of the cab. He stood over Dad's window and paid the fare. Dad was ready to drive off but Taylor stopped him. Dad always explained that he meant to apologize but Taylor cut him off before he could speak.

"'I work for Jack Kennedy,' Taylor said. 'I work arm in arm with him every day.' He leaned in closer to me. 'I want you to know that Jack Kennedy ran for President because he believes in people like you. This building behind me is filled with people like me who stopped everything in their lives to work with him.' Then he locks eyes with me and says, 'Mr. Barnes, you've got good reason to be frustrated but as sure as I'm standing here Jack Kennedy is going to make a difference in your life.'"

To be polite, Dad exchanged phone numbers with Taylor but put him and his promise out of his head the moment he pulled away from the curb.

Dad was done with hoping for hope.

Instead, he took advantage of his sister's offer to watch Lincoln and Franklin while Mom spent the next two days in the hospital with me. Working a marathon shift, he sustained himself on black coffee and an occasional catnap. He was so bleary-eyed when he drove us home, it didn't even occur to him that the black Buick sedan parked outside our apartment building on South Capitol Street carried Mr. Taylor.

"I thought he had forgotten about me," Dad was sure to remind us each time he spoke of that morning. "I had certainly forgotten about him."

Taylor emerged from the car to explain that he'd been trying to contact Dad for days. He reached into his suit pocket for an envelope—an envelope that altered the course of our destiny. And made my life possible.

It was job. A job that paved the way for us to work our way into the middle class. It turned out that Hobart Taylor, Jr. was being tapped by President Kennedy to lead a new agency that he wanted to create: the Equal Employment Opportunity Commission. The opportunity he found for my Dad was to work as an apprentice to a jet mechanic for a then new company starting in Connecticut: Drummond Aerospace. The first ever press release issued by the EEOC was about my Dad and his story.

—⁓—

That nearly fifty-year-old EEOC press release was sitting on Hank's desk.

"Your response," Hank repeated.

"In order to have this conversation," I said, "you first have to ask whether racism and sexism still exist."

"So you're saying Connecticut is racist?"

"I believe in the core decency of people in this state and I couldn't and wouldn't run for this office if I thought otherwise. However, we have not achieved the goal of living in a state or a country where gender and race don't matter."

"Isn't it true that the only way to create a colorblind society is to adopt colorblind policies?"

"Hank, I'm the descendant of slaves. In just a few short years, my family has been able to achieve something that had escaped them for more than two centuries: to realize the dream of entry into the American middle class. Were it not for the policies that you now question, I'd be locked in the same prison of poverty and hopelessness as everyone who has come before me."

"Well, you've done a lot better for yourself than gaining entry into the middle class. You were a partner at the most prestigious firm in the state . . ."

"I'm not sure I understand the point you're trying to make. Even with the existence of the policies you now criticize, my father was never able to reach his full potential."

"Mr. Barnes, my point is that *your* children will."

I caught Monica, Mildred and Gene out of the corner of my eye. They looked more worried than when the interview began.

Black candidates aren't allowed to talk about race. "If you're talking about race, you're losing," Aidan advised Macey Robinson when she was running for State Senate back in '98. An African-American woman, she fought Aidan hard on this point. "It's not fair but it's a dead end for you," I watched him tell her over and over again. She eventually relented and now serves as the President Pro-Tem of our state senate.

My conversation with Hank about race had gone on way too long.

"Hank, I suppose it all boils down to this. If you believe that we are, in fact, a color and gender blind society, then affirmative action isn't an issue that we can discuss. If, on the other hand, if you believe the data that women are not receiving equal pay and promotions for equal work or that people of color still face many of the same challenges in housing and the workplace that they faced a generation ago, we can then have a dialogue about it."

"That's a clever response," Hank said, smiling. "I'm not sure the premise of the statement is fair so let me just ask you this simple question and hopefully I can get a one-word answer: As you sit here today, do you believe that affirmative action is a necessary evil?"

"I don't think there's anything evil about it."

"You support affirmative action?"

"I do."

Hank changed the subject. He turned to my education plan, defense spending and the growing inequality in the state, but it was all largely irrelevant. The buzz would be about the brown candidate talking about his support for racial quotas.

—w—

"You know what this is?" Keisha asked, hovering over me while I tried to nap on Monica's couch.

In protest, I refused to open my eyes.

"I honest-to-God had just fallen asleep. I have to get up in twenty-five minutes to spend my Sunday evening out in Ridgefield to talk to a bunch of people who won't vote for me."

"Well, I'm tired too. But I want to win."

I opened one eye.

She shoved a piece of paper in my face.

There was no writing on it.

I closed my eye.

"Thank you for disturbing the few moments of peace I've had in the past two days to look at a blank piece of paper," I said.

"It's blank because it's the PACER case report for Alistair Kincaid."

I sat up. And took the paper from her.

PACER is the federal court's case tracking system. Any case that is a matter of public record can be viewed by anyone with access to it.

"When did you run this? I asked.

"Five minutes ago." Keisha sat next to me. "I thought it was weird that there was never anything in the paper about his indictment after we were told by the office that it was coming. So I searched the court system. Nothing."

"It could still be coming."

"After almost three months?" Keisha asked, popping her gum. "But just 'cause I thought you might say something like that, I got this." She handed me another piece of paper. It was an internal Clay Pittman case assignment spreadsheet dated May 15th. She had circled the line on the spreadsheet showing Dudley Saltonstall as the attorney of record for Alistair Kincaid.

"Where did you get this?" I asked.

"Oh, cut the Boy Scout crap." She said, seething.

"Keisha, we can't do stuff like this."

"Wait a second," she said, standing. "We're dealing with people who got a federal indictment to go away in exchange for Saul Berg's pension and you're worried about me snatching a case assignment sheet?"

"But you don't know that's true."

"What else do you need to know?" she asked, slapping her thigh before standing. "Kincaid's life was on the line with the indictment. He calls his buddy Saul and says, 'Hey, the guy you appointed U.S. Attorney is about to send me to jail for the rest of my life.' Saul takes care of it. And the payoff was this stupid Nutmeg Medical deal."

"But Saul said over and over that his wife had only a nominal interest in Nutmeg Medical. And he disclosed it."

"Well, they're getting the money some other way."

"We couldn't prove that in a million years."

"We don't have to prove it," she said. "This is politics."

"But even if I leaked this stuff, I'd have to violate the attorney-client privilege. You understand this as well as anyone. The only reason I know these things is because I represented Alistair. This doesn't change anything."

"Do you know who I spoke with today?" she said in a way that I knew she wasn't going to wait for an answer. "Nancy Perez."

I exhaled, put both hands on my head and leaned back. "Please set up a call with her. She probably thinks I forgot about her."

"You can tell her yourself tomorrow," Keisha said. "She wants to work for you."

"Good," I said.

"You know why? Because this weekend Saul was campaigning with Mayor Brocco in East Haven *in front* of the My Country store talking about their support for the Latino community. Like the shooting—*the murder*— of her first born child never happened. It's all forgotten."

I looked down at my feet and rubbed the top of my head.

"These people have no shame!" Keisha yelled at me. "They will say anything and do anything to win an election. And you're sitting there telling me you're worried that the guy who's bribing a senator is gonna come after you for telling people about it?"

"Keisha," I said calmly. "What Nancy had to watch this weekend was horrific. You know how that sickens me." I got to my feet. "But you also know that I took an oath. And the point is that I don't know for sure he did this."

"You're nuts. And wasting the time of people who are killing themselves to help you get elected." She headed for the door. "I'm taking this to Aidan."

"Don't!"

Keisha stopped.

"Give it to me," I said. "I'll talk to him about it."

"When?"

"Tomorrow."

XVIII

Our campaign achieved a new first during Monday call-time. We were shut out. In our many weeks of dialing for dollars, we were always able to raise at least a few thousand dollars. Today, we couldn't raise a single dime.

"School's out now. Everyone's starting their summer vacations," Rachel said, rationalizing the morning when we struggled even to get a live voice on the phone.

We grew so desperate that we grabbed the voter identification list for the afternoon session. We figured that if we could, at least, find some voters to talk to we might get lucky generating some small donations. We went zero for about two hundred.

I shut things down for the day when the clock struck 4:00 p.m. and texted Aidan.

What are you doing?

He answered right away, setting off a rapid exchange.

The same goddamn thing you should be doing. Killing myself on the phone, trying to raise money . . .

I'm coming over . . .
Why?
Need advice . . .
Here's my advice: Make more goddamn fundraising calls!
Be there in 10 mins.

I left my car behind and headed down Main Street into what was an oppressively hot late-June afternoon. Rush hour was just getting started, creating gridlock all the way back to Hartford Hospital.

I mumbled to myself as I strode past the federal courthouse and the Hartford Public library. "Quinn, you have to be the first candidate who can't stop people from voting for someone they don't even like. It's pathetic." A petite gray-haired woman walking toward me clutched the strap of her handbag and moved near the street to avoid me.

My phone rang.

"This is Quinn."

"John Quincy Barnes?"

"Hello, Lucy."

"Now you don't sound very excited to hear from me," she said.

"Really not a good time."

"You feeling better about things?"

"No Lucy, I'm not."

Lucy inhaled and exhaled slowly. "John Quincy, you know the difference between us?" she asked.

"Silicone and hair dye?"

"Goodness gracious! Now if I could only get you to channel some of that emotion in Saul's direction," she said. "The difference between us is that you think we're all equal. That we're all the same."

"I don't follow," I said. "And I really don't have time for this—"

"It holds you back from doing what you have to do," she said. "See, I wake up every day knowing I'm not one of the masses. I'm special. And I have a billion dollars to prove it. It liberates me."

"Liberates you to do what?"

"To do the things necessary to be the leader. I'm supposed to be the leader. I don't worry myself one bit about how I get there."

Annoyed. I just hung up.

I passed a homeless man in front of the Wadsworth Athenaeum digging soda cans out of the garbage. He was black, mid-fifties, with long black and white hair that made him look like he'd been hit by lightning.

He picked his head out of the garbage can just as I passed. I made eye contact and nodded. I would have kept on my way down the street but for his standing up, bowing out his chest, and staring at me. I couldn't tell if he was angry, confused or just surprised that I'd acknowledged him.

"Are you okay?" I asked.

"Conspiracy! Oh, CONSPIRACY!" he hollered. His outburst scared a little girl walking with her mother. She clung to her mother's leg and they scurried behind me on the sidewalk.

I waved with both hands to try and calm him down. "It's okay. I'm just gonna—"

"Hide your monstrous face!"

"—be on my way." I backed away in the direction of Bushnell Park and could still hear him yelling as I scurried over to the CityPlace building to get to Aidan's office.

I was going to tell Annie about the conspiracy man, but she was on the phone when I stepped into the reception area. She winked at me as I turned down the hall toward Aidan's corner office.

The door was shut. I knocked and waited. Not hearing anything, I knocked again and pushed the door.

Aidan was face down on his desk.

For a moment, I held out hope that he might have been sleeping. When he didn't respond to my calling—and then shouting—his name, I rushed to his side.

I sat him up in his chair and loosened his tie. I put my ear to his mouth to wait for a breath. After I got a faint one, I slipped my right arm behind his back and my left under his knees and carried him to the couch against the wall. His head slumped on my shoulders like a baby falling into sleep.

I dialed 9-1-1 from the phone on the end table next to the couch. The operator asked questions that seemed to go on forever. I answered them as best I could. After I gave her the address, I hung up even though she had more to ask.

I tried to call out to Annie but couldn't get any words out. I held Aidan tightly and rocked him back and forth. My tears fell silently on his starched white shirt as I waited for the ambulance.

XIX

"Quinn?"

I clenched the chair's arms. I didn't have to open my eyes to see Brooke. I could feel that she was there.

I stood and hugged her tight in the dim light.

"What time is it?" I whispered.

"Two."

We moved to Aidan's bedside.

"Who's watching the kids?"

"Your mom is there." Brooke leaned on the corner of the bed. "What did the doctors say?"

"That they can't believe he can still tolerate the pain. Most patients would have been on morphine for weeks by now."

We both just looked at him for a good bit without saying anything.

"I can't tell how sorry I am," I said, "I know I've made a mess of everything."

"Let's not do this now." She placed her hand on my shoulder and kissed me. "Besides, I knew I wasn't signing up for a carriage ride when I married you."

"I must surely be close to dead if Brooke Wolcott is here." Aidan's hazel eyes were wide open.

Brooke and I parted. She sat at the foot of the bed next to his left leg. I sat to his right.

"Well, this is quite the party," Brooke said, patting the bed.

"What happened today?" Aidan asked.

"You're exhausted," I said. "You passed out."

"I know that," Aidan said, irritated. "I mean with the campaign."

"Can we talk about something other than the campaign?" Brooke asked.

"The campaign is why my eyes are open. So, no."

"I really have no idea," I said.

"Well," Brooke began, "the morning news cycle focused on Quinn the fascist, who is hell-bent on taking poor children away from their parents. This afternoon's coverage revisited Quinn's gang life and featured an interview with a member of the gang that Quinn never joined. And oh, I almost forgot, tonight we learned that Quinn hates America and all the white people in it, which as his wife I found particularly noteworthy."

"But things are definitely looking up," I said. "There was hardly any coverage of my debacle with Hank Daniels."

Brooke, unamused, continued, "Every spot still ends with the 'Do you know the real Quinn Barnes?' question."

"Their discipline is pretty impressive," Aidan said.

"Are you insane?" Brooke asked. "Our children—and our friends—and our entire town are seeing this."

"I mean their message discipline and the politics. The politics are clever." Aidan said. "Anything else on Nutmeg-Gate?"

"No," Brooke and I said in stereo.

"There's a little chatter on the blogs," Brooke said. "But none of the mainstream press is talking about it."

"We're taking on too much water," I said.

"Too much water?" Brooke said. "This ship has sunk."

"Not yet," Aidan said. "We just need more money. We need to get a bio piece out and start telling Quinn's story."

"In almost three months of fundraising," I told him, "I'm at a hundred and eighty thousand in commitments—and we've collected less than half that. Unless you had a magical day yesterday, we still haven't even broken two hundred."

"Well, then we need to be better at leveraging earned media. We have to get you doing more interviews and using them to tell your story."

Aidan reached for a cup of water. Brooke took his hand and returned it to his chest. She grabbed a cup of water from the nightstand and slipped a straw inside. She helped him take a sip. His eyes danced back and forth while he took it in.

I hated seeing him look helpless.

Brooke wiped his mouth and then his neck with a towel. Relieved, he took a deep breath and got back to work.

"Whaddya have tomorrow?" he asked.

"The plan for tomorrow is to go through a big stack of photo albums and watch *Mr. Smith Goes to Washington* right here in this room," I said.

"Well, you're gonna be watching *Mr. Smith Goes to Washington* here by yourself. I'm gonna be making fundraising calls and working on your campaign back in my office."

"Aidan, you're almost out of time," I said. "Let's just spend what time we have left without all this chaos."

"You don't get it. You still don't see it."

Aidan's eyes welled up. He wasn't blubbering. Just tearing—like a child being told he had to go to bed—and there was nothing he could do about it.

"This thing is about destiny," Aidan said, looking to Brooke for help.

"How about this?" Brooke asked. "We'll get you two or three interns and all the tablets and laptops that you need."

"I need my phone back," he said.

"We'll get your phone and we'll just consider Hartford Hospital our newest campaign office."

"Will that make you happy?" I asked.

"If everything can be here first thing in the morning," he said.

"I'll call Monica and take care of it myself," Brooke promised.

"Are you gonna help him?" Aidan asked, looking to Brooke.

Brooke swallowed.

"Help with the campaign?" she asked.

Aidan looked at me. "Did you tell her that she's forgiven?"

"I'm forgiven?" Brooke said. Her neck was reddening.

"You didn't tell her?" Aidan asked, his eyes one me.

"I didn't have a chance," I said.

"You were supposed to tell me that I'm forgiven?" Brooke asked with a smile on her lips but not in her eyes.

"Well, not exactly," Aidan said. "There's a story that goes with it. He was supposed to tell you the story."

"Why don't you tell it to me," she said.

"When Quinn was sixteen, he wanted to drive more than anything. I mean he would call me every day to tell me the world was gonna come to an end if he didn't get his drivers' license." Aidan took a moment to catch his breath. "So the day comes for his driving test. He passes and takes the bus to my office to show me his permit and asks me to lend him money."

"To buy a car?" Brooke asked.

Aidan nodded. "And for the insurance."

"I asked for an advance," I said. "There's a big difference."

"So I told him, 'Hell no. I'm not advancing you a dime. You don't have the money for a car, so you're not getting a car.' I never game him a dime for anything. I made him work for every penny."

"That's touching," Brooke said, sarcastically.

"Quinn goes berserk," Aidan went on. "Tells me, 'You have this big pile of money and you won't give me an advance? You're the meanest, cheapest bastard on the planet. I hate your f-in' guts!'" Aidan laughed, which made him cough.

"I'm not getting the point," Brooke said.

"I told him, 'I forgive you.'" Aidan looked to me. "Well, that stopped him cold. He said, 'you forgive me?' He had the Devil's fire in his eyes."

Aidan was out of breath again. I finished the story for him.

"Aidan said, 'Sonny, a long time from now, after I'm gone, you're going to beat yourself up over all the times you said mean things to me or told me how much you hated me,'" I explained to Brooke. "'Please don't,' he said to me. 'They're just things people say during bad times. I know you didn't mean it. I forgive you.'"

"Is that what you were trying to tell me at the waterfront?" Brooke asked me.

"I've just been wanting to apologize for what I said and didn't want you to feel bad about what you said. So we could move on."

Brooked slipped under my arm at the foot of the bed and we embraced.

"Please stop with the displays of affection," Aidan pleaded. "Makes me uncomfortable."

Brooke smiled and planted a kiss on my lips to make Aidan squirm a bit longer.

"To answer your question, Aidan," Brooke said, her arm draped around my neck. "I have never and will never stop trying to help Quinn."

XX

In February 1860, Connecticut Governor William A. Buckingham was facing a predicament as old as America. He was up for reelection in April and very much wanted to win. It was clear to the governor that he was in for a tight race and in need of something that would give him an edge on Election Day.

Governor Buckingham and the Connecticut Republican state chairman, Nehemiah Sperry, put their minds to finding a man who might campaign and make some speeches in Connecticut to help improve their chances in the spring election. They set their sights on a man who was causing quite a stir with his outsider against-all-odds campaign for president: Abraham Lincoln.

Lincoln was in New York City giving what eventually became known as his Cooper Union Address. Sperry invited Lincoln to come to Connecticut. Lincoln replied that he had to first visit his son Robert in Exeter, New Hampshire but agreed to give a talk in Hartford. Additional dates were soon added to the calendar and plans were set for a six-day odyssey—most of it with Governor Buckingham by his side—across Connecticut.

On Monday afternoon, March 5th, Lincoln arrived by train in Hartford. Always trolling for an extra vote, he used the time before his address to walk up Asylum Street and stop at the Brown & Goss bookstore, where he bumped into the editor of the Hartford *Evening Press*, Gideon Welles. Customers and curious onlookers recognized the man from Illinois. Word spread up and down Asylum Street that the giant killer was in town to speak about the issue that would determine how people on Asylum Street and all the other streets in the state and the country would live for centuries.

Governor Buckingham acted as master of ceremonies for the big event at Hartford Town Hall. The *Connecticut Courant* reported, "The hall was filled before the appointed time for the appearance of the speaker, and when he took his position on the stand he was greeted with applause which was almost deafening . . . ."

"Whether we will have it so or not, the slave question is the prevailing question," Lincoln told the capacity crowd before getting to work on his central theme: that slavery threatened and would continue to threaten the values of republicanism. "A regard for future generations and for the God that made us require that we put down this wrong."

The *Courant* reported the following day that, "The speech of Mr. Lincoln at the City Hall, last night, was the most convincing and clearest speech we ever heard made."

On Tuesday morning, Lincoln toured the Sharps Rifle Works and Colt Armory in Hartford before taking an afternoon train down to New Haven. The New Haven *Palladium* enthusiastically advertised the event: "GRAND RALLY! - FOR BUCKINGHAM AND THE UNION! - THE HON ABRAHAM LINCOLN, OF ILLINOIS, WILL ADDRESS THE FREEMEN OF NEW HAVEN, AT UNION HALL ON TUESDAY EVENING, MARCH 6, 1860. PUSH ON THE COLUMN!"

Abe fittingly appeared at Union Hall on Union Street in New Haven. The largest room in the city was filled to capacity. Abe underscored his concern that the institution of slavery would threaten the long term viability of the country. "Does anything in any way endanger the perpetuity of this Union but that single thing, Slavery?" he asked. "Let us not be slandered from our duties, or intimidated from preserving our dignity and our rights by a menace," he said in closing. "But let us have faith that Right, Eternal Right makes might, and as we understand our duty, so do it!"

Lincoln was a big hit in New Haven. The *Palladium* reported that "There was witnessed the wildest scene of enthusiasm and excitement that has been seen in New Haven in years. For several minutes, everybody was cheering."

Things were looking up for Governor Buckingham.

The following evening, Lincoln took a train north to Meriden where he spoke at the Town Hall on East Main Street before heading over to Woonsocket, Rhode Island the next day, then back to Norwich, Connecticut—Governor Buckingham's home town—for what was yet another wildly successful event. "Cheer after cheer went up for the noble champion of Republican principles, and some minutes elapsed before the applause subsided sufficiently to allow him to commence his address," reported the Norwich *Bulletin*.

On March 9, the contingent landed in Bridgeport, where Lincoln would give his last speech in New England. He spoke in Washington Hall, an auditorium at what was then Bridgeport City Hall—it's now McLevy Hall—at the corner of State and Broad streets. The speech in Bridgeport went much like the others. There was humor and fun interspersed with the cold, hard logic of Mr. Lincoln's position. When it was all over, Lincoln received a standing ovation, visited with the crowd for a bit and then took the 9:07 p.m. train that night back to Manhattan.

When the state held elections at the beginning of April, Governor Buckingham won reelection—but by just 541 votes. Buckingham went on to serve for the next seven years and was warmly remembered as Connecticut's Civil War governor. As to Abe, Connecticuters point to the time he spent here as providing the providence that would propel him to snatch the Republican nomination a few months later at The Wigwam convention center in Chicago, and, of course, to change the course of the nation and the world.

Shut out on fundraising and without any discernable strategy for the next few days until Thursday's press conference, I proposed at our daily campaign meeting that we trace Lincoln's steps across Connecticut. As far as I was concerned, the race was over and I thought it might be a neat thing to tell my grandchildren about—that I campaigned the same path as Lincoln. I was also in desperate need of inspiration. Not to try to win the race. I was certain the race was over. I was just looking for something to help me get through the next few days before I made it official.

I still wasn't sure how to tell everyone about my decision. I hate giving people bad news, which I suppose is ironic because I always want my bad news right away.

"Is this a good idea?" Monica asked in response to my proposal.

"It kinda looks like the black guy trying to play the race card by locking arms with the guy who freed the slaves," Keisha said. Gene, sitting next to her, nodded in agreement.

"You've been saying that campaigns are about the future," Nancy said in a way that showed she wasn't certain it was okay for her to speak in a staff meeting. "Isn't this about the past?"

"A stunt about the past," Monica said.

"We're not going to tell anyone that it's Lincoln's trail," I said. "I'm just going to do it."

"Well, then, what's the point?" Monica asked.

"Karma," I said.

"You mean superstition," Keisha countered.

"Does anyone have a better idea about how to spend the next few days?" I asked.

"Okay, let's put together a string of events for Hartford, New Haven and Meriden tomorrow," Monica said. "We'll keep it small and intimate."

"I don't think that will be a problem," Rachel said.

"He can do Bridgeport on Thursday morning before his press conference," Monica said.

"Can you put the Bridgeport Summer Read program on the schedule?" I asked. "It's a pilot project that I keep hearing about at the Marin school down there. They're bringing in at-risk kids for some kind of summer reading camp."

If morale was already low, my request took the air out of the room. Even a volunteer working on her first campaign knows there are no votes in a grade school and would read it as the first open sign of my intent to fly the white flag of surrender.

"It will give me a chance to talk about my education plan," I said, although it came out like a cheap afterthought. "And the education gap."

"Why don't you guys put something together and I'll have a look," Monica said. "And Quinn, go home and get some rest tonight. We really need to try and get things on track these next few days."

—⟋⟍—

I sat behind the wheel of my Jeep, not sure where to go.

I couldn't really go home.

Brooke would be asking me a million questions and I just didn't feel like talking about any of it. I definitely didn't want to tell Mom about my decision. She'd try to hide her disappointment and tell me that it was all okay and that she was proud. Which would make it all worse.

I took the top down. Headed down to Founders Bridge and sped over the Connecticut River to Route 2 to crisscross the eastern half of the state. I didn't put on the radio because I wasn't in the mood for company. I just listened to the wind rush past as I headed all the way up to Thompson near the Rhode Island state line, and then down to Plainfield. Lost in thought, I was almost surprised to find myself an hour later on the winding narrow roads around Ledyard and Uncasville. With the summer solstice sun gone from the horizon, I turned west and headed home.

I sat in the driveway and adjusted the seat back for a few minutes. I had long missed dinner and figured I'd relax by watching Brooke and the kids for a while before heading in to help put the kids to bed.

Through the two large wood-framed windows I could see her cleaning the kitchen while she talked on the phone. She waved her hands about and looked to be getting more talking done than cleaning. I figured she was speaking to her mother.

The windows adjacent to the kitchen featured the boys chasing their sister around the dining room table. She put up a good fight until they decided to pursue from opposite directions and cornered her. In an impressive display of athleticism, she jumped up on the table to escape to the family room but slipped on the table cloth—knocking chairs over and nearly tipping the antique china cabinet handed down to us from Brooke's grandmother.

The kids froze. I followed Brooke's march from the kitchen to the dining room.

With hands on hips, she admonished the three of them. Mom appeared at the bottom of the stairs and joined in. They both pointed upstairs. Eliza led the way and the boys followed.

My phone rang.

"Can you get down to the lockup in East Haven?" Keisha asked.

"What's going on?"

"Gene's apparently fallen off the wagon."

XXI

I stood with my back to the wall of brown cinder blocks outside the lockup and waited for the guard to buzz me in. He was in no hurry. I got the sense that he was making me wait just to show me that he was in charge.

When the thick gray metal door finally buzzed, I pulled on the bars and stepped into the interior of the jail. Another guard was waiting to give me a second pat-down. When he was done, I followed him down a long corridor. We took a right at the end, entering the wing of holding cells for the defendants who had been arrested that evening. The first cell held an obese red-haired man tattooed from head to toe.

"Are you a lawyer?" he asked.

We continued walking until we got to the fourth cell on the right.

Gene was in an orange jumpsuit, sitting on a cot. His elbows were on his knees and he was staring into space. He either didn't know I was there or didn't want to acknowledge me.

The guard started to walk away.

"Can you let me in?"

He smirked and raised his eyebrows at me. Most lawyers speak to their clients through the bars. Shaking his head, he opened the cell and locked me in.

I sat next to Gene.

"What are you doing here?" he said flatly.

"At the moment, I'm going to try to get you out of jail."

"They're not letting me out of here."

"The standard is whether you're a danger to yourself or anyone in the community." I stood and paced the length of the cell. "Your last arrest was years ago and I think it's safe to say that you're not going to harm anyone."

"They're not letting me out of here," Gene repeated. "They caught me red handed."

"Tell me what happened."

"Nothing much to tell. I busted into a nursing home to score some oxy."

"Why?"

"I'm a drug addict, you idiot."

"I meant, why did you go to a nursing home?"

"It's where the drugs were."

"What do you mean that they caught you red handed?"

Gene lay back on his cot and slipped his hands behind his head. "I went there to find some oxy. I found it. And the police were there to arrest me before I could get out."

I pulled out a notepad from my briefcase and sat by his feet. "What time did you get there and how did you enter?"

"We're not doing this."

"Like hell we're not doing this. If they charge you with distribution, you're looking at a mandatory minimum of twenty years and will probably get more. You'll die in jail."

"For fifty oxys?" Gene lifted his head and looked at me.

"That's how the federal sentencing guidelines work," I said. "And they can and have charged people with distribution for a lot less drugs." Gene drew a deep breath and laid his head back down. "Just sit tight," I told him. "Let me put some things together for your bail hearing and we'll get you out."

"I'll talk to my lawyer about it," he said, staring at the ceiling.

"What lawyer?" I asked.

"You're not my lawyer."

"What do you mean I'm not your lawyer?"

"I have a federal defender representing me."

I stood. "So you're not going to let me help you?"

"Not with this."

"What's gotten into you? I thought things were going fine."

"I need for you to just stay out of this," he said.

"No."

Gene sat up and grabbed my arm. It felt like my bicep was caught in a vise. "Now listen to me. I'm bad news for you and this campaign." His eyes were fire red.

"Gene, the campaign is almost over."

"Whadda you mean? When?"

"Soon. I'm suspending it at the press conference on Thursday."

"Well, I'd hate to see that happen." Gene lay back again. He seemed to calm quickly. "But I've decided this and I'm gettin' another lawyer," he said evenly, staring at the ceiling again.

"I don't know what to say to that."

"Don't say anything!" he said. "You talk too damn much sometimes. Just go away."

Gene turned his back to me and faced the wall.

I walked the length of the cell two or three times with my arms folded, trying to figure out what to do. How to tell him that right now it was more important to try to fix his problems than to worry about having disappointed everybody—including me. I just couldn't find the right words and figured I'd let it sit for a few days.

I noticed a blanket folded under the cot. I laid it over his back. I called for the guard to let me out. And left.

XXII

Aidan looked weak. As weak as I've ever seen him. The dawn's light creeping through the white venetian blinds highlighted that there was no color whatsoever in his face—or at least the part of it that wasn't covered by his oxygen mask. I would have thought he was gone but for the modest rise and fall of his chest and the signal from the screen on his life support confirming that his heart was still beating.

I was praying for him to slip away. There was nothing left to be gained from continued suffering but I also knew there was no way Aidan would give in. It's not in his nature, but more importantly, he probably didn't trust me to follow through with it all—and for good reason.

Aidan lifted his finger to get my attention.

His hazel eyes were open. They looked alive as they moved back and forth—but trapped in a body that was near its end.

I lifted his mask over the top of his head.

"What time's the press conference?" he asked.

"Noon. But I have to head down to Bridgeport this morning so I'm going to have to leave soon."

"Sonny, you understand that this is your last real chance," he said, his voice a raspy whisper. "You have to try and shake things up today."

"I'm getting out," I said firmly. "There's still time to salvage things. I can hang a shingle and maybe run after Saul retires. This is going to be his last go-round and I'd have a lot better shot then. I started telling the staff about it earlier this morning."

Aidan's eyes welled up. Tears bled down the side of his face. He didn't have the strength to wipe them away himself.

"Six years isn't going make much difference," I argued. I tried to wipe his face with my handkerchief; he used whatever strength he had left to turn away. "He'll be gone soon and I'll either get in or find someone to go fight for our issues."

I sat next to him on the bed and waited. His reply came soon enough.

"He's gotten to you. Probably made some kind of crazy promise that makes you think you can get your life back."

"I'd like my life back."

"What life? You're not living—not living for someone like you."

I exhaled and reminded myself that each word spoken could be our last. "Aidan, you have pushed me every minute of every day—and there were a lot of years when it was pure misery—but I understand it now. I know it's made all the difference in my life. But this is different. I'm a grown man and this is taking me down a road that will ruin a lifetime of hard work. You can't want that for me."

"Sonny, everyone must ask the question: Am I meeting my destiny? The only thing that makes death tragic is to have known your destiny and ignored it."

"Does that apply to you? Have you lived your own life asking that?"

"In my way, yes. But this isn't about me. It's about you."

"So it's true that this has nothing to do with Saul? You made me do this because you're not satisfied with me?"

"See it the way you want to see it. I'm an old man who was taking one final stab at making sure a Mozart didn't spend the rest of his life as a bricklayer." Aidan struggled to clear his throat. "And I got news for you. I promised your father on his deathbed that I'd make sure you'd get to something big. Something important—"

"Please don't bring my father into this."

"—and now I'm on my way to see him and I have to tell him I failed."

"How am I a failure? I kill myself giving to everything and every cause under the sun. There's not a moment of rest or peace in my life."

"In almost 50 years of politics, I've never had a candidate that could do what you have the potential to do. If you want to go on being a partner at some big law firm representing companies that are buying up the politicians that are ruining this country—you go do that and be happy. That's a fine legacy."

Aidan's enemies always cited his mean streak as the thing that made him impossible to deal with—or defeat. I'd seen it hundreds of times but never like it was being directed at me now.

"Warms my heart," he said, "to know that all those kids living in shitty neighborhoods will be living in the same place and going to the same crappy schools long after I'm dead and gone."

I just wanted him to stop. I grabbed the Styrofoam cup from the nightstand and tried to make him drink. He turned his head away in defiance.

"Go away and let me die in peace," he said, looking out the window. "I'm ready for it now."

I put the cup back on the nightstand, reached for my suit jacket draped over the chair and left.

—◊—

The Marin School ranks 530th out of 530 Connecticut public elementary schools. Barely a third of its students are proficient in reading or writing. It's held this dubious distinction for eleven years running without a single politician, including Saul, ever so much as making a single mention of it or the other schools facing similar challenges.

The Marin School's problems are a product of the Bridgeport school district's utter dysfunction. In July 2011, city officials threw up their hands and voted to dissolve their school board rather than try to address the school system's $18 million budget shortfall and infighting among members. It was the first time in state history that a municipality asked for the state to take it over. The Supreme Court eventually ruled the takeover illegal and ordered a special election. A few months later, Bridgeport and its schools were back at square one—hopelessly divided and at a total loss as to how to solve their budgetary and other problems. All the while, another generation of students and parents were left facing the same issues as the one before without any real progress.

Today, Marin was the perfect respite from my problems, lending me the opportunity to do something I actually like to do. Sitting around and talking with some kids.

With Gene in the lockup, Graham had taken over the driving duties. It was pretty quiet in the car as we sped down the scenic Merritt Parkway toward Bridgeport. Mildred and Graham probably figured that I wasn't in the mood to talk much with Aidan in such bad shape. That was true, but there simply wasn't much to talk about if the campaign was going to be wrapped up by day's end.

I stepped from our car to greet the lens of Saul's video tracker, Devin.

Gavin was on a mission to catch me in a gaffe—or at least find words that could be edited into a gaffe. It was like a soccer team being up 11-0 but doing everything in its power to score a twelfth goal. It was overkill but Saul wasn't going to leave anything to chance.

Devin didn't give any thought to invading my space. He followed me up the concrete walkway to the front of the large brick school and through the hunter green metal doors.

Ms. Breen, the Marin teacher who created the Summer Read program, was waiting for us.

"So glad to meet you," she said, using both her hands to shake mine. "The children are so excited."

We followed her down a long hallway to the second to last classroom on the left. In the brightly decorated room the children were seated orderly on the floor, legs crossed. They smiled and waved as I entered with their teacher.

There was a child-sized table and a chair next to it. I left the chair for Mildred and sat on the floor with the kids. Saul's tracker sat on the table behind the children.

Ms. Breen gave a short introduction after which I read *Click Clack Moo*. Some of the kids got up to read along over my shoulder. When I was done, a girl with cornrows dressed in a yellow pleated dress took the book from my hands and replaced it with another, *Giggle Giggle Quack.* She wedged herself beneath my arm while I read the second.

"You talk funny," she said, interrupting me.

"Talicia," Ms. Breen said from her chair on the side of the room, "that's rude."

"I have an education," I said. "I speak like someone who went to college and then law school. Can you understand what I'm saying to you?"

"Yeah," Talicia said.

"Well, that's all that matters."

After I finished off *Giggle Giggle Quack,* I placed Talicia on the floor in front of me. I gave the third graders a short talk on the three branches of government and explained my Senate campaign.

"Did you know the president is black?" Talicia asked, moving on to another topic.

"Yes, I'm aware of that, thank you," I said. "What made you think of that?"

"I don't know. I supposed it means you can be a senator."

"It means a lot more than that," I said. "It means you can be a senator. Or whatever else you want to be."

"But *I* can't be a senator," she said. She was quite certain of herself.

"Don't be silly," I said. "Why would you say that?"

"I'm from Bridgeport. The President is black but he ain't from Bridgeport. And neither are you."

Ms. Breen squirmed in her chair.

"I'm from the north end of Hartford—which is just like Bridgeport."

"Bullshit," a husky boy yelled from the back.

Ms. Breen stood. I started in before she had a chance to speak.

"I grew up on Albany Avenue in Hartford, Connecticut," I said. "The only difference between the two of us is that I went to college. Are you going to college?"

"Trey can barely read," Talicia said. "He ain't goin' to college."

"I can too read," Trey fired back.

"Good. Then when someone asks you if you're going to college, I want you to say, 'Yes. I'm going to college.'"

"My Mom says college costs lots of money," a girl with pigtails sitting next to him said. "We don't have lots of money."

"What's your name?" I asked.

"They call me Nefi," she said.

"Her name Nefertiti," Trey yelled out, giggling.

"They make fun of my name, so I just have people call me Nefi."

"But Nefertiti is a queen's name," I said, smiling at her.

"I know. It means a beautiful lady is coming," she said, waving at her classmates to remind them of her connection to royalty.

"Well, Nefertiti," I said. "I want you to say it anyway. We'll figure out a way to help you pay for college."

"No one in my family ever went to college," she said.

"Doesn't matter," I said. "Just keep telling yourself that you're going to college and it will happen."

Trey raised his hand and waved wildly as if his pants were on fire. "You figure you gonna beat that white man?" he asked.

Saul's tracker stood to make sure he had the best shot available to record my response.

"His name is Saul Berg," I said. "You should call him Senator Berg—"

"Yeah, Senator Berg," Trey said. "You gonna beat that white man?"

"The thing I want you to remember from me coming here today is that any person in this room can rise above their circumstances. Get your education and there's no limit to what you can accomplish. Including being a Senator."

"You don't sound like you think you gonna win," Trey said.

"This state is mostly white people," Talicia said. "They ain't gonna let him be senator."

"Don't say that," I said sternly. "Besides, the president is black."

"Yeah, but white people here are rich," she said.

"You're not going to accomplish anything in life making excuses about being different," I said. "And I'm not going to lie. Being different is hard. It means roadblocks are going to be thrown in your way that other people don't have to deal with. But there are no excuses. None. You just keep going after what you want."

"You're wrong," Trey said.

"I'm wrong?" I said, looking to him. "Wrong about what?"

"About being different," Trey said. "We're all the same. It's just the rules that are different."

"The rules?" I asked.

"Yeah," Trey said. "I'm a football player. And last Saturday we had to play these rich white boys from Darien."

"He sits the bench," Talicia said.

"Don't matter. I'm still on the team," Trey said to Talicia. "Anyway," he said, turning back to me, "before the game, my coach says, 'you see those boys from Darien? They think they better than you. But you know what? They just the same as you. They have two arms, two legs, and they put their pants on the same as you.'"

"You have a very good coach," I said.

"Yeah. And then he says, 'When you get on that field and step in between those lines, the rules are the same for everybody. Everybody's the same. They got no advantage.'"

"I think I see where you're going," I said.

"It ain't about being different. It's about the rules. We need to be makin' the rules the same for everybody. Otherwise, we have no chance at anything."

"Trey," I said. "That may be the most insightful thing I've heard since this campaign started."

"What 'insightful' mean?" he asked.

"Smart," I said.

Proud, Trey stuck his tongue out at Talicia.

"Why are you here?" Nefertiti asked. "No one here can vote."

"That's a good question. I suppose I'm looking for inspiration."

"What's inspiration?" Talicia asked.

"Something that makes you feel better. It gives you energy to do something good. It can be just about anything but for me it's usually an image. Like a picture."

"Well, did you find your picture?" Nefertiti asked.

"I think I did."

"Tell me about your algorithm."

"What do you want to know, sir?" Graham asked, looking at Mildred and me through the rearview mirror.

The car swerved onto the Merritt Parkway's newly installed rumble strips. Mildred held on to the door handle.

"How about telling us about it while keeping your eyes on the road," she said.

"Yes, ma'am." Graham stiffened his arms on the steering wheel. "Well, it predicted the Congressional election in the Second District last cycle by 150 votes—five months before the election."

"It or you?" Mildred asked.

"Well, I wrote the algorithm—and the program."

"Have you ever tested it in another race?" I asked.

"Tested, sir?"

"Yes, how do we know it would work again—or work in a statewide race?" I asked.

"I guess I don't understand," Graham said. "There's nothing to test. You're counting the votes one by one."

Graham peeked at us both through the mirror.

"The road," Mildred reminded him.

Graham obeyed. Mildred took out her notepad.

"How is this possible?" she asked.

"Old-fashioned polling is about quarantining small samples and making an educated guess about how larger groups of people are going to behave. My program thinks of voters as individuals. It analyzes the whole thing at the atomic level."

"Atomic level," Mildred said, adding the phrase to her notes.

"It collects every piece of information about a person—social media information, consumer data, and voting information—and develops a composite picture of everyone. Every individual voter."

"What do you mean by consumer data?" I asked.

"Everything. Where people shop; what they read; where they vacation; everything a person does helps predict how they're going to behave in a voting booth. Once you have the picture, you give them the information they would need to vote for you."

"How do you get it—the consumer information?" Mildred asked.

"Lots of ways, but you can just buy a lot of it."

"Exactly how many votes are you projecting that I'd need to win just the primary?"

"One hundred and twenty-one thousand, five hundred and eighty seven."

Graham sounded like a computer program himself.

"What would it show if you ran the program today?" I asked.

"It has you losing by twenty-nine percentage points."

"But it can't help us figure out how to win," Mildred said, "it's just an interesting science project."

"But it does. It shows you the people you have to contact and what you have to say to them. Right now we're wasting time calling and trying to reach people who wouldn't vote for Mr. Barnes in a million years. This shows you who will vote for him and what specific part of his platform we'd have to share with them to get their vote."

"I want you to put together a memo that shows me what you would have to do to make this work for us and the game plan to execute it," I said.

"It would take me about a week and a half."

"You have two days."

"And I'm still driving for you?"

"No. Raymond can drive. Or Mildred."

"I can?" she asked.

"I'll get to work."

Graham leaned on the accelerator as we came out of the West Rock tunnel and headed north to Hartford.

XXIII

M ary Silliman's situation was looking grim. Six months pregnant, her world in idyllic Fairfield had been turned upside down. Her husband had been kidnapped and was being held captive on Long Island. After careful consideration, she concluded that the only way to change her circumstances was do something that was not in her nature: commit an act of violence.

It was the spring of 1779 and the American Revolution was raging in the colonies. It wasn't so much a revolution as a civil war for Mary Silliman and scores of colonists like her. Many of her neighbors in Fairfield were Loyalists and openly advertised their allegiance to the Crown by painting a black Tory band atop their chimneys. They didn't like it one bit that Mary's husband, Colonel Gold Selleck Silliman, spent the war years working against them. He patrolled Connecticut's southwestern border for the Loyalists who were vexing Patriot towns and families along the coast, worked to fend off the British raid on Danbury in 1777 and prosecuted cases against Loyalists in his capacity as state's attorney. One night, in May 1779, a Tory who had previously done some carpentry work for the family got together with eight other Tories, crossed the Long Island Sound in a whale boat and snatched up Gold Silliman and his son, Billy.

Mary was beside herself. She appealed to General George Washington, Connecticut's Governor Jonathan Trumbull and anyone else who might be able to help with a prisoner exchange to earn her husband's release. Every effort failed.

Mary's children needed a father and she wanted her husband back. So she resolved to do what would be unthinkable to her under normal circumstances: she directed some men to kidnap a prominent Tory who might be exchanged for her husband. They settled on Chief Judge Thomas Jones, a Tory leader on Long Island. On November 6, they crossed the Sound and snatched Jones and a young man named Willet, whom they hoped to exchange for Billy.

A few months passed. On April 27, 1780, a boat that Mary had hired departed Black Rock Harbor with Judge Jones aboard in hopes of returning him in exchange for Silliman. By coincidence, that very same day Silliman's New York captors had chosen to free him. So both prisoners returned safely home.

I was thinking about Mary Silliman as I set my eyes on the orchestra of reporters, camera crews, bloggers, government workers and political junkies waiting for our incongruous motorcade at the corner of Trinity and Elm streets in Bushnell Park. I've never been able to figure out if she would have gotten her husband back by just trying to reason with people and relying on the karma built up by being a good person. Or whether it was that raw act of aggression, snatching up Judge Jones, that helped her get what she wanted.

I suppose I've always believed that it was both.

A green Prius led the way, followed by a red Volvo station wagon, and then Mildred's black town car, which carried me in the back. We pulled up to the curb and immediately found ourselves in a mass of people. Television cameras rolled and photos snapped furiously as staffers jumped from the cars and got in position for the big event. I was still trying to jot down a few notes on the back of some scratch paper when a volunteer opened my door.

The advance work looked first-rate for a renegade campaign. The gothic marble and granite Capitol building—with the sunlight dancing brilliantly on its gold leaf dome—framed the small stage and lectern for the audience.

My mouth was dry and my hands were shaking. I firmly grabbed the hand of each supporter as I passed them to disguise my uneasiness.

"That was a real . . . good . . . fight," Jack Crowe said, gripping my shoulder like we were old friends. "Gonna write something up that will make your children proud."

Monica pushed me forward.

When I made it up to the stage, I turned and waived to the crowd.

After receiving a few waves in return, I tapped on the microphone to make sure it was working.

"We can hear you," a gruff fifty-something man in a Teamsters t-shirt said from the front row; he wore a red button with the "Stickin' with Saul" message emblazoned in white letters.

"Thank you," I said right back to him.

"Hope you got something worth hearing," he said, folding his arms over his chest.

People settled in. I reached for the bottle of water placed under the lectern for me. Again, I gripped the bottle tightly to hide my fear.

I took a sip, pulled my scrap of paper from my pocket and kicked things off.

"Thank you all for coming. What I have to say isn't going to take long. In fact, I feel sort of guilty that so many of you have come out to hear such a short announcement."

"I wanted to have this press conference near the Capitol because this is a difficult day for my family and the dome is something that comforts us. I suppose it actually does much more than that. It reminds me that just about everything you do in the few short years that you get on this planet matters a great deal. And if you're passionate about doing things that will make a difference in the lives of others, the things you do can echo long after you're gone."

I sipped my water and took stock of the crowd.

"I'd like to start off with a confession: I've made a big mistake. I've been walking around for the past three months lying to myself—and to you—about who I am and why I'm in this race."

Our supporters looked at each other quizzically. Jack, sitting in the front row, elbowed the reporter next to him.

"I also have to confess that these attacks have wounded me. Deeply. I know you're not supposed to be in politics if you can't stand having terrible things said about you. But when I hear that the principal opposition to my candidacy is that you don't know me—that I'm not like you—or that I'm different and extreme, it brings me back to one of my life's greatest struggles."

"So I'm despondent right now. In addition to these attacks, this race has taken my wife and kids away from me and every minute that goes by when we can't be together is agony . . . but I'm pressing forward."

Rachel, Raymond, Mildred, Melissa and Keisha stood and led our supporters in applause. Dozens held up their phones and cameras and took photos.

"The reason we're going to continue on with a renewed determination is simple: Saul Berg is wrong. He's dead wrong. I'm not just talking about his views on the need to increase defense spending, his indifference to the threat of income inequality or his obsessive commitment to practicing the politics of self-promotion. I'm speaking to something more fundamental. When Saul says that I'm not like you and that I'm different than you, he's wrong. In fact, I believe you're all just like me."

I paused and collected the nods from the friendly faces and ignored the others.

"We're all mortified as the rules that ensure we live in a fair and just society—organized labor that gives working people a voice, a properly funded public education system, a social safety net that ensures the elderly can live with dignity—are being dismantled. We're frustrated by a government that not only has lost its ability to function but has become the playground of corporations and special interests that manipulate it to their selfish ends. Finally, and perhaps most importantly, I know we're all pained to see how we just don't seem to care about each other anymore—especially those with the least among us: the homeless, the sick, the destitute. So many claim to believe that 'I am my brother's keeper' but so few seem to live it."

I tucked the notes into my jacket pocket. I didn't need them to finish.

"Now, I haven't done a very good job of showing this all to you and I take full responsibility for that. But I promise you that we're going to start over. Starting tomorrow, we're going to run a new kind of campaign. The kind of campaign that reminds you of what we all have in common. A campaign that speaks to our collective struggle. A campaign that will bring about true change."

I let the audience have their applause.

"Now, there are some people in this state—powerful people—who do not want us to continue. I imagine that as I stand here and speak to you, they're dialing their cellphones and barking orders to destroy us and what we're fighting for. They're bigger than us. They're stronger than us. And this will not be easy."

"I ask that during what I'm sure will be the difficult days ahead, you remember this: Our world is being turned upside down not because of the people who are wicked and corrupt, but because of people who can't find the courage to do anything about it."

"So let us come together. Work together. Face our fear together. And fight for our shared ideas and ideals. Let's go Fight for Change."

XXIV

"Now calling number thirty-three on Your Honor's presentment calendar, the United States versus Eugene Allen."

The federal public defender, Bryce Hamilton, gathered her files and pushed to the front of the crowded courtroom. Gene was in good hands.

Attorney Hamilton was the hard-charging star of the Federal Defender's office. A Trinity College and Yale Law School grad, she cut her teeth defending death penalty cases in Alabama during the late 90s. After five more years prosecuting police brutality cases in the Civil Rights Division of the Justice Department in Washington, she returned home to Connecticut to take on some of the toughest cases in the Federal Defender's office. The *Connecticut Law Tribune* profiled her career a few years back and quoted her saying, "As long as there's a breath left in my body, I'll be representing the reviled, the despised and the people no one wants to think about. That's the only way I know to protect myself."

I joined her at the counsel table reserved for the defense and we waited for Gene to emerge from the lockup.

"Good morning, Your Honor," we said, in stereo, to Judge Steely.

"Good to see you, Mr. Barnes," she said, peering over her reading glasses. "Good to see you again, Ms. Hamilton."

The lockup door cracked open and Gene emerged, handcuffed in his orange jumpsuit. He looked back and forth as he oriented himself to the courtroom. When he found us at the defense table, he walked straight over and shook Bryce's hand. He didn't look at me.

"He doesn't want to hurt you," Bryce told me earlier that morning from her car as she made her way to the courthouse. "He feels like he's let you down and figures the best thing he can do right now is to go away."

"He has let me down," I said from the parking lot outside the courthouse. "But I'm not giving up on him."

"I think he can make bail if I can say he's gainfully employed."

"So tell them he's still working for me."

"Are you sure?" Bryce asked. "Don't you have to clear that with your people?"

"No," I said. "Just do it, if it will make a difference."

Bryce, standing barely five feet tall, pulled Gene down to her to provide him with some final instructions. He placed his hand on her shoulder to stop her. "I've got it all," he said. "Don't worry about me. Worry about the judge—and the prosecutor."

Devin Cane, the Assistant U.S. Attorney, moved to the prosecution table on cue. He was joined by a much younger prosecutor whom I'd never seen. The clerk handed Judge Steely the case file. Both the defense and the prosecution waited as she read through our respective papers.

I stood with hands behind my back. I couldn't resist the temptation to peek at the elderly Devin Cane. A few years past his prime, Devin had been a ferocious prosecutor in his heyday. He also wasn't a bad candidate. He ran for Congress in '92 in the Third District— which includes New Haven. He had a great resume, but Aidan had his sights on another candidate—a woman Aidan was hell-bent on getting elected. When Aidan asked him to step down until something else opened up, Devin thumbed his nose at him, which was a big mistake for Devin. He managed to secure Saul's endorsement but Aidan and his machine ran roughshod over him. That was the end of Devin Cane's short political career.

Overweight and now balding, Devin still appeared refined and polished. His gold cufflinks showed slightly beneath a well-tailored jacket. His pocket watch chain created a flawless U shape across his belly.

"Okay, I've read both your submissions," the judge started off. "Let's dispatch with the representation issues first." She pulled her glasses down. "Mr. Allen, it's my understanding that Mr. Barnes previously represented you and that you would like a new lawyer."

"Yes, ma'am—I mean, Your Honor," Gene said, correcting himself. "I want a new lawyer."

"That's fine, and Attorney Hamilton is here to enter her appearance in this matter," the judge said. "But can I ask whether this is your decision and your decision only?"

"To get a new lawyer?"

"Correct."

"Well, yes," Gene said, sounding unsure of why the judge was asking. "Attorney Barnes is a good lawyer and all but he represented me a long time ago and . . . but that has nothing to do with this all here. I want Attorney Hamilton to be my lawyer."

"Thank you, Mr. Allen. And with that representation, I'm going to grant Mr. Barnes' motion to withdraw as attorney for this case and accept Ms. Hamilton's appearance." Judge Steely paused for a moment to sign the order. "Mr. Barnes, you're excused."

"Thank you, Your Honor," I said. I grabbed my bag and made my way up the center aisle.

"Can you give me a few minutes after this is over?" Jack Crowe asked, pulling on the hem of my suit jacket.

"Sure," I said. I found a seat in the rear of the courtroom.

"So, Mr. Cane," Judge Steely said, "is the government looking to hold the defendant?"

"Yes, Your Honor."

"Why?" Attorney Hamilton asked, looking at Devin and breaching well-established court decorum. Attorneys aren't allowed to argue with each other, only to address the judge or witnesses. Devin ignored the interruption before continuing his presentation to Judge Steely.

"The case represents yet another episode in a long line of menacing conduct threatening our community," he said, checking his notes. "I'd remind Your Honor that the assisted living facility that he burglarized is also the home of several elderly residents and our final charging decision will reflect that."

"Judge, we're literally making a federal case out of fifteen doses of OxyContin," Bryce said, again interrupting. "A drug which I'd add he was seeking to address chronic back and knee pain he suffers as a result of four years of college football. Moreover, I have three separate opinions from three doctors that he could receive prescriptions for these drugs if he had the money to pay for them." Bryce waved a small stack of papers while she made her point.

"Your Honor, the defendant is a convicted drug dealer," Devin said.

"Only because the government thinks that sharing drugs with other addicts counts as distribution," Bryce said.

"A two-time convicted drug dealer."

"My client is in jail because he has a sickness and is poor," Bryce said. "And black," she added for good measure, looking at Devin.

The courtroom erupted.

Federal judges keep gavels on the bench but they don't ever use them to restore order. They don't have to.

"I'm going to say this one time," Judge Steely said, quieting the courtroom. "If there is any member of the gallery who cannot watch these proceedings without making outbursts, they will immediately be removed by the marshal." She looked down at Attorney Hamilton. "And Ms. Hamilton, one more ad hominem attack like that and I'll hold you in contempt and report you to bar counsel. Do you understand me?"

"Yes, Your Honor."

"Good," Judge Steely said. "Now, Mr. Cane, you want to hold Mr. Allen pending trial."

"Correct, Your Honor."

"From what I can see here," Judge Steely said, looking over Gene's file, "he's lived in Connecticut his entire life and doesn't seem to have ever really traveled outside the state except to play in some football games over twenty years ago. How is he a flight risk?"

"If convicted, he's likely going to spend the rest of his life in federal prison."

"Ms. Hamilton," Judge Steely said, looking to Bryce.

"It's a specious argument. Where would he go?" Bryce asked, her palms facing the ceiling. "Also, I confirmed this morning that Mr. Allen will continue to be gainfully employed if released pending trial."

Judge Steely made a note. "I think I understand your respective positions on danger to community. Do you have anything to add to your prior representations, Mr. Cane?"

"Only that the defendant's entire adult life has been spent in and out of jail. He's never been gainfully employed on a consistent basis and that there is no reason to think he has either the means or where-withal to do anything but continue to prey on the community."

Bryce started to speak. Judge Hamilton cut her off.

"I'm setting bail at twenty thousand dollars. Mr. Cane, you're obviously free to ask the court to revisit the issue when you have an indict-ment." She looked to Gene. "Mr. Allen, you're going to be drug tested weekly and I'll be notified immediately if you test positive."

"Mr. Allen understands, Your Honor," Bryce said. "And I'd note for the record that his test following his arrest was negative."

"Thank you. We're adjourned."

Devin made a note on his court file. Gene reached out and shook hands with Bryce to thank her. Her hand disappeared in his big mitt. She pushed up on her toes to pat him on his back. I slipped into the hallway followed by reporters.

Monica and Keisha waited for me in the corner. Monica looked nervous. She didn't want me anywhere near this courthouse or Gene but understood I had to take at least a few questions.

"Short and sweet," she said in my ear, feigning to remove a piece of lint from my shoulder. "You were here to satisfy your obligations as a lawyer. That's it."

I nodded and turned to face the gaggle of reporters gathering behind me.

"Mr. Barnes, why are you here?" Jack Crowe started off.

"I'm here to satisfy my obligations as an attorney. I was previously the counsel of record and I obviously had to participate in these pro-ceedings before a new lawyer for Mr. Allen could be appointed."

"Is Mr. Allen your friend?" Jack asked, following up.

"I was here today because I was Mr. Allen's lawyer." I caught Bryce emerging from the courtroom out of the corner of my eye. She joined the crowd. "But yes, Mr. Allen has been and forever will be my friend."

Monica patted me on the back to signal for me to try and wrap things up.

"So a candidate for the United States Senate is friends with a drug addict?" Jack asked, refusing to let anyone else get a question in.

"We're supposed to have compassion for people, even if they're trapped in wrongdoing," I said. "I don't condone drug use but I also know that we're all flawed, including you, Jack."

Mark Conner from the *Fairfield Clipper* patted Jack on the back.

"I'm not going to turn my back or forget about a person during a period of struggle," I said. "In fact, I'm running a campaign to fight for people whose lives have been reduced to nothing but struggle each and every day."

"Will you be Gene Allen's employer when he's released?" Jack asked.

"I expect to see him at work first thing tomorrow morning."

Monica took a step back and joined Keisha against the wall behind me.

"Mr. Barnes," Sue White from the AP said, raising her hand, "*The Left Nutmeg* is reporting this morning that it has hard evidence that Senator Berg's wife executed a side letter agreement with Patriot Enterprises International—some type of consultancy agreement—to facilitate the sale of Nutmeg Medical to Patriot."

"I saw that report earlier this morning," I said. "I really can't comment."

"They're reporting that they have a copy of the consultancy agreement and it's worth in excess of four million dollars," she continued.

"Again, you'll have to ask Senator Berg about that."

"They're actually alleging a conspiracy," Mark Conner noted. "The report claims that Rivka Berg's interest as well as that of other investors in Nutmeg Medical was managed by Alistair Kincaid's firm—"

"It . . . is . . . a . . . blog." Jack said, looking back at Mark. "We're talking about a bunch of kids in their parents' basement making things up while they eat cereal out of a box."

"—and that Kincaid had serious legal troubles that mysteriously went away after the deal went through."

"All I can say is that you all will be the ones who will have to compare Senator Berg's comments at his press conference with what's outlined in this report," I said, casually. "And assess if they can be reconciled. I don't feel comfortable commenting on it."

"Mr. Barnes," Pamela Foggerty asked with her cameraman shooting over her shoulder, "yesterday Nancy Perez and her supporters were canvassing for you in New Haven. Were you aware of that? And is she now a part of your campaign?"

"Since I'm the one who asked her to do that—after she joined my campaign and thankfully accepted my apology for not attending the protests she organized for her son—yes, I'm aware of it," I said. "I suppose I should also add that I've let go our consultants who advised me against it."

"You're not concerned that voters will question your affiliation with the mother of a reputed gang member?" Pamela asked.

"Alarico Perez is dead because of the color of his skin," I said. "If people aren't willing to ask the right questions to understand that fact, I'll still sleep well at night."

Sludge Hammer yelled a question over the crowd. "There's a rumor that Brooke Barnes will be joining you on the campaign trail for these last three weeks. Is that true?"

"If she were here, she'd remind you that her last name is Wolcott."

"But will she be joining you?" Pamela asked.

"I certainly hope so."

XXV

Six weeks to the primary. We threw the political playbook out the window. There would be no more waving at parades or shaking hands at town fairs. I was determined to run the campaign that I've always dreamed of running.

Rachel and her team leveraged our social media platform to organize a Walk for Hunger in working-class New Britain during the July 4th weekend. Eliza, Pierce and Benjamin even helped by posting and spreading digital invites. We had no idea whether anyone would show but everyone was willing to give it a try.

When we arrived at Stanley Quarter Park, we were greeted by more than three thousand walkers from all over the state. Bridgeport came in two school buses decorated with the clarion call, "Fight for Change." Greenwich led a brigade of gold-coasters wearing red, white and blue t-shirts broadcasting the same message. Members of the service employees union from Norwich, Hartford, Waterbury and a dozen other towns were apparently competing with one another to come up with the biggest and most colorful signs.

Keisha, Gene and Nancy organized the volunteers from the backs of three rented U-Haul trucks. As people dropped off food on a truck's tailgate, they received a campaign t-shirt—if they didn't already have one.

There were more reporters than I'd ever seen. I didn't recognize most of them and assumed they were from out of state.

"Quinn Barnes, today's tracking poll has you within 17 points of Senator Berg," a blond male-model-looking reporter said to me. "Is this latest movement in the numbers a result of you getting your message out or going negative with Nutmeg-Gate?" He jammed a microphone in my face.

"We have and will continue to speak about our vision for a more just and stronger Connecticut," I said. "We're still a long way from achieving our collective goal but this is obviously good news."

"Is it really senatorial to organize and run a food drive?" another reporter beyond my line of sight asked.

"I think that if every elected official in this country skipped one fundraiser to organize a food drive, it would inspire their constituents and make us a stronger country."

Monica pushed me up on the back of one of the rental trucks. Nancy handed me a bullhorn. I thanked everyone for coming and for their support. And did my best to remind them of why they were there.

"If we keep doing the same thing, nothing will change."

"If we keep voting for the same people, nothing will change."

"Small individual acts can inspire an entire state to change—or an entire world to change!"

The food drive was such a big hit that we repeated them across the state for the next few weeks and decided to ride the wave of what felt like growing momentum by declaring all of July public service month for the campaign. By mid-month we were directing our supporters east to Groton, south to New Haven, west to Danbury and north to Enfield to help build houses with Habitat for Humanity. Gene drove Brooke, Mildred and me to each location each day so we could pitch in and spend a few hours with our supporters. Monica and our advance team were masterful in making certain the media could follow our whereabouts by posting a tracker on our website. We were swarmed at every stop.

"Brooke Wolcott, are you concerned that you and your husband are not actually speaking with voters during these final critical weeks of the campaign?" Sue White asked us as we stepped from the car in Danbury.

"This is who we are and this is how we'll lead," Brooke said, grabbing my right hand.

"Today's tracking poll has you closing to within 12 percentage points for the first time," Sue said. "What will you and your husband be saying to voters during these final days of the campaign?"

"We're going to continue to speak to them through our actions," Brooke said.

We devoted the final week of July to the state's most resource-strapped high schools. We picked up trash, painted over graffiti and did whatever small repairs we could muster. This, however, got under Saul's skin. We were met by police and security guards at Harding High School in Bridgeport toward the end of our week long effort.

"Everyone has five minutes to get off the property," an officer said to me when I arrived at Harding.

"And if we don't leave?" I asked.

"You'll all be under arrest for trespassing," he said.

"You're really going to arrest a bunch of kids and volunteers for raking and cleaning the school they attend?" Brooke asked him, stepping in front of me. "In front of all these cameras?"

"We're prepared to do that, ma'am," he said.

"I think you might want to have your police chief speak with Saul before you try something like that," Brooke said, not giving an inch. "Because we're all prepared to have you arrest us."

The officer retreated to his patrol car. We went on with our plans. He just sat and watched us for the remainder of the morning.

By the time we made it up to Stevens High School in East Hartford that same day our volunteers had all been removed and the gates were locked.

"The Berg campaign is calling this a cheap stunt," Jack Crowe said as we met with our supporters in front of the school. "This is a cosmetic gimmick that doesn't focus on any real issues that relate to education."

"Is there a question somewhere in there, Jack?" I asked, smiling. "Or do you plan on just printing your own statement?"

"How does cleaning up a bunch of school yards effect any real change in education?" he asked.

"When we let our schools fall into such disrepair, the message we send to the kids attending them is that we don't care. We don't care about their school. We don't care about them. And we don't care about their performance." I turned away from Jack to speak directly to our volunteers. "We're doing this today because sometimes a small gesture can change how someone thinks and feels about themselves and might even allow a sliver of hope to enter into their lives. That's why we're here today and that's why we will continue on."

We had our volunteers clean up the sidewalks outside the school and empty overflowing garbage cans. Brooke decided on the spur of the moment that she wanted to plant flowers. She had Gene and a group of volunteers go buy as many trees and flowers as we could plant before the sun set.

When they returned, Eliza, Pierce and Benjamin helped Brooke haul four trays of Peace Lilies over to the front gate. I joined them.

Brooke and I kneeled together with the kids and dug in. We planted Peace Lilies on any patch of ground that we thought could sustain them.

"I'm happy," I said to Brooke as we worked in the dirt.

She stopped to kiss my cheek. "I'm happy, too."

"No, I mean this makes me happy," I said. "That we're fighting together. Side by side. It's all I've ever wanted."

Brooke shook her head and smiled. "Quinn," she said patiently, "how about you think of this as our just working together?"

"That's not how it comes into my head."

"Well, then, maybe you can just use different words." She stopped working to wipe the perspiration from her forehead. "Sometimes just using different words can make a world of difference."

"I'll try."

Pamela Foggerty set up her live shot for her evening update behind us while we worked. I didn't really listen to her report. Brooke and I were too busy watching the kids work—and reveling in them doing something for someone other than themselves. I did pick up the last part of Pamela's commentary.

". . . as the sun sets here in East Hartford, questions abound regarding whether what Barnes volunteers are referring to on social media platforms as Senator Berg's Lockout has backfired on Saul Berg, and will do nothing but draw more attention to Quinn Barnes and what must now be described as a movement for change."

XXVI

"Nine for nine." Rachel yelled from across the basement. "And I've got a list of four people that *called you.*"

Success with the first nine targets on our call list for the day didn't make asking for money any more enjoyable but at least it felt like we were coming to life.

"Give me the list," I said. "And let's plan on circling back with the big donors who said 'no' to us in the spring."

"Bryce Hamilton is here to see you," Keisha said from behind me. I turned around to find her staring at her phone with her free hand on her hip. "You have five minutes here and then you have to start your interviews." She didn't look up while she spoke.

"How many do we have?"

"Nineteen."

"How many are TV?"

"Four."

"How many are bloggers?"

"Eleven. Do you want to me cancel on some of the bloggers?"

"No. But I want you to stay with me to keep us on time." I pulled my headphones off and pointed upstairs to Rachel to let her know I was taking a break. "Where's Bryce?" I asked Keisha.

"In Monica's office."

The bullpen was buzzing. The GOTV team had taken over the entire south side of the increasingly crammed office. State congressional district and town maps covered every inch of wall space. Melissa and Nancy were holding court with the more than three dozen staffers who would be charged with leading the effort to get our supporters out to the polls in one week. Monica was drowning in a sea of volunteers at her desk. With a phone wedged between her shoulder and neck, she answered questions and gave directives between whatever conversations she was having on the phone. Mildred, Raymond and Gene were organizing a shipment of lawn signs to be delivered to people our Voter ID team had identified as supporters. Gene was doing all the lifting.

I slipped into Monica's office to find Bryce waiting for me in one of the visitor's chairs.

"Looks like you have a legit chance at becoming a senator," she said, standing to shake my hand.

"We're still a long way off from that, and this last surge may turn out to be too little, too late. But we have a chance." I slipped into the chair behind the desk and crossed my legs.

"He has five minutes," Keisha announced as she closed the door. She leaned against it and resumed managing my day from her iPhone.

"Bryce, I wish we had more time—"

"It's okay," she said.

"—but we have to get straight to it. Is there any way to keep Gene out of jail?"

"Well, I don't think anything will happen—certainly not a trial—before the Primary or Election Day. I don't think you need to worry about—"

"It has nothing to do with the election. You need to think of him as my brother."

"Funny that you said that."

"Why?"

"Because he said the same thing."

"Well, how can we keep him out of jail?"

"Under normal circumstances, I could probably talk the government into knocking it down to a simple possession case involving a junkie."

"But he's attached to me—"

"And everyone's on my ass. Nutmeg Medical is calling for him to be tarred and feathered. Mayor Brocco is reminding everyone four times a day about the big scary black man stealing from East Haven's blue-haired invalids. And don't think Saul's not in the U.S. Attorney's ear to make sure they make life as painful as possible for Gene—to get to you."

"This U.S. Attorney's office doesn't work like that."

"Like what?" she asked, smirking.

"They don't get this involved in politics."

"And what planet are you from?" she asked, raising the corners of her brown, almond-shaped eyes. "Because on the one I live on, it has happened, it's happening now and it will happen in the future."

"What kind of plea have they offered?"

"Nothing. That's how I know Saul's involved. Normally, they'd offer a generic felony to give everyone a chance to get it over quickly. He'd have ten years hanging over his head but let me argue for downward departure at sentencing to minimize the damage."

"Your first interview is here," Keisha said, cutting in. "I have to go help them set up. You have two more minutes." She cracked open the door and slid out.

"When are they telling you that they'll have an indictment?" I asked.

"They haven't said. Which is also bizarre, right? This case could be indicted in a day and it's been almost two weeks."

I stood.

"You should obviously let me know if there's anything I can do to help." I offered my hand to her. "I'll take care of paying for his drug treatment."

She shook my hand. "His tests have all been negative. He says he's happy he got caught before falling off the wagon."

"Well, he still needs to go to counseling."

"That's great, but I really just need you to put some fight in him."

""I don't think that will be a problem for Gene."

"Well, right now he just wants to plead guilty and go to jail."

"Why?"

"He still thinks that's the only way to protect you."

XXVII

"Why is she pitching?" I asked Pierce, annoyed.

Caught up in the game—and surprised to see me—he gave me a double take from his seat on the end of the bleachers. "They're out of pitchers." He followed it up with a look that said, "Don't blame me."

"John Quincy, stop being so crabby," Mom said from her seat next to Brooke in the stands. "Just sit down and watch the game."

"Yeah, Dad," Ben said, emboldened by my mother's reprimand. "Don't be a crab."

I stared him down to remind him which of us was the parent.

I kissed Brooke on the lips and then Mom on the forehead. Gene gave Pierce and Ben fist bumps. Gene then followed me out to the center field fence to watch the end of the game.

One week before the primary, everything is a campaign event—or at least fodder for the media. I could feel eyes and cameras on my back as we headed to center field by walking along the fence along the third base line and making a right when we got to the end. I shed my suit jacket and rolled up my sleeves. Gene stepped back to give me some time alone.

"Hi, Mr. Barnes," our centerfielder, Brian, said from just a few feet away.

Brian was thoroughly out of position in center field. He was our hardest throwing pitcher but he couldn't outrun a one-legged sloth.

I waved. "What number hitter is this?"

"Ninth," he said.

The scoreboard reported that we were ahead 3-1 in the final inning of play. We had no outs. The problem was that Eliza had never been on the mound in a game. She played with her brothers in the backyard, but playing in the championship game of an all-star tournament—where she was the youngest player on the field—was not a situation where she was in position to succeed.

I cursed her coach.

Her warm-up pitches were a mess. When she couldn't get the ball over the plate she started aiming like she was throwing darts. Her last two warm-up tosses didn't reach the plate.

She lucked out with the first batter she faced. He went down swinging on a pitch in the dirt. The lead-off batter, however, was a much more seasoned hitter and made her pay for lobbing the ball over the plate. He doubled by ripping a shot to left field. She walked the number two batter, bringing the winning run to the plate. Rattled, she walked him also, loading the bases.

I looked over to Brooke. She was trying to provide encouragement, but our opponents—and their parents—smelled the blood in the water. The place was getting loud. And Eliza was melting down.

I could tell from her body language that she was on the verge of tears. Her coach couldn't tell, but I could. The sight of him walking out to the mound pushed her over the edge. She took a knee and started bawling.

There aren't many things worse than watching your child struggle and not be able to save her—or at least help her. I weighed hopping the fence and heading to the mound but figured it would make a bad scene even worse. Her coach asked her for the ball. She stood—and pushed him away.

The field quieted down as the spectacle unfolded.

She was now in a full-blown confrontation with her coach.

"Are you sure?" I heard him ask.

She nodded.

Eliza wanted to stay in the game. And continue battling.

She walked to the back of the mound and removed her hat. I'm still always amazed to see how much hair she fits under that thing. She took her time to fix her ponytail and pull it through the back of her cap before pulling it down tight on her head. She wiped her cheek with the back of her sleeve and looked out to me.

She kept her chin low. I searched for a way to send her a private message that might help in a park filled with people. I reduced my coaching to just a word.

"Aggressive," I said, just loud enough so she could hear me.

She nodded and got back on the mound.

The first pitch to their clean-up hitter came high and hard to the inside part of the plate. The batter jumped back in the box and the catcher's mitt popped. The umpire rightly called it a ball. The batter stepped out of the box. He spit on his hands, took two practice swings and got back in the batter's box looking determined to hit the ball to Massachusetts.

The second pitch was in exactly in the same spot as the first. This time the batter took a tomahawk swing, shooting the ball right back at the mound. Eliza threw her hand up to defend herself from injury and knocked the ball down. She went to the ground also. By the time she got to her knees the runner on third was halfway home. She lurched forward at the ball lying a few feet in front of her and tossed it underhand to the catcher. He caught it and touched home plate. Two outs.

The number five hitter was even bigger than their cleanup batter. He strode to the plate with Ruthian confidence. Not at all fazed by the moment, he took his practice swings like he was about to take batting practice. He had to be twice the size of Eliza.

I could see that she didn't have many more pitches in her so I was hoping she could get the first few over the plate. She obliged by reaching back and letting a fastball go. She fell off the side of the mound as the ball sailed right over home plate. The batter sent the ball high and deep to center. It first looked destined to land over my head but the wind blowing in from behind me knocked it down.

Brian lumbered back toward me. I could feel the ground vibrating beneath my feet. Each step he took without falling down looked like a miracle. His luck ran out a few feet short of where he needed to be to catch the ball and he went down in a mass of flailing limbs in front of me.

"Stay with it," I said as calm as I could manage.

Like a car sputtering as it runs out of gas, Brian fell forward from his knees with his gaze fixed on the ball.

And made a perfect backhand catch.

The celebration ensued on Brian's back as player after player piled on while he tried to get to the dugout. The only part of Eliza's body that was visible in the pile was her hair sticking out.

"Great game," a voice said from behind me.

I turned. A clean-cut young man smiled warmly at me. His blonde hair was parted neatly to the right. The two of us were the only people at the ballpark in suits.

Gene stepped between us to protect me from the stranger. When the guy started to reach into his breast pocket, Gene started after him.

"It's okay," I said, trying to prevent a scene.

"Easy now big boy," the man said, sneering.

Gene balled up his fist.

"Don't react to him," I said sharply, looking up to Gene. "That's what he wants you to do. He doesn't matter."

I grabbed Gene's arm. He opened his hand and stepped back to stand with me.

"Can I help you?" I asked evenly.

The stranger pulled a folded piece of paper from his pocket.

"Just want to leave you a memento to remember this great game," he said, grinning as he handed it to me.

I unfolded it and read the message beneath the seal of the U.S. District Court for the District of Connecticut:

YOU ARE COMMANDED *to appear in this United States district court at the time, date, and place shown below to testify before the court's* **grand jury**.

"Thank you," I said, determined not to give him the satisfaction of a reaction.

"Will see you in two weeks," he said. He turned and headed into the crowded parking lot.

"Who was that guy?" Gene asked, still staring at the FBI agent as he disappeared in the crowded lot.

"Don't worry about it," I said. "I can take care of it. It's actually good news."

XXVIII

"Campaign meeting!" Monica announced. "Campaign meeting!" Staffers scurried around our cramped Gambrel Colonial in the tiny borough of Fenwick in Old Saybrook.

Fenwick and its beach sit at the exact point where the Connecticut River flows into the Long Island Sound. I thought it would provide a great mid-week break to allow the team to recharge their batteries and have some fun as we headed down the home stretch for what would be five days of non-stop campaigning.

Keisha planned a day of activities that was the perfect diversion. We started early, on the beach, playing Frisbee and Wiffle ball. Pierce, Benjamin and Eliza then gave everyone body surfing lessons in Long Island Sound, confirming to me that we clearly had the least athletic campaign team in the history of American politics.

We drove golf carts down Bridge Street, crossing South Cove, for a barbecue lunch at Dock & Dine. Afterwards, we headed to Old Saybrook Center for a matinee production of *Julius Caesar* at Kate Hepburn's Art Center.

We gave everyone the night off except for a group of senior staffers who headed back to the house with us for our campaign meeting.

Our dining room table can only comfortably seat about six. Gene helped me pull the table apart to slip the leaf in and make more room. Brooke took the seat at the head of the table and Monica settled in next to her. Mildred sat opposite Brooke. Raymond and Keisha book-ended her.

After Gene helped me add additional chairs, Melissa, Nancy and the GOTV team filled in one side. Members of the finance, polling and voter ID teams filled in the other side and the vacant chairs against the wall. Eliza, Ben and Pierce took drink orders and scurried back and forth to the kitchen as they dropped them off. I sat in a chair reserved for me in the middle. Gene sat against the wall behind me.

"What's first?" Brooke asked from the head of the table.

"Polling," Monica said, turning to Samantha.

"Ma'am, as of about ten minutes ago, the number is seven."

"Ma'am, as of about ten minutes ago, the number is seven."

Applause. The back benchers stood up and held up their cans of Diet Coke and bottled water, saluting the room.

"What was it three days ago?" Brooke asked

Samantha rummaged through some papers. "Eight."

"And three days before that?" Brooke asked, taking notes.

"Eleven."

"We may not be closing on him fast enough to catch him but thanks," Brooke turned to Monica. "Let's get a release out tonight on these numbers—and start tweeting this now."

Monica and Samantha nodded.

"What's next?" Brooke asked.

"Voter ID," Monica said, looking to Graham.

"Well, you just sort of heard about voter ID in the polling data," he said, stammering. He sent a handout around the table while he gave his report. "We continue to utilize all available voting and other data to target likely voters at the micro level."

Based on all the knitted brows and glances exchanged around the room, no one could really make heads or tails of Graham's handout. I stepped in to make sure I, at least, understood the salient points.

"What does the data say most voters want to hear from us?

"Well, our profiling shows that seventy-one percent of likely voters rank the economy and income inequality as their top priority. We take that and message our calls with our income inequality talking points, follow up digitally with your public statements on it, and for this issue, we do a mail drop that features only this issue."

"Has Nutmeg Medical been coming up?" Brooke asked.

"No, they want to talk about issues."

"Nutmeg Medical is an issue," Monica said.

"I'm sorry, ma'am," Graham said. "I meant issues relating to our platform."

"Why do you only mail-drop for the people that want to hear about income inequality?" Brooke asked, "and not the other issues?"

"Cost. Our program doesn't cost any money—other than the costs associated with gathering data. But snail mail is expensive so we only spend it on the most important issue."

"What does your model say would happen if the election were held today?" I asked.

"Well, no offense," Graham said, looking to Samantha, "but this is more precise than polling. We're literally counting votes until we get to the 121,587 that we project we'd need to win the primary."

"So where are we?" Brooke asked.

"We need 12,517 more votes."

Brooke did some math on a sheet of paper. "That would mean we're barely within single digits. We're 9 points out. Not 7." She looked to Samantha for an explanation.

"It's a different kind of analysis," Samantha said. "It means—theoretically—you've identified the voters you need to identify and contact to win the election."

"So you both agree we're getting close?" Monica asked.

"Yes," they said in unison.

"Monica, did you tell me we're going to have an endorsement tomorrow?" Brooke asked.

"The Council for a Livable World. Your husband is apparently the only candidate that was able to answer their board's trick question."

"Okay. Good. Let's do this," Brooke said. "We're going to have some money coming in. Let's mail drop on every voter contact, not just the income inequality contacts."

"Got it," Graham said.

"What's next?" Brooke asked.

"Get-Out-The-Vote . . ."

XXIX

"What are you doing here?" Pierce asked.

"Dad, this is a total embarrassment," Ben said. "Did Mom make you do this?"

Leadership camp for the boys was my idea.

Having them attend it at Choate was Brooke's.

Founded in 1896 in Wallingford, Choate Rosemary Hall is simply the most prestigious prep school in the world. Its alumni include world-renowned scientists, Oscar winning actors, and numerous world leaders, including President John F. Kennedy.

I raised the predictable objections about the kids being around entitled children and concerns about diversity. Brooke went on a week-long campaign, bombarding me with facts and figures to refute my arguments.

I'd like to say I relented—which would suggest that I, at least, had some say in the matter—but the truth is that Brooke just ignored my protests and signed them up. After driving through the campus, I was glad she did. The place looked spectacular and with kids from all over the world attending, it was an experience that I wanted Pierce and Ben to have.

"How's it going, fellas?" Gene asked them while he offered them each a fist bump.

"Mr. Gene," Ben said, looking much happier to see him than me, "not one of these kids can hit a baseball."

"Or play any sports," Pierce added.

"Sports are fun but you definitely don't get to do them forever," Gene said. "It's more important to learn how to be a leader, like your Dad."

They drank in Gene's counsel until he got to the part about me. When they rolled their eyes.

"Well, it's career day," I said, looking inside the auditorium where the camp attendees were starting to gather. "And one of your counselors asked a few special parents to speak about their professions."

"Dad, you're unemployed," Ben said. "You got fired from your law firm."

"This is just too embarrassing," Pierce said, shaking his head. "Besides, most of these kids are Republicans."

"How do you know that?" Gene asked.

"They're always complaining about Obama at lunch."

"Well, I think I can do five minutes on American government for a room full of sixth graders without offending anyone," I said.

Pierce and Ben spun around and entered Getz Auditorium. Gene and I followed.

Gene stood in the rear against the wall. I took a seat on the edge of the stage with two other parents.

The first speaker, Mrs. Lopez, talked about the renewable technologies company that she founded, which specializes in wind and solar projects. I was dying to get her opinion on whether she thought the government was subsidizing the industry at the levels necessary to spur growth, but I knew the boys would be mortified if I asked a question. I just folded my hands on my lap and listened. The next speaker was Dr. Tisdall. He spoke about his research in the field of nanotechnology and potential medical benefits in being able to direct control of matter on the atomic scale. I was so fascinated by his work that I couldn't help myself. I started to raise my hand but Gene appeared and put my arm back down at my side.

He leaned down to deliver his message in my ear.

"They need you back," he said.

"Back where?" I asked.

"Headquarters. They say it's urgent."

I turned to find everyone, including the boys' counselors who were now staring at me.

"I'm sorry," I said. "But I have to take a rain check."

I looked to Pierce and Ben who were both slumped down in their chairs. Neither of them looked back at me.

The car pulled up to the curb and I could see Monica pacing back and forth in the bullpen. As soon as I made it through the door she grabbed me by the wrist and dragged me into the first empty office she could find. She closed the door behind us and shouted, "Five!" She jumped into my arms and nearly choked me to death. When she finally let go, she handed me a crumpled piece of paper.

"Okay," I said, trying to calm her down. "That's good, but we still may not be able to make up five points in 24 hours."

"We're ahead!"

"Are you sure?" I asked, looking it over.

Giddy, she crossed her arms and twisted back and forth—and could not stop smiling.

"Will you calm down?" I told her. "Tracking polls don't mean anything."

"They meant something when you were behind."

"Who knows about this?"

"You, me and our kids doing the polling."

"Let's keep it that way."

Monica hugged me again. This time she was pinning my arms to my torso. And started sniffling.

"Please calm down. You're going to jinx everything."

There was a knock at the door. Monica was full out crying before I could open it. Mildred joined us with the evening's itinerary in hand. "You ready, Senator?" she asked grinning.

"Don't say that," I said. "We haven't won anything yet. And how do you know about this?"

"Voter ID calls are the same as a poll. And they're running strongly in our favor."

"Really?" Monica asked, releasing me and embracing Mildred. Mildred tried to back away but Monica wouldn't let her go.

"By how much?" I asked.

"Fifty-two to forty-six," Mildred said, still hog-tied by Monica.

"Who knows this?" I asked again.

"Everyone working on your campaign, you fool." Monica finally let go of her. "That's why they call it voter ID. Your volunteers know we're ahead."

"Call a campaign meeting," I ordered, ushering them both to the door. "Remind them that we still have to execute tomorrow and can't take anything for granted. We have to work even harder now."

"Are you coming to it?" Monica asked.

"No. I need to go see Aidan."

—⅏—

Daniel sat at Aidan's bedside staring at his hand. Aidan was asleep. He looked to be wincing beneath his oxygen mask as he struggled to get the air in and out.

I was probably in the room for a good five minutes before Daniel noticed I was sitting across from him.

"How long has he been asleep?" I asked.

"He just fell off."

"Is he taking any morphine?"

"No," he said. "Said he wanted to be clear-headed to talk to me."

We sat together for at least another five minutes. We didn't share a word—or even move. We just stared at Aidan.

"You okay?" I asked.

Daniel snorted. "Under the circumstances? Yeah, I'm okay."

"I just mean you're dealing with a lot. It can't be easy that the campaign got thrown on top of all this. Do you think it makes sense to reach out to your sponsor?"

"I said, I'm okay."

More silence.

"Well, I really appreciate the help on the campaign," I said, tip-toeing. "I obviously understand if you're not going to be around much . . ."

"He'd kick me in the ass if I wasn't out there working for you." Daniel rubbed his forehead. "This is what he wanted for you."

"For the state."

"Who do you think you're talking to?" Daniel turned to me, his forehead wrinkled.

"Listen," I said. "The thing that I want to make sure gets said is that I'll never be able to pay you back for sharing your father with me."

Daniel stood.

"I'm going to get something to eat," he said. "You want something?"

"No, I can't stay long. I have to get out tonight."

Daniel left.

I went to Aidan and took his hand. It felt cold. I used my hands to warm it.

When it was time to go, I leaned over him and put my lips near his ear.

"Hold on," I whispered. "We're almost there."

XXX

August 13th. Primary day. My eyes didn't open at 4:00 a.m. I was stirred awake by the sound of a staffer logging on a computer. I opened my eyes to the sight of gray and white ceiling tiles from the couch in Monica's office.

Beyond tired, my whole body ached. My knees and feet were swollen; my arms and stomach were sore. I couldn't quite figure out how that could have happened and massaged my forearms to bring my body to life.

I tried to thumb through my emails as I reached for a clean shirt from the hook on the back of the office door. Hundreds of notes poured in. I didn't even try to read them. I went down to the bathroom with my shaving kit, got myself cleaned up and headed over to see Aidan.

The sun hadn't yet risen but his room looked like Grand Central Station at noon. Aidan was managing to sit up in bed. His oxygen mask had been replaced with oxygen tubes hanging from his nose, and he was giving the orders and instructions he'd given every Election Day since long before any of the staffers were born. The GOTV plan had been baked weeks ago but it seemed to make him feel good to repeat things.

We didn't talk much. We both knew there's little a candidate can do on Election Day. Monica and Mildred arrived and pulled me off to the corner to give me a bunch of instructions that went in one ear and out the other. They went to work on my suit, removing lint and brushing out the wrinkles while talking over the day's itinerary. Aidan reviewed the protocols he wanted followed with his poll watchers and legal team. I kissed him on the forehead before I left. It's not something I'd ever done before. He didn't react; he just kept on talking.

The first stop was the senior center in Pentfield, to vote. Brooke was waiting for me in the lobby. She looked like she had walked off the cover of a magazine, wearing a contoured black and white sheath dress. She had no tolerance for anything that smelled of being a trophy. And I appreciated her indulging me for one day—or at least one morning of one day—to play the role of the candidate's wife. We voted and did the obligatory fluff interviews with the media, who far outnumbered the early morning voters.

I was wedged in between Monica and Mildred in the back of the car while Gene drove south on the Merritt for Greenwich, Stamford, Westport and Norwalk. They woke me when we arrived at polling stations to step out and spend time with our volunteers and say a few words to the bloggers and reporters the campaign had arranged to meet us. By mid-morning we were on our way to Bridgeport and I had pieced together enough catnaps to be functional.

Monica had set up small rallies in the bigger cities. We did three in Bridgeport, and the energy from the crowds provided all the adrenaline I would need for the remainder of the day. It had nothing to do with the signs, balloons and cheers; there was some type of palpable force behind it all; it surrounded everyone and penetrated everything.

"I've been doing this a long time, and it's never felt quite like this," Monica said as I stepped down from the stage in New Haven.

That's how it also went in New London, Groton, Norwich, Willimantic and then back in Hartford by evening rush hour. The scheduled events were over by six so we took to the streets of Hartford until the polls closed. We rendezvoused with volunteers and walked up and down Main Street and shook the hand of every commuter at every red light that we encountered.

Horns honked.

Drivers hollered, "Fight for Change!" from their cars.

At one point, it felt like a hundred consecutive commuters waved and extended their hands for a high five.

A trio of police officers approached me near Asylum Street. I expected a stern warning about obstructing traffic but instead received a series of fist bumps and pats on the back. "Fight for Change, my brotha, Fight for Change," the last of the three told me.

Working our way down Main Street, we landed at the door of the Ramada Plaza Hotel right as polls closed. The lobby was a sea of staffers, volunteers and media. The extra lighting from the television cameras was blinding.

I shook hand after hand as Monica pushed me to the elevator. When the doors finally closed, I asked Monica, "Any issues at the polling stations?"

"Lines were a little long in Bridgeport and New London but things cleared up late in the day."

"Make sure you check with Aidan first, but we should let our poll watchers and voter protection teams go for the night. No need to keep them up."

She nodded.

The doors opened on the fifth floor. We were greeted by another staffer who led us to a suite at the end of the hall.

"I'm going to lie down," I said.

"I wish I could," Monica said.

"Me three," Mildred added.

"It's going to get called late," Monica told me. "We'll wake you when we have to."

The doors to the suite opened to a roomful of staffers, none of whom I recognized. People in suits worked their cellphones—although for the life of me I couldn't figure out what work they could be doing with the polls closed. Kids working on laptops snacked on cheese, crackers and fruit from platters littering the room's landscape. The garbage cans overflowed with empty soda cans.

It struck me as ironic that a bunch of liberal activists wouldn't recycle.

I waved to the room. People applauded between their calls and faux multitasking. I migrated through the crowd to get to the bedroom. The only thing between me and a mattress was a well-dressed man with his back to me.

"Excuse me," I said.

He turned to me.

Sometimes when you see someone you know out of context, it takes a second to recognize them.

"Albert—Albert Money?" I said, trying to feign that I wasn't struggling with his name. Albert was a former teammate whom Aidan had set up in what eventually became a very successful process-serving business. I hadn't seen him in a few years, but he was dressed to the nines in one of his signature Armani suits.

"Good to see you, Q. And congratulations on a great race."

Something was wrong. I could read it in his face. Albert pulled an envelope from his inside breast pocket.

"Q, I've been given special instructions as to how to deliver this to you and you only." He handed me the envelope and put his hand on my shoulder. "Again, congratulations. Hope this all works out."

I pushed open the bedroom door and locked it behind me. The envelope was white and plain and had just my name on it. My hands started to tremble when I turned it over.

I recognized the stationery.

I turned on a lamp and sat on the bed.

I stared at it for a moment to mentally prepare myself.

A deep breath.

And tore it open.

My Dear Son:

If you're reading this, it means that my will could no longer sustain my body.

Please don't spend even a moment lamenting my not being able to see your greatest triumph. I am certain that you have succeeded and I ask that you take comfort in knowing that my last thought was of knowing you've achieved the impossible. I couldn't be more proud.

The hardest part may still be ahead. If there is a way for me to be by your side, I will take on the Almighty himself to find it. Regardless, please know that I was just a spectator these many years. The greatness was always within you. I just tried to help you see it.

It was surely providence that brought us together as I've never loved anything on this planet the way I have loved you.

I've always believed that my destiny was to help you achieve yours.

Press on with fury.

Aidan

I curled up on the bed, the way I curled up when I was a child. I wept—and was overwrought with guilt about it. I kept thinking about my own father's passing. It just hadn't hit me like this. I tried to understand it—and then rationalize it—but there was no explaining how in the course of human interactions we sometimes develop bonds and love that completely defy custom and convention. If I'd had a thousand tongues I could not have expressed the depth of my devastation. I could feel the hurt deep in my bones and joints—and heart.

I felt as if I could not get up.

A boom echoed from the other side of the door—the kind of sound you hear when someone looking to barge in learns too late the door is locked. An opus of knocking ensued followed by shouting and yelling. For an instant, I thought the building might be on fire.

I sat up and used the corner of the bedspread to wipe my face. I slipped my jacket back on and walked to the door. I leaned my forehead against the door for a moment of meditation before pulling it open.

"Saul is on the phone!" Monica yelled, jamming a phone in my face. Behind her stood a roomful of people bear hugging and fist bumping each other in jubilation.

"Quinn Barnes."

"Quinn! This has to be a special night for you and your family and I wanted to offer my congratulations—and concession." Saul spoke without a hint of acrimony or the realization that more than three decades of elected life was about to come to an end.

"Thank you, Senator. It was an honor." Monica shushed the room so she could eavesdrop. "I'd appreciate the opportunity to come sit with you next week to get your thoughts on how to handle Lucy in the general. We only have a few weeks."

"Well, enjoy the night with your staff and family. I know it's a special one. Best of luck."

"Thank you, Senator."

Monica jumped up and down like red ants were eating at her feet.

"I have Leader Steed on the line," a volunteer I couldn't see hollered from across the room.

My cellphone rang and *Brooke* appeared on the screen.

"The governor is on the phone!" Mildred yelled.

"The governor of what?" a volunteer asked.

Monica and Mildred pushed me back into the bedroom and set up a makeshift office at the table in the corner to accept my phone calls before we had to head downstairs for our acceptance speech. Staffers, elected officials, party brass and hangers-on streamed in and out to pat me on the back while I took my calls.

"Berg just announced he's staying in the race," a student volunteer reported, rushing in the room.

"Staying in how?" Monica asked.

"Gonna form his own party. They're calling it 'Connecticut for Saul.'"

The script for my acceptance speech was shoved in front of me. Monica cleared the room. After we had some quiet, she stood over the sheets of paper spread across the table and started coaching me about how to handle this late-breaking news.

"Forget it," she said. "Ignore it."

She stared at the pages to consider the matter further and then changed directions.

"You can't ignore it," she said. "Say something like, 'He's a typical politician trying to hold onto power'—use your Jimmy Stewart stuff . . ."

She went back and forth about how to handle Saul's creating the chaos of a three-way race. Finally, she called our communications director—and then changed her mind two or three more times about how to respond.

"You're not listening to a word I'm saying," she said, arms crossed.

"Not really."

"You okay?"

"I'm okay."

"Good. 'Cause there's no stopping us now."

She grabbed my jacket from the back of the chair and handed it to me.

I pulled Aidan's letter from my pants pocket and transferred it to the left breast pocket of my jacket.

I got up.

And led the way downstairs to the ballroom.

XXXI

Hundreds To Attend Coyle Funeral

HARTFORD, CONNECTICUT (AP)—*Aidan Coyle, the man who turned the Democratic Party into the dominant force it is in Connecticut politics, will be laid to rest today.*

> *The former state chair and party leader succumbed Tuesday after a year-long fight against pancreatic cancer. He will be buried in Cedar Hill Cemetery.*
>
> *Funeral services will be held at St. Joseph's Cathedral in Hartford, the city where he lived all his life.*
>
> *Coyle, who died at Hartford Hospital, kept his grip on the state party despite his infirmity, engineering John Quincy Barnes' primary victory of over long-time Sen. Saul Berg last week.*
>
> *Coyle is credited with playing a substantial role in the nomination, election and re-election of every Democratic member of Connecticut's congressional delegation for the past generation.*

Aidan would have loved his funeral.

St. Joseph's holds about nineteen hundred people and it was pushed to capacity—with even the side chapels bursting with mourners. The pews were filled with all kinds of people. Advocates for the homeless sat next to congressmen. Union workers shared pews with CEOs. Democrats prayed with Republicans.

Looking back over the gathering from our seats in the second row, the blend of race, religion and creed was a testament to a life well-led. There wasn't enough room to accommodate the media—who were crammed together beneath the stained glass windows on the side of the church.

Aidan liked to say, "What's a good funeral without a little politickin'?" and it would have made him ecstatic to see all the negotiating and bargaining that was going on. The minority leader of the State Senate was in the aisle bending the governor's ear about his budget. Progressives from our Congressional delegation were caucusing about how to drive support for accepting immigrants from Central America into the state. A peace activist was questioning Saul in the row behind us about his upcoming vote on the Iran Threat Reduction Act.

I also met many members of Aidan's extended family for the first time.

"Aidan talked about you so much over the years, I feel like I know you," his cousin Jim Flood from Boston said to me before the service.

Keisha, Gene and the rest of our team broke up all the deal making so we could start the service.

Daniel did a bang-up job kicking off the eulogizing. He was serious, thoughtful and moving.

"For much of my life I felt like I was in competition with so many of you for my father's time. But as I look out at all of you and we reflect on his many accomplishments, I'm proud to have shared him with you." He finished by turning to the casket and speaking directly to Aidan. "Your work and your song will echo far beyond the years you shared with us. You made the world a better place. We love you."

Governor Tate lightened the mood when it was his turn. He talked about his start in politics and how Aidan helped him snatch victory from the jaws of defeat back in the 80s—and the Irish whiskey they shared door-knocking on cold October evenings. By the time members of our Congressional delegation jumped in, things had become a bit bawdy and turned into a full-blown roast. Each anecdote started with more Irish whiskey.

I was up last.

"When I lost my own father, Aidan stepped in. I've spent a lifetime trying to repay him for all he's done for me. I realized these past few days that it would take me ten lifetimes to finish."

I wanted to devote the rest of my time sharing anecdotes about Aidan's kindness to me and his unending devotion to people in our state. But that's not what he would have wanted. Just as he would have cringed at the notion that I spend even a moment mourning his loss when there was so much work to do; he'd expect that I use the unique opportunity of having every key politician, activist and reporter captive to deliver a full blown assault on Saul. That would make him proud. That would make him smile as he looked down on all of us.

I'd selected my words carefully, mindful that the whole thing could easily backfire if people got the sense I was delivering a cold, calculating political speech. I was determined to do both—to honor my second father and to speak the words that would make him proud.

"As you've heard throughout the morning, politics was everything to Aidan and from the time I was a child—not much older than my own daughter, Eliza—he was imparting his views, his philosophy about politics and politicians." I looked to Eliza sitting on my mother's lap next to Brooke and the boys, before turning back to the congregation. "If he were here, I think he would put it this way:

"A politician must be the champion of the facts necessary to lead a responsible public discourse—and the sworn enemy of lies, rumors, false accusations and nonsense." I scanned the audience as I spoke but made sure my gaze landed on Saul when I delivered the part about lies and false accusations.

"A politician must be accountable and understand that their charge is not simply to highlight their triumphs," I said, still keeping my attention focused in the general direction of Saul and his team. "But hold themselves accountable for their failures so we can all work toward a more perfect union."

I gave the attendees a good bit about the need for politicians to be perpetual idealists. And how they should spend every moment of every day working to stamp out the cynicism and negativism that corrodes our political culture. I could see Aidan rolling his eyes. I got back to the heart of the matter to close things out.

"Aidan's life was a testament to these ideals and the cause of social justice, economic justice and human dignity."

I paused to let the smattering of "amens" roll through the pews.

"In his final months, he was mindful that we are headed into perilous times. He wanted the people of this state to have a choice between the economic inequality that excludes so many from so much and a society that embraces equity, fairness and generosity. While we're all shaken by his loss, I for one resolve to honor his memory," I said, looking to his casket, "by redoubling my efforts to advance the causes that were his life's work—and hope you will join me."

The kids were well behaved on the way to the cemetery. Eliza sat on Monica's lap while Pierce and Benjamin talked about their memories with Aidan. It was a comfort to just to be sitting next to Brooke.

After we pulled into Cedar Hill Cemetery, I left the family behind to resume my pall-bearing duties. It was a glorious late-summer New England day. The tips of the trees were just starting to show some orange and yellow, signaling the end of summer and the inevitable march towards fall.

The giant mass of mourners followed us as we made our way to Aidan's final resting place. I let his family sit in the chairs beneath the white tent. I stood behind them with Brooke and the kids.

This is the part where it always becomes real for people—unmistakably final.

. . . we therefore commit his body to the ground; earth to earth, ashes to ashes, dust to dust; in sure and certain hope of the resurrection to eternal life . . .

This is the part when everyone usually cries.

Including me.

Daniel stayed with his father as the guests cleared out. He wasn't quite in the mood to thank everyone for coming, and people understood. I left him alone.

We drifted back to our car. I felt a hand on my shoulder as the family piled in before me.

"Q, wanted to offer my condolences for your loss."

"Albert," I said. "Thanks for coming. It means a lot."

"Wouldn't have missed it for the world," he said. Brooke got into the car and he closed the car door behind her.

"Is everything okay?" I asked.

"Everything's fine. But Aidan charged me with one final duty and he was very clear that he wanted me to be discreet in all my dealings."

"What duty?"

"I'm the executor to his estate."

"Okay."

"And we need to talk."

"Is it urgent?"

"Yes."

"Can you give me a preview?" I asked

"Well, it's about Aidan's estate. It's considerable."

"Why don't you just connect with Daniel in the morning? He'll be home."

"Aidan has left his entire estate to you."

"Are you sure?"

"Quite. But there is an important condition."

"I think I already know what that might be."

"He wants you to use the funds to win the election."

"I can't do that."

"I'm just the messenger."

"Who knows this?"

"Only you."

"What about Daniel?"

"The will has to be made public after probate is granted. He'll know then."

Brooke lowered the window. "Quinn, the kids are hungry."

I shook hands with Albert. We parted. I slipped into the car and buckled my seatbelt.

"What was that about?" Brooke asked.

"Nothing," I said. "Just offering condolences."

"Are we taking off tonight?" Monica asked.

"No," Brooke answered. "We're going to meet at headquarters after the wake."

XXXII

"What's first?" Brooke asked from the head of the table.

"The debate," Monica said from the first chair to her left. "We're finally having a debate."

Mildred, seated next to me in the center, started clapping. The rest of the long table—and the back benchers sitting against the wall—saw it was okay and joined in.

I hate debates.

People make too big a deal about a candidate's mistakes or gaffes. The formats don't lend themselves to a real exchange of competing ideas. And there's never enough time to fully answer a question.

Despite months of complaining about Saul's refusal to agree to a debate, it made me grouchy knowing one was now on the calendar.

"What time will it be?" Brooke asked.

"Time?" Monica asked back.

"He's terrible at night," Brooke said. "Worse than terrible late at night."

"I've noticed that," Mildred added. "His worst event of the day is always his last event of the day."

They went on as if I wasn't there—or supposedly leading the organization.

"Let's see if we can negotiate a lunch debate," Monica said, making a note.

"Breakfast would work also," Brooke said, running her hand over the back of her head, "and try for an amphitheater. He does better in an arena. It's more like court."

"Why don't you three figure this out off-line," I said. "Just make sure we book plenty of time for debate prep. Also, can we negotiate a Hartford venue? I'd have the home court advantage."

Monica nodded.

"Or Wesleyan," Brooke said. "Middletown would come out strong for him."

"What's the latest on our polling looking like?" I asked, turning to Samantha.

"We have one in the field tonight but based on the three or four out there now, it's basically tracking as a three-way tie."

"What do you mean by basically?" Brooke asked.

"Everyone is in the 19 to 22 per cent range," she said, looking nervous that Brooke might fire her for giving bad news.

"Are we ahead in any?" Brooke asked.

"One—but again, they're all within the margin of error."

Brooke made a note. "As soon as you're done with the one in the field I want you to bring it to me," she said. "And to Monica."

She nodded.

"Money?" I asked, looking to Rachel. I know she wasn't the finance director but wasn't sure where I was supposed to be looking.

"We're in the red."

"How can that be?" I said testily. "I'm the Democratic Party's nominee."

"We're working on it," Monica intervened.

"We're eight weeks out from a general election," I said. "If we're going to do an ad buy, it had to be done days ago."

"Lucy and Saul have probably already bought up most of the time," Brooke added.

I turned to Graham. "Can't we do our magic voter targeting thing again?"

"We can but we still need *some* money to run it."

I stood.

"Where are you going?" Monica asked.

"Downstairs to make some fundraising calls," I said, as sharply as I could, to let everyone know this had to be addressed. And that I was annoyed.

"Who are you going to call at this time of night?" Brooke said, almost laughing.

"Anyone I can," I answered, heading to the doorway leading to the basement.

Brooke was right.

It's pointless trying to make a fundraising call in the late evening hours, let alone past 8:00 p.m. I was just in a foul mood and wanted to get away from everyone. I felt bad about snapping at Samantha but figured Brooke would smooth it over.

It did give me time to think about Aidan's estate and our money situation. Had Saul gotten out of the race, the floodgates would have been open, but his big donors and corporate money were staying with him. My primary win wasn't big enough to pry them away, and the handful of donors who had written big checks for me in the primary were already maxed out.

The money from Aidan's estate could be a difference maker for us. But I knew it wasn't fair to Daniel.

I was certain that Aidan didn't mean for it to be a slap in the face to Daniel. Or a rejection of him. He loved Daniel—in his own way. A way that some people may not have understood but I did. Aidan was just always funny about money. He never believed in giving an individual person large—or small—sums of money. He always thought that kind of charity made people complacent. Took away their edge. It's why he refused to lend me even a few hundred dollars for a car that he knew I needed when I was a teenager.

A cause, on the other hand, was a whole different matter for him. He gave generously to causes and movements because he believed he was contributing to an idea or an ideal. The truth was that if I had decided not to run for the Senate, he'd probably have donated the entire estate to some charity.

But I was also sure Daniel wouldn't see it that way.

I put my head down on the desk to think it through. But a long and emotional day caught up to me. I nodded off.

I wasn't sure how long I had been sleeping before I heard Brooke. "Shush," she whispered.

I could hear her and another person tip-toe around the room clicking off desk lamps and powering down computers before they settled just behind me.

"Is he okay?" Monica asked.

"One never knows," Brook answered.

Silence.

"He's not someone who's ever going to tell you about his problems," Brooke said. "Or ask for help."

"Does he even think we're doing a good job?" Monica asked.

"Of course. Why would you even ask that?"

"He just gets so grumpy sometimes. It makes me feel like I'm failing him."

"Quinn's had a hard life. He's had to overcome things that you can't imagine and he's done it by convincing himself that his only hope is himself—that he can do anything and everything by himself. It's why he has no real friends. He just compartmentalizes all his problems and keeps going. Sometimes I curse Aidan for making him like this but then I look at all he's accomplished—including this—I just try to love him he way he is."

"He has to understand that this is not something that any one person can do," Monica said.

"Being married teaches you that if you can't learn to accept the things that make you crazy about the person you love, then you can't be married."

"Even if that means you never really know if you're near a cliff?" Monica asked.

"Even if you never know whether you're heading over a cliff."

More silence.

I felt Brooke's hand run up and down my back. She kissed my neck.

"Let's go home, Baby."

XXXIII

In almost twenty-five years of practicing law, the numbers of clients I've ever permitted to testify before a federal grand jury is zero. Hundreds of clients and just as many subpoenas and I never once let a client go in there.

I've taught the lessons about the grand jury to law students at Connecticut State for over ten years. While the grand jury is secret, the target can never know what the grand jury knows—and you can be certain that the grand jury knows everything there is to know about you before you sit in the witness chair.

The grand jury is even more complicated for politicians. If word got out that I took the Fifth just weeks before an election, everyone would assume that I was guilty of something. It's not supposed to be how the system works, but that's how it is.

I figured that Bryce was right and that Saul was engineering the whole thing when I was served with the subpoena at Eliza's game. Saul had been looking at the same polling numbers as us. He's been in the game too long not to know that when a challenger is gaining on an incumbent in the days before an election, he'll likely win. When he saw that we were actually ahead, he conceded the battle of the primary and had moved onto the war of winning the general.

But now, he wasn't going to leave anything to chance. And if holding onto power required him to manipulate the most sacred and powerful aspect of our government, he was going to do it. I was sure of it the moment I set my first foot in the grand jury room.

Dale Treecut was waiting for me behind a large oak table.

A long-time operative in Saul's political organization, his service had been repaid by the senator's nominating him to serve as U.S. Attorney. Nothing in his resume would have made him qualified to serve in the post but senators are free to nominate anyone they want. And Saul wanted his guy in this spot as an insurance policy, for just this type of problem.

The U.S. Attorney normally wouldn't ever appear in the grand jury room. He'd leave the day-to-day work of prosecuting cases to the hundreds of assistant U.S. Attorneys on his team. I figured his presence gave me the opening I might need to get through my testimony without taking the Fifth.

I mouthed "Good morning" to the twenty or so grand jurors seated at desks, organized in four rows behind Dale. I recognized the court reporter from my days in the office. I nodded. She smiled.

"Good morning, Dale," I offered as I sat.

Dale lifted his head. He was just the type of guy who would be annoyed that I didn't address him as "U.S. Attorney Treecut."

"Morning, Quinn," he said dryly. "We'll get started in just a minute."

He made more notes while two or three grand jurors returned from their bathroom break. I bowed my head to each of them as they sat at their desks. When everyone was in place, Dale fixed his red and white paisley bow tie and stood.

The sergeant-at-arms administered the witness oath and we began.

"Mr. Barnes, please state your name for the record," Dale said.

I complied and provided him with the other generic information he requested including my address and date of birth. I kept the tone light and waited patiently for my spot.

"Mr. Barnes, I would like to call your attention to April the thirtieth of this year."

"Great," I said, trying to keep the proceeding conversational.

"That was a busy day for you, correct?"

"Well, yes. That was the day I announced my candidacy for the Senate."

Dale turned to his pile of papers, removed the first sheet from the stack and stepped closer to me. "I would like to ask you some questions about your campaign."

"You want to ask me questions about a political campaign?" I feigned surprise for the benefit of the grand jurors.

"Yes. About your campaign's finances and other matters," Dale said.

"Can I make a statement to the grand jury?"

Dale stopped cold in his tracks. He played poker but I could tell he was off balance.

"After I ask my questions," Dale said, his voice turning to steel.

He stepped closer.

"I don't think so. I'm going to make my statement now," I said, as if I didn't have a care in the world.

"Then I'll have to find you in contempt," Dale said.

I had him.

Most prosecutors learn about the operations of the grand jury by watching other prosecutors. They don't actually study or even read the rules. Dale was a political hack and barely a lawyer—and he was misleading the grand jury.

"Ladies and gentlemen of the grand jury," I said, standing. "Before we proceed I want to make sure you understand some important principles about the grand jury. The most important one is that you are an independent body. The prosecutor does not control you. You control him."

The foreperson spoke up. "But doesn't he have to ask the questions?"

"I said I *like* to ask the questions first," Dale said. He still had on his poker face but I figured that even the grand jurors could see he was getting defensive. "I said you can ask questions after I'm done." Dale returned to his chair, ceding the stage back to me.

"You control everything that happens here," I said. "You decide what witnesses to call, what questions to ask. And if you disagree with the prosecutor *on anything*—you win."

Some of the grand jurors took notes.

"Isn't he our lawyer?" the foreperson asked.

"No," I replied. I held both hands up for emphasis. "That is absolutely not true."

"I said I serve as your legal advisor," Dale said, his voice breaking. "It's a little different than being your lawyer."

"It's a lot different," I said. "You can ask him legal questions but you need to consider the source."

"Does this mean you're not going to answer any questions?" a thin gray-haired African-American woman asked from the back. I guessed that she was a librarian. It was a total guess. She just looked like a librarian to me.

"No. I'm going to answer any and every question you may have. I just wanted to make sure you knew all this and that I can only be held in contempt for failing to answer your questions—not his."

I started back to my chair.

Dale stood.

I offered another piece of advice before retaking the witness chair.

"One more thing," I said, holding up my index figure. "There have been several cases in the past few years of the grand jury being abused to advance political agendas—which is totally inappropriate. Six cases in fact."

There was a lot more writing, and I waited patiently for them to get it all down.

"Are you accusing me of misconduct?" Dale asked, his face red.

I kept my voice as calm as lake water. "All I'm saying is that I haven't done anything wrong." I turned to the grand jury and spoke right past Dale. "The most important thing you need to understand is that Dale Treecut is my political enemy. I'm fighting for a twelve dollar minimum wage, family medical leave—"

"This is outrageous!" Dale was right on top of me.

I just kept talking.

"—unemployment insurance, absolute universal health care, and the people he works for and their friends don't like it. They'll do anything they can to stop me and that's why I'm sitting here."

Dead silence.

Dale took a half step backwards. He ran his hand across his head to calm himself.

"Are you ready for my questions now?" he asked.

"I don't think we're going to have any questions today," the foreperson said. "We're going to want to talk about this a bit more before we go forward."

"Can I make a suggestion?" I asked. I didn't wait for an answer. "If you tell me what issues you're investigating, I'll be happy to come back with whatever documents or information you need to figure things out."

Dale tried to cut this off. "Don't give him any—"

"It's about all these people on your payroll," the librarian said, "—that Perez woman, Gene Allen—and how you're getting all this information—"

"Information," Dale said, raising his voice again. "Please stop—"

"And your wife and her hotel rooms," another grand juror muttered from the back.

"Thank you," I said. "Am I excused for today?"

"Yes, for today," the foreperson said.

XXXIV

Monica waited with Samantha for me in the rear entrance of the Center for the Arts in Madison before a meet-the-candidates breakfast sponsored by the Daughters of the Union Veterans. Monica paced the red and gold carpet like a panther. Nine days out from Election Day, the *Free Press* was reporting "Senate Seat Up For Grabs." "Independent Vote Key to Victory in Senate Race" was the lead in the *Gazette*. The *Sludge Report* maintained its commitment to the highest standards of journalism with "Three Way in Connecticut is Tight— And Enticing."

I couldn't tell if she was worried about our poll numbers or the upcoming event. I wasn't much concerned about either. The appearance was nothing more than each candidate taking the stage, one after another, to deliver a rehashed version of our stump speeches. As to the polls, I figured the papers had it about right.

"How we doing, Samantha?" I asked.

Samantha jumped into report mode.

"Good but not great," she said, fumbling through a brown folder with papers sticking out.

"Has Brooke seen all this?" I asked.

"Yes," she said, pulling an Excel sheet from the folder.

She started to hand me the paper. I put up my palm to let her know I didn't want to read it. "What did Brooke say?" I asked.

"She thinks you're winning. Even though there's only one poll where you're beyond the margin of error. And it's only one point."

"Then why does she think we're winning?"

"'Cause you're still ahead in the other polls," Samantha said. "Even though you're within the margin of error . . ."

"So it's trending in our direction," Monica said, finishing her sentence.

"What do you think?" I asked Samantha.

"I think that even if she's right, it's all razor-thin," she said. "Make a mistake in the debate, or just say something stupid—it's gone."

I fixed my tie. "I'll try not to say anything stupid."

Monica led us through a maze of hallways to get us into the lobby.

Saul's people were gathering on the other side of the red and gold carpet. They all wore red shirts with white "Stickin' with Saul" letters. Saul was nowhere in sight that I could tell.

Lucy and her supporters camped out about thirty yards away. She was taking questions from reporters beneath a chandelier. She wore a white shirt with an oversized collar beneath a tapered navy blue jacket with gigantic gold buttons. She looked like a cross between a Union general and Michael Jackson. As soon as she picked me up from across the room, she led the mob of reporters and cameras over to us. And greeted me by wrapping both arms around my mid-section and pulling me close.

"I do love this, John Quincy Barnes," she said loudly for the reporters, still holding me in a bear hug. "Any woman that got ahold of him would be crazy to let go. He is just delicious!" She planted a big kiss on my cheek and held it, leaving her gigantic red lip prints on my face.

Her crowd laughed. My staffers were stunned. Monica was fuming.

Monica jumped into action and pulled a tissue from her purse to clean up my face. In what seemed like the same motion, she pushed me toward the corner of the lobby, separating our two flocks. I took a few questions from reporters. When it was time to start the event, Monica pulled me aside. Her face was still sour.

"Why are you mad at me?" I asked. "What was I supposed to do?"

"You're not telling me something. And it's something that Lucy obviously knows."

"I don't know what you're talking about."

"I can't help you if I'm in the dark."

My phone rang. The 203 area code signaled that it was coming in from New Haven. I held up my finger and stepped back a few paces to take the call.

"Quinn Barnes."

"Quinn. U.S. Attorney Treecut here."

Dale sounded calm. Like the entire episode days before hadn't occurred.

"What can I do for you?"

"The grand jury would like you back."

"When?"

"Wednesday at nine."

"I'll see you then."

XXXV

Aidan's office somehow looked bigger to me without him in it. I closed the door behind me.

Daniel busied himself packing up books and papers.

"You going to move in here?" I asked.

"Definitely not," Daniel said. He didn't look up. He just kept working on packing boxes.

"Is now a good time to talk?" I asked.

"I know why you're here," he said, still not looking at me.

"You do?"

"Yup."

"You know about your Dad's will?"

"Yup."

"When did he tell you?"

"In the hospital. The night we found out you'd pulled ahead in the primary," he said, finally looking at me. "He wouldn't take any morphine so he could redo his will."

I collapsed on Aidan's couch.

"Congratulations," Daniel said dully.

Daniel sat in Aidan's chair. We listened to about twenty ticks of Aidan's grandfather clock before attempting to finish our conversation.

"Well, it doesn't matter," I said. "I'm not taking this money. It belongs to you and I'm going to get it to you as soon as his estate gets through probate."

"It doesn't matter?" Wrinkles massed on his forehead. "My father has figured out a way to reject me. Forever. That doesn't matter?"

"That's not what I meant. And that's not what this means. I suppose I don't know what to say."

"You know what I'll always be trying to figure out?"

"I think this is one of the moments where we should probably both go off alone to think."

"What I still don't get," Daniel said, "Is if you listened to all those lectures, took all those backhands and worked all those hours for him, just to set yourself up for today."

I stood.

"'Cause God knows," he went on, "I wasn't going to put up with his insanity to get his money. Hope you're happy."

I turned and walked out the door.

XXXVI

The questions were hurled at me one after another:

"What's your monetary policy and how does it differ from the current Fed Chairman?"

"How much does a quart of milk cost?"

"What percentage of the federal budget goes to education and how can you make it more efficient?

"What's the capital of Niger?"

"Are there people who will vote for you because of the color of your skin?"

"Are there people who will vote against you because of the color of your skin?"

"Please name the specific programs that you would cut from the defense budget?"

"How do our laws currently define an 'automatic weapon' and how does it need to be modified?"

"What are Connecticut's five largest exports?"

I wanted to tear my ears from my head.

Debate prep could be kind of fun when I was an operative and got to play the role of the moderator or the GOP candidate. It was pure root canal as the candidate.

"No! That was awful." Brooke said, critiquing my attempt at explaining why my position on defense spending won't cost the state jobs. She stood behind Monica, who was sitting at a table in her role as pretend moderator. "Start off with a general statement, like 'Our nation's security and the security of our citizens always has to be our first priority.' Then go on attack. Say something like, 'Unfortunately, Senator Berg has lost sight of that as evidenced by his vote on the Iran Threat Reduction Act' and then only give specifics if there's any time left."

"Broad concepts—big value statements," Monica added.

"Big value statements?" I asked, wincing.

"Yes," Brooke said. "You haven't even once said that you love Connecticut."

"Is anyone running on an 'I Hate Connecticut' platform?" I asked.

"Just do it," Monica said.

Brooke nodded—which meant I had to do it.

I loved having Brooke around but I could tell that even the staff felt sorry for me. It was the same way parents on a Little League team feel bad for the coach's son; he's the kid who always gets it the worst.

"And please stop hunching over every time you take a note," Brooke said. "You're bent over like a question mark."

I stood up straight.

"And smile, for God's sake," Brooke said, raising a small green bottle of Perrier to her lips. "You look like you're miserable."

Mercy intervened in the form of a kid delivering a half-dozen pizzas.

"Dinner break," I announced, stepping down from my pretend podium.

I grabbed a bottled water from the faux moderator's table. Brooke came to me.

"You're getting better," she said, pushing up on her toes to plant a kiss on my lips.

"Honey, you do realize that I'm the leader of the team."

"And?" she asked, drinking her water.

"And it's hard for me to lead when you're berating me like this."

"Stop being so sensitive. In seven days you're going to be in the ring with two vicious, cold-blooded killers and I can't get you ready by playing patty-cake." She finished her water. "You'll be thanking me after it's over."

And so it went. Two additional hours of torment until it was finally over. I did feel a world more comfortable by the time we wrapped up. As I milled about the room to thank everyone for their input, I could see that our team was feeling better also.

"You're ready, Q," Gene said, slapping me on the back.

"You got this," Keisha assured me.

"You're gonna make us so proud," Nancy said.

Brooke and Monica camped out in Monica's office to go over my itinerary for the campaign's final days. I waited for Brooke in the next office. She came to get me after they finished.

"C'mon. Let's go home"

"Can we talk for a minute?" I asked her.

She stepped in the office and pulled the door behind her.

"Let me start off by saying that this is going to sound crazy and nothing may come of it," I said. "But is there any way Saul—or Lucy—can claim you're having an affair?"

"Why are you asking me this?"

"About a week and a half ago I had to give testimony to the grand jury."

"You what?"

"Can we just focus on the problem and try to fix it?"

"Quinn, you can't keep doing this to me. You can't say, 'Oh, let's just try and fix a problem that I didn't trust you enough to discuss with you at the point when it could have actually been fixed.'"

"It's not that I didn't trust you. I was just trying to figure it out on my own. I'm at a point where I can't, so I'm talking to you about it."

She hung her head in her palms.

We sat in the stillness.

She gripped the corner of the desk, took a deep breath, and raised her head.

"So you're the target of a grand jury investigation."

"I'm actually not sure what's going on. And I already said that this may not amount to anything."

"Quinn, had you told me about this when it happened, I'd have shown you that it's insane to think that this could wither on the vine in the middle of a political campaign. What would possibly make you think you could navigate a grand jury investigation without anyone finding out?"

"Honey, it's not like I'm a stranger to the grand jury. I know how it works . . ."

"You know how it works," she said, monotone.

"It's a secret proceeding. If they don't indict—and I'm not sure they will—no one will know. Had I told anyone about it, I'd risk it getting out."

"Even me?"

More stillness.

"No," she finally said.

"No what?"

"There's no way anyone could even make that claim. Even though you cause me more pain than anyone I've ever known by asking me that."

Brooke didn't cry. I could have sworn she would. She'd cried about a lot less over the years. She just stood.

Finally, she said, "Let's go home."

"I'm okay with sleeping here."

"No," she said, taking my hand. "Even when you drive me into a state where I can't stand to be in the same room with you, I realize that we have to stay together. Otherwise, I'll never break through with you."

I grabbed my jacket with my free hand.

"Is there anything you want to ask me?" I said.

"No. I already know the answer."

She reached for the light switch. I placed my hand over hers. We left the darkness behind us and went home.

XXXVII

"Mr. Barnes, how long has your wife officially been on the campaign staff?" Dale asked, taking the lead on the questioning from his desk, positioned center front.

"That's hard to say."

"Why?"

"Because she hates politics."

Laughter. Dale sat as still as a statue.

I did my best to look confident and carefree.

But I was scared.

While I knew I hadn't done anything wrong, a constellation of innocent facts taken together can be made to look like I had. And Brooke was right. At this point, it wasn't likely that any of this would wither on the vine.

"But when did she assume an official role with the campaign?" Dale asked again, after things settled down.

"She's never had a paid position." I looked around, trying to make eye contact with all the grand jurors. "But as the candidate's wife, I suppose she's always part of the campaign."

"And what about Nancy Perez and Gene Allen? He asked.

"What about them?"

Dale stepped closer. The grand jurors readied their pens.

"They are both paid members of your staff, correct?

"Yes."

"What do they do for the campaign?"

"Ms. Perez helps coordinates volunteers. Gene Allen takes care of various tasks."

"Like what?" Dale crossed his arms.

"He drives me to events, delivers equipment and signs to our offices, helps our advance people set up stages," I said. "Gene is a big man so he basically gets assigned to anything that weighs over fifty pounds."

No one laughed. Or even smiled.

"What are their qualifications to work on your staff?"

"Are you serious?" I asked.

"Mr. Barnes, please just answer the question," the foreperson said from behind Dale.

"It's a political campaign," I said. "The only qualifications are a willingness to work twenty hours a day for little or no money and live on stale pizza."

"Had either Nancy Perez, Gene Allen, or your wife, Brooke Wolcott, ever worked on a campaign before this one?"

"No."

"And Ms. Jackson?"

"Keisha Jackson has worked for me for more than ten years. She's probably the most capable person on our staff."

"Capable of anything, you mean," Dale said.

"I mean that she's one of the brightest, efficient and talented people on our team."

The grand jury is always advised the transcript of its proceedings will be made available to them if they need it, but everyone was writing like they were charged with producing their own.

"And Ms. Jackson, Ms. Perez and Mr. Allen were issued campaign smart phones?"

"I suppose. Keisha actually takes care of those types of things."

"But your campaign provides phones to personnel for campaign business."

"Yes."

"Mr. Barnes, just a few more questions," Dale said as he sat on his table and struck his best professorial pose. "Do you consider yourself responsible for all the actions of your campaign staff?"

"Well, at this point, we have more than a thousand volunteers and a paid staff of almost two hundred. No leader of a large organization can possibly see what all those people are doing at every minute."

"But you're the leader," Dale said. "And you've said publicly on many occasions that 'Leaders must always be held accountable.'"

"Not exactly in this context, but yes, I'm the leader and responsible for the official acts of my organization."

"Mr. Barnes," the foreperson said. "I think we have just one more question. Do you remember saying to us that you were concerned that all this fuss was being stirred up by your political enemies?"

"I do."

"Is Mr. Coyle your political enemy?"

"Aidan Coyle?" I asked, puzzled.

"No. I'm sorry," the foreperson said, shaking his head. "Daniel Coyle. Is Daniel Coyle your political enemy?" he asked.

My pulse quickened. I could feel my heart beating hard beneath my starched white shirt as I tried to process the question.

A wave of memories rushed over me. Baseball games when we were kids. Studying after school in Aidan's office. Birthdays. Weddings. Unable to make sense of the question, I went into lawyer mode.

If I answered yes, I'd be questioned about why and forced to give details. And I didn't really have any.

If I answered no, the questions would stop but Dale and the grand jury would have the answer they wanted. The one that could have me trapped.

I didn't have much choice.

"No," I said. "Of course not."

Treecut stood. "Thank you. I think we have everything we need."

My heart sunk. It was stupid to testify. I could never have known everything the grand jury knew, and I could read in the smugness of Dale's grin that they had information that had me cornered.

Desperate, I did the only thing I could do.

"Can I make a request?" I said, standing.

"What is it?" Dale asked.

"Can I come back?"

"No," Dale said. "The grand jury is going to vote on an indictment right after you leave here today," Dale said.

"Why do you want to come back?" the foreperson asked.

"Because I want to present you with something that I believe will change your minds," I said.

"What makes you think their minds are already made up?" Dale asked, placing his knuckles on the table.

"When can you come back?" the foreperson asked.

"The election is six days from today," I said. "I can be back the day after the election."

"We can't do that," the foreperson said. "We'll be here on Friday at 9:30. If you have something to show us, we'll have a look. If you're not here, we'll vote."

—⚍—

Gene held the passenger side door open for me. He wouldn't look me in the eye. He had the look my kids sometimes have when they know they've done something wrong and are wondering if I know about it yet. He turned on the radio as soon as he got in.

I needed some time to think about the best way to approach things with him. I bought myself a few minutes by checking my email and then looking over my itinerary for the next few days. By the time he turned on the Chapel Street entrance to I-91 north toward Hartford, I'd figured out the best way to start the conversation.

"I know what you did," I said.

"You're not supposed to know," he said. "That was the point of it all."

"Well, any cub prosecutor could have figured this out." I reached out and turned off the radio. "And it's going to be a huge mess."

"Let me explain the whole thing to you—"

"Stop talking," I said, cutting him off. "I'm not your lawyer anymore and if they asked me what you said to me, I'd have to tell them."

"Well, then, you can tell 'em this," Gene said getting loud. "You didn't have any part of this and that's the truth. You just keep your mouth shut and let me take this plea after they charge me."

"It's not that simple now," I said. "Other people are in jeopardy."

"Not if you just don't say anything."

"How could you possible know that?" I asked.

"My lawyer told me so."

The hum of the tires on the pavement was the only sound all the way from Hamden until the ten minutes or so it took before we were passing through Meriden, when Gene finally broke the silence.

"Q, you need to face something that's always bugged me about you. You walk around thinking I could have been like you. That the only reason I've spent my days on this earth in and out of jail while you've been in a suit is because of luck or some school that you had that I didn't."

"Because it's true," I said.

"Maybe for somebody like Ms. Keisha but it ain't true for me."

"And why does that bug you?"

"Because it means you don't understand yourself." Gene gripped the steering wheel with both hands and exhaled. "Do you know why I got after Dex that night?"

"At Bowling Green?" I asked. "What does that have to do with any of this?"

"You were about to break. You were the leader. The one we all looked up to and you were about to break—or be broken. I could see you couldn't take any more and something had to be done." Gene held his fist up. It just sat there suspended in air while he searched for his next words. "This is sort of like that. But a world more important than a football game. You're the leader. The special one. I could see that you were about to be broken. So I did what I had to do."

"But I'd never want you to do something that's against the law."

"I know that. That's why I kept you out of it. And why I'm ready to take what's coming to me."

"What would make you think I'd ever let you sacrifice yourself for me?"

"Because I'm asking you to. I didn't think it'd come down to this but I'm okay with it. 'Cause there's not much I can do to make anything of this life of mine anyhow. Can you imagine what it would be like to live all these years and not have one thing to look back on to be proud of? This is my one chance to do something positive—something special. Let me do this one thing."

I shook my head. "There has to be another way."

—⟋⟍—

Six days from Election Day, the bullpen looked like a crowded college bar. Our volunteers were so busy that I was barely acknowledged as I zig-zagged my way to Monica's office.

Both Brooke and Monica were waiting for me.

Stress hung on their faces.

"So?" Brooke asked. She sat on the corner of the desk.

"About what we expected."

She pinched the bridge of her nose.

"I've seen lies on the eve on an election. But this?" Monica said. "An indictment?"

"We're getting in the way of people's money," Brooke said, steadying herself. "Every word that comes out of his mouth threatens someone's money. I know as well as anyone that they'll stop at nothing to put a stop to it."

"But what would they even indict you for?" Monica asked.

"They don't tell you exactly what they're thinking. The best I can tell from their questions is that they're going to claim that members of our campaign staff conspired to break into Nutmeg Medical to steal a copy of Rivka's consultancy agreement and then leak it to the press—"

"But that's a lie," Monica said. "He broke in to feed a drug habit."

"No, he didn't," Brooke said. "I knew it didn't make sense that his drug tests were negative."

"They can't prove this!" Monica said. "Did you ask Gene or Nancy or Keisha if any of this is true?"

"He can't," Brooke said. "If he did that and the government asked him what they said, he'd have to tell them every word."

"Are you allowed to tell us what the grand jury said?" Monica asked.

"Oddly, yes," I said. "Grand jury secrecy rules don't apply to witnesses."

"So do they have a case?" Monica asked.

"It's hard to say. Based on their questions, they're going to claim that one of them—probably Nancy through her contacts with the service employees—got Gene keys to the building and the office. Once he found the consultancy agreement, they'll say, he took photos of the pages with his campaign-issued phone and sent them either to Nancy's or Keisha's campaign phones. And that they then leaked them to *The Left Nutmeg*."

Monica leaned back and put her feet up on her desk. "And Gene used the drugs as a curveball to cover it up?"

"Yup."

"Could they charge you?" Monica asked.

"Oh, they're planning on it," I said. "They'll charge a conspiracy. They'll claim that because none of them had any experience working on a campaign, the real purpose of them being on paid staff was so I could direct them to do something just like this."

"Would that hold up in court?" Monica asked.

"No," I said.

"But it doesn't really matter," Brooke said. "It'll take months to sort this all out. They just want to be able to say he's been indicted before Tuesday."

"But let's not let them turn this on us," Monica said. "Gene and Keisha and Nancy. They did a good thing."

I shook my head.

"Quinn," Brooke said, "the information leaked to the press is true information. They didn't make it up or tell even the slightest lie. Saul and Rivka are the liars. They were hiding this from the public . . ."

"Exactly," Monica said. "The people have a right to know this. It proves that he used his office for financial gain."

"Can we move on?" I asked. "You're not going to get me to condone burglary and theft." Brooke and Monica looked at one another. "I have to go back there on Friday."

"The grand jury?" Monica asked. "The debate's on Friday."

"Why do they want you back?" Brooke asked.

"I told them I wanted to present them with something that might change their minds."

"What's that?" Brooke asked.

"I don't know yet."

Brooke and Monica looked at each other again.

"How are you seeing this play out?" I asked Brooke.

"Normally, the indictment would be irrelevant," she said. "They would have what they want by just spending a few days throwing around the words grand jury, investigation, fraud." She stood and milled around the room while she thought it through. "It seems to me this is different. They now need an indictment to make the case that our wrong was worse than theirs. The grand jury is going to be acting like the referee."

"Agreed." Monica said. "Everyone knows they're dirty. They have to show that we're dirtier than them. They need the indictment to do that."

"The timing of a Friday indictment would be perfect for them," Brooke said, still musing and not talking particularly to either Monica or me. "Gives them enough time to move the polls and keeps us from really being able to respond. And what a bombshell for the debate."

"Are we sure this is right?" I asked. "Why wouldn't they just start leaking it now? Everyone knows that ninety-nine percent of cases get indicted . . ."

"It's too risky for them now," Brooke said. "You actually did a smart thing by asking for more time."

"I'm going to write down that you said that," I said.

"If they leak it and the grand jury doesn't indict," Brooke went on, "they'll lose for sure."

"She's right," Monica said. "They'll look like they abused their power to try to cover the whole thing up."

"Was there anything else?" Brooke asked.

"No," I said, looking at my phone to figure out where I was supposed to be next.

"Are you sure?" Brooke grabbed my arm. "What about that other thing you asked me about?"

"Is there something you two need to share?" Monica asked.

"No," I said.

XXXVIII

"Can I take your order, sir?" Benjamin leaned over with a paper towel draped over his forearm.

I held up the handwritten menu to the candlelight in our dining room. There was only one choice listed.

"Lobster tail and clam chowder."

"Mom?" he asked, looking to Brooke.

"Lobster tail and clam chowder."

He walked over to my mother. "Grandma?" he asked.

"Gumbo!"

Ben looked confused.

"That's not on the menu," Eliza said, trying to help him. "We only have lobster tail and clam chowder."

After seventy-two hours of marathon campaigning, Brooke had mandated a night off. Or at least a family dinner without checking e-mail and taking phone calls.

Our rallies and town halls couldn't have gone better. Our crowds weren't just strong; we were talking to overflowing auditoriums and filling up small parks. To the outside world, we managed to make our beat-up jalopy look like a sleek silver jet airliner rocketing across the sky.

I even accepted the coaching regarding message discipline.

"Now, just say the exact same thing you just said this morning, the exact same way," Monica said, as I took the stage in Plainville.

"No ad libbing!" Brooke shouted in my ear.

I felt bad for our staffers who had to listen to the same jokes, told the same way, over and over again.

Saul looked to be playing the percentages. And playing it safe. He kept his events small and intimate. "Come Have a Cup of Joe with Saul," his campaign broadcast day after day as he focused on his strongholds of Waterbury, Trumbull, Stamford, Fairfield, Naugatuck and Wallingford. The images from the news reports showed diners that looked full and Saul shaking hands and getting pats on the back from the supporters filing through; but Brooke, at least, suspected he was keeping his events small out of necessity.

Nutmeg-Gate continued to hit Saul hard. He kept his messaging about it simple and disciplined. "I didn't break the law," he said whenever the subject was raised. "And there's no connection between any official action I took and the sale of Nutmeg Medical." But as Election Day crept closer, it was clear it had taken a sizeable toll on his campaign. I figured he'd be up by ten points without it. We might even be ahead by ten if I was talking about it. But I was determined to try and win on our ideas.

Lucy seemed to have disappeared altogether from the campaign trail and had apparently decided to rely on her air attack.

"I'm not a career politician," she said, looking into the camera from a table in what looked to be her dining room. "I'm a wife. I'm a mom. I'm a grandmother." As images shifted to still photos of her behind a desk, her voiceover added, "I've been bankrupt. Lost everything and come back and rebuilt." She finished her pitch, surrounded by a diverse-looking crowd of supporters and declaring, "I understand the struggles of real people and I'll bring a totally different perspective to Washington."

Like all of Lucy's ads, it was well-done and hard to miss if you watched TV for at least fifteen minutes. But the time for her to get on stage with us, and be prepared to answer questions ranging from changes in local mill rates to the appropriate level of funding for stem cell research, was quickly approaching. According to the blogosphere rumor mill, which Graham kept me apprised of, she was devoting all her free time to debate preparations.

"*Connecticut Alex* has learned that Lucy McCann has locked herself in with staffers to master some finer points of geography and other facts that are commonly known to sixth graders as debate night approaches. McCann was apparently unaware that the Netherlands is a country and was unable to correctly name the Allied Powers of WWII."

I would have preferred spending the evening on both my grand jury presentation and my own debate prep, but had to comply with Brooke's directive on shutting out the outside world for a few hours to unwind. Unfortunately, my brain doesn't ever really shut off.

I thought about texting Daniel to invite him over to eat with us. I even pulled out my phone and started typing a message but then deleted it. I wanted to get Aidan's inheritance straightened out before talking to him. Maybe that would smooth things over—if it was still possible to do so. And Gene. And Keisha. And Nancy. They were all in big trouble for trying to do something for me. And I felt responsible. It always kills me that people who have the least are always willing to give the most.

Pierce and Ben managed to get our dinners—which were pur-chased earlier, with my mother's help, from Frescas—on plates and warmed in the microwave. Eliza worked on our drinks.

"Dad, your phone is ringing!" Eliza yelled from the kitchen. "It's Ms. Monica."

"Leave it!" Brooke yelled back from beneath the exposed beams of our dining room.

Pierce and Benjamin wore oven mitts to deliver our dinners to the table. Eliza took care of our club sodas. And we were ready to eat.

"Do you like this better than gumbo?" Eliza asked my mother.

"I'm not sure it's better but it's just as good."

"Do you miss living here in Connecticut?" Ben asked her.

"I do," Mom said. "I miss being around you children."

"Why do you live down South anyway?" Eliza asked. "Mom says she'd never let us live there—"

"Eliza," Brooke said. "You mind your manners."

Mom just smiled. "Well, Louisiana is my home and I've always fig-ured that it belongs as much to me as anybody else. Would you let anybody make you leave your home?" she asked, tasting her mint julep that she'd made herself in a mason jar.

The three of them shook their heads "No" from their bench.

"I didn't think so," she said, cutting off a piece of her lobster tail. "Did you know your Daddy always loved going down South?"

"He did?" Pierce asked, confused.

"He absolutely did," she said. "He'd stay with my sisters in Opelousas in the summers and do all kinds of stuff with them on the farm. When he was just about your age," she said, looking to Ben, "he even helped birth a calf."

"What does that mean?" Ben asked.

"Well, if a heifer is having trouble giving birth to her calf," Mom explained, "you have to stick your hands up inside her to pull the calf out."

Ben and Pierce dropped their forks. Eliza spit her food out.

"Yuck!" Eliza said. "That's absolutely disgusting."

"It was all gooey and smelled awful," I said. "And the heifer was in pain so she was pooping the whole time. It was pretty gross."

The kids twisted their faces as if they smelled it from their chairs in Pentfield.

"Quinn, is that really necessary?" Brooke asked. "We're trying to eat dinner."

I pointed to the kids' plates to get them focused back on eating dinner.

"How come you have light skin and Daddy's so dark?" Eliza asked my Mom.

"Eliza!" Brooke said. "I've told you a thousand times, it doesn't matter."

"I know," Eliza said. "I just wanna know."

"Well, your Daddy favors his father," Mom explained. "He had dark skin. But your Momma's right. It doesn't matter. Things like that only matter to crazy people."

"Like people that have that flag on the back of their trucks?" Eliza asked.

"The Confederate flag," Pierce said, clarifying the point for his sister.

"Mom and Dad always say that we're in danger when we see that flag," Ben said. "And the Nazi flag."

"Well, that certainly sounds like good advice, but you shouldn't worry on that too much," Mom said.

"Why am I called black if my skin is so light?" Eliza asked.

"Eliza," Brooke said. "Please stop obsessing about this. None of this matters."

"Well, if it doesn't matter," Eliza said, "I declare myself 'caramel!'"

"You can do that," Mom said. "But the world is going to keep calling you black."

"Who made all these crazy rules?" Eliza asked.

"Crazy people," Mom said. "But again, you shouldn't spend so much time worrying about crazy people."

"Why not?" Eliza asked.

"Because there's more good people than bad in the world," Mom said. "And you can make *yourself* crazy worrying about the bad ones. You don't want to let them distract you from getting what you want and being what you want to be. You just take things as they come."

There was a loud knock at the kitchen door. Pierce ran to go answer it.

He reappeared a moment later at the dining room door with Monica standing behind him.

"This couldn't wait an hour?" Brooke asked.

"No, Ma'am," Monica said. "I really am sorry."

Brooke and I retreated into the living room. Monica followed while the kids finished their dinner with Mom.

Brooke sat and crossed her legs on our citrus-colored Joplin couch. I stood behind her. Monica pulled her iPad out of her bag and activated it. She handed Brooke the blog post that she had bookmarked. I read it over her shoulder:

THE SLUDGE REPORT
Bombshells and Betrayal in Barnes Camp

HARTFORD, *November 1st—Quinn Barnes looked like a man with a lot on his mind as he watched his daughter Eliza in her Little League all-star game from the outfield in early August. "He watched from the outfield—separate from his wife who sat in the bleachers—and it was like he was not there," says a* *witness who saw the Senate hopeful at the event. "He just stood behind the centerfield fence, gazing off."*

He had good reason to be distracted. Ousted from his family home, he was coming to grips with his childhood friend and confidant taking up with his wife, Brooke Wolcott. Here's what the Sludge Report knows now:

- *Quinn Barnes was exiled from the marital home last spring by his wife, Brooke Wolcott;*

- *Wolcott, who has always refused to take her husband's last name, kicked Barnes out of their home to devote herself to her longtime lover, family friend and campaign treasurer, Daniel Coyle;*

- *Wolcott was missing completely from the campaign until after the primary and reportedly only joined the campaign recently to be near her boy-toy, Coyle. According to unnamed sources, the two have carried on their longstanding affair during the campaign;*

- *Barnes and Wolcott are said to have an "open marriage" in which they are free to have sexual relations with other partners.*

- *Coyle's only comment to the Sludge Report is that "Both Quinn Barnes and Brooke Wolcott are not what they appear to be. They are devious pathological liars and the people of Connecticut need to realize this before Election Day."*

The Sludge Report has been told that members of Connecticut's mainstream media are aware of the story but none have had the courage to report it. Stay tuned to find out: whether Wolcott will sign an affidavit denying the story (doubtful) or take a lie detector (even more doubtful) or whether law enforcement will be looking into whether campaign funds were misused to carry on their affair (likely).

Brooke closed the cover of Monica's iPad case and handed it back to her.

"If this is politics," Brooke said, "then politics is like swimming in a sewer."

She crossed her arms over her stomach and gently rocked back and forth. I came around the front of the couch to sit next to her.

"Okay, so this is one of those really surreal moments that only a campaign manager ever experiences," Monica said, almost whispering. "But is there any—"

"No," Brooke said, looking up. "None."

"You're sure," Monica said, still whispering.

"Yes," I said.

"Terrific." Monica sat in the French loveseat across from us. "You have to understand that if most campaigns could leave a flyer on the windshield of every car in the state on the eve of an election claiming their opponent was a child molester, they would do it. That's how you have to see this."

"This is it," Brooke said.

"This is what?" Monica asked.

"This is the moment that explains why no sane person would ever dare do something as crazy as run for elected office," she said. "I knew we should have been bombing him on Nutmeg-Gate." She looked at me, jaw clenched. "That was true information. Instead, we're letting them slander us and win with made up lies."

"We can't go back in time," Monica said. "Let's talk about what we need to do to respond."

"Respond to who?" Brooke asked. "Do you have any idea how long my family's lived here? What they've built?"

"How many hits does this blog post have?" I asked.

"A few thousand in the first hour or so." Monica opened her tablet and navigated to the Sludge Report's home page. "It's tracking at about eight thousand now and I figure it could go as high as a hundred thousand by tomorrow."

Brooke covered her face. She started crying.

"We can't talk about this now," I said to Monica.

"How are the children supposed to go to school tomorrow?" Brooke said through her tears. I ran my hand up and down her arm and pulled her close.

"We're going to get a denial out tonight," I told Monica. "Send me the statement and I'll review it from here."

"But there are going to be more questions," Monica said. "What about the affidavit? What if Daniel has more to say?"

"Set up a press conference before the debate," I told her. "I'll answer this before the debate."

"Do you need help putting something together?" Monica said.

"Any candidate who can't answer a question about crap like this doesn't deserve to be a senator," I said.

XXXIX

" **D**o you swear the testimony you're about to give is the truth, the whole truth and nothing but the truth, so help you God?

"I do."

Dale sat quietly at his mahogany table. He looked the way I figured he'd look working inside his office. A handful of papers were neatly stacked in front of him. His Waterman fountain pen made notes on a yellow legal pad.

"Mr. Barnes," the foreperson started. "This session is really for your benefit. I believe you have something you would like to present to us?"

"I do, and thank you." I stood and stepped in front of the grand jurors to deliver the summation of our case.

"I can't win the case," I said.

Jurors looked at one another. Dale grinned.

"I used to be a prosecutor," I said. "I'm well aware that when the police caught Gene Allen red-handed like that, it meant that you could charge him with drug distribution, burglary and theft—and also wire fraud for using the campaign cell phone to transmit Rivka Berg's consultancy agreement."

"It actually means even more than that," Dale said.

"It does," I said, looking right over him to the grand jury. "The federal conspiracy statutes probably allow you to charge several people from the campaign."

"Including you," the foreperson said.

"Including me," I said, nodding. I tucked my hands in my front pockets as I moved to the left side of the room. "And I'm not here to present you with an alibi or some kind of forensic evidence, like you might see on a TV show, that would establish the facts are different from what you believe them to be." I walked back to the center and stopped. "I am, however, going to present you with something more powerful than any of those things. Something that will change the way you think about this case. Something that I'm hoping will help you see your way to a No Bill and letting us go on our way. Knowledge. And the power that comes with it."

Dale snorted and then smirked. He put his pen down and looked up to me from his desk. I kept speaking as if he weren't in the room.

"I want you to know that Mr. Treecut has a power known as prosecutorial discretion. It enables him to stop a prosecution to serve the ends of justice."

"Ahh," Dale said with his finger raised. "Mr. Treecut won't be exercising that power in this case."

"You, as grand jurors, have a similar power: it's called nullification."

Dale popped up out of his chair. "We're not doing this. There is no way I'm going to sit here and let you instruct them to disregard the law." His carotid artery bulged from his neck. "I'll have you removed from this room before that happens," he said, pointing to me.

"Information and knowledge are power," I said calmly. "If you can control information, you can control people. And Dale Treecut is trying to control you right now."

Dale slammed his hand on the table. "That's it. I'm having the marshal remove you right now!"

"Mr. Treecut, I'm not prepared to order that," the sergeant-at-arms said.

"You'll have the opportunity to tell us if you think he's saying something that's wrong," the foreperson said.

"As grand jurors," I continued, migrating back to the center of the room, "you have the power to decide whether it would be fair and just to apply the full force of the criminal law to an accused person. This power that you have is the reason why we have you jurors sitting there instead of computers. Because you're supposed to be the conscience of the community. You're supposed to decide if the law should be applied or if it should not."

"He's trying to get you to disregard the law," Dale insisted. "As if one person can be above it. He wants you to just ignore the law."

"It's not a request for you to show any disrespect for the law. *It's part of the law.* It's as essential as reasonable doubt." I paused, making a point of making brief eye contact with as many grand jurors as I could. "You decide, considering all the circumstances of the case, if you should brand the defendants as criminal." I sat on the corner of Dale's desk. "Think about the Boston Tea Party. No one would say that breaking into a ship shouldn't be a crime. But in those particular circumstances, should people be convicted of doing that? Or the Fugitive Slave Act. Grand juries in Connecticut routinely declined to indict citizens who refused to return runaway slaves back to the South. Or Prohibition. That's the kind of question before you."

"That's not the question before you," Dale said, standing. "He's talking about historic cases that happened generations ago."

"Juries use this power every day. They nullify marijuana and other drug cases all across the country. And notice what Mr. Treecut is not saying. He's not telling you that you don't have this power—or that a judge could even review it. He just doesn't want you to use it."

"But we're not talking about just a drug case," the foreperson said. "That was just to throw us off. We're talking about the burglary and the theft of that private document." He pointed to one of the papers on Dale's table.

"And the use of your campaign cell phones to send it all back to your team and the blogs," the sergeant-at-arms said. "That makes it wire fraud."

"But there's a context," I said. "The most important thing in the world is the outcome of an election." I got back on my feet. "The winner of an election could change this state—for better or for worse—for generations. Gene didn't take this information so he could make a big pile of money. He did it to so people could make an informed choice on Election Day."

"It still doesn't sit well with me," the librarian said.

"I suppose the question you're going to have to answer is this: Would it have been okay with this all staying a secret? For a politician to stand up and say something that obviously was not true to hold onto power? Or do you feel like it was something the people had a right to know? Because that's the decision Gene had to make."

I paused to let my words sink in. When the note takers were done writing, I returned to the center of the room.

"And as you're about to cast your vote, I want you to have one thing on your mind: the lengths the Bergs are willing to go to distract everyone. Do you remember when you asked me if Daniel Coyle was my political enemy?"

"We know all about that," the foreperson said.

"Know about what?" I asked.

"That the affair business isn't true," he said.

"You shouldn't be discussing other grand jury business with a witness," Dale reminded him.

"Well, you're the one who wasted our time with that nonsense," he told Dale. "So, I suppose I'll say what I like."

"I take it that you spoke with Mr. Coyle and don't credit his testimony," I said.

"Not a word," the foreperson said flatly. "After Mr. Treecut asked his questions and we got to him, the whole story fell apart. It took us a whole hot minute to see that Coyle was working with the McCann and Berg campaigns to push that lie."

"Then can I ask, Why would you take an action that rewards this kind of behavior?"

"Because two wrongs don't make a right," the librarian said from the back.

"It sounds like you have a grip on all the issues that are before you," I said. "Can I ask that you let me know your decision as soon as you make it?"

"You know they can't do that," Dale said, looking at me.

"We'll figure out a way to let you know," the foreperson said.

—⚉—

"How'd it go?" Gene asked, holding the door for me at the corner of College and Elm Street.

"Not sure," I said, out of breath from hustling downstairs and dashing across the New Haven green to try and stay out of sight from any reporters.

Gene shut the door behind me and jumped in the driver's seat.

"Where we headed?" he asked.

"Up to Hartford."

"HQ?" he asked.

"No, CityPlace," I said. "We're going to see Daniel."

My head snapped back as he hit the accelerator and we sped toward Route 34 to get us on the interstate.

XL

I stepped off the elevator into Coyle & Coyle's law offices to find the twenty-first floor deserted. Annie wasn't at the receptionist's desk, which looked cleaned out. As I walked the long corridor to Aidan's office in search of Daniel, the majority of offices were unoccupied. Only a few even looked like someone had left any possessions in them.

I'd assumed that some lawyers would move on after Aidan's passing but that Daniel would largely keep things together. I would never have imagined a wholesale exodus.

I wouldn't have thought Daniel was even in the building but for his promise to be in Aidan's office from our text exchange the night before.

D: I want to see you. Q

Good. Want to see you too.

When and where?

Dad's office. Noon.

As I neared the cracked door of Aidan's office, I heard one of those unique sounds that's unmistakable to the ear. Someone was rummaging through an ice bucket and dropping cubes in a glass.

I drew a deep breath. And pushed the door open.

Daniel sat behind the desk gripping Aidan's Ravenscroft crystal decanter at the neck as he filled his glass. The decanter was nearly tapped out and he put it down heavily next to the ice bucket.

When he finally looked up at me, bags under his eyes, I stopped in my tracks.

A 10-mm Glock was sitting in the middle of the desk, pointed in my direction.

Daniel kept his bloodshot eyes on me while he drank.

He put his glass down hard on the desk after he gulped the whole thing down.

"Sit down, Quinn."

He said it like he had all the power. And he did.

I sat.

"I knew you were gonna be trouble for me the first day we met," he said, reaching to refill his glass with whatever was left in the decanter.

I shook my head.

"How can you possibly still be living in a day from a lifetime ago?" I asked.

"The past is never dead," Daniel said, putting the decanter down. "You remember that gem, don't you, Quinn?"

"That's not what it means. It doesn't mean you're a prisoner to your past."

"Are you saying Dad was actually wrong about something?"

"I loved Aidan but he wasn't right about everything," I said, sitting perfectly still.

"Do you know what he said to me that day on the way home in the car?" Daniel asked, calmly. "While he was reaching back and *beating . . . my . . . ass?*" His face filled with rage in an instant.

"He wasn't right about that either."

"I kept telling him—*pleading with him*—that I fought as hard as I could. And do you know what he told me in between each one of his backhands?" Daniel gritted his teeth. "'Quinn did it! He's no bigger than you! And he did it!'"

"I really don't know what you're looking for from me—"

"Yup, I knew that day that as long as you'd be around, he'd be comparing me to you," he said, calm again. "And I'd never live up to you. You destroyed my entire life, Quinn."

"Your life's not over," I said. "And it's up to you to make it turn out the way you want, not me."

"My entire life," he said, his eyes blank, gazing over my head. "You've destroyed my entire life, Quinn."

"So you're going to shoot me?"

"Shoot you?" he asked, grinning. "I don't even have the guts to shoot myself."

"Then why are you keeping that Glock so close?"

"'Cause I wasn't gonna let you come in here and smack me around like him," he said, starting to cry.

I've always believed that where there's life, there's hope. And I've tried not to give up on people—especially people close to me—no matter how far they've fallen. But there was nothing I could ever do to help Daniel. Maybe someone else could, but not me.

I stood and retrieved an envelope from my breast pocket. An envelope that held the documents transferring Aidan's estate to Daniel.

I tossed it on the desk and said all there was left to say.

"Goodbye, Daniel."

XLI

When I was in school, I always studied until the moment the test hit the desk. With a press conference and a three-way debate ahead of me—both of which required my absolute finest performance—I was going to work until I had to take the stage. I sat with the family as we sailed together down I-91 in Mildred's Town Car for my press conference and debate. And my head was already in the debate.

I had narrowed the hundreds of potential questions down to a list of twenty or so that were most likely to come up. I studied each response and how I wanted to say them. After I got through them three or four times, I turned to my pre-debate statement. I first went over the words, trying to visualize how it was all going to look and feel. I filled up the margins on both sides of the page with reminders.

"Honey, you're mumbling," Brooke said, nudging my shoulder.

I looked up to find Pierce, Benjamin, Eliza and Brooke staring at me. Mom was laughing.

"Are you scared, Daddy?" Eliza asked.

"Not so much scared—just nervous. I suppose it feels about the same as scared."

"Why?" Benjamin asked.

"A lot of people are depending on me."

"Do you have to win this debate to win the election?" Pierce asked.

"Yes. But first I have to give a speech about what Saul and Lucy are saying about Mommy and me."

"I wish you hadn't done this," Eliza said.

"I know this is hard," I replied.

"I just can't take people talking about my parents." She turned to Brooke. "You were right that Daddy shouldn't have done this."

"Please don't say that, Honey," Brooke said. "I was wrong."

"You were wrong about something, Mom?" Pierce asked.

I smiled.

"Dead wrong. We don't ever want you to sit quiet and do nothing when a bully is making people miserable on the playground."

"Are you mad, Mommy?"

"Not mad," she said. "Just ready to speak up."

"Daddy, I know what you need to do," Eliza said.

"What's that?" I asked.

"Be aggressive."

"I'll try."

—⁓—

We drove by the Garde Art Center on our way to the hotel. Lucy's gigantic red, white and blue coach sat in front of the theater. "Lucy!" ran the length of the side of her gaudy monstrosity. Her slogan, "It's Time to Change Washington" was splashed across the back end.

Orange "Stickin' With Saul" lawn signs were planted on both sides of the street. Our team was getting started handing out white and blue "Fight for Change" placards to volunteers to hold up.

We cut down State Street toward Eugene O'Neill Drive to get to the hotel. People were pouring out of the Marriott lobby. Gene pulled into an alley and then down an unmarked ramp to deliver us into the hotel's basement. Monica and a half dozen staffers were waiting for us.

The kids looked like they were having fun—traveling like secret agents to get to unused hallways and private elevators up to our floor. They chased each other down the hallway and then fought over who was going to stick the key card in the door.

Monica gave them all jobs to keep them occupied. Pierce and Ben helped our volunteers rearrange the furniture into what would become a makeshift command center until Election Day.

I slipped into the bedroom and laid my notes out on the coffee table in front of a couch wedged into the corner. I sat and worked with whatever time was left.

A knock broke my concentration.

My pulse rate went up.

"It's time," Brooke said.

—⁌—

The ballroom was already decorated for election night. A fifty-foot banner with a forty-foot blue "Q" in the middle encased our campaign slogan, "The Right Experience. For the Change We Need."

I couldn't help but think back to the retail phase of the campaign: when we met with small crowds and spoke with every person who showed up for a gathering. The scale of this event was enormous. Thousands of supporters from across the state were holding up signs and chanting "Fight for Change." I couldn't find anyone in the crowd who wasn't wearing a Barnes campaign button or t-shirt.

Brooke and I entered from the rear of the ballroom. A roar went up as she stepped through the door. Dressed in a white mock turtleneck sweater and skirt, perfectly cut to accentuate her hourglass figure, she stopped at the door. First she waved then she held up her fist. Whistles and shouting layered over the applause. When I came into view behind her, the thunder was deafening. It was as close a thing I had experienced to stepping into a football stadium filled with thousands of crazed fans.

Monica appeared with our security—which looked like a half dozen or so rugby-playing interns in blue jackets and khakis—and we migrated through the crowd to the stage. The media were stationed on a platform that ran the length of the room's back wall. Additional camera lights went on when Brooke and I took our seats.

"All three affiliates are picking it up live," Monica shouted between us.

I reminded myself that the people I needed to convince were not in the room. They would be watching through the television cameras.

Monica took to the podium and fed the crowd some red meat to keep them riled up. I pulled my notes from my suit pocket. I blocked out the crowd and everything around me while I ran through my remarks one final time. The outside world came back to me when Brooke stood to introduce me.

We embraced. I rubbed both her arms from her elbows to her shoulders and kissed her again before she left my side for the podium.

I can tell in an instant when she's uncomfortable. Her expression fades. Her neck reddens. Tonight, though, she looked just fine.

She wanted to be up there.

She started slowly. She thanked our supporters in the room and all around the state; reminded everyone to reach out to their family, friends and neighbors in the lead-up to Election Day; and then got to my introduction.

"I'm here to introduce you to the love of my life, the next senator from the great state of Connecticut." I moved to the edge of my seat to ready myself for center stage. "But I've changed my mind."

The room calmed. Some people looked at one another. Others chuckled, not sure if they'd missed a joke.

"As you know, there's a debate tonight. A debate which immigrant parents here in New London are hoping will lead to a discussion about which candidate is best suited to help their 17-year-old pay for college; a debate that a homeless family in New Britain is longing to lead toward them getting into a permanent home; a debate that the families of twenty-six victims of the horrific tragedy in Sandy Hook are praying will identify the candidate who will make certain there will be no more tragedies like Sandy Hook."

Applause.

"Instead, we're on a path to have a debate about lies, rumors and innuendos. A debate that will start in the gutter and end in a sewer. A debate that will reward the two people—Saul Berg and Lucy McCann—who put it there. So here's what I'm going to ask you to do: Make this the last election."

Brooke paused and let things settle. She looked straight into the bank of cameras before continuing.

"Make this the last election in which a politician is able to use the levers of government to make false accusations and hold onto power. Make this the last election where a candidate thinks that her road to high office is by distracting you from a discussion of the issues that will have an impact on you and your family for generations. Make this the last election that hinges on a debate over manufactured scandals and bald-faced lies. And when you're standing in that voting booth, I'm asking you that you make them pay. That you show the Saul Bergs and Lucy McCanns of the world that from this moment forward, there will be consequences for lying, slandering and cheating to win an election. Make them pay by voting for Quinn Barnes."

The packed ballroom erupted in applause. The chant "Make them pay" overtook the room. People stamped their feet in beat with the chant. I could literally feel the podium shaking.

Brooke let them carry on for about a half minute before she held up her arms to settle things down. The chant seemed to grow louder before it finally subsided and she could finish.

"Quinn is fond of telling and listening to stories. Stories are part of his DNA. It's not only how he finds inspiration, it's how he communicates. It's one of the things I love about him. So, I want to close with a story that he told me when we first met. It's a story about a grandmother . . ."

"Many years ago—1958 to be exact—racial tension across the nation had hit a fever pitch. The Civil Rights movement was gaining momentum throughout the South and this 78-year-old grandmother had taken notice. She decided that she was going to travel from New York to Tennessee to teach at a workshop on how to conduct non-violent acts of civil disobedience."

Brooke wasn't using any notes. She was just talking.

"The Ku Klux Klan didn't want the workshop to go forward and guaranteed certain harm to anyone who attended, including this elderly, gray-haired woman. But this grandmother was undeterred. She called her best friend—who was a spry 71 years old—and the two of them flew to Nashville, rented a car and headed to the workshop. They made their way through the heart of Klan territory. The only protection the two women had as they literally traveled through the valley of the shadow of death was a loaded pistol sitting between the two of them."

Brook slipped her hands up and down the lectern before resting them at the bottom.

"The 78-year-old grandmother's name was Eleanor Roosevelt."

The room erupted into more applause. There wasn't any catcalling or whistling. Just a kind of respectful clapping.

"I've thought about this story for many years and never fully understood it. Why would someone who had already given every breath of her life to every cause under the sun disregard the bounty that the Klan had placed on her head to attend a meeting, during a time in her life when she should have been spending her nights in front of a fireplace with her grandchildren? I now know the answer."

"This country requires unending sacrifice—especially during the times in our lives when it's inconvenient. This means that during the years you should be resting, you still have to fight. It means that even when your job or livelihood is threatened, you have to press on."

"Vote for ideas. Vote for idealism. Vote for hope and change. Vote for Quinn on Tuesday."

Grand slam home run.

Supporters crowded the stage while Brooke waved to the crowd. She started to the right and finally came back to the left where she hugged Monica.

And then kissed me on the lips.

"Now you go get 'em," she said, looking into my eyes.

XLII

"Good evening. I'm Tom Monahan and welcome to the first and only scheduled televised debate between the three candidates for U.S. Senate. As your moderator, I'd like to introduce you to the three candidates. They are incumbent Senator Saul Berg of the Connecticut for Berg party, the Republican nominee, Lucy McCann, and the Democratic nominee, John Quincy Barnes. Welcome to all of you."

Aidan always counseled candidates that debates are irrelevant and the most important thing—especially in a close race—is to keep your head down and play it safe. "Don't take chances. Don't overreach," he'd say. "You're just going to spend 90 minutes talking to your base."

I made some last-second notes on the single sheet of paper that I brought with me to the podium as Monahan walked through the debate's ground rules.

I had to get a lot more done than just talking to my base.

I circled my talking points about the grand jury investigation and practiced one final time in my head as to how I would deliver them. When I was done, I looked up and found Brooke in the front row. She looked calm. Monica, on the other hand, was chewing on her fingernails from the seat next to her. She looked like a twelve-year-old squirming in the waiting room of the dentist's office. I had to suppress a laugh.

Keisha waved to me with just the fingers of her left hand from her seat next to Gene and Nancy. I could have sworn that Raymond was affectionately locking hands with Mildred off to the right. I tilted my head slightly to have a look but my eye was drawn to an elderly African-American woman sitting in the row in front of them. It was a face that I recognized but it was out of context.

She wore a Fight for Change t-shirt and a pair of jeans. She nodded at me when we made eye contact.

I nodded back at the librarian from the grand jury.

I put a big X over my grand jury talking points.

"I want to start off by joining Brooke Wolcott in denouncing a report that doesn't even rise to the level of journalism," Saul started off affably. "It was a vicious and unfounded attack that has no business in this debate."

The applause was strong. Some people stood. I figured Brooke had boxed him in. He was cutting his losses and doing the best under the circumstances—and his best was pretty good. He was subtly placing all the blame in Lucy's lap.

"I agree!" Lucy hollered, out of order. "Let's just dig in and start talking about the issues."

Saul raised his overgrown eyebrows at Lucy before continuing his opening statement.

"I'm one of the senators who is able to reach across the partisan divide to get things done, and that's helped me deliver for Connecticut," he said from his center position on stage. He was cool, smooth and senatorial. "It helped me save 31,000 jobs at the sub base in New London. Jobs that would be in jeopardy if my opponents have their way—"

"Don't put me in that rodeo!" Lucy said, interrupting—but picking up some laughs. "I'm for jobs. And the freedom and security those jobs deliver."

The lines in Saul's forehead placed his annoyance at the interruption in full view but he stayed focused. He didn't look at Lucy, me or the audience. A professional politician of the highest order, he directed his attention to the cameras and the cameras only. Saul Berg wanted to keep his job and was bringing all his considerable abilities to bear to save it.

"My experience and seniority help me return money to Connecticut. Money that creates projects and new companies and the jobs that come with them. Quinn Barnes runs around this state acting like he invented concern about income inequality. He's missing that everything I do for this state is about addressing income inequality: creating job opportunities for working people. He's missing it," Saul said, finishing as he pointed in my direction. "But don't you miss it."

His supporters, disregarding the debate rules, exploded in applause from the center section of the theater. I put a big check on my notepad. Saul was impressive but he was playing in my sandbox.

"Can I ask you all a question?" Lucy asked, starting her opening statement. She labored to tone down her Carolina accent. "If your repairman can't fix something after twenty-four years of trying, don't you think it's time to try something else?" Lucy's army of Tea Party Patriots stood and started shouting an apparently staged "Try Something Else" chant. One of them stood up holding a "Revolt Against Socialism" sign. He was getting close to Monica. I was afraid she might hit him.

After regaining order, the moderator restated the debate rules, and admonished the audience to follow them.

"Mrs. McCann, you may continue," he said.

"I don't have nothing else. That's all I needed to say."

More applause from the Tea Party faithful. More restating of the rules. More admonitions. Security guards removed the guy with the "Revolt Against Socialism" sign.

After I got the preliminaries of my opening out of the way, I kept it simple, short and to the point.

"Ladies and gentlemen, facts are stubborn things. They retain their power for people who are willing to listen and acknowledge them. So I'd like to start off by providing you with a few facts that I'd like to discuss with you this evening."

Like Saul, I poured all my energy into the lens.

"The 85 richest people on the planet have more wealth than the bottom 50 per cent. That's 85 people with more wealth than three and a half billion. In our own corner of the world, we're the wealthiest state in the wealthiest country in the world and our state is the most unequal of the 50—"

"Socialism—Socialism—Socialism," a rotund dark-haired woman yelled from Lucy's section on the right. Her brethren seated around her joined in.

Monica stood. A pack from our team stood with her. Even Mom got to her feet—which got Gene to his feet to protect her.

I glared at Monica and put her back in her chair with my eyes. Our staffers followed.

"I'm asking that we have a discussion. Not a shouting match or a name-calling contest but a sober debate about what these facts mean. Inequality stifles economic growth. Alleviating it and promoting growth are intertwined. They're connected, so you can call me a Socialist, a Communist. You can call me a Socialist Communist if you like. I really don't care. This issue is the single greatest threat to the country right now. How do we find a way for the millions of people in this state and across the country—with their faces pressed up against the window of opportunity—to realize their dreams like the generation before us?"

Applause. I told myself I wasn't going to judge my performance based on the level of applause. But it was strong. And it felt good. It also didn't go unnoticed by Saul.

"You're a handsome young man who says these things with a warm smile. But what does this mean?" Saul asked, holding his hands up like a soccer player complaining that he didn't get a call. "Are you saying we should redistribute wealth through the tax code or some other way?" he asked.

I was supposed to be making an uninterrupted opening statement, in which I was entitled to offer soaring rhetoric to the electorate. Neither Saul nor Lucy was going to let that happen. The debate was on.

"Over half of all U.S. tax subsidies go to just four industries: oil and gas, financial services, utilities and telecommunications," I said. "On top of that, thirty of the largest companies in the world had an effective tax rate of zero last year. Just so we're clear: They're getting government giveaways and not paying taxes. Is that corporate socialism? How is this happening?"

Gary H. Collins

"It happens because of the free market system," Lucy said, not really looking to make a substantive point as much as she was just trying to stay in the mix.

"If the free market system includes buying Congress to make sure companies get all the subsidies and all the tax breaks," I said, "while the middle class continues to tread water, then you're right."

"But Son," Saul said, holding up his finger, "you're not answering the question—"

"Please don't call me 'Son,'" I said. "I'm a grown man discussing serious issues—"

"The question is whether you're going to prosecute a war between the classes," Saul said.

"I think Warren Buffett has said it best: 'There has been class warfare waged and it's been a rout' for the one percent.'"

Monahan broke in above the applause.

"We're going take a moment for a station break and when we return, we're going to turn to the questions segment of the debate. Please stay with us."

The handlers for all the candidates rushed the stage like they were working the corner of a heavyweight prize fight. Saul's people got to him first. Careful not to be overheard, they covered their mouths while they whispered. Lucy's team looked nonplussed.

Brooke and Monica brought me a fresh bottle of water.

"You're doing great but you have to come off this," Monica said, turning her back to the other candidates. "You're scaring the independents."

"How do you know that?" I asked.

"We have a focus group at the hotel," Monica said. "You're scaring them."

"What do you think?" I asked, looking to Brooke.

"You're doing great. Maybe even winning," she said, brushing a piece of lint off my shoulder. "But remember: crazy never wins. You've made your point. Just move on. Show 'em you're not a one trick pony."

I made a note.

"Thirty seconds!" the stage manager yelled. "Please clear the stage."

Monica grabbed my empty water bottle.

Brooke rubbed my back and drew close to whisper. "You got us all here so just trust yourself and do what you think is best." She softly kissed my ear. "I'm so proud of you."

The handlers scurried off the stage. The stage manager gave us the countdown.

"We're back," Tom announced. He walked the audience and candidates through another set of instructions and admonitions. Saul cut him off again.

"Tom, if I may?" Saul said, not waiting for permission to continue. "We're trying to have a debate and I think what just transpired was an emotional rant. So I'd like that we spend a moment so that I can get an answer to my question."

"Which question is that, Senator?" Tom asked back.

"How does Quinn Barnes plan on redistributing the wealth as part of his plan to make everyone equal?"

Tom and Saul probably went back fifty years but Tom was mad. His cheeks turned a light shade of red.

"Senator," Tom said, "I allowed everyone some leeway in the first round but we have a format and rules that I'm going to ask that we try to follow—"

"Tom, can I go ahead and answer this question so that we can all get back on track?" I asked.

Tom exhaled. "Go ahead, Mr. Barnes."

I turned to the camera.

"Ladies and Gentleman, what you just heard—disguised as a question—was a stunt. A cheap political stunt that demonstrates why Saul Berg isn't worthy to continue serving as your senator."

"I just want an answer to my question," Saul shouted from off camera.

"Saul Berg figures that he's not doing so well in this debate. So, he thinks that if he can call me a name—dressed up as a question to scare you—he might be able to keep his job."

"I want an answer to my question!" Saul hollered again.

I continued ignoring him and just kept talking to the camera.

"He's a politician. He's thinking that if I don't answer the question, he'll get to label me as the guy who's going to redistribute your wealth. And that even if I do answer the question, the only thing you'll remember is that I'm the guy looking to redistribute your wealth."

"Now you've got me thinking you're looking to redistribute wealth," Lucy said, still straining to stay relevant. She picked up a smattering of laughter and lots of grins.

I smiled along with everyone else. "I'm for common sense solutions to make sure the system isn't rigged against working people: Make sure young people have access to food, education and health care so they can fulfill their aspirations; limit tax breaks, subsidies and loopholes that are being allowed to companies to only the ones they actually need; and finally, yes, we need the top one percent to pay a greater share so that we can unlock our economy's growth potential in a sustainable way."

Applause.

Tom took the reins back. "Let's turn to our round of questions."

There were no surprises in the questions. Energy, the environment, a touch of foreign policy. Any one of which could be answered by a junior campaign staffer. They, however, transformed Lucy into a train wreck.

Uneasy at the podium, Lucy shifted back and forth like she was anxious to get to the bathroom. The worst of it was watching her fumbling through the index cards where she had her answers written down. She couldn't find the right card when asked a question about the environment, so she read the answer on the card that she could find.

"I know you and your drive-by media have an agenda to push but I'm going to talk about what I want to talk about: the national debt . . ." She proceeded to read the card and there was no mistaking—by anyone—that she was reading.

"A bloated bureaucracy creates wasteful spending that plagues our government . . . ," she recited from the card.

Had I been watching on TV, I would have changed the channel.

Out of what seemed to be an act of mercy, Tom threw her a softball question about what committees she would want to serve on if elected.

She just stammered and muttered, not able to name a single one. Lucy was done.

Everyone was relieved to get to the part when the candidates were allowed to ask each other some questions, marking the close of the debate.

"Mr. Barnes," Tom said to me, "Please select a candidate and pose a question."

"Thank you," I said. "Senator Berg, I'm going to keep this short."

"That's why you'll never be a good politician," Saul joked.

I waited for quiet.

"What's your plan?"

"My plan?" he asked back.

"Yes, you had a good bit to say about my plan to address our disappearing middle class. What's your plan?"

Saul sipped his water, touched his tie, and answered the question the way a seasoned politician answers questions.

"I thank you for that question and he opportunity to finally lend my views on the subject. I'd start off by saying that I have never and will never vilify people for being successful—as you've done throughout your campaign. There are structural issues—changes in our economy that stem from the technology revolution—that create unique challenges in terms of job creation. We're not going to meet these challenges by tearing people apart—pitting neighbor against neighbor—the wealthy against people who aspire to be wealthy. We need to build bridges. Bring people together. So we can all prosper as a nation."

Saul looked to Tom before going ahead with his question.

"Quinn, as I look out to your supporters, I can't help but notice a two time convicted felon—who's currently out on bail for a series of other felonies—is sitting among them. Do you think it's appropriate for a United States senator to harbor criminals?"

My supporters booed.

"It's a fair question," I said, waving to my faithful to simmer down. "The short answer is, I'm doing what my parents would have wanted—what they would have expected."

"Your parents would have wanted you to condone and support drug abuse and theft?" Saul asked.

More boos.

"My mother is here tonight." I looked to Mom. She lifted her hand from the arm rest to wave at me. "She and my father used to tell me a story when I was child about our family history and how a public servant who worked for John F. Kennedy made a difference in our lives. I used to think the story was about the importance of an election. But's it's not. It's about our willingness to fight for people who've been forgotten by everyone else. Those are my instincts. Those are Brooke's instincts. That's why we're in this race. I'm hoping the voters will understand that. If they don't, they won't understand anything else we're saying. I suppose we'll find out the answer on Tuesday."

XLIII

"Why do you suppose bad people win elections?" I asked.

"What's wrong with you?" Aidan said, looking down at me from his desk. "Mrs. Ella T. Grasso's about to win. She's gonna be the first woman governor ever to be elected in the entire country."

"But not all your candidates are gonna win," I said, showing him the exit polls I was responsible for updating. "All these bad people are gonna win too."

""Sonny," he said, looking over my work, "The first rule of politics is that you don't win every race."

"But the people on the other side are bad, right?" I asked. "We're good and they're bad."

"I never said that." Aidan rummaged through the top of his desk in search of his lighter.

"But you said if our people don't win, people like my parents won't get their Truesovelt fair shake. If the other side won't give my Mom and Dad a fair shake, aren't they bad?"

"It's Roosevelt," he said slowly as he pulled a cigar from the box he kept next to the phone. "And that's very clever reasoning. It's gonna make you a great leader someday."

"But what's the answer?"

"All people are good and bad at the same time." He lit his cigar and leaned back in his chair.

"Are you sure?" I asked, confused.

"I'm certain."

"Even those three boys I fought for Daniel?"

"Sonny, you're only eight years old and this is gonna be hard for you to understand. But one day those kids are gonna feel mighty sorry for what they called you and what they did."

"I don't think so. They just grit on me at school. I think they want to jump me."

"You shouldn't worry about that," he said, placing his cigar in the ashtray on the corner of his desk. "Trust me when I say that won't happen."

"But I don't see how there can be one pound of good in any one of those boys. Or in those people that won't give my parents a fair shake."

"Think about it this way," he said. "The people who are bad don't think they're bad."

"How do you show them that they're bad?"

"Well, first you have to learn how to make a good argument. They teach you how to do that in law school," he said, leaning back. "Then you have to become a leader and reason with people."

"Does that always work?"

"No," Aidan said, looking as if he was sorry to disappointment me. "It only works with evolved people."

"What's 'evolved?'"

"It means smart."

"What about the people who aren't so smart?" I asked.

"We just do our best with them," he said exhaling and then checking his watch. "Why don't you run out to Annie's desk and grab my call sheets so we can do our best to make sure as many good people as possible win today."

I obeyed. I walked down the long hallway to the reception area. My head barely reached the doorknobs of the offices I peered into along the way.

Daniel was lying on the couch in the reception area watching cartoons on the console TV. Annie smiled while she worked behind her desk. She looked mighty busy stapling papers and writing things down. I was afraid to interrupt her. I just stood there waiting for her to notice me.

"Here you go," she said cheerfully. She handed me a stack of papers—with a red lollipop on top.

"These are Mr. Coyle's call sheets?" I asked.

"They are," Annie said, still smiling.

"Ms. Annie, can I ask you why you're so happy?"

"A woman is going to be governor!" she burst out.

Not sure what to do or say, I jammed the lollipop in my pocket, smiled back at her and ran to Aidan's office. I reached the doorway to find him staring out the window looking north up the Connecticut River against the orange, yellow and red backdrop of the New England fall foliage.

I handed him his papers and returned to my place on his couch.

"Mr. Coyle, can I ask you one more question?"

"Why don't you call me Mr. Aidan. And you can ask me as many questions as you want later but right now I have to make some phone calls," he said, paging through the papers I just handed him. "Why don't you just sit there and listen to how I talk to these people."

"But could I ask you just this one, now?" I asked, distressed.

Aidan tossed the papers onto his desk and sat on the front of it. "Of course," he said. "What's bothering you?"

"Does what you said mean you, too?"

"Does what mean me?"

"That you're good and bad. That there's a bad part of you?"

Aidan laughed out loud. "Well, Daniel's mother would probably tell you I'm all bad."

My eyes grew as big as cookies.

"I'm joking," he said. He came over to the couch and sat next to me. "Sonny, I've got a feeling we're gonna know each other for a long time 'cause I want to help you. How about I just do my best to show you my good parts. And you just keep trying to be more good than bad."

"Why are you gonna do that?"

"Do what?"

"Help me?"

"I'm honestly not sure," he said. "I want you to keep asking all these questions but you're gonna have to accept that there's not an answer to everything. And most of the time there's no way to explain why we feel a certain way about people. Why we love some and hate others."

"But there has to be a reason," I said. "I mean, this office ain't filled with all Daniel's friends."

"Maybe it's the good part of me," he said. "The part's that innate."

"What's 'innate?'"

"It's the good stuff that's deep inside us. In our hearts." Aidan tapped the left side of my chest with his long index finger. "When something special touches your heart, you should do your best to try and hold onto it."

"Mr. Aidan?"

"Yes, Sonny."

"You're full of words," I said.

Aidan laughed a deep-throated laugh. "Sonny, you really are a wonder."

"What I meant to say," I said, stammering, "is that I really like you, Mr. Aidan."

"I like you too, Sonny."

"Are you my friend?" I asked.

"Think of me as a coach," he said. "Like your football coach."

"How long do you figure you'll be my coach?"

"As long as you need me, Sonny. As long as you need me."

I heard Hank Daniels saying my name in the distance. I tried to go back to sleep so that I could stay in Aidan's office. But then I heard Saul's name.

I could see the TV's glow creeping through my eyelids but didn't open my eyes. They were burning and I didn't plan on getting up until I had to.

I could feel Brooke take my arm and snake it around her shoulder as she laid her head on my chest. She surfed the channels for updates on the race but settled back in on Hank. The volume wasn't quite loud enough for me to make out whether there was any news but I figured Brooke would wake me if they were ready to call the race.

There was a low knock at the door.

"Can I come in?" Monica whispered.

"Sure," Brooke whispered back.

I could hear Monica dragging a chair to our bedside. Brooke put the TV on mute.

"Has he gotten much rest?" Monica asked.

"Quinn? The world could be on fire and he'd sleep like the dead." Brooke said. "Have you slept?"

"I closed my eyes for a few minutes at one," Monica said. "I'm done with all this if they don't get it right."

"Don't say that," Brooke said. "We'd be lost without the die-hards. You can't take the losses too hard."

"Normally, I don't," Monica said. "I mean there are lots of races where my candidate loses and I know the voters did the right thing. They picked the better candidate. But if they can't see this . . ."

"If they can't see this, then you have to fight even harder."

A cell phone rang.

"Barnes for Senate," Monica said, whispering.

I pushed myself up and leaned against the headboard. Brooke clicked on the lamp next to our bed. I closed my eyes again.

"Sir," Monica said, shaking my shoulder.

I opened my eyes.

She handed me the phone.

"Quinn? Quinn? Can you hear me?"

Adrenaline shot through my heart. I sat up and put my feet on the floor.

"I can hear you, Senator," I said.

"Quinn, I know this has been a tough race but I hope you will accept my heartfelt congratulations."

I couldn't just forget about all he'd done. Everything he'd called me. The lengths he was willing to go to ruin my family. I know it was part of the politician's code. It's all just business. The rules that everyone understands before stepping into the arena.

"Thank you, Senator."

Monica turned on the overhead light. Brooke turned up the television. Staffers started pouring into the room. The volume in the room seemed to go from one to one-hundred in an instant. Some people sat on the edge of the bed. Others crowded around the TV. People activated their phones and started making calls.

"You're going to make a great senator," Saul said. "I hope you'll feel comfortable reaching out to me if you ever need any advice or if there's anything I can ever do to help."

Brooke would expect me to let him have it. Tell him how awful a person he was. I took a deep breath.

"Thank you, Senator."

I handed the phone to Monica and joined Brooke.

We took the stream of handshakes, hugs and kisses from our couch in front of a table of empty water bottles and trays of half eaten fruit and cubes of assorted cheese.

Monica dropped the text of my acceptance speech on my lap. "You okay?" she hollered, gripping a champagne flute filled with beer.

"Can you get everyone out of our room?"

"What?" she asked, leaning down, cupping her ear with her free hand.

"The room—can you clear the room for five minutes?" I shouted.

She jumped on the coffee table in front of us, planting her left foot in a small pile of leftover cheese.

"Everybody out! Out!" She stepped down and started pushing people out of the room. "We'll rendezvous downstairs in twenty minutes. Twenty minutes!"

Brooke didn't wait for the room to clear before collapsing in my arms and putting her feet up on the table. I wrapped my arm around her back and cradled her. She closed her eyes. And I closed mine.

"All clear, sir," Monica said in my ear. "Will be back in fifteen to wake you."

I opened one eye. "Thank you," I said. "For everything."

"Thank you, sir. This is the most important thing I've ever done."

I winked at her.

My eyes were closed but I stayed awake. I pulled Brooke close and locked my hands around her back.

She dug her chin into my chest.

Bliss.

"What do you figure we do now?" I asked.

"We'll work on it tomorrow."

Brooke exhaled. I reached down for her hand.

"Why don't you go get in bed?" I said. "I'll be back in an hour."

"Oh, I'm coming with you."

"You don't have to," I said. "I can go do this by myself."

Brooke looked up and arched an eyebrow.

"Brooke," I said, trying again. "Do you think you'll be able to make it downstairs with me?"

"Much better," she said, resting her head back on my chest.

"I love you, Brooke."

"I love you too," she said, "We should tell each other that more often."

About the Author

Gary Collins serves as the President of the Council for a Livable World. With more than 100,000 members, the Council is the nation's largest political action committee devoted to advancing a progressive agenda on national security and nuclear disarmament issues.

Gary was formerly a candidate for US Congress from Connecticut's 2nd Congressional district. He's previously served as a strategist and senior advisor to several candidates for statewide office in Connecticut, including Ned Lamont for US Senate in 2006.

A lawyer by training, Gary formerly served as an executive at a fortune 10 company. Prior to that, Gary was a partner at one of the oldest law firms in Connecticut, where his practice focused on government investigations. His partnership was preceded by his service as an Assistant United States Attorney in Washington, D.C. during the Clinton administration. He taught government investigations at the University of Connecticut, School of Law from 2004-12 and is the co-author of the ABA best-seller, *Warning the Witness.*

A noted author and commentator, Gary sits on the board of several non-profit organizations and is the founder of the Collins Foundation, Inc., which invests in initiatives that improve educational opportunity and strengthen community organizations in Connecticut, with a special emphasis on individuals from under-represented and disadvantaged backgrounds.

Gary H. Collins

Gary received his Juris Doctorate from Vanderbilt University School of Law in 1991. He graduated from the State University of New York at Buffalo in 1988 where he earned a Bachelor of Arts degree in Political Science.

He lives in Portland, Connecticut with his wife, Amy Salvin-Collins and their two sons, Grant and Harrison and is reputed to be a helluva youth basketball and baseball coach.

Made in the USA
Las Vegas, NV
18 January 2022

41752379R00184